## CORNERED!

Ann Rodick is a witness to murder. Now on death row, the murderer appoints his brother, Billy Quirter, to avenge him. So Ann goes into hiding, changes her name, her looks, and gets married. Now she is Ann Burley of Arrow Junction. But Quirter is still on her tail. But so is Bob Saywell, the local merchant who makes everybody else his business, particularly such a pretty woman as Ann. No matter that she's married to momma's boy, Ted. Or that the town doctor, Hugh Stewart, is also showing an interest. Saywell knows how to get what he wants. But when Quirter hits town one snowy night, all bets are suddenly off.

## THE LONG RIDE

Harry Wells set up the bank heist with military precision. But what he hadn't figured on was the panic of his young accomplice. He didn't figure on newlywed Allan Garwith being in the right place and the right time and snatching the bag right out from under him. So when he finds out that Garwith and his young wife have suddenly answered an ad to join a carpool to San Francisco, he answers the ad as well. But so does John Benson, an F.B.I agent with a very good hunch on the stolen money. And Margaret Moore, recently divorced and anxious to get away from it all. And Miss Kennicot, man-hungry librarian out for a little adventure. This is one cross country trip that none of them will forget.

James McKimmey Bibliography
(1923-2011)

**CRIME NOVELS**

The Perfect Victim (1957; expanded from "Riot at Willow Creek," *Cosmopolitan*, 1957)

Winner Take All (1959)

The Satyr (1960)

Cornered! (1960)

24 Hours to Kill (1961)

The Wrong Ones (1961)

The Long Ride (1961; expanded from "The Long Ride," *Cosmopolitan*, 1960)

Squeeze Play (1962)

Run If You're Guilty (1963; expanded from "Death Trap," *Cosmopolitan*, 1962)

Blue Mascara Tears (1965)

A Circle in the Water (1965)

Never Be Caught (3 novelettes, 1966: Never be Caught, And Then She Was Dead, Kill Him Again)

The Hot Fire (1968)

The Man With the Gloved Hand (1972)

**JUVENILE FICTION**

Buckaroo (1979)

**As Benjamin Swift**

Playoff (1981)

**As Dewey Daniels**

The Martindales' Nightmare (1981)

# CORNERED!

— — — —

# THE LONG RIDE

## by James McKimmey

**Stark House Press • Eureka California**

CORNERED! / THE LONG RIDE

Published by Stark House Press
1315 H Street
Eureka, CA 95501
griffinskye3@sbcglobal.net
www.starkhousepress.com



ISBN-13: 978-1-944520-12-0

Book design by Mark Shepard, SHEPGRAPHICS.COM
Cover design by James Heimer, WWW.JAMESHEIMER.COM



First Stark House Press Edition: October 2016

# James McKimmey
## by Bill Crider

When I first started collecting paperback originals, the two imprints I looked for were Gold Medal Books and Dell First Editions. I had no idea that Knox Burger worked as an editor at both of these places, but I knew that the books they published were usually just what I was looking for. I also knew that they both published John D. MacDonald, whose name on the cover was practically a guarantee that I'd like the book. In 1958, however, when Knox Burger left Dell for Gold Medal, MacDonald stopped writing for Dell. I don't know if Dell was looking for a new writer to take MacDonald's place on the roster, but 1958 was also the year that Dell published James McKimmey's first novel, *The Perfect Victim*.

I didn't buy the novel then, but I was already familiar with McKimmey's name. For several years around this time I had been reading science fiction almost exclusively, and McKimmey had published quite a few stories in the last of the pulps and in the SF digest magazines, mostly *Planet Stories* and *If*. He also wrote Ki-Gor stories for *Jungle Stories*, but those were published under a house name.

Not a lot has been written about McKimmey, but Jason Starr provided an excellent introduction to a reprint of *Squeeze Play*, which led to a thoroughly interesting correspondence between Starr and McKimmey, with a lot of information on McKimmey's friendship with another SF writer, Philip K. Dick. At one time there was an excellent interview with McKimmey on Al Guthrie's *Noir Originals* website, but that site has been taken down. It can be found by using the Wayback Machine, however, and I've quoted several things from it in this essay. The interview is in print form in *Paperback Parade* #64, and perhaps a used copy can be found by those who might be interested if they engage in diligent searching. Aside from those sources, nothing much about McKimmey exists. While there might a dearth of information on McKimmey, however, his novels can speak for themselves, and the two reprinted in this volume are fine examples of his work.

One thing that McKimmey says in his interview with Guthrie is that

John D. MacDonald's influence on him was "rather huge." He adds that while he "never remotely approached John's readership or, certainly, his earnings, . . . the desire to do it was always there." What McKimmey doesn't say is that one of the ways that some of his novels resemble Mac-Donald's work is in their use of the "Grand Hotel" plot, in which a number of characters with little or no previous connection come together in a situation that puts pressure on all of them. As the pressure increases, the question becomes one of how people will react and which ones will do what the reader expects, or doesn't expect.

McKimmey doesn't trace his use of this technique to MacDonald's novels, however. He says he learned it when writing from editor Malcolm Reis when writing for *Planet Stories* and *Jungle Stories*. McKimmey was having trouble writing longer-length stories, and Reis told him to think in terms of a movie, to move the camera around to get different points of view. After he started to think in those terms, McKimmey said, "it made all the difference for me." He adds that "using that technique in my novel-writing that produced whatever that branch of crime/mystery writing most of my books might represent."

The two novels reprinted in this volume are fine examples of that technique. In *Cornered!* there's a terrific opening scene set in a service station, a scene that could come right out of the current TV series *Fargo*. It's cold, and it's snowing, and the scene is both darkly comic and suspenseful. It ends with a big bang.

Two gangsters have come to the small town of Arrow Junction to kill a woman named Ann Burley, the woman who sent their boss to prison for murder. Eventually a good many people are trapped by the killers in the store owned by Bob Saywell, a local bigshot who's figured out who Ann Burley is and who thinks he can use what he knows to his advantage. Ann's husband, Ted, is an abuser with other problems as well. Hugh Stewart is a local doctor whose skills are far beyond those of most general practitioners. Like Ann Burley, he's hiding out in Arrow Junction, but for very different reasons. To complicate things even more, he and Ann have fallen in love. The Reverend and Lottie Andrews are driving home from a ministerial conference. Sam and Gloria Dickens are returning from a visit to Sam's hometown. At first no one other than the reader is aware that killers are headed for Arrow Junction.

McKimmey manipulates the plot and orchestrates the cast (which also includes the local law, outside Saywell's place) with a sure hand. The story moves right along, with McKimmey's economical prose switching points of view and giving us insights into all the characters while never letting up on the suspense. There are any number of small surprises and payoffs along the way as we discover which characters are going to act in the ways we expect and which are not. Some will be cowardly, some will perform little acts or heroism, and some won't survive. McKimmey makes the reader care about all of them.

In fact, it's clear that like John D. MacDonald's "Grand Hotel" novels, *Cornered!* is as much a novel of character as it is a crime novel. Today it would probably be called "a novel of suspense," of which there is plenty in the story. It's the attention to the characters, however, that elevates it above many other paperbacks of the period.

And the same is true of *The Long Ride*. Before I talk about the book, though, I have to give a little background. Once upon a time, in 1961 when this book was published, I was a college student. Located in the student union building on the campus where I was a student, there was a map of the United States. Cards were provided so that people who were driving to any location could leave a name and number, and those looking for a ride could get in touch with them. Alternatively, someone who was looking for a ride but didn't see anyone going to the right city could leave contact information in the hope that a driver would see it and get in touch. That might seem a bit quaint now, but I suppose it must have worked well enough in those days. The map was there for my entire college career, and there were always cards from people who were driving or who were looking for rides.

The only reason I mention this is because that's more or less the setup for *The Long Ride*. McKimmey gathers a disparate group of people who are going to California from somewhere in the Midwest and who are looking for a ride. They respond to a newspaper ad, and find themselves in a station wagon owned by Mrs. Landry, a woman of a certain age who drives as if she's trying to win the Indy 500. That's a stressful situation, indeed, but it's made much more stressful because of who's in the station wagon with Mrs. Landry.

Before the long ride begins, however, there's another suspenseful setup, just as well done and exciting as the one in *Cornered!*. The book opens with two men preparing for a bank robbery. We learn almost immediately that one of the robbers, Harry Wells, is a violent man and a killer. He's ruthless and devoted only to himself.

When the robbery takes place, like so many bank robberies in books like this one, things turn violent and go very wrong. Wells, in a gun battle with the police, has to ditch the loot in order to escape.

A one-armed man, Allan Garwith, is a small-time crook married to a young woman named Cicely, who's desperately trying to make their marriage work. Garwith is an abuser and doesn't really care about Cicely.

While she's out, he witnesses the robbery. He also sees Wells hide the money. Garwith isn't going to pass up an opportunity like that, so he takes the money for himself. Now he needs to get out of town, but he doesn't have the means. So he and Cicely sign up for a ride to California with Mrs. Landry.

Harry Wells signs up, too. It's no coincidence. He knows that Garwith must have the money, and Harry will do what it takes to get it back. If he can figure out where it is. Garwith doesn't have it with him.

Another passenger is Miss Kennicott, a librarian who's going to California for a great adventure. She's going to get more adventure than she bargained for, but she's not going to get what she really wants.

Margaret Moore is also in the station wagon. She is a somewhat mysterious but beautiful woman who never likes to stay in one place for very long. California seems like a good destination to her.

The final passenger, John Benson, is an FBI agent. The FBI suspects Harry Wells is the robber, but they don't know who has the money. Benson also knows that Garwith lived in an apartment near the bank. The only way to keep an eye on the two men is for Benson to travel with them.

A good deal of the novel's suspense derives from what the readers know that most of the people in the car don't know. Mrs. Landry and Miss Kennicott are oblivious to the drama being played out around them. Mrs. Landry wants them all to sing to make their journey a cheerful one. As if that's not bad enough, Miss Kennicott clearly has her cap set for Benson. One's ability to enjoy *The Long Ride* is dependent to a certain degree to a tolerance for Miss Kennicott. She is, no question, one of the most annoying characters in all of McKimmey's fiction and might well make one wonder if McKimmey once had an unpleasant experience with a librarian.

As in *Cornered!*, several of the characters are given extensive backstories, but the primary ones are those for Garwith and Wells. One of McKimmey's strengths is giving even minor characters backgrounds that do a lot to explain their actions, and once again it's easy to see why McKimmey thought of himself as writing novels of character that just happen to become crime novels.

Both *Cornered!* and *The Long Ride* have the virtues that made paperback originals so exciting in the 1950s and early 1960s. They're well written in clean, economical prose, and they have clever, fast-moving plots. McKimmey also provides shifting points of view that reveal much about the characters and increases the reader's empathy for them. Even in the brief summaries above, it's evident that he drew from all sectors of society and that he enjoyed writing about what makes people tick.

*Cornered!* and *The Long Ride* have been out of print for more than fifty years. That's far too long, and it's good to have them back.

June 2016

# CORNERED!

by James McKimmey

# Chapter One

There were two men in the car. One was short, lean and dark. He was a tense man with quick dark eyes beneath black eyebrows. He wore a dark brown topcoat, matching hat, and tight-fitting leather gloves. He sat behind the steering wheel waiting for the service station attendant to come toward the pumps through the swirling snow.

The second man was not much taller, but he was heavier. He tended to roundness: his face was round, his hands were round, his puffy, fish-like eyes were round. He was dressed almost identically with his companion, but the color of his coat and hat was a lighter brown; the color almost matched that of his hair and eyebrows.

The attendant had arrived, and the darker, smaller man lowered the car window.

"Yes, sir?" the attendant smiled. His name was Corly Adams. He took pride in running his station. He wanted to run his station better than anyone else in Graintown. Corly was always happy to oblige, always happy to serve. It was good business, and Corly just liked to be engaged in everybody's affairs. When Corly went to heaven he only hoped there was plenty to do and a lot of folks up there to do it for.

"Fill it up," the darker man said.

"You bet your life!"

"Legs are killing me," the man with the round face said.

"Sure," the darker man said. "Everything kills you."

"Going to get out and stretch."

"Sure. Get out and stretch. You'll die otherwise."

The round man got out ungracefully, his topcoat bundled around him like a thick blanket. The dark wiry man got out too, smoothly and quickly. There was something about him that made his smallness seem less small. His face wore a set expression, and only his eyes moved. But it was somehow a look of animal endurance, not one of fragility. He held his small gloved hands in front of him and carefully rubbed one over the other.

The round man came around the front of the car. He looked like an outsized child bundled inside his topcoat. His teeth were chattering.

"This cold kills me."

"You should have died a thousand times today."

"You're losing your sense of humor, Billy."

Billy Quirter looked through the falling snow and noticed Corly

Adams adjust the nozzle of the gasoline hose into the car's tank, then brush a hand over the rear license plate.

The round man's voice hushed a little. "I wonder what Tony's thinking about right now?"

"Shut up," Billy Quirter said.

"See? You don't want to tense up too much, Billy. I've been watching you."

"Maybe it's listening to you, Al."

"Now, Billy." Al Poli slapped his hands together again, teeth chattering. "This goddam cold, huh? The middle of nowhere and all this cold and snow and crap. I'm going to freeze to death."

"I don't know who's worse off," Billy Quirter said, "you or Tony. All they're going to do with Tony is cyanide him. You, it's your legs killing you, the cold killing you..." His waspish voice trailed away. His eyes had never moved from the actions of Corly Adams.

"We're going to find her in time, ain't we?" Al Poli asked.

"Shut up, Al."

Al Poli shrugged, trying to burrow deeper in his topcoat.

Corly Adams came around the car. "You come from Nevada? I saw your license plates."

"Right," Billy Quirter lied.

"What part?"

"Vegas."

"Las Vegas! That's some town, I hear! All those movie stars!" Corly lifted the hood. "How do you like this new Chevy? Nice car, huh?"

"Sure," Billy Quirter said.

Corly Adams pulled the oil stick. "What do you do in Las Vegas, anyhow?"

Al Poli looked at Billy Quirter. Billy Quirter shoved his right hand through the first and second buttons of his topcoat. Al Poli put his right hand into the pocket of his topcoat.

"Business," Billy Quirter said.

"Fine! Well, your oil's okay." Corly looked across the car's engine as a half-ton truck moved in beside the other pumps. "What do you say, Henry!" he called. He slammed the hood down and turned to Billy Quirter. "Say, you fellows'll excuse me for a minute, won't you?"

"You got a map of this country?" Billy asked.

"You bet! A whole pile inside the office there. Just put out by the Chamber of Commerce. Take one and keep it!"

Corly Adams hurried to the newly arrived truck. Billy Quirter said, "Watch him, Al. He's nosy." Al Poli nodded. Billy Quirter walked toward the office.

Henry Dawson in the half-ton truck yelled to Corly Adams, "She's going to blizzard if she keeps it up!" But Al Poll could not catch the words. Snow blew in powdered gusts across the roof of the station office and around the pumps. Al Poli tried very hard to listen carefully. But he heard only voices, not words. The wind blew the words away.

The conversation would have meant nothing either to Al Poli or to Billy Quirter.

The point of Corly Adams's conversation with Henry Dawson was that Henry Dawson owned a few head of cattle that Sheriff Joe Bingham, who had decided he preferred cattle to a new campaign, was interested in buying. Henry Dawson had no telephone on his small ranch. So the retiring sheriff, with only twenty-seven days of term remaining, had left word with Corly Adams that he would like to speak to Henry Dawson when Henry came to town. While Billy Quirter walked into the office and Al Poli tried unsuccessfully to overhear the conversation going on in the whipping snow, Corly Adams was happily obliging Sheriff Bingham by talking to Henry Dawson.

"Said he wanted to see you first thing, Henry. Think I know where he is right this minute."

"Well, I ain't got nothing against talking cattle with Joe."

"Why don't you sit still? Maybe I can fetch him over here right now."

Cony turned and waved at Al Poli. "Be with you in a second!" He trotted toward the office as Billy Quirter was coming out, map in hand. "See you found it! Be right with you!"

Corly Adams fairly bounced with enthusiasm. It pleased him to be middle man for this piece of business. It pleased him that he knew just about where Sheriff Joe Bingham would be this time on a Friday morning. He telephoned the Sell-Rite Drug Company. Sure enough Sheriff Bingham was over there having a cup of coffee at the fountain counter.

Outside Billy Quirter returned to Al Poli. "What the hell's going on?"

Al Poli shook his head. "Yakked with the guy in the truck there. Then busted back inside and picked up the telephone."

A small muscle flickered beside Billy Quirter's mouth. They had been traveling for two days and three nights at high speed. They had a little over two days left. At that time Tony, Billy's half-brother, would be breathing cyanide pellets. Tony wanted the girl dead before that happened. Tony wanted that girl absolutely dead, so he could breathe those pellets knowing that the witness who'd got him into that death cell was getting the same as he was getting.

Billy took a breath. Tony had told him to knock the girl off, and he'd always done what Tony had told him to do. Moreover, Tony had promised to filter out word to Billy, using a prearranged code, about where to pick up that fifty thousand dollars he'd put away. But only if Billy chopped the girl in time. Billy Quirter rubbed a gloved hand across his mouth. He swung around as Corly Adams bounced back into the driving snow.

"Sorry to hold you up!" Cony said. "Where you fellows heading anyhow?"

"East." Billy kept his right hand inside his coat.

"Bad roads out that direction. You ought to have chains on. You got chains?"

"Yeah."

"I can put 'em on for you. No time at all."

Billy Quirter looked down at the map. On one side was a detailed map of Graintown and its neighboring towns. On the other was a map of the state. Arrow Junction, Billy Quirter saw, was a crossroads ten miles east on Route 7.

"How about Route 7?"

Corly Adams shook his head. "Gravel road. Maybe haven't put a snow plow through there since she started to storm. Haven't got a report yet this morning. I wouldn't try that without chains, mister."

Billy Quirter looked at Al Poli. Al Poli was no help. Billy finally said to Corly Adams, "Put the chains on."

"Do it real fast!" Corly Adams said, and shouted to Henry Dawson in the half-ton truck, "Hold right on, Henry. He wants to see you. He'll be right over!"

Bill Quirter moved back in the less windy area in front of the office. Al Poli moved with him. Al Poli's teeth were chattering again. His large fish eyes kept blinking. "Maybe we shouldn't wait for those chains, Billy."

"Now you say it. You talk when you're supposed to shut up, and you shut up when you're supposed to talk. Why don't you shut up now?"

Al Poli ducked his head against the snow and cold. Billy Quirter looked nervous and that frightened Al Poli. "Listen, Billy. Croaking that old buzzard in Sacramento—"

Billy turned black, furious eyes on Al Poli. "I keep telling you! You don't want to get paid for this trip?" Billy rubbed his gloved hand across his mouth again, looking back at Corly Adams. Murder was not new to Billy. He'd been committing it for his half-brother, Tony Fearon, all the years since Tony had got into the rackets. Almost nobody was wise;

he was just Tony's brother hanging around without even an active finger in the operation.

But now Tony was locked up in condemned row in that California prison. Billy didn't have Tony's personal reassurance that he was doing a good job so far. All he had was the help of a spaghetti-spined Al Poli.

All of that increased his nervousness. All of that kept him worrying about having killed the girl's father in Sacramento. Well, the hell with it. They'd made it look like a simple robbery and beating, hadn't they? And the ransack of the croaker's apartment had produced the lead they were looking for.

The girl may have disappeared after that day in court when Tony was convicted and had yelled his threat about getting her. But Billy and Al Poli had gotten one good lead: a note written in the old bugger's hand: *Annie—2346 Adams Street, Omaha.*

Billy and Al Poli had followed it out. She'd changed her last name from Rodick to Brown. She'd worked for a little while as a secretary in Omaha. Blonde, now, not brunette. Then she'd married some farmer from out in the sticks. They didn't know the farmer's name. But they knew the name of the small burg was Arrow Junction.

Now they were ten miles away. Close. But they couldn't afford any mistakes now.

"I'd put her up on the rack," Corly Adams yelled to them, "only I got Emil Bronsen's Nash up there, see?"

"What the hell do we care about that?" Al Poli said to Billy.

"Shut up, Al."

Corly Adams rattled a tire chain. He grinned and yelled at Henry Dawson in the truck, "How's the missus, Henry?"

"I mean this boy yaks and yaks," Al Poli said.

Billy Quirter shifted his feet nervously. Quite suddenly he didn't like any of this. Corly Adams seemed purposely clumsy in mounting the chains. There had been that telephone call. Billy didn't know what Corly Adams might have smelled out. The car switch in Vegas should have been good. You could always count on Nick Pappas for a clean car. But somehow Billy kept feeling something was going wrong.

It all happened quickly.

The light blue Ford sedan rolled up behind the half-ton truck. Corly Adams straightened and turned. A tall, lean man with a broad-brimmed hat stepped out of the Ford. Billy Quirter identified only one word that Corly Adams uttered:

*"Sheriff..."*

Billy saw the metal star pinned on the lapel of Joe Bingham's mackinaw. Billy's right hand came from under his coat. The gun in his hand leaped twice, spouting tongues of flame into the blowing snow.

Corly Adams watched Sheriff Joe Bingham sit down suddenly on the snow-covered concrete. Corly remained frozen for a fraction of a second, then spun around. He took one look at backing, gun-carrying Billy Quirter. Then he threw himself under Henry Dawson's half-ton truck in a single swift motion.

Al Poli was swearing. It was a steady aimless swearing, performed as he tried to make his brain catch up with what had just happened. Henry Dawson, shock-eyed, ducked under the window of his truck.

But Billy Quirter judged the situation in an instant. Their car was still up on the jack. They couldn't use that. What to do next?

While Billy was wondering that, the right hand of Sheriff Joe Bingham had moved laboriously under his mackinaw to close around his own gun. The gun came out and up. Al Poli fired at the same moment the gun in Sheriff Bingham's hand kicked.

Sheriff Bingham, in that last minute of his life, did not know which of the two men had shot him first or if it mattered. He simply fired at the larger, easier target.

Al Poli slid down to the snow like a thick blanket collapsing. It would have taken a better county coroner than Grain County owned to have determined who died first: Sheriff Joe Bingham or Al Poli.

Billy Quirter paused only once before he fled from sight. He looked back and saw the silhouette of Corly Adams lying under that truck.

With accurate speed, Billy Quirter aimed his gun at the man he was certain was responsible for all that had just happened.

When Billy Quirter disappeared, Corly Adams lay flat beneath that truck, a bullet gone cleanly from temple to temple. It was Corly's chance at last to find out how much there was to do in heaven and how many he could do it for. The only man alive remaining in that snow-swept station that morning was farmer Henry Dawson. Farmer Dawson had not been touched by hand or bullet. But it later took five of Graintown's strongest men to pry him out of that truck....

It was some time later that Tony Fearon, much larger than Billy and pasty white with prison pallor, heard the news of the shooting in Graintown.

But he'd already got the news about that old man being killed in Sacramento. So far, neither the cops nor the newspapers had tied up the old man's death with the threat Tony Fearon had made the day he'd been convicted; although one San Francisco daily had noted the fact that the old man, beaten to death and robbed, was the father of the key witness who'd accidentally been on the scene the night Tony had gunned fellow-gambler Mickey Haveland in a burst of temper. Nobody but that girl, that witness, had taken Tony's threat seriously. That was too bad. They should have been smarter, just like Tony should have been smarter in the first place and let Billy take care of Mickey Haveland.

But that was done now, and Tony was going to die. But not before he knew that the girl was dead. Billy was on this one. No matter how Billy made Tony's skin crawl, he was the best assignment killer in the business. The cops had thought for years he was just a hanger-on who'd bummed his living off Tony. But Tony made Billy earn his living. Billy, weird bastard that he was, had earned it well.

The death of the old man in Sacramento had come out of no simple beating and robbery, Tony knew. It was Billy at work, trailing that girl, to nail her once and for all.

And that was all Tony Fearon was praying for—that Billy would bring it off. It was no matter that the girl's involvement had been entirely accidental. The only thing that mattered was that her testimony had put him where he was now, and she was going to pay for it. Tony Fearon had focused all the hate in his system on just this one thing.

It was not with the faintest surprise or self-questioning that, at death's edge, he found himself praying not to God, but to one of the best gunmen west of the Mississippi River.

# Chapter Two

When Billy Quirter had first looked at that map picked up in Corly Adams's service station, he'd labeled Arrow Junction a crossroads. Arrow Junction was more than that to its citizens. It was All of Life.

Within the town were one church, one combined garage and service station, one combined lumber yard and hardware shop, one post office, and one general store. The general store offered a grocery section, a small meat counter, a lunch counter, a small but varied collection of drug sundries, and plenty of animated conversation by its owner and proprietor, Robert Saywell. Robert Saywell's enterprise was known as the Arrow Junction General Store or more familiarly as Bob's. It was the focal point for the community.

Bob Saywell was fifty-three years old and a leader in the community. He was a bristling, rather short man of considerable girth. His hair, straight and white, showed off a pink complexion that somehow seemed ageless, despite the crinkling lines. Bob Saywell had lived in Arrow Junction all his life with the exception of two years spent in Kansas City during his eighteenth and nineteenth years when he'd clerked in a shoe store and learned that it was more important for him to perform at a responsible level within Arrow Junction's small sphere than to enjoy the more exotic fruits of Kansas City living on a cheap clerk's level. There were, after all, the annual trips to Chicago to season an otherwise restricted existence.

At the moment there was a lull in the store. Besides Bob Saywell only Charlie Bacon and Dr. Hugh Stewart were in the room, both seated at the lunch counter.

It was a little past ten-thirty. Dr. Hugh Stewart, young and handsome, was drinking a cup of coffee. Charlie Bacon, in from his farm three miles west of town, was eating an early lunch. The news of the shooting in Graintown ten miles away had not yet arrived.

Bob Saywell moved along behind the counter, brushing plump hands against his white apron. "How do you like that coleslaw, Charlie? You don't get coleslaw like that every day. Got the recipe for Martha last time I was in Chicago. I wouldn't take five hundred dollars for that coleslaw recipe. Got it from a cook there in the Enright Hotel where I stay. The management would have a fit if they knew that fellow gave me that recipe."

Charlie Bacon looked up, then down. He tasted the coleslaw again, paused, nodded, suddenly convinced that the coleslaw was something very special. Bob Saywell was a good talker.

The fact that the coleslaw was just plain coleslaw that Martha, Bob Saywell's wife, had made up in the same way she'd always made it up did not prove Bob Saywell's statement a deliberate lie—not in Bob Saywell's mind. Bob Saywell did not lie. He merely invented a little as he talked.

"Quite a storm," Dr. Hugh Stewart said.

Bob Saywell moved down the counter a little, straightened a napkin holder, then looked back at Hugh Stewart. "Did you say something, Doc?"

"I said it's quite a storm, Mr. Saywell."

"Oh, sure, Doc. It's quite a storm."

Dr. Hugh Stewart did not realize the extent of harm Bob Saywell had done him during these past months. It was not that Bob Saywell said or did anything definite. It was just that when business lulled and Bob Saywell chatted with this customer or that, it was quite easy for Bob Saywell to wonder aloud about the advisability of seeking Dr. Hugh Stewart's services. You had, after all, some pretty good doctors you could trust over in Graintown, Drs. Orwell and Nordly. And you never knew about a young fellow like this, full of just school training and no real experience. He was a stranger to Arrow Junction, wasn't he? How could you get to know anyone in only eight months? And wasn't there a little something funny about him anyway, with that quiet way of his and all?

Hugh Stewart, of course, did not know why Bob Saywell would attempt to damage him, since it was a well-known fact that the Arrow Junction area could use another doctor. But the truth was that there were two specific reasons why Bob Saywell opposed the presence of Dr. Hugh Stewart.

The first was that it was necessary for Bob Saywell to remain constantly influential in Arrow Junction. He wished to share this influence with nobody, with the possible exception of Reverend John Andrews. And Reverend Andrews was, in reality, no competition with that halting, ineffectual manner of his. It was just that Reverend Andrews was a representative of the Good Lord, and Bob Saywell was not going to compete with that, but rather join forces. There was nobody in or around Arrow Junction who attended church services with greater regularity than Bob Saywell.

But Hugh Stewart was a threat to Bob Saywell's monopoly on influence. Bob Saywell knew well enough how most folks got to worshiping a doctor once he was established. The idea then was simply to prevent Dr. Hugh Stewart from becoming established. By so doing Bob Saywell not only retained his own power, but proved once again that he could make or break a man in this community, a proof that certainly did not displease him.

The second reason for Bob Saywell's opposition to Dr. Hugh Stewart made itself apparent just at the moment Bob Saywell rounded the counter and walked over to recheck his supply of drug items.

Ann Burley walked into the store.

Dr. Hugh Stewart looked up and smiled at her. There was a fleeting but noticeable exchange of looks between them that Bob Saywell did not fail to see. There was a quickening in Bob Saywell's blood at the sight of Ann Burley. His mouth turned dry, and a pulse showed visibly at his throat. The looks between Ann Burley and Hugh Stewart sent a small rage of jealousy through him.

Still, even that whipping jealousy, even the persistent desire for a continuing monopoly of influence in Arrow Junction, evaporated from Bob Saywell's mind as he continued to stare at Mrs. Ted Burley coming along beside the counter. The cold had put a blush in her cheeks. The powdery snow had caught in her pale-blond hair and was now suddenly melting and shimmering like white jewels. Bob Saywell's mind skipped to that newspaper clipping he'd placed beneath the flour canister in the kitchen. His palms turned moist.

"Morning, Mrs. Burley!" he exploded. "Quite a storm, isn't it?"

There was a troubled look in Ann Burley's eyes. But Bob Saywell did not notice that. And it was not evident in her voice when she said, "Yes, it is, Mr. Saywell."

Once again Bob Saywell let himself think exactly how it would be with Ann Burley. He let his mind wheel through a cascading flight of imagination. There was a note of pure beauty in Ann Burley's face. The blond hair (that was dyed, Bob Saywell was certain) set off those dark eyebrows of hers, enlivened those brown eyes. And Bob Saywell had seen well enough last summer how Ann Burley looked when she walked down the sidewalk wearing those thin summer dresses.

He came forward to meet her, fairly bristling. He was absolutely going to make that trip over to Graintown today to see what he could see, even through the storm. He was going over to the Graintown library and check the newspaper files and prove what he was certain about anyway. That newspaper clipping under the canister was about the impending execution of a killer on the West Coast named Tony Fearon. It contained a review of the trial, including mention of a threat Tony Fearon had made when he'd been convicted, a threat that he would make certain the girl who had been the witness against him would be killed before he died.

Oh, Bob Saywell's brain was canny. He had a good memory. And he could remember the news stories way back at the time right after the trial when a reporter attempting to interview the girl had revealed she'd completely disappeared from California.

Well, she'd gone to somewhere. And Bob Saywell was pretty sure he knew just where. Oh, she was something all right, so clean and ladylike around a community like Arrow Junction, when in truth she was nothing but a big-city floozy mixed up with something degraded and criminal, bringing that degradation and criminality right along with her.

Bob Saywell swallowed, trying to hold down the excitement he felt when he thought about what she really was, what it would really be like if he could...

"Saved you some real fine special chops, Mrs. Burley!" Bob Saywell, pillar of Arrow Junction society, babbled. "You just come take a look...."

Just then George Herbert burst into the store. "You folks heard yet? Terrible thing in Graintown! A shooting right there in Corly Adams's station. Corly dead! Joe Bingham dead! Henry Dawson was there. Saw it all. They say Henry's like to being crazy. Keeps staring at people like he don't know where he's at. Nobody knows how it come about. Just these two fellows came in and started shooting. One of them dead too. Say he's some kind of gangster from out in California. Other fellow got away. They're looking all over for him! I tell you…"

Dr. Hugh Stewart was the only one who noticed the color go out of Ann Burley's face. He barely caught her before she fainted.

# Chapter Three

The storm was biting in by midafternoon that day. There was cold wind and driving snow. Drifts were building steadily along the snow fences of the fields. Roads were gradually becoming more difficult.

There was a good amount of confusion in the courthouse in Graintown. Sheriff-elect Harvey Jenkins and Deputy Wade Miles were not at all certain of their next move. But the sheriff had notified the State Police, and gradually some order was being restored.

The roads leading in and out of Graintown were being blocked this minute. Each car was being stopped and checked. Some preliminary searching had been done through the town, but nothing intense yet.

"We'll get him, don't you worry," Sheriff-elect Jenkins had said, assuming authority prematurely by twenty-seven days, doing it with a great deal of outer bluff to belie the confused uncertainty and fright he felt inside.

The truth was that ever since he'd viewed that body of the late Sheriff, Joe Bingham, he was shaking inside with the kind of fear he hadn't felt since the threat of his infantry company being shipped overseas during World War I, a threat evaporated at the last minute only by the Armistice. The truth was that Harvey Jenkins wished to bloody hell he'd never run for the office of sheriff in the first place, just to try to get a little prestige by beating a weak candidate like Ed Madison.

But despite Sheriff-elect Jenkins's promise, no trace had yet been found of Billy Quirter; and Billy Quirter had now been identified by West Coast bulletins as the half-brother of a killer awaiting execution in a California prison. That was enough, along with the knowledge of Quirter's performance in Corly Adams's service station earlier that day, to make Harvey Jenkins know that the capture of Billy Quirter was going to be dangerous, nasty business.

Sheriff-elect Jenkins felt sick to his stomach, and he kept remembering how, when he was a child some fifty years ago, he used to solve being frightened by running to his bedroom, jumping into bed and pulling the covers over his head....

Billy Quirter, when he re-examined that Chamber of Commerce map, saw that Arrow Junction was not a crossroads. There were, in fact, no two roads to cross, but simply one road that came in one side and went out the other.

Billy was hunched inside a woodshed on the north rim of Graintown. The shed was open on one side. That side faced a snow-covered field. Unfortunately the wind was cutting straight in. Billy was shivering steadily now. His skin had a bluish tint along his jaw. He'd lost his hat. Snow was sticking to his black straight hair.

But Billy was all right. He was thinking quite clearly.

He ran his finger along the line indicating Route 7 which split through the center of Arrow Junction. Then he ran his finger along the other line, the red one indicating railroad tracks. They would be watching Route 7 closely, Billy was certain, but maybe not the railroad. The railroad yards were straight east of where he huddled in that lean-to.

He shoved the map in his pocket and pulled the topcoat tighter around his thin neck. He moved out carefully. Billy didn't care a damn for anything now, including his brother. If Tony had let Billy handle that gambler instead of losing his head and lousing it up, why, he wouldn't be where he was. Getting that girl and grabbing the fifty Gs were the only things that mattered in the world right now.

And nobody was going to stop him.

# Chapter Four

Ann Burley lived one mile west of Arrow Junction, just one eighth of a mile of dirt road off Route 7. You could see the house from the graveled snow-covered highway even through the continuing storm. Bob Saywell, when he drove by on his way to Graintown, slowed just a little, eyes narrowing above his fatty pink cheeks. Dr. Hugh Stewart's car was parked in the yard. There was yet no sign of Ted Burley's pickup truck.

Bob Saywell could still remember with pumping anger how Dr. Hugh Stewart had carried the limp figure of Ann Burley to a table. He could remember how he'd rubbed her wrists, touched her forehead gently. Bob Saywell could feel his own fingers twitch as he thought about that.

Bob Saywell swore. It was not a profane swearing. But rather a vicious repeating of Biblical declaiming: "Thou harlot! Thou slut!"

Because he was almost sure now. By the time Dr. Hugh Stewart had revived Ann Burley, insisting that he drive her home, Bob Saywell had hurried back to the kitchen. He'd taken the newspaper clipping from under the canister and looked at it again carefully. There was almost no doubt. The vague familiarity of Ann Burley's face when she had first arrived in Arrow Junction with Ted Burley was explained. She was Ann Rodick. The witness in that trial.

Bob Saywell's cheeks fairly quivered. She'd lied about her identity to Ted Burley. She'd lied to every decent citizen in this community. Now there had been the appearance of those gangsters in Graintown. And Ann Burley had fainted when she'd heard about that.

All right. Soon he would absolutely confirm it. And then....

Bob Saywell was traveling on Route 7. Route 7 created, in effect, a long S over a span of three hundred miles. Arrow Junction was very near the center of that S.

There were, at that moment, two cars traveling toward the center.

One of them was a 1948 Ford sedan containing Reverend and Lottie Andrews, who were just returning toward Arrow Junction from a ministers' conference in Babcock. The other was a new Chrysler containing Sam and Gloria Dickens, who were returning to the West Coast from a visit at the small town of Bannerton, Sam Dickens's old home town.

Of the two cars, only Sam Dickens's carried a radio. The strongest beam you could get was from the direction in which Sam Dickens was driving. West. The beam came from Station KWTC in Babcock. Right now a local announcer at KWTC was relating the latest news on the hunt for Billy Quirter. He was doing it with a monotoned twangy Midwest accent, and the words were merely an irritating hum of sound in the ears of both Sam and Gloria Dickens. Neither was listening carefully enough to realize that the search for Billy was going on in the path of their intended route. Both were angry, as the Chrysler rolled with slow uncertainty through the storm.

Finally Gloria reached out and snapped off the radio. "Some goddam sport."

Sam Dickens shifted his hands on the steering wheel. He was a large man with beefy hands and a florid face. He would be forty-seven on his next birthday, and right now his neck ached as though he were going to be ninety-seven. Good God, he thought, what a trip! But to Gloria he said, "Now take it easy, honey. And do you have to swear?"

Gloria uttered a four-letter word that made Sam Dickens's face turn even more florid.

"You know I don't like you to swear, Glory. That word in particular."
Gloria said it again.

Sam Dickens sighed, looking sideways at his wife—his third wife, to be exact.

She was twenty-two years old. When Sam had first seen her in the chorus line at that hotel in Las Vegas his throat had caught just like a kid falling in love for the first time. She'd been beautiful, with those long shapely legs and that tantalizing smile. He'd made up his mind instantly. Four weeks later they'd gotten married.

Now, well, she certainly didn't look like she did when she was dancing. But after ten months of marriage he'd gotten used to this other look of hers: like a kid, hair in a pony tail, wearing a blue striped sweater and black matador pants, not even using any makeup except a little lipstick.

So, Sam Dickens thought, she was just a kid. Still, he knew, she had real potential. She was a lot smarter than she'd like you to think. Once, before they were married, Sam had walked into her hotel room and found her reading Sophocles, for God's sake. It was her second time through. *King Oedipus, Oedipus at Colonnus, Antigone.* And she knew what the hell it was she'd read, although she had some kind of juvenile notion that she ought not to make anything out of it. She had a really big heart. Out of the money she'd saved from dancing she'd bought Sam the camel's hair topcoat he was wearing right now, the most expensive coat he'd ever owned, and he'd owned some good ones. And guts. You didn't get in Gloria's way when her back was up. She'd become a foster child when she was eight and went through five homes. She'd learned how to handle the hard knocks with the toughest of them. But at times she seemed to revert to being the child that she really was underneath that flip front of hers. That was when Sam realized the difference between their ages. It took something like this trip to do that, but, by God, this trip had really done it.

"Return to the womb," Gloria said. She hiked her legs under her and stared out the window at the swirling snow with grim boredom.

"What?" Sam Dickens asked.

"I said return to the womb. That's what this was. My God."

"All right. What's the matter with that?"

"It's proof of retarded development."

"Glory, you dance real good. You've got nice legs and a real sexy smile. Sometimes you show a real good brain. But as an amateur psychologist you stink."

Gloria used her word again.

Sam Dickens compressed his lip. "So it didn't work out so well. So what? That's life, isn't it?"

"This is life? This crummy country? Look at the snow. It keeps snow-ing and snowing. So I like snow. But I like something else once in a fat while. It snows out here like a horse—"

"Watch your tongue, Glory. Don't be so foulmouthed."

"It's this stinking country. It's enough to make anyone foul-mouthed. Even a lady, which I ain't."

"You're a lady. You just hate to admit it, for some reason. You've got some notion that—"

Gloria uttered her word for the fourth time.

Sam Dickens didn't try to argue any more. There wasn't any use. He couldn't really blame Gloria anyway. The whole trip had been a mistake. So this state was home. Or rather had been. It certainly wasn't any more. He'd forgotten altogether what it was like. And he couldn't blame Glo-ria, what with the way it had gone. And Gloria had never been east of Las Vegas in her life.

"You know," Gloria said, "I keep thinking about your aunt—the one with the nose."

"All right, Glory. Lay off."

"Now she was something. What a sweet old soul. I'll bet hers was the original witch's in a snowdrift. Talk about cold! That old tweet would freeze an Eskimo's—"

"Glory, I'm telling you. I'm going to stop at the next service station and wash your mouth out with soap."

"You and how many others, I wonder?" Gloria said insinuatingly.

Sam opened his mouth and closed it. His face flushed even more. One thing he'd learned for certain. He'd made himself the best producer in Hollywood he could. But that was just about all he was now. He cer-tainly wasn't a kid in the old home town any more. Going back to Ban-nerton was positive proof of that. Apparently Bannerton felt the same way about him. And what Gloria had just needled him about in a round-about way, well …

What was he supposed to do? So he'd walked away from the big Car-well kid's insults. That had made Gloria mad. Good God, he thought, I can't fight every young punk in Bannerton that comes along and dis-likes me because I got out of the damned town and did something with my life.

Sam's hands gripped over the wheel tightly. All right. So maybe in some basic way she was right.

Juvenile or not, right or wrong, sometimes there was honor in not run-ning away. Because the Carwell punk wasn't the only thing he'd run away from. He'd also run away from the situation in Hollywood.

Maybe that had avoided a showdown between him and Johnny Masters. But only temporarily. Sooner or later he was going to have to face Masters. Fight him, in fact. Not with fists. But he was going to have to fight him just the same so the studio would know whose policy it was going to be when he produced a picture: his or Masters's. With Masters's young bull drive it was going to have to be one of them.

So he'd run off from that and gone barreling back to his old home town.

Why? To find something he'd left back there? His parents had been dead for years.

What the hell was he looking for anyway, going back to Bannerton? Return to the womb, Gloria had called it. Maybe she was right. Because when you were forty-seven and in real trouble with your career, maybe it looked better back in that direction.

Once again Sam Dickens glanced at Gloria. She was still sitting with her feet under her, still gazing stubbornly out the window.

Sam's mind, no matter how he fought it, kept going back to Marge. How long had they been together? Thirteen years? That dull ache hit him again. He thought of how she'd looked that last time he'd seen her alive, when she was dying in that hospital bed with a stinking disease nobody could do anything about.

But it was no good thinking about Marge. It was no good thinking about Morla either. He should have known it was no more than a horrible loneliness for Marge that caused him to marry Morla. Now it was Gloria. And Gloria was really bitched off.

"Look, honey," he said, "why don't you turn the radio on again? Find some music. Music always cheers you up."

"Not the kind of music they play around here. Ring dang doody, ring dang do. It's got as much class as an old cow's—"

"Knock it off, Glory."

"Lullaby in turd land."

"Damn it, Glory—"

It wasn't any use. She was right. Walk away from everything that smacked of reality. Including the reality of Gloria's foul mouth. How could anyone look as beautiful as Gloria did when she was on stage and still come up with the dirtiest talk this side of Brooklyn?

But that was the way she was. It didn't change anything else about her, certainly....

Light was growing dim, the storm seemed to increase. Now Sam was able to drive no faster than forty-five miles an hour. They were coming into a little place. Bostwick. He remembered that. There was a motel up ahead. They couldn't drive all night. They wouldn't even come close to hitting Cheyenne until late tomorrow.

Moreover, he was feeling a warm desire. He'd never quite got over that, ever since he and Gloria had been together. Now it was all the more intense.

"What do you say we stop for the night, honey? Get some rest and a fresh start tomorrow. How about it? We're both a little on edge, I think."

Gloria shrugged.

He parked and registered. Others had been slowed by the storm. The motel was almost filled. There was one unit left, a double cabin.

Sam unloaded their bags into the cabin, while Gloria took off her coat in the second section. A blast of snow-filled wind hit Sam's back as he closed the door. The sudden warmth felt good and comforting. He took off his coat and hat and tossed them over the bed in the first section. He looked in the second section as Gloria was pulling the blue striped sweater over her head, then slipping off the matador pants.

She stood, touching her hair, looking at herself in a mirror, wearing only the expensive and brief lingerie Sam had bought her. She was built, Sam thought; she was a lot of things, but one thing she certainly was was built.

"This is nice, isn't it?" he said, smiling.

"Yeah," she said shortly, and disappeared into the bath. He listened to the shower running, then got out the leather flask of Scotch from his bag. He walked into the second section and arranged two glasses on the bureau. When she came out, he said, "We can have a nightcap together."

She had on a short pink nightgown. "All right," she said, the edge less in her voice.

"Do you want ice?" he asked. "I can walk up to the office and get some."

"No," she said. "It's all right."

He suddenly felt better; when she looked at him like that and talked to him like that, something got a little tight in his throat. He came out of the bath in pajamas, poured two drinks and carried them over to the bed where she was sitting, legs pulled up under her.

"Cheers, baby," he said softly.

"Blood in your eye." She suddenly gave him that smile of hers. He could not help laughing.

"Baby, baby," he said, putting an arm around her, burying his face against her neck. He put his drink down. He moved his face up and kissed her. He looked into her eyes. All of a sudden he wanted to explain to her about that Carwell kid, so that she would understand perfectly, so that it wouldn't be in their way.

"Glory, listen," he said, whispering, "about that Carwell kid—"

She suddenly stiffened.

"See, Glory—"

"Why couldn't you have done something, Sam?"

"Honey, listen—"

She moved away from him now, enough to make him free her entirely. "I'm tired, Sam."

"Glory."

"You just didn't do anything."

In a moment, he knew, it was going to be just like it had been in the car. Why did she have this juvenile notion so deep-rooted? He felt himself angering. "Damn it, Glory—"

She looked at him, anger flaring in her eyes. "I'd like to get some sleep."

He stood up, putting her glass down hard on the bureau, carrying his own into the next section. He closed the door behind him. He sat down and finished his drink. He shook his head, sighing, as the anger evaporated.

He wasn't thinking about Billy Quirter at that moment, because he'd paid no real attention to that news broadcast. He wasn't thinking about Ann Burley or Dr. Hugh Stewart or Ted Burley or Bob Saywell, because he didn't know them.

He was only thinking about Gloria, realizing with a kind of surprise that, despite everything, he really, honestly, was in love with that kid.

# Chapter Five

Reverend John Andrews was driving in the direction of Arrow Junction from the opposite end of the S formed by Route 7. He was not thinking of Billy Quirter any more than Sam Dickens was, because, not having a radio in his ageing Ford, he had not yet heard of Billy Quirter at all. But he was thinking, in a vaguely general way, about Ann Burley, Dr. Hugh Stewart, Ted Burley and Bob Saywell, because all of them were actively or inactively a part of his congregation.

Specifically Reverend Andrews was thinking desperately about what he was going to say to his flock that next Sunday morning. The trouble was that although Reverend Andrews felt his faith so strongly that the intensity of it often gave him actual physical pain, he could seldom communicate that faith to his flock.

In the three years that Reverend Andrews had been the minister for the Lutheran community of Arrow Junction, there had been numerous times when his wife Lottie had gotten up in the middle of the night and found the good reverend on his knees making an impassioned appeal to the heavens to give him more adequacy of communication.

But that did not mean he wished to be exactly like Reverend Maynard Styles. Now as he and Lottie were driving home from the Babcock Ministers' Conference, Reverend Andrews was even more certain that he did not want to be exactly like Maynard Styles.

"It was a nice conference, wasn't it?" Lottie asked. When Lottie and Reverend Andrews had been married, Lottie's daddy, Horace Teliwinder, had described his daughter as, "Just a big little girl." That was twenty-three years ago. Lottie was an even bigger little girl now. But she had retained that tiny voice, and nobody, including Reverend Andrews, thought of her as anything but a little girl. She adored her husband. Though the Reverend was smaller-boned, an inch shorter and a good deal leaner, nobody ever thought of large Lottie as anything but Reverend Andrews's little girl.

"Yes," Reverend Andrews said, "it was a nice conference, Lottie."

"The food was so good."

"Yes, it was."

"Dear, you seem so blue."

"No, I'm not. I'm feeling very thankful that the Good Lord allowed us to make this journey with so much enjoyment."

"I know that, dear. But even if you're grateful to the Good Lord, that doesn't mean you can't be blue, does it? I wish you'd tell me. You always keep things to yourself."

Reverend Andrews shook his head. "I don't know, Lottie. We should always think well of our brothers, particularly our brothers who have rallied to the call of the Lord and taken up the yoke of duty. But—"

"You're thinking about Maynard Styles, aren't you? I know what usually makes you upset. You think Maynard is—well—"

"Don't say it, Lottie. Let's leave judgments up to the Good Lord."

"Well, I can't help but feel that Maynard isn't always thinking about the Good Lord."

"Now, Lottie."

"It's true. He didn't seem to be thinking so much about the Good Lord when he kept going on about how much the church in Babcock was paying him. And then about that extension to his house."

"Jealousy is the Devil beckoning, Lottie."

"I do wish we could have a little more money. But I'm not jealous, John.

It's just that Maynard seems to be more concerned with worldly things than a good minister ought to be."

"He's doing very fine work, Lottie. You know that."

"I know that. And he talks an awful lot about it too. Just because we all grew up in Arrow Junction, I sometimes think he tries to make us jealous. Talking on and on about his programs over KWTC. I don't think that's the way the Good Lord likes things to be done."

"Now, Lottie," Reverend Andrews repeated, but Lottie had opened the tap that allowed the whole disturbment of being around Maynard Styles wash through his mind. Even as he prayed for an unembittered attitude, the Devil kept beckoning.

Maynard Styles was a tall broad-shouldered man with a handsome and strong profile. There was the strength of Samson in his looks. Reverend Andrews, when he examined his own insignificant features in the morning mirror, often wondered at the Good Lord's oversight in this unequal distribution.

Moreover Maynard Styles owned the voice of thunder, a voice that caused Reverend Andrews something very close to shame when he compared it to his own slightly rasping sound that always seemed to fog in the middle of particularly emotional utterances.

Yes, Maynard Styles certainly owned all the physical assets that a good minister would want to own. But for a good number of young years Maynard Styles had been quite deaf to the clarion trumpet of the Lord. Reverend Andrews well remembered one evening in 1932 when Maynard Styles had been discovered drunkenly passed out in the middle of the main street of Arrow Junction.

But of course Maynard did change his ways after he'd gone off to agricultural school at the University.

He'd come back loudly proclaiming his new dedication to becoming a worker for the Lord. Reverend Andrews had never heard a more enthusiastic vocal pledge to reform than Maynard Styles had made.

And the truth was that Reverend Andrews had never been sure that the switch from farming to preaching had been done entirely for spiritual reasons.

Reverend Andrews's career had produced one long siege of austere existence as he and Lottie moved from one tiny community to another, finally winding up back in Arrow Junction. But a minister's life could produce something else, as Maynard Styles had proved.

Maynard Styles had been able to settle comfortably, if not grandly, in Babcock. He had his three-times-a-week broadcast over KWTC, which brought his voice to so many that it would be no time at all before he went on to Omaha or even Chicago. He had his large house with its fine study and fireplace. He had his good gabardine suits, his Stetson hats, and that new De Soto. Reverend Andrews was not at all sure that Maynard Styles could have done so well materially at farming as he had done at ministering. Certainly there would not have been so much ego satisfaction in plowing the land.

Reverend Andrews tried to shake free from that kind of thinking. Judgments, as he'd told Lottie, should be left up to the Lord. And if sometimes distributions seemed unequal, well, the Lord often saw to balances in His own way.

"Storm seems to be getting worse," Lottie said. "It's a good thing they've been through here with the snow plow. I wonder if they've been through between Graintown and Arrow Junction?"

"Let's hope so."

"Are you hungry, dear?"

"I am a little, yes."

Lottie lifted from the back seat one of several cardboard boxes left over from the conference. It was filled with cold fried chicken.

"I think maybe I'll just keep driving through tonight, dear."

Reverend Andrews settled himself more firmly behind the wheel. In truth he had to keep driving because he didn't have enough money to stop at a motel for the night. But Reverend Andrews nonetheless sent up his prayers of gratitude. The windshield wipers were working fine. The heater was giving out good heat. The time spent driving might very well solve his problem of what to say on Sunday. Reverend Andrews was suddenly more content.

They had plenty to eat, after all. There was a gigantic quantity of fried chicken in the back seat. Despite the fact that Reverend and Lottie Andrews had consumed enough fried chicken over the past twenty-three years never to want to hear a chicken cackle, you couldn't deny that it was always good chicken. The Good Lord was just, Reverend Andrews reminded himself.

"Here, dear," said Lottie. "You can have the wishbone this time."

# Chapter Six

Earlier that day, Dr. Hugh Stewart had watched Ann Burley open her eyes in Bob Saywell's store and known the feeling about her he'd been trying so hard to avoid could no longer be avoided.

That had been at late morning. He'd driven her home. He'd taken her into her house. He'd been with her alone.

Now, as the wind increased and darkness moved in late that afternoon, Hugh Stewart paced his small office on the second floor of a building facing the main street of Arrow Junction.

A quiet man, Arrow Junction had labeled Hugh Stewart. They had even developed a form of distrust for it, neatly prodded along by Bob Saywell. But the quiet was but an outward control for Hugh Stewart to cover the inner fires.

Hugh Stewart walked across the office and stared at the turbulence outside. This storm—it was like the storm that had begun in him early and continued to reappear, seasonally, with the same inclemency that storms built and raged over these Midwest fields.

Hugh Stewart stood silently, a tall man who did not look tall because of the slim well-proportioned body. The slimness, like the quiet, was deceptive. He was a little over six feet. But he weighed one hundred and eighty-one pounds. Nobody in Arrow Junction would have guessed that. There were a lot of things about Hugh Stewart that nobody in Arrow Junction would have guessed.

He turned, looking at the simple neatness of his office. It was clean, normal, economically equipped. He was now a small-town doctor. And he was not even successful at that. Hugh Stewart lifted his hands and looked at them.

They were large hands with long, strong fingers. He had not used those hands with the true skill they owned since he'd gotten here. He smiled bitterly. He wondered what Dr. Emil Ludgaard would think about that. Perhaps, he thought, Emil Ludgaard would understand. Perhaps Emil Ludgaard had understood a lot about him.

Hugh Stewart had never talked anything but medicine and surgery with Emil Ludgaard. In those terse working days the walls of that New York clinic formed a barrier against anything else.

"You could be a great surgeon, Hugh," Emil Ludgaard had said in his softly clipped, European-accented words.

Emil Ludgaard was a great surgeon himself. He did not make mistakes in judgment. He never lied. It was an occasion when he offered the faintest compliment.

"You could be a great surgeon, Hugh...."

Yes, Hugh Stewart breathed to himself, a great surgeon....

His mind raced back through the tunnel of time; those childhood parentless years. He'd been just seven months old in 1926 when that Atlantic boat had sunk and killed both parents. But he'd been saved, handed ashore to an aunt who was too busy, too pretty, to want an orphaned infant seven months old.

Later he'd learned something about his parents through this sister of his mother's. He'd learned about their gaiety, their money, their whirlwind life of excitement. But he'd really understood nothing. Not even later when the Crash had disintegrated the family money and sent the aunt to sudden poverty and too much alcohol, when she'd finally drawn a razor across her wrists.

He'd been found in that small apartment with her. Hungry. Dirty. Screaming his lungs out. He had not understood then. But later he did, through the lean and lonely years of being shunted from family to family. The same fire blazed inside himself, he'd discovered, that must have blazed inside his parents and his aunt. But the elements around him were different. He learned to case the fire in armor.

But he had not been entirely unlucky. There had finally been Uncle Ben, clear on the opposite coast in California.

Uncle Ben had given him understanding and love. It was a quietly good time with Uncle Ben, who was not really his uncle but the uncle of his father. There was a neat picket-fenced cottage. There was a room of his own. If he'd felt any insecurity before, he lost it with Uncle Ben.

Uncle Ben had worked with him and been proud of the results. It was high school by that time. It was study and athletics. He'd accomplished both. Honor student. Star halfback.

He'd achieved his accomplishments quietly, trying to hide the fire. But the fire exploded now and then. Twice with girls which only gave him a reputation that was not uninviting to other girls. They were a little afraid of him. The bolder and better-looking of them searched him out. When, almost invariably, he continued with his quiet and his armor, they went away puzzled.

The fire exploded in other directions too. He found a sudden switch of interest and discovered medicine. As a result the athletic drive lessened. The summer after high school he worked with an ice company, loading cakes of ice. But every night he'd gone home and pored over books. The hunger for medicine became full-blown.

Uncle Ben had been steadily behind him. Grayer now. More bent. Working at his factory job with uncomplaining good humor.

"You want to be a doctor, Hugh. I'll help all I can...."

But Hugh had refused help then. He would not be a burden to Uncle Ben. He'd gotten a football scholarship. He played adequate but uninspired football for three years, getting all the pre-med he could, and working as a janitor to pay for the small room he rented.

Then the Army. When he returned home, the hunger was greater.

Uncle Ben said, "Now let me help you, Hugh. You can't waste more time. Medical school will take all your time...."

He worked, earning what he could when he could at whatever he could find. He went to school the year around. Uncle Ben helped him. It wasn't nearly enough. But somehow it worked out. He made it. Uncle Ben, white-haired now and thin, cried the day he graduated.

Then came internship and residency. He knew, of course, what kind of doctor he wanted to be by then: the best kind of surgeon. The power of the desire was so great that it frightened him.

He took long and hard walks at night, wondering at the flames inside him. Once, in the blackness of a cold winter night, he felt the flames might explode and disintegrate him, leaving nothing but a flashing brilliance in the night, then only blackness. That was the first time he got really drunk, waking up in the cheap room of a girl with whom he could not remember being. He was spent and dry and shaking....

Uncle Ben was behind him always. "It's right for you, Hugh. Being a good surgeon. I've talked to doctors who work with you. They believe in you."

And Hugh had replied, "It's more study and more money, Uncle Ben. It's for somebody else. I've got to pay you back now—"

But Uncle Ben had insisted. And the hunger was great.

New York then. The finest specialists in the profession. The final, truest training, the honing of a talent to razor's edge.

He'd worked harder than ever before, the fire steadying to a red-coal glow. He'd worked with a dedication that allowed for nothing but work, using the money from Uncle Ben without questioning.

Then that final specialized training was almost over. He'd reached a zenith; they would use him for one of the most important operations any young colleague of these professional masters had ever performed in the clinic, proof of his achievement. Uncle Ben would, at last, realize the fruits of his belief and help.

But the red-coal glow was again fanned into flames the night before the operation. Uncle Ben died. He died almost penniless, having given

Hugh all he could and more. He died without knowing the final victory.

Once again Hugh Stewart gave in to the flames. He woke up in a jail cell this time, five hours after Dr. Emil Ludgaard himself had successfully performed the operation Hugh Stewart was to have performed.

He woke up black-minded and exhausted, empty and grim.

"It's all right, Hugh," Dr. Ludgaard had said, his tired blue eyes avoiding Hugh's, "You broke up that tavern terribly. They'll raise hell at the clinic. But I'll smooth things." Dr. Ludgaard, like Uncle Ben, would not let him down. "These things happen, Hugh. You thought a great deal of your uncle."

"No," Hugh said. "It was more than that. It was—"

He had not been able to explain. He didn't know. It was simply that finally he no longer trusted himself. The flames would steady to coals, but they did not cool and die. They were always waiting. The kind of talent he now owned was not a talent to be offered unreliably.

He'd decided. He would settle for being a general practitioner. A country doctor. Not a specialized surgeon. This would demand all his energy. The work would come at him in a steady stream. But it would not be likely to build to excruciating delicacy. A country doctor's duties required of a man all his general medical ability, but it was not often channeled to that final thin blade. In emergency that could be left to others.

But now here he was. Out of touch with all he'd learned in the clinic. Out of touch with Emil Ludgaard. Lost in the center of a corn-belt flatland. The escape from delicate life-or-death responsibility he'd wanted had been more complete than he'd bargained for. There was no responsibility so far. Nothing.

Yet the flames had flickered again, threatened to blaze once more.

Hugh Stewart sat down at his desk tiredly, rubbing hands through his hair. Ann Burley. He hadn't counted on that at all.

Yet he could think of nothing else. Her face was etched in his brain. It was the way she'd looked when, after he'd kissed her, she'd turned her face away from him, trembling....

There had been no forewarning. Nothing of substance said between them. They had stood apart in that farmhouse. In Ted Burley's farmhouse...

But the unsaid, unadmitted communication was as real as though it could be seen, like spitting sparks along a high-tension line. They'd come together roughly. She'd met his fire-driven passion equally. Then they had stopped.

He'd left swiftly and returned to his office. Now here he was as the darkness crept into an unlit room. The emptiness, the grimness, had returned.

He was startled when the knock sounded on his door. He stood up, frowning. There were so few knocks at his door. He opened it, blinking in surprise.

Ann Burley stood there, blond hair rumpled, wide-spaced brown eyes staring at him as through long distances and a hundred hurts. There was a bruise darkening her left cheek. Blood showed at the corner of her mouth.

"May I come in?" she asked as though dazed.

He helped her in quickly.

# Chapter Seven

Ann Burley had awakened that morning with a premonition of disaster.

The day was like any other winter's day on a farm outside Arrow Junction. The snow was falling, and a lot of snow fell on Arrow Junction in the winter of every year. The wind and cold and amount of snow were reaching blizzard proportions. But there had always been blizzards in Arrow Junction's history. Snow, cold and wind. The flat barrenness of the country and the old, inadequate farmhouse. It was pretty much like any other winter's day.

But at midmorning, when she was alone in the small house, Ann had opened herself to a self-examination more intense than any she'd ever committed before. It was an effort to recheck the events that might have led her to this premonition of disaster.

She had started in this world twenty-seven years ago, an only child of parents spread vastly in age. Her father was already middle-aged when she was born, her mother barely twenty. As she grew older her mother seemed to want to grow younger. But her father continued to want to ease into a restful twilight of old age. Her parents convivially separated when she was seventeen. Ann chose to distribute her affections equally by going away to school. Her father remained in Sacramento, her mother moved to Los Angeles.

She spent two years at college in Santa Barbara. When she went to work in San Francisco at nineteen, she was extraordinarily pretty. She worked first in an insurance office on Sansome Street, then in an advertising agency on Montgomery Street.

It was a smooth transition from girl to woman. There were impersonal visits with her father in Sacramento. The variance in their ages created a chasm, yet the relationship was always pleasant.

The time with her mother was spent absorbing the gush of her mother's emotion, her silliness, her attempted deception of time. She had begun to realize the foolishness of her mother.

Yet Ann's life was smooth. Her beauty saw to that. The male attendance was vast. She did not fall truly in love. The emotions she experienced were but infatuations which started quickly and ended just as quickly. She simply enjoyed life, a fast clear-running river of activity and work. That she might have viewed marriage with suspicion as the result of her own parents' debacle did not consciously enter her mind.

So went her existence. Until that chance moment when she'd walked along her street in the dusk and saw one man kill another, and the river had gone to rapids, cascading into dangerous and deadly currents.

It was a chance incident. She had never heard of Tony Fearon. But she plainly saw him kill a man that evening: stepping forth from a large black car, firing at the man standing before one of the white houses built flush on a steep San Francisco street. She saw him kill and flee in the heavy black car.

It made no difference to her the reasons behind Tony Fearon's reason to kill. The thing had been done and she'd seen it. She'd reported it and become a part of it. The river had run into rocks, and the river was her life.

The trial was a blur. Gambling was at the bottom of it. Tony Fearon headed one group or syndicate, and the slain man had moved in.

But that made no difference to Ann. All that did matter was that she had witnessed the murder and had the obligation of swearing in court to what she saw. Tony Fearon was convicted, judged guilty and sentenced to death. Despite endless and desperate legal maneuvering the sentence had held. But Tony Fearon had, that day of sentencing, promised loudly that he would know the destruction of this girl who had sounded his death knell....

That had been over a year ago. Now the end was approaching. The date for Tony Fearon's final breath was coming near. Ann had been running ever since the end of that trial. But where had she run? And what good had it done? That morning, she asked herself exactly that.

It was a day like any other winter's day on a farm outside Arrow Junction.

You could look across the farmyard and see the snow lying white and new on the ground and on the sheds and on the roof of the barn beyond.

In the snowless days the farmhouse and the sheds and the barn were ugly to the eyes with their weather-gray nakedness. But now the snow was a bright and fancy decorator. Yet, snow or not, Ann had not really complained since she married Ted Burley eleven months ago. There had been plenty of reasons. But she had tenaciously ignored these reasons, telling herself steadily that she had not married Ted Burley solely to escape the threat of Tony Fearon in the anonymity of Arrow Junction....

Ted Burley had arisen that early morning from the cot bed he'd chosen to sleep in almost from the start of their marriage. The cot had been Ted Burley's since he'd been four years old. From the second bed in the room, the large iron-framed bed that had been used by Ted Burley's parents before they died and left him the farm, Ann watched her husband arise. Ted Burley walked heavily into the kitchen, his shoulders hulking beneath the fabric of long underwear. He put on a pair of overall pants and started a large pot of coffee.

Ann got up then too, looking at the alarm clock to realize there were still fifteen minutes before their normal time to arise. She switched off the alarm lever and put on a wool robe over her flannel pajamas. She stopped in the living room to light the stove and followed her husband into the kitchen.

"I would have gotten the coffee ready."

"I've already done it." Ted Burley walked to the back door and looked sourly through the top frame of glass at the still-dark morning.

"You got up before the alarm again."

"Said I would last night."

Ann knew he'd said no such thing, but she did not argue. "What would you like? Scrambled eggs? Bacon?"

"Yes," he said, and there was almost a pouting tone to his voice.

"All right, Ted," she said gently. She did not yet like to admit that talking to him as she would a child was something required. She had thought when she met him in Omaha that he was a very strong man.

She set the kitchen table and poured beaten eggs into a frying pan. "Sit down, Ted. It'll be ready in a minute."

"I wish you'd quit nagging me." He remained standing at the kitchen door, staring out grimly.

She started to retort, then did not. Her mind this morning kept switching back to her father. She'd had a dream that something horrible had happened to him and awakened in the middle of the night in a bath of terrified sweat, seeing his face smashed and bloody. It was a foolish dream, but the memory still sent her blood cold.

She placed bacon and scrambled eggs on Ted's plate. "There you are.

I don't mean to nag."

Silently he sat down and began eating. She poured a cup of coffee for each of them and sat down across from him.

"You going to eat or not?" he asked.

"When you've finished. I wanted to get yours ready right away."

"Easy life, isn't it? I got to eat on the run and go out and work my hands down to a nub. You haven't anything else to do but eat breakfast whenever you feel like it."

"Don't be mean, Ted."

"I'm not. I give you a good life. Maybe it isn't good enough for you though? Maybe you liked it better in Omaha?"

"Ted, why all this—" She spread her hands. "Eleven months! It still ought to be a honeymoon, and we don't even—"

"You shut up about that, do you hear? I told you once. I won't any more!"

"Ted—"

"I mean it! I know what you're talking about! Take a filthy mind to think about that all the time. Where'd you get that mind of yours? Where'd you learn to think about that all the time?"

"Can't you understand? There's nothing filthy about a man and wife—"

"I told you!" he said menacingly.

She looked at the vivid flush of his face. For the first time since that memorable moment of their first night together in this house or any-where, she thought he might hit her again. She had a fleeting thought of Dr. Hugh Stewart. She had a strange impulse to get up suddenly and flee to him for protection.

But Ted Burley did not hit her. He'd done that just once so far, and that had been after their first night of married love. That night Ann had found out a lot about Ted Burley.


She did not know Ted Burley when she married him. Their courtship had been only a month long. He'd come to Omaha from the farm, a lonely man who needed her desperately, he'd told her. He'd been thirty-one and large and, even in his wind-burned and raw-boned look, hand-some enough. He'd seemed to Ann as capable and strong as her ideal-istic concept of a noble frontiersman.

But she was on the run. She'd left San Francisco and gone to her fa-ther in Sacramento because she did not trust her mother with the knowl-edge of where she was. Only her father knew that she'd dyed her hair from dark brown to blond, that she'd then gone to Omaha and assumed a new name of Brown. Only her father had her Omaha address. He had not written to her since she'd got married. She had not written to him.

On the run, she had chosen what seemed solid protection in the form of Ted Burley.

She'd met him at the Stockyards Exchange where she'd gotten a job as a secretary. He'd come once on business, then returned again and again. Suddenly they were married. And Ann had gone home with him to the farmhouse outside Arrow Junction and the bed of his mother and father.

It was there, eager with a love she was certain was real, that Ann found that, despite his large size and rugged look, Ted Burley was but a prudish child.

She'd sensed his nervousness and had thought it was simply a strong man's hidden shyness. So she'd done the advancing, and he'd been caught up by it, driven to a wild emotion. She'd willingly accepted the drive of it, no matter how brutal and selfish. When it was over he hit her.

She did not understand, and he didn't care that she didn't. He'd left her alone. His soul having been exposed, he seemed to hate her. He slept in his child's bed that night; he'd slept there ever since. For weeks on end he would contain his emotion, then he would unleash it as though he were using a whip on her. Then the same withdrawal again. She began to understand more about the child within the man's exterior. But she could not mature the spirit of him....

"Don't like my bacon so damn well done," he said.

"I tried to do it the way you like."

"Maybe you don't know how to do anything the way I like. Maybe it's too bad you're here and Ma isn't. She knew everything there was to know."

He stood up and disappeared into the parlor. He reappeared dressed and shoved his thick arms through the sleeves of a heavy mackinaw. "You going to town today?"

"I'd planned on it."

"Well, I don't have chains on the sedan yet. I didn't count on that today. I got to go clear over to Webster in the truck in this damn storm."

"If I knew how, Ted—"

He laughed harshly. "You couldn't do anything in this world if I didn't watch you. And I don't have time to be teaching you how to put chains on a car! I'll do it myself."

She looked at him in honest wonderment. Then she said, "Did your mother know how, Ted?"

"Sure she did! She did it lots of times!"

She examined him closely, nodding.

"Got to get going," he said, pulling a wool-lined cap over his hair, unfolding the flaps down over his ears. "See you try to keep from getting sassy with every man in town, do you hear?"

Her examination of him turned from curiosity to amazement. For a moment she was ready to laugh. He'd only started this kind of thing recently. She could still not believe he was serious. But he was, she saw, dead serious.

"Ted, you don't honestly believe that I—"

"Damn, yes!" He left the house, slamming the door against a gust of snow-driven winter wind.

By midmorning over coffee she had become entirely introspective. And she had again allowed her feeling of fear to be felt fully. She thought of how Tony Fearon must be sitting in his cell right now, dreaming, she was certain, of how it would be when he knew she was dead, just as he'd threatened....

Shortly after that she got into the old sedan that Ted had readied earlier with chains. She drove into Arrow Junction and parked outside the Arrow Junction General Store.

She walked inside and saw Dr. Hugh Stewart. When they exchanged smiles, something warm and strange happened to her. It was a feeling of having seen someone truly familiar again, as though suddenly everyone in this community including Ted had become strangers—everyone except herself and Hugh Stewart. She walked down the length of the counter, noticing Charlie Bacon, then Bob Saywell as he came around the end of the counter.

At that moment George Herbert had burst into the store and announced what had happened in Cony Adams's service station that morning. Ann could not be certain. But it seemed exactly what she had been waiting for—a positive sign that death was approaching on the run.

The trouble in Graintown could have been the result of any two hoodlums, any pair of bandits. But the premonition in Ann Burley, as she fainted, had become an engulfing terror.

# Chapter Eight

When Dr. Hugh Stewart drove Ann Burley home at midday, Bob Saywell immediately prepared to make his trip through the storm to Graintown and the public library. As Bob Saywell passed the Burley farmhouse and noted the automobile of Dr. Hugh Stewart parked in the farmyard, Billy Quirter was on his way to the railroad yards.

Billy was cold. But he moved with a deadly determination. He ran from the back of a woodshed through a grove of elms and oaks. The wind whipped at him, slicing through with its cold to the inside of his bones. The snow now was like fine white sand, granular, stinging when it struck Billy's freezing face. But Billy darted relentlessly from cover to cover.

The railroad yards were on the northeast edge of Graintown. At the east end was the train depot. Outside the depot, the tracks moved westward a short distance to the switch-offs for the cattle and hog pens on the tip-end of Graintown's small stockyards. At that point lay two alternate tracks that carried the stock cars to the loading chutes. Two boxcars stood here in unused snowy solitude waiting for some future loading of beef or pork.

Billy Quirter made it to one of those boxcars, shoved a door open with hands grown numb with cold, and crawled inside. The cold had frozen out the smell of livestock and had, in fact, sterilized the interior with the freezing temperature. This was fortunate for Billy, because Billy hated filth desperately. Billy closed the door. From a corner he picked up a ragged blanket left by a previous transient, shook it, then wrapped himself and crouched in one corner out of the raging wind and snow to wait until he heard the sound of a train on the main tracks.

He did not know it, but he would have to wait most of the afternoon. Besides the snow-clearing engine, there were but two trains going through Graintown; the 7:30 in the morning going west, and the 4:07 in the afternoon heading east in the direction of Arrow Junction.

Despite his discomfort Billy was patient. The blanket stopped most of his shaking. He actually felt a kind of pleasure in this silent waiting, with a good view of the boxcar's sliding door. His gun was warm in his hand beneath the blanket. He could easily kill the first thing that came through that door.

Ann Burley, that afternoon, found herself in a deeper emotional crisis than she had ever dreamed she would be in when she'd started that particular day.

She had awakened from her fainting late that morning, looking up at the face of Dr. Hugh Stewart. The fact that she had known Hugh Stewart only slightly did not diminish the feeling that his was the single face she cared to see at that moment.

He drove her home. Alone with him in the small farmhouse, despite her efforts to avoid it, there was an unsaid but strong attraction between them. She tried very hard to avoid that. But then her mind turned back to her fear. She had to find refuge somewhere. She ceased to fight the attraction.

She sat up on the sofa now. Hugh Stewart walked across the room, turned, smiled. "You look better."

"I feel better," she said weakly. Then she lied, "I don't know why it happened."

"Could have been several things. It's possible, you know that—" He shrugged. "Pregnancy?"

"No."

"Well, you can't always be sure. Perhaps—"

"No."

He nodded finally. "Maybe we ought to check you over more thoroughly. Drop into my office. I'll—" He paused. "Maybe you have your own doctor in Graintown."

"Yes," she said. "I haven't had any reason to go to him. But Ted—it's more or less family with him."

"Certainly," he said, and she was sure she saw a flicker in his eyes. "But I suggest you see him. Several things, you know, could cause fainting like that. It's always worth checking."

"I'll do that."

She met his eyes for a moment, then she could look at him no longer. She knew nothing about him, and yet it was as though he were someone long familiar to her and that they had always known about this feeling.

He seemed suddenly uncomfortable. "I'll be going. Your car's still in the village—"

"I'll drive in with Ted when he gets home." She stood up. "Thank you so much, Doctor."

"My pleasure. Give my regards to your husband, won't you?"

She nodded and moved toward the door just as he did. He reached out and took her in his arms roughly. She met his hunger with hers, digging her fingers into his back.

She broke free and turned away abruptly, trembling....

He left quickly. She heard the sound of his car moving through the farmyard. Still trembling she felt as though she had just smashed everything she'd tried to be with Ted Burley. That was a little past noon.

At four o'clock that afternoon, Bob Saywell knocked on her door.

The unexpected sound had given her a moment of terror, until she looked out and saw his car. Then she opened the door, unusually annoyed by the sight of his fat smiling face.

"Just wanted to see how you were, Mrs. Burley."

"I'm fine, thank you."

"Well, that's why I stopped. To find out." He smiled. His jowls seemed to quiver faintly. There was peculiar brightness in his eyes. "May I come in? A little cold standing out here."

"Yes," she said, covering her annoyance. "Come in, Mr. Saywell."

He stepped inside briskly, slapping his gloved hands together. He removed his gloves and wiped his shoes carefully on the throw rug in front of the door. "Take it Ted's not around. Knew he was going on over to Webster. Take it he's not back."

"No, he's not back."

"Now this is a real pretty little house you've got here, Mrs. Burley. Twice as pretty as Ted kept it before he married up with you. Just about as pretty, I'd say, as his ma kept it before she died!"

Ann watched him walk around the room, looking at the furniture, touching things; there was an odd jauntiness to his manner; some of his perpetual obsequiousness was gone. He stopped finally, his face wreathed in good humor, eyes steadily bright. "Sit down, Mrs. Burley. I want to talk to you. Sit down over there in that chair of Ted's ma. The light's real good there. I can see you better."

Ann was surprised by the commanding tone in his voice. "You want to talk to me, Mr. Saywell?"

"We can cut the monkey business. Just sit down, Mrs. Burley. Or should I say Ann?"

"I'm afraid I don't—"

"Or should I say Ann Brown? That was your name before you married Ted, wasn't it? Or should I just ay Ann Rodick?"

She stared at him disbelievingly. Rodick, her own name! The name she'd changed to Brown when she'd gone to Omaha. He nodded, jowls jiggling. "Oh, I struck a nerve there, didn't I? Oh, you'd better sit down now, Mrs. Burley. I do believe you might faint again."

She did sit down now, weakly, still staring at him. "How did you find out?"

"Now you never want to think old Bob Saywell hasn't got a good brain, you know. Didn't build that business I've got by being dumb. I'll bet you never thought it took brains to build that kind of business, did you? I'll bet you thought Bob Saywell was just somebody cutting up the chops for you? You think maybe it doesn't take any brains to get to be a leader of a little community like this?"

"Mr. Saywell, please! You've found out my real name. I want to know how and why!"

"Well, I'll tell you," he said, grinning wickedly. "I've got a good memory, Mrs. Burley. There was a trial out there on the West Coast. Made good reading. Some of the newspapers even around in this state printed it up. Seems one fellow shot another. Seems a girl saw it happen. That was you, wasn't it? I checked that, you see? I had a clipping, but the picture of you wasn't good. So I just drove on over to Graintown and had them dig out some old newspapers out of their files. And there it was, a real good picture. What I thought was true, wasn't it, Ann Rodick?"

"I don't deny it! So you know then why I changed my name and the color of my hair. You read about Tony Fearon's threat!" She said it desperately, thinking that surely the tone Bob Saywell was using was not abusive. What reason would he have to be anything but sympathetic?

"Oh, yes. I read all about that. Yes, indeed. And I wonder—does Ted know about this?"

He'd come nearer, standing with his paunchy belly just in front of her, pink cheeks rosy in the light from the windows.

She shook her head, completely confused. "No, of course not. There's been no need—"

"I just wonder what he'd think about this. You take Ted. He's thin-skinned, that lad. Oh, not a lad now. But he always was real sensitive. I know people hereabouts. I know Ted, and I knew his ma and his pa. Ted is what you might call a mamma's boy. Most people might not think that just to look at him, but that's what he is. I wonder how it'd be if he knew you'd married him and all the time using the wrong name?"

"Mr. Saywell," Ann said, standing up, "I don't like the tone of your voice. You've found out something. But it has nothing to do with Ted. I've deceived him about nothing more than my name. I had a reason for that—my safety."

Bob Saywell suddenly laughed. "You're a tricky one, aren't you?"

"What are you talking about?"

"I mean that way of yours. That kind of angel-like way. That's a good way to put it, isn't it? Angel-like. All blond and wide-eyed and kind of like a baby stare you've got. Only the hair isn't really that color, and you aren't any angel, are you, Mrs. Burley?"

She shook her head, unbelieving.

"No," he said, "you aren't that at all. Otherwise, why did you faint away there in my store, Mrs. Burley? I wonder if you'd tell me that?"

"You come in here? Insult me? Insinuate things? Question me? In my own home? You have no right whatever to—"

"You didn't tell me why it was you fainted!" he said, leaning closer to her. "Now why don't you? Why don't you tell me it was because of all that bad business in Graintown this morning. Huh? Yes, sir! This gangster, this Mr. Tony Fearon, he threatened to get you killed before he was executed, didn't he? Now just maybe that was it. Now maybe you thought those fellows doing that shooting in Corly Adams's station was fellows maybe this Mr. Tony Fearon sent out to get you. Was that it, Mrs. Burley?"

She stared at him in shock. "What are you after, Mr. Saywell?"

"Did I say I was after something? Now maybe I am. I wouldn't be at all surprised if maybe I am. But I haven't said anything about it, have I? I'm just trying to get everything straight. Ann Rodick, the girl mixed up with those San Francisco gangsters! I just wonder what Ted would think of all that? I wonder what the whole community would think of that? Mrs. Burley turning out to be mixed up with a dirty group of California gangsters—'specially now that Corly's gone and been killed and Sheriff Joe Bingham likeways? Now that's a shame. People liked Corly and Joe a lot around here. I wouldn't wonder if they might just get up and want to maybe use the tar and feathers once they found it was all your fault!"

"Mr. Saywell, I'm beginning to think you're crazy! What kind of warped mind could you have to accuse me of being mixed up with them? I had nothing to do with anything but accidentally being in a certain place at a certain time. God knows I wish I hadn't been! But I was and I can't help that. What right have you to say anything is my fault?"

He was closer to her now, so close she could see the texture of his rosy skin. On close inspection it lost its cherubic look. You could see the wrinkling and the blemishing and the drying pores.

"Now I'm going to tell you something," he said. "Something I just heard on the car radio, loud and clear, while I was driving from Graintown back here. This fellow they're looking for, this Billy Quirter, he's this Tony Fearon's brother. What do you think of that!"

Hearing that was like a hard blow to the pit of Ann's stomach. There was first the sharp pain, then a spreading dull sickness. Tony Fearon's brother! So it was true!

"You see?" he said, smiling with his mouth but chilling her with his eyes. "I know exactly who you are." She realized, looking into those eyes, that he was honestly condemning her—that, in reality, he thought her no different than Tony Fearon! It was a warped mind behind those eyes, she knew; warped by the narrowness of the world in which it had been spawned and aged, warped by a false sanctimony, made worse by long years of dulling his conscience until he had become a stupid hypocrite, and dangerous because of it.

If he released his knowledge, it would be like pulling the world down on her head. The newspapermen would descend. Everybody would descend. And Billy Quirter, brother of Tony Fearon, would know exactly where she was. She would again have to depend on the police to protect her. But could they protect her for a lifetime?

"I think you'd better get out of here!"

He tipped his head, gazing at her with absolute confidence. "You're fooling me. You're trying to bluff me. I don't bluff, Mrs. Burley. Not Bob Saywell. No, sir. You're scared, Mrs. Burley. I can see that. You don't fool me at all."

"I told you," she said, voice tightening. "Get out!"

"Yes," he said, "I will—when I've said my piece. And I think you'd better listen to that, Mrs. Burley." It was his sureness that frightened her.

"Go ahead then," she said. "Say it."

"Now that's better," he smiled, shifting his feet to bring himself an inch closer to her. "Now that's a whole lot better! Yes, I'll say it. I'll say that you've brought an evil to this community of ours...."

He talked on, and the drone of his voice, now wheedling, now sharpening with viciousness, amazed her with its self-righteous conviction. And somehow his words, his face, the turning of his brain seemed to merge with the identity of Ted Burley, her husband. Somehow the personalities fused. And that was because, she realized, it was really a single mind speaking, the mind of a community with a single attitude of narrowness and backwardness.

"... so you see, Mrs. Burley, Bob Saywell, if he were a gambling man, which he's not, would hold the cards, if he played cards, which he does not. Do you get my point? I mean this escaped gunman, this Tony Fearon's brother, is prowling around somewhere. Now I know that. And you know that. Everybody around here knows that. But my point is that it seems nobody but you and me and him knows just why. Now we, all three, know, don't we? But now that gangster, maybe he don't know just exactly where you are, so he can do what we know he's trying to do. How about that, Mrs. Burley? That's about right, isn't it? That's maybe what you're counting on, isn't it? With your hair colored different and your name changed and living out here on this little farm of Ted's, why, who'd think it was really Ann Rodick here, just the person this fellow's after? Am I right?"

She did not answer, so he went on.

"You're not going to let the word out so this fellow can come and do what he's after, are you? Not by a long shot! So it won't be you telling. And that leaves matters pretty much in the hands of Bob Saywell, doesn't it, Mrs. Burley?"

She blinked, in one sense disbelieving, but in another realizing with frightening clarity the extent of his viciousness.

"You're threatening me," she whispered. "In God's name, why?"

"You ask me why. Now I'm getting to that. Because this community doesn't deserve this kind of blight you've brought into it. This community stands for something—it stands for the word of the Bible, the Good Word. And it doesn't deserve any of the dirtiness like you're mixed up in—"

"You filthy—!"

"Oh, no! Don't you talk to me that way! The devil calling the angel evil, is that it? No, that's no good, and you know it. *You're* the evil here, and hereabouts we live by the Good Word, do you hear that? I take pride in this little community of ours. I take pride in doing what I can to lead this little community of ours over the rough rocks and see that nobody gets hurt too bad. Some of us were picked by the Lord to see their fellow man gets a straight chance at things. No, sir. I take pride and care with this community. I got a responsibility to it, I'll tell you!"

Almost subconsciously, Ann realized that Saywell's left hand had drifted up, touching her arm now, fingers opening, closing again, around her bare flesh, lightly, like the test of a python. It was a detached realization because her mind was still confused by this blather of words flowing at her, like the parody of some outlandish sermon performed by a revivalist fanatic.

And Bob Saywell, having rationalized his position sufficiently, revealed the single motive behind his entire strategy.

"Don't you see?" he whispered, eyes blazing. "I can protect you! I can keep you safe! I won't tell. No, sir! You can count on that!"

Ann, now with his hand on her, knew exactly what he wanted. There was no mistaking it in his eyes, the quiver of his face. "And why won't you tell?" she asked, her voice going cold, despite the rising fear she felt of him.

"Why?" he breathed. "Because I'll be nice to you and not tell. You see?

And the reason I'll be nice to you, is because you'll be nice to me—"

Both hands now were on her, squeezing tighter—the fat, blubberlike face coming closer to hers.

"Oh, yes," he whispered, "you will, won't you? You'll be just as cozy as a bug in a rug with old Bob Saywell! That fellow will never find you. No, sir. Not as long as you're nice to old Bob Saywell. And you will be, won't you!"

She twisted from his grip and brought the flat of her right hand sharply across his fat and quivering face with all her strength. The sound of the slap, cracked like a small rifle report.

Bob Saywell's face flushed. His, eyes squeezed smaller, and he took a step back, still quivering.

"You'll be sorry for that!" he whispered hoarsely.

"Get out of here," she said, the anger sweeping through her. "Get out of here!"

Her anger seemed to frighten him, but he stood locked for a moment more, head pulled closer to his fat narrow shoulders. "I'm going to give you a little more chance, is what I'm going to do! And you'd better be smart enough to see that Bob Saywell is nobody to fool around with. Now you get over your snottiness with me, do you hear? You think twice before you ever do again what you just done. A little more chance, and that's all. And then—"

He put his lips together, wheeled and walked out. The door slammed shut behind him. Ann, staring at the door, shook her head unbelievingly. She was in deadly danger, and what had this man just tried to do? She simply could not yet believe in the man's utter hypocrisy, his utter blackness.

There was, then, the sound of a pickup truck coming into the barnyard.


As Ted Burley pushed his large-framed figure from his truck, his eyes caught the figure of Bob Saywell emerging from the farmhouse. He stared at Saywell with thin eyes.

Bob Saywell suddenly smiled. The rosy tint of rage remained in his face, but it seemed merely the effect of the winter wind.

He yelled immediately, "Hello, there, Ted! Glad to see you!"

Ted Burley nodded curtly.

"Just come back, Ted?" Bob Saywell said, hurrying up.

"Yes." A frown cut between his heavy eyebrows. "Looking for me?"

Bob Saywell instantly saw the suspicion written into Ted's face. And Bob Saywell rarely lost an opportunity.

"No, sir. Not this time, Ted. You didn't hear about the missus fainting there in my store?"

"Fainting? No! Been gone all day."

"Sure enough she did, Ted. Kind of gave me a worry there. So I went over to Graintown on business and coming back, passed your house. I thought I'd look in and see how she was. She appears to be fine now."

"Don't know what would make her faint."

"Don't think it was anything at all," Bob Saywell said. "You know how women are. No, sir. She looks fit as a fiddle now. Just something a woman does now and again."

Ted Burley nodded, still examining Bob Saywell intently.

"Tell you, though," Bob Saywell continued, "you'd better talk to Dr. Hugh Stewart about it. He was the one who saw to her there in the store."

Ted Burley's frown deepened. "Saw to her?"

"He was in the store at the time. Did for her there on a table." Bob Saywell grinned faintly. "Then he took her home."

Ted Burley shook his head, anger and confusion obvious in his face. "He had to bring her home?"

"Well, I don't know that he had to do that, but that's what he done. Just to make sure, I suspect. I imagine he knows what he's about, don't you, Ted?"

Ted Burley nodded slowly. "I reckon he does."

"Well, it's good to have a doc around close. Course, you and me, Ted, we always went over there to Graintown and Doc Orwell. You can't be too sure about your doc, I always say. I mean, that's one man you always want to be sure about. Right, Ted?"

"You're pretty right, I'd say." Ted Burley blinked, trying to get his thoughts straight. Bob Saywell pressed his advantage.

"Well, I don't want to talk on about Doc Stewart. Just that somehow he always—well, I don't know. Just impressed me as kind of out of place here in our little community. He's got big-city ways or something. Oh, I'm not saying there's anything wrong with someone who's from a city. Now I guess I know your missus came from Omaha. And your missus is certainly all right! Maybe I'm just small-town all the way through or something, Ted. Maybe it's just me. Don't doubt your missus can understand Doc Stewart a good bit better than I can. She seemed to be real pleased to see him there, when she woke up. Wouldn't doubt they've got a whole lot in common. Probably accounts for that long visit they had."

"Long visit?" Ted Burley asked, face darkening now.

"Well, Doc Stewart took her home there in late morning. When I went by in the afternoon, why, there was Doc Stewart's car still parked in your yard. Don't doubt they get along real fine, Ted. Well, I got to get going. You take it easy now, Ted."

Bob Saywell waved a cheery hand, ducked his head once again into the fatty folds of his neck and hiked off to his car. Ted Burley immediately strode toward the back door of the house, a habit taught to him by his mother, so he could kick the snow from his boots at the stoop and not track the front-room rug.

Ann came into the kitchen as he was stripping off his mackinaw.

"Ted," Ann said. "I'm glad you've come home." She was, in fact, quite glad he'd come—there was a familiarity in his presence that, at this moment, belied the true feeling she had for him. In comparison to the recent presence of Bob Saywell, he seemed an almost refreshing sight.

Ted Burley did not answer. He washed his large hands silently in the kitchen sink.

"Ted—"

"What was Doc Stewart doing bringing you home?"

"Ted, I fainted in the store!"

He turned, his face twisted into an unbelievable fury of jealously.

"How long did he stay?"

"I don't know, Ted. I didn't time how long he was here."

"What happened while he was here?"

Ann shook her head. "Ted, listen to me—"

"Don't have to!" he said, churlishly. "Just want to know what happened!"

His face made it plain that he was creating the blackest pictures available to his invention.

"I *told* you!" he whispered hoarsely.

"Ted, *please!*"

"*Right in this house!*" he said, his voice suddenly lifting in power, nearly screaming.

His hand came from nowhere. It struck her solidly across the cheekbone, sending her pitching across the kitchen floor. Half sprawling, she shook her head, amazed at the blow, yet understanding that somehow he'd perceived something *had* happened between her and Hugh Stewart.

She didn't argue or defend, only saw the pace of his large boots toward her. She scrambled to her feet, grabbed a coat from the hallway, and ran from him. She ran outside to the snow and the bitter wind, and she kept running. She thought he was following her. Her flight became panic, stumbling through the ever-increasing snow, the wind stinging her cheeks. She ran.

Ted Burley stood in the doorway and looked after her disappearing figure. He did not follow. Instead, panting with rage, he allowed his wild imaginings to increase in tempo. The lust rose in him, not to strike her again, but to avenge her in the same way he was sure she had cheated him. It was a wild moment of anger and physical desire, both at high peak. Standing there, large body tense, rough-hewn, face strained and lined with fury, Ted Burley looked every bit the man. But inside, the child raged in an infantile tantrum.

"The dirty whore," he whispered. "The dirty whore..."

## Chapter Nine

The 4:07 train going east out of Graintown was, because of the storm, thirty-two minutes late that afternoon. But before its arrival and departure, Sheriff-elect Jenkins had sent a detail of volunteer assistants to check the railroad area. The detail was to have been headed by Deputy Wade Miles, but Miles had been asked to check the west roadblock before he joined the group. The group of volunteers was not about to investigate the area until given the immediate leadership and moral support of Wade Miles. Thus, while Miles made his check at the roadblock set up by the State Police, the volunteer searchers at the railway depot stamped around the tiny waiting room and talked in angry terms of what they were going to do when they found Billy Quirter as they smoked and spit.

At 4:39 the train pulled in from the west. But by that time Deputy Miles had been diverted by a report that a local housewife had seen a man behind her garage on the north side of town. A quick personal check, accompanied by State patrolmen, convinced Wade Miles that the housewife was having hallucinations. When Wade Miles reached the Graintown depot, the 4:39 had pulled out as the volunteer searchers stood determinedly in the protection of the depot's waiting room, watching the arrival and departure of the train like vigilante statues.

"Hell, Wade," one of them said to the deputy, "he couldn't of got on that train or we would of seen him."

"Well, damn it," Wade Miles said, "if you couldn't search that train, let's still search the area anyway. Let's go! Joe, call Arrow Junction and have the train searched there."

So the 4:39 was now on its way in the direction of Arrow Junction. And Billy Quirter was on it.

Thirty seconds after the train had started moving, Billy started running toward it, keeping the cars between himself and the depot up the tracks. At the last second, he'd vaulted up to an empty freight car, kicking like a monkey, and shoved himself through a partially opened door. He'd made it, minutes before Deputy Wade Miles arrived to mobilize the fear-frozen volunteers into belated action.

But as the train got underway, Billy realized he still had a problem. The map had told him the tracks ran through Arrow Junction, but he had no way of knowing whether or not the train stopped there. It was a chance he had to take.

Reasonably, Billy struck a match and looked at the map again. The distance by highway from Graintown to Arrow Junction was exactly ten miles. But it was hard for Billy to estimate how long it would take that train to make those ten miles.

It took, in fact, a little over eleven minutes. The train, in fact, stopped at Arrow Junction at approximately 4:50.

But Billy, at the end of nine minutes, began to worry, thinking that the train would not stop at Arrow Junction. He pushed himself close to the space created by the partly opened door and looked at the heavy snow whipping by in the ever-increasing gloom. He thought, one minute outside of Arrow Junction, that the train had gone beyond the town.

He slid his legs through the doorway, squirmed around so that he was facing the direction the train was moving, then jumped.

He missed a switch handle by inches, a collision that would have performed a sudden and complete castration. He hit a heavy drift of snow, which softened his fall and slowed the momentum of his roll. But an unpracticed jumper like Billy was bound to land awkwardly. Billy did, with crushing impact. He was bruised. His knees hammered through the snow clear to the underlying cinders. But it was his left arm that, in the shock, took the real punishment.

Dr. Stewart would have diagnosed the result as a simple fracture of the left radius at the point of the nutrient foramen.

Billy only knew that he had broken his damned arm.

Swearing viciously, he held the wrist of that arm and lay in the snow like a rifle-shot jackrabbit. The wind blew, whistling over the back acreage of Ben Swanson's farm on the opposite side of the highway from Ted Burley's place. At that moment Billy was just exactly one half mile from the intended target of his gun, who was then making her way into Arrow Junction proper. But Billy didn't know that. He did not know, in truth, where the hell he was.

Blinded by wind and snow and pain, he finally staggered off, away from the tracks, until he ran into the barbed wire fence Ben Swanson had replaced only that previous spring. Billy caught that in the face and back of his right hand. A barb ripped a neat cut across his right cheek and another stabbed his hand. But both wounds were superficial, the cold clotting the blood quickly. Billy, undaunted, moved through the strands, swearing a blue streak, and staggered on across Ben Swanson's field, until he shoved into Ben Swanson's barn.

This was what Billy wanted. He wanted protection from the infuriating wind and snow and cold. He found it here, and letting the broken arm hang, climbed with one hand and numb feet to the loft of Ben Swanson's barn. There, in the hay, he squirmed into relative warmth, teeth set tight against the pain of that broken bone.

He was, in effect, a wounded animal now—lying small and insignificant in the dark of the great barn. Tony Fearon had a peculiar momentary loss of confidence at that moment in his California cell, wondering if, finally, the one dream he clung to in the face of death would go smash—and Billy would not, finally, make it.

But if Tony had seen his younger brother at that moment, his confidence would have returned full force. Billy was merely temporarily postponing his moving. Wind, snow and cold, broken bone, barbed wire and torn skin had not stopped Billy. Billy was only waiting for the morning now, to move on. He had a good view toward the entrance of that barn; anyone opening that door during the night would have gotten the entire new clip of bullets in Billy's waiting gun. But fortunately nobody did.


As Billy waited in the barn, Dr. Hugh Stewart helped Ann Burley to a chair in his office.

"What happened?" he asked her softly.

She started to speak, then shook her head. He carefully wiped the blood from a corner of her mouth. She tried again. "It was Ted."

He felt a quick flare of anger. Ted Burley was her husband, but that was no matter now. No man should ever have hit her. He tried to keep calm. "Why?"

Again she shook her head. "Not now, Hugh."

He nodded. "All right." He looked at her, head bent, sitting in that chair. He looked at the unconscious grace of her posture, the fine mold of her hands clenched over her knees, the shape of calf and ankle.

"You'd better take that coat off," he said.

She looked up, and her beauty, even bruised, caught him by surprise, as it did every time he looked at her. She stood up, and he put his hands around her to take the coat as she slid one arm free, then the other. He held the coat, and they stood inches apart.

"Ann—" he said very softly.

"You're too close to me, Hugh," she said.

"All right," he said, but he didn't move away. Instead he brought his hand in, touching her arm.

"I don't want you this close."

He put his hands on both her arms. "That's not true, is it?"

"I don't care if it's not true," she said. "It can't be this way."

"You're here, aren't you?"

"I couldn't help coming."

"Why not?"

"Please, Hugh—"

"You can tell me and mean it, I won't touch you."

"I won't tell you," she breathed.

His arms were around her now. He held her gently at first. Then, as she tipped her head back, eyes closed, he lifted her carefully. There seemed no effort in the action, only the absolute movement. He saw her face, pale against the dark leather of the office couch. He saw her lips, soft-looking, soft-red against the paleness of the bruised face. He moved his own face down, his hand touching a button below her throat, loosening it. She did not resist....

Much later he offered her a cigarette. She shook her head. He lit his own, looking at her.

"Are you sorry?" he asked.

Her voice was soft, her eyes and mouth were soft. "No."

Moments passed. He smoked his cigarette. She raised her chin finally. "But I'd better explain everything," she said.

"Some things don't need explaining."

"Not some things. Other things do. I've got to tell you everything, Hugh."

He nodded. "All right."

Slowly, carefully, she told him.

He remained silent for several moments when she had finished; he was controlled now, despite hearing of the childish meanness of Ted Burley, of the blackmailing effort by Bob Saywell. He looked down and saw that his knuckles were white from his grip on the desk. He released his grip carefully. "Billy Quirter—Tony Fearon's brother. You've got to tell the sheriff in Graintown."

"No," she said.

"Listen, Ann. You've taken a lot of punishment. Why go on?"

"There's nothing else to do until Tony Fearon's dead, and even then—"

"That's right. Even then his brother's alive. You've got to stop running, Ann. You can't run forever."

"I can try," she said.

"But why? Why not tell the sheriff what you've told me, and—"

"No. Because what good would that do? Will it stop Quirter?"

Hugh Stewart took a breath. "You've been running so long you don't know what's valid and what isn't any more. From the start, from Ted Burley on, you've been running. Searching for protection. Ted Burley's farm, a little shelter in the middle of a state like this. It's the middle of nowhere to Tony Fearon—you were sure of that. That's why you married Ted Burley, isn't it?"

"I don't know why I've done anything," she said.

"You don't love him. You couldn't. Otherwise what just happened between us—"

"Maybe I'm cheap."

"Ann, shut up. That isn't true, and you know it."

"Hugh, I've tried so very hard with Ted. I didn't want to—"

"How can you deal with a child? For God's sake, Ann, don't let the warps of some of these people in this town get into your mind. That's no good that way. Listen to me. You can't live a lie any more. It doesn't breed good. It only breeds bad—like the honorable Mr. Saywell. That's all you'll get out of it. Don't you see that?"

She shook her head. "If I thought the only reason I married Ted was simply to—"

"Damn it, Ann," he exploded, "is he worth this kind of consideration? To hell with him. I say that to you straight, and I don't give a damn about the morals or the propriety of my saying it. He's a child, and that's not your fault, is it?"

"I married him, Hugh."

"You married him for protection."

"Was that remotely honest?"

"It was human, wasn't it? Is it impossible for you to admit that you're human like the rest of us? That you can get scared like every other man, woman and child in the world? What's so indecent about that?"

She shook her head, and he knew she wanted to give in now; but he knew the habit had grown deep-rooted. He stood up, moving toward her. "Ann—"

"No," she said. "Don't touch me again, Hugh. I can't think when you do. I've got to think."

"All right," he said at last. "But remember one thing—you can't keep on running. You've got to stop sometime. Your life's in danger. Your marriage to Ted Burley is a sham. And it's a sham primarily because of the fact that if you told him what you've told me about who you really are, the marriage would come apart on that and that alone. That's no real marriage, Ann. If you're going to think, please think about that. I'm selfish. I'll admit that. I want you. Do you understand that?"

She looked up at him. Then she said, "Please. Not now, Hugh."

He nodded. "I'll leave you alone—you'd better stay here tonight. Lock the door when I leave, and don't open it to anyone but me. We'll talk in the morning."

"Yes," she said. "Thank you, Hugh—"

He opened and closed a hand. "I love you, Ann," he said simply. Then he was gone.

From the window of the office just darkened, she watched him make his way to his car parked at the curb below. The wide main street of Arrow Junction was now simply a straight white mark between store buildings, like a wide strip of adhesive tape.

Hugh Stewart's car coughed, spurting gray exhaust clouds into the snowy wind. Then it moved slowly down the street and turned left at the near intersection. She watched the car disappear from the shifting circle of light created by the swinging street lamp hung in the very center of the intersection. Then she watched his lone car lights moving along the small off-street. The lights disappeared then, shut out by the invisible but real framework of cottonwoods and elms clustered thickly at the next intersection.

Still, Ann continued to look out, beyond the wind-swaying street lamp, hung like a metal dish above the intersection, beyond the dark shaft of the small street and the invisible leaf-stripped cottonwoods and elms, beyond to the black of the night and the snow and the wind and the deepening cold. It was, now, an unseeing look—while her thoughts turned slowly. But if that look had been properly focused, capable of X-ray vision and telescopic power, it would have, at that moment, stared straight into the black cold eyes of Billy Quirter as he lay, gun tucked against belly, in that silent barn.

# Chapter Ten

Shortly before dawn the next morning, Sam Dickens swung his legs over the mattress and sat up on the edge of the bed in his section of the motel. He sat that way for a moment, feeling the soreness in his back created by the sag in the mattress. It seemed that ever since he and Gloria had left home, they had yet to find a room that did not have a sag in the mattress. He tried to shake the sleep from his mind, staring at the closed door leading to Gloria's room, thinking it certainly wasn't anything else but a sagging mattress that had made his back sore this morning.

He stood up, shivering with cold, and walked over to look at the thermostat. Mouth set grimly, he yanked it over to full temperature, then disappeared into the bathroom.

Presently, shaved and showered, dressed and warm now with the finally heated room, he was feeling normal again. Normal and faintly sardonic—and, if he would admit it, scared all over again. He'd been thinking again about that upcoming business with Johnny Masters. He lit a cigarette and looked at Gloria's closed door. He'd purposely made some noise getting dressed and repacking his bag, in the hope that it would awaken her, fresh and restimulated. Now there was the faint rustle of her movement in the other room.

He smiled, feeling a lot better all of a sudden. He had not realized, until this trip, just how much he really felt for Gloria. If it hadn't done anything else, coming out here had taught him that.

He sat down, listening to the activity on the other side of the door, finally hearing the snap of her suitcase going shut. He grinned and stood up hopefully, thinking now that everything would be all right.

The door swung open, and Gloria paused, not wearing slacks now, but one of her good dresses and the mink coat he'd given her. Her hair was sleekly done up, her makeup expertly applied. Her beauty was like a vision. He had not, he was certain, ever seen a more lovely creature in his life.

"Glory," he said softly, smiling.

She looked at him coldly. The momentary softness of last night was, he realized, totally gone in the cold light of the morning. "Do you want to get the bags into the car? I want to get to Cheyenne and on a plane and out of this country! I've had it!"

"Glory—" But now he was angry again himself.

She walked to the door, the calves of her shapely legs swelling with each movement. She swung the door open, and fierce cold and powdered snow blew in with the wind still raging from off the prairie beyond.

"What a beautiful, gorgeous, stinking morning!" she said, striding toward the car. Sam followed, his mouth set grimly.

As Gloria and Sam Dickens stepped through the unrelenting storm toward the new Chrysler, Billy Quirter climbed from the hayloft. In the raw, open cold once again, his arm hurt like the blazes of hell. But nothing in this rotten world was going to stop him....

And still coming east, pushing his ageing sedan through the snow drifting across the ribbon of Route 7, the good Reverend John Andrews fought fatigue doggedly, while Lottie had, hours ago, given up, and now slept.

Just before Graintown and the waiting roadblock, Reverend Andrews too had almost given in to his fatigue and swung off to the right, with the idea that he might impose himself and Lottie on the good people of the Harry Harkins farm. The swing took him on a detour around the south edge of Graintown, a road so bad that when Reverend Andrews had finally decided against the intrusion, he kept going and picked up the main road again, missing the roadblock. Now he was just a mile and a half away from Arrow Junction.

He had almost dislodged that bitterness he'd fought earlier—the bitterness caused by his feelings about Maynard Styles—that prod of the Devil's pitchfork—and pretty soon he would be home in Arrow Junction. Within another half mile, he was feeling the warmth of the totally unselfish, grateful only for the chance to be alive and in the Good Lord's calling. He was a mile out of Arrow Junction now. And it was just there that he saw the figure of the small topcoated man stumbling onto the highway.

Reverend Andrews brought his old sedan to a lurching halts, feeling a quick compassion for this soul caught in the storm.

He swung open his door, as Lottie, awakening, straightened in her seat.

"Hello, there, neighbor!" Reverend Andrews called. "Here, get in the car! You're going to freeze to death out there!"

The man came toward the car, a frail-looking figure, whipped by the savage wind. All the pity in Reverend Andrews's heart went to him. He pulled his seat forward to allow the man, gripping his left arm tightly, to get inside to the back seat. Under the dome light, he caught a glimpse of the man's face. He saw the cold, frosty look of it, and the pity rose even more fully within him.

"You look frozen," Reverend Andrews said. He turned, as did Lottie, looking at the unfortunate man now seated in the back seat.

"Frozen, yeah," the man said, shaking visibly.

"Car break down?" Reverend Andrews asked worriedly.

"Car broke down, yeah," the man said, twisting his head a little.

"If there's anything we can do right now—you look absolutely frozen," Reverend Andrews said. "Otherwise, we'll—"

"Yeah." The man released his grip on his left arm. His right hand disappeared inside his coat. When it reappeared, it was gripping the handle of his gun. Billy Quirter said, "Here's exactly what you do. You knock off the chatter and kick the engine over. We're going to Arrow Junction. Now move!"

It was a morning of early rising for everyone except Ted Burley. At that moment he lay snoring, blindly drunk for the first time in his life. Beside him lay Greta Blummer, snoring in equal tempo. Her large and bare breasts rested against Ted Burley's muscular arm, her right hand lay absently across the inside of his naked right thigh. How Ted Burley got to be in the unclothed company of Greta Blummer in her lonely farmhouse four miles south of Arrow Junction, Ted Burley, at this moment, did not know nor care. But when he awoke later that morning, he would know, and the knowledge would frighten and shame him. But right now he was oblivious to all.

Bob Saywell was up and moving.

His conversation with Ann had not been, to him, entirely unsuccessful. The results of it had been, in essence, very similar to some very typical results he'd had with customers in his store. There were a few people in and around Arrow Junction who did not buy as much as they could from Bob Saywell, going, instead, to Graintown and using the three larger groceries there. This saved them money, because Bob Saywell was up a cent or two on most canned goods and a bit more on meats.

However, Bob Saywell knew how to keep at it. He took a variety of approaches. With some he emphasized service. With others he emphasized quality. With a few he emphasized the point that trading with him was the best loyalty you could show to your own home town of Arrow Junction, because where would you be if you didn't have his general store to come to in case of emergency when you couldn't get to Graintown? With some few others he was required to resort to veiled threat—a cutting-out approach, designed to make the subject feel guilty, threatening him (indirectly but effectively) with possible deletion from the close Arrow Junction circle of society of which nobody doubted Bob Saywell was the hub. It all depended. But the main thing was you didn't get discouraged. You kept at it. And the undeniable fact was that there was little buying potential in Arrow Junction that did not, finally, give in to Bob Saywell.

Ann Burley, then, was hardly any different from a lagging customer of his store. He'd scored as well as he'd expected to score in that first inning. There were plenty of innings coming up to score harder. It was this positivism that had started Bob Saywell's brain turning on an axis created out of pure and absolute lubricity.

It had started the night before, when, after climbing into bed with Martha, Bob Saywell's mind switched back to his encounter with Ann. The proximity to Martha at once started the sharp pangs of desire—not because Martha was desirable, but because she was so undesirable that the contrast between Ann and her, even though Ann remained but a mental picture at the moment, became all the more urgent in its effect.

Martha did the cooking, the dishwashing (at store and home), the housework, the sewing, and the going-to-meetings required to attune one's spirit to the whole of Arrow Junction's. Martha, in effect, worked like a horse. But she never questioned it, would never rise up against it. This was all in the world that Martha knew about marriage, and it was all Bob Saywell cared for her to know.

That she was a flop in the department of physical love as well as incapable of procreation did not, of course, deny the fundamental fact that she was a woman. And when Bob Saywell reached close proximity in their large bed, he had often enough reached desire, but seldom these latter years had he taken advantage of his marital opportunity. Martha was submissive, but she really did prefer the obligations of cooking and cleaning the house a good bit more.

Of course, Martha could not help an inability to conceive. But Bob Saywell had never been disappointed that they'd had no children. Who, if Martha were busy being pregnant and wiping children's noses, would do the work?

So, despite certain lacks, Martha was nevertheless a woman and Bob Saywell liked to waste no opportunities available to him. But on this evening, Bob Saywell was not even concerned with getting his due from Martha.

Most of the time Bob Saywell spent in saving his emotion for fairer pastures—his trips to Chicago, for instance. Now there was the mental image of good-looking, clean-formed Ann.

So Bob Saywell suddenly decided he could stand no more of this proximity. He decided to get up and get dressed and out of the house and into the store, where he could entertain his thoughts for another hour or two in total privacy—it was Martha's day off from the store anyway, her day to get things at home in order.

" 'S matter?" Martha murmured.

"Snoring," Bob Saywell said.

"Sorry," Martha mumbled, rolling on her side.

"Think I'll get up," Bob Saywell grumbled. "Go down to the store. I'll get my own breakfast."

"Mmmm," Martha uttered.

Thirty minutes later Bob Saywell unlocked the back door of the store. He turned on the thermostat, the grill, and started up the coffee, and in another twenty minutes was comfortably ensconced at the counter of his own store, warm, a cup of fresh coffee tantalizing his sense of taste and smell, the thought of moments to come with Ann Burley teasing his libido. It was a nice moment, exciting, pleasantly introspective for a man used to facing the public almost every hour. He was shut now behind the pulled shades of the broad windows and the glass-paned door.

The storm roared outside, the wind blew, the snow came down, the temperature stayed at its freezing level. Bob Saywell barely heard the old sedan of Reverend John Andrews cough its way down the main street and come to a stop directly in front of his store.

# Chapter Eleven

One going east, one going west, Reverend Andrews and Sam Dickens had arrived at Arrow Junction almost precisely at the same time. Both drivers had something in common: the controllers in each car (Billy Quirter in one, Gloria in the other) were hungry. The sign denoting food served in the Arrow Junction General Store performed the beacon.

Gloria was the first to step outside, running lightly and easily through the snow with a dancer's grace. She rapped quickly on the glass pane of the door. Sam Dickens came up behind her saying, "Honey, they're not open—" But Gloria paid no attention to him.

Sam Dickens sighed, and turned to look disinterestedly at Reverend Andrews's old car. Gloria's knocking was insistent. Finally, face perturbed, Bob Saywell jerked up the shade, preparing to shake his head. He looked at Gloria in her mink. Quite suddenly he unlocked the door and swung it open.

"Why, you folks come right on in!" Fat cheeks puffing roundly with a smile, Bob Saywell motioned Gloria inside. Then his eyes flickered to Sam Dickens, on to Sam's new Chrysler, then to Reverend Andrews's car as the good reverend, face set, climbed out.

"Yes, sir," Bob Saywell said, his nostrils twitching faintly with the scent of Gloria's expensive perfume. "Come in!" Then Bob Saywell boomed to Reverend Andrews. "Come on out of the cold, Reverend! Tell Lottie to hurry up and get herself warm with a cup of Bob Saywell's good coffee!"

Bob Saywell laughed, glancing at Gloria, who was now seating herself at the counter, checking her reaction to his good nature and generosity in opening for them.

By now Lottie Andrews had gotten stiffly out of the old sedan. And Bob Saywell saw that a third party had gotten from the car, a small man in a dark coat who carried his left arm peculiarly. Reverend and Mrs. Andrews moved rigidly toward the store, eyes looking at Bob Saywell in an odd, fixed manner. Bob Saywell was puzzled. He stared at the stranger, trying to fix the man's identity. He could not.

But again his cheeks puffed with a smile. "Got someone with you, Reverend? Why, that's fine. I'll get things going in here, and we'll all be cozy, eh?"

The reverend and his wife had gone past Bob Saywell. Now Billy Quirter stepped inside. Bob Saywell slammed the door shut.

"Yeah," Billy Quirter said to a suddenly paling Bob Saywell. Billy's gun was out and pointing straight at Bob Saywell's ponderous belly. "Cozy. Right. A nice, cozy little party! Lock the door, fat boy. Pull the shade!"

Billy Quirter's eyes flickered over the room. His mouth twisted faintly with a smile, as he sized up the beauty of Gloria. Then he looked back at Bob Saywell.

"Don't stand there and quiver, jelly roll. Do what I say, huh?"

Bob Saywell, at last, moved into fast and frightened action. "Yes, sir," he mumbled. "Yes, sir!"

The door locked, the shade drawn, Billy Quirter's smile widened. "Now this is real nice. Now let's keep it nice. I got an arm here that's busted. But that don't hurt my shooting arm at all."

He grinned. He slipped his finger from the trigger of his gun and let it slide expertly back in his palm, holding the gun out for everyone to see. It was a German P-38, and Billy loved the pistol; the serial numbers had been filed from each part where they appeared, but it was otherwise in perfect condition. To Billy, it was a symbol, and so he, in effect, worshiped the gun. He liked every part of it: the black look of it, the short snout of it, the front sight that could cut a man's face like the tip of a beer-can opener, the heavy trigger guard, the curving and ridged grip of the butt. He could remember the first time he'd fired it, shooting holes in pasteboard boxes with targets pasted over their sides out in the country. He remembered the sweet kick of the gun in his hand, the sharp report, the faint orange flare of the muzzle blast, the neat holes it had left in the pasteboard; perhaps others would remember a first baby or a first lover, but Billy remembered the first shooting of his gun.

He knew everything there was to know about that gun now. He knew the combinations of safeties, the tension of the magazine catch and thumb safety and hammer and trigger, the weight of it in his hand. He knew how to care for it, how to disassemble it with lightning speed, how to rub the oil on the steel and look down the shining and spiraling grooves of the bore to detect the faintest foreign particle. He knew, as well as he knew anything about it, its balance.

He held it lightly now, testing that balance. Then he placed it carefully on one of Bob Saywell's tables just in front of him, looking at the group staring back. He smiled. Then his hand leaped out and came back with the gun palmed neatly. It was a heavy gun, but not to Billy. In Billy's practiced hand, it was light as a plastic toy. He slipped his forefinger through the trigger guard, then suddenly let the weight of the pistol go entirely on the finger. The muzzle tipped around, up, and back, so that the barrel pointed at his own forehead. He jerked his hand slightly, and the gun spun, flashing darkly. He spun it backward, then forward. It snapped neatly into position again, the barrel pointing in the direction of the awed group.

Billy grinned again. The demonstration had been almost childish, but it had served its purpose. One thing was apparent: Billy was one with the gun, and nobody was going to forget that.

"You see how it is?" he said. "One good arm, one good hand, that's all I need. So everybody just stay calm now and don't say anything and don't do anything, huh? Just you, fat boy. You get on the telephone and get a doctor over here. And that's all you do, see? Or I'll bust that balloon gut you got and see what pours out. You savvy that, fat boy?"

Bob Saywell savvied instantly. He hurtled back through the store to the telephone on the wall.

"Just dial and say it's an emergency and tell him to get over here and hang up!" Billy snapped from the other end of the room.

Bob Saywell turned, staring at Billy with helpless panic. "Can't dial. No dial. You got to crank and ask Marie!"

Billy frowned in momentary puzzlement, then understood "All right then. Crank, jelly roll, and ask Marie!"

Bob Saywell cranked. His voice came out in a high tremolo in answer to Marie's voice at the switchboard in the telephone office three blocks away. "Doc Stewart's office, Marie!"

He waited for what seemed an incredible time, sweat oozing on his forehead. Marie rang the long and a long, over and over. There was no answer.

"It's pretty early," Marie said. "I'll try his house, Bob."

Bob Saywell nodded dumbly.

A short and a long this time. Repeated once. Then Doctor Hugh Stewart answered.

"Me, Doc!" Bob Saywell quivered. "Bob Saywell! Got an emergency over here at the store. You got to get over here!" He put the receiver back on the hook and turned around, looking at Billy Quirter in wild pleading, asking with frightened eyes if he'd done exactly the right thing.

"Okay, jelly roll," Billy Quirter said. His sharp dark eyes had examined Bob Saywell thoroughly. He was satisfied. Bob Saywell was no threat. Billy relaxed just a little, feeling the prickling of a peculiar new kind of power he'd never felt before. He'd spent most of his days in the shadow of Tony, doing his work with no recognition, Tony always being the front man, always taking the spotlight. This was different. It was all right. It even seemed to help the burning pain of his arm.

Billy's eyes brushed over the others, trying to analyze them. The preacher. The preacher's fat wife. The guy from the Chrysler. The guy's broad. Billy's eyes stopped on Gloria. She was everything Billy had always imagined to be desirable; she closely resembled the visions he'd seen on the screens of dark movie houses where he'd spent so much of his lonely time. Billy smiled faintly. He jerked his head a little toward the kitchen and said:

"Fat boy, you get back there and lock that back door if it ain't already, huh? Then get some eggs on. Make yourself useful. I'll tell you what. Breakfast for everyone! How's that? We're all going to have breakfast!"

Billy grinned as Bob Saywell stumbled over himself to do what Billy had ordered.

Billy looked at Gloria. "I like him. He's eager. He likes to please. How about you, sweetheart?"

Gloria looked at him with cold calm.

Billy shrugged, then motioned his gun at Reverend Andrews and Lottie. "Sit down at a table, Reverend. Breakfast's coming up."

"May God have mercy on you," Reverend Andrews breathed, his hand finding Lottie's.

"That's right," Billy said. "May God have mercy on us all. Especially anyone who gets funny, huh? Now you and your wife sit down, Reverend!" The smile went, the voice hardened.

Reverend Andrews guided Lottie to one of the tables where they sat down. Lottie kept staring unbelievingly at Billy, but she kept her chin up firmly.

Billy rounded the counter and came up the back side. Bob Saywell had a high stool he kept there to sit on when he conversed with customers over the counter. Billy sat down on that, overlooking the store. Bob Saywell nervously broke eggs onto a hot grill at the rear of the store.

Billy looked at Sam Dickens. "What's your name, Jack?"

"Dickens."

"Dickens what?"

"Sam Dickens."

"Oh. I thought it was Dickens something. I like that—Dickens. It's the name of a book, ain't it?"

"I don't think so," Sam Dickens said.

"Well, who cares? Do you care, Dickens?"

"No. I don't care."

"That's the stuff," Billy grinned. "I like you. You look smart to me. Is this your wife?"

"Yes."

"See? Now that's one of the reasons I know you're smart, Dickens. You got to be smart to have a wife looks like this."

Sam Dickens said nothing. Gloria looked at Sam, then back at Billy Quirter.

"Sam Dickens, huh? What's her name, Sam?" Billy smiled wickedly at Gloria. "Mine's Billy, sweetheart."

"What's the point?" Sam Dickens finally said. "What are you after anyway?"

"Now I said you were smart. I meant that, Sam. Now a smart man in a case like this keeps his mouth shut from asking what he's not supposed to. I mean, he just answers what he's asked. Now you're a smart man, Sam. See, I can tell it takes a smart man to own a car like you got outside and a wife like this here one. And that mink coat she's wearing, you don't afford that from being dumb, huh, Sam? Now I didn't ask you to ask me what the point was or what I was after. That's my business. I asked you to tell me what Mrs. Dickens's name is."

Gloria looked at Sam Dickens, anger flaring in her eyes. Then she said to Billy Quirter, "The name's Mrs. Dickens. I'm his wife. His name is Dickens. I'm Mrs. Dickens. Okay?"

"Gloria, listen," Sam Dickens pleaded. "He means business. Isn't that obvious? That's a gun in his hand."

But Billy suddenly laughed. "That's all right, Sam. I like your wife. I really do. Lots of pepper, huh?"

Sam Dickens had his hands on the counter. He opened and closed them without answering.

Gloria's mouth tightened. She looked at her husband, then away.

"Now this gun in my hand," Billy said. "Are you scared of it, Dickens?"

Sam would not lift his head.

Billy nodded. "He is, Gloria. Gloria—I like that name."

"That's grand."

Again Billy laughed. "You kill me, Gloria. Why don't you come around the counter and pour us all some coffee?"

"Why don't you climb a rope?"

Billy's face suddenly froze, the dark eyes thinned a little.

Sam Dickens said, "For God's sake, Glory! Don't—"

"Shut up!" Billy snapped. He stared grimly at Gloria. "Now I mean it, sister. I told you to do something. I said come around here and pour us some coffee. Did you hear me?"

Gloria met his stare steadily. "Go to hell."

Sam Dickens opened and closed his mouth. Suddenly Billy's face wreathed into the broadest smile he'd yet demonstrated. "No kidding! What a broad, huh? I mean it! Beautiful and sheer guts!"

Gloria said, "Why don't you pour the coffee, smart boy? I could use some."

Billy shook his head in pure and obvious admiration. "Smart, Dickens. Real smart to grab a dame like this. How'd you do it? Well, never mind. I'll tell you what. *You* pour the coffee, Dickens. Now you ain't going to tell me to climb a rope, are you?" Billy smiled jovially at Sam Dickens. "Come on! Make like a bus boy, huh?"

Sam Dickens sat motionless for a second. Then he stood up and walked slowly around the right side of the counter to the glass coffee containers. He got cups from the shelves and poured five cups.

"Distribute," Billy grinned.

Sam Dickens carried two cups to the table where Reverend Andrews and Lottie sat. He came back and carried two cups to the counter for Gloria and Billy. Then, as if sensing that Billy would demand it (in his mind was the memory of a western he'd produced in which the bad man said to the good man, "Ain't you going to drink with me, pardner?"), he took the final cup for himself.

"Fine, Dickens," Billy said when Sam had reseated himself. "Now that's real fine. He did that good, didn't he, Gloria?"

Gloria didn't answer.

Billy grinned, his enjoyment of this outweighing the pain of his arm. "What do you do for a living, Dickens?"

"Motion pictures," Sam Dickens said quietly. "I'm a producer."

"No kidding," Billy said. "The movies, huh? Now I could give you some real material, Dickens. Not that slop you put out. What the hell are you doing in this little dump anyway?"

At that Reverend Andrews stood up, started to speak, found a fuzziness in his throat, cleared it, and finally said, "I'll thank you not to swear in here."

Billy looked at him in utter astonishment.

Gloria half turned, looking at the reverend. Sam Dickens also looked back.

"I might remind you," Reverend Andrews went on doggedly, "I am a clergyman."

Billy sat there for a moment, then carefully got off his stool and walked along behind the counter until he was even with Reverend Andrews. The movement jolted pain through his arm, but he ignored that. He stood there, one arm limp, the other crooked up, carrying the gun in his right hand so that it half pointed at the reverend. "Yeah," he said, eyes thinning. "Yeah, you're a clergyman. You told me in that car, remember? You're a preacher. So what, huh? That makes you God, maybe? You yak about it so much maybe that's what you think?"

"I think nothing of the sort. I am merely of the Good Lord's calling—"

"The Good Lord's calling!" Billy said meanly. "He called you, did He? When did the call come in? Long distance, straight from Heaven? Person to person, maybe? You're a nut is what you are! How about that, Reverend? You hear voices, huh?" Suddenly Billy's tense look disappeared. "I'll tell you something." He smiled now, delighted with his train of thought. "I hear voices too." He walked back to the stool and reseated himself, looking at the reverend all the while. "All the time! Only my calls come in from the other direction. Direct. Person to person. Guess from where?"

Reverend Andrews forced himself to stand there despite the paleness of his face. But he was silent.

"Sure," Billy said happily. "A direct line to down under. Straight from the Devil himself, Reverend. Do you believe that?"

Reverend Andrews was silent for a moment, then very quietly he said, "Yes, I do."

Billy blinked, his eyes shifting just in time to see the faintest quirking at the corners of Sam Dickens's mouth.

Swiftly Billy's gun dropped in his lap, and his right hand lashed out, the flat of it cracking against Sam Dickens's cheek. The movement was fast as lightning, and the blow had a surprising impact. It half turned Sam Dickens on his stool.

"Funny?" Billy snapped to the surprised Sam Dickens. "You think something's funny, Dickens?"

Sam Dickens, his cheek flaming red where Billy's hand had struck it, was silent for a moment. He shook his head. "No," he said softly.

"Good." Billy's gun was back in his hand now. "That's good. I thought you thought something was funny. I'll let you know when something's funny. All right, Dickens?"

Sam Dickens nodded faintly.

Billy's tense look disappeared entirely. "Now sit up and drink your coffee." He looked at Reverend Andrews still standing determinedly by the table. "You sit down, Reverend. I didn't think you were a trouble-maker. Is that what preachers are for? To be trouble-makers? You just caused me to bust old Sam here in the face. What's your Boss going to think of that? You better sit down, Reverend. You don't want to be a trouble-maker, do you?"

Reverend Andrews licked his lips and slowly sat down.

Gloria Dickens, startled by the slap, but once again poised, said, "Why don't you take a swing at me? Just for good measure."

Billy grinned. "I'm afraid you might swing back, honey. Besides I wouldn't want to hurt those pretty features of yours. You're a doll, do you know that?"

"No kidding? I'd always thought I was real ugly."

"Honey, you kill me."

"Maybe I would if I had a chance."

"You ain't going to get a chance. Old Sam here ain't going to help you get it anyway, is he, Gloria?"

"No," Gloria said, glancing angrily at Sam, "I guess he's not."

"Then we're all happy," Billy said, looking toward the rear. "Where's the breakfast, jelly roll?"

"Right away, right away!" Bob Saywell chattered. A moment later he scurried up with a large plate of eggs and bacon. He placed it obsequiously in front of Billy, then backed up and looked hopefully at the gunman, giving the impression of wringing his hands without actually doing it.

Billy placed his gun in his lap again and started eating ravenously. He paused suddenly, looking sideways at Bob Saywell, fork poised in air.

"Well, feed the rest of the animals, chunky. We're all at the trough this morning!"

"Yes, sir!"

Bob Saywell had never given such service. He served the entire room in unbelievable time, then stood panting, waiting for Billy's next desire. Billy motioned with his gun. "What's the matter with that doc?"

"Ought to be here any minute! Yes, sir! You can count on Doc. A good man! The best, Doc Stewart!"

"I don't care what his goddam name is," Billy said, carefully looking over the counter at Reverend Andrews. "I just want to know where he is." Reverend Andrews flushed, but he did not get up.

Bob Saywell, in desperate but futile eagerness to produce Dr. Hugh Stewart, looked as though he might have to run to the back of the store to the small lavatory.

Hugh Stewart solved Bob Saywell's dilemma at that moment by rapping on the front door.

Billy's fork clattered onto his plate. His gun was again in his hand. He looked at a quivering Bob Saywell.

"Now, listen, jelly roll. This is closed shop today, you hear? I mean to everybody, but that doc. Now you go over and look past that shade. If it's the doc, let him in. And he'd better come in alone, or I'll put a hole right through your pink little head, see? I mean that like I never meant anything in my life, chubby. Now, go!"

Bob Saywell went, around the counter, scooting to the door. He peered out, then unlocked the door. Dr. Hugh Stewart stepped inside.

"Now shut the door and lock it!" Billy snapped from behind the counter.

Bob Saywell did just that. Hugh Stewart stared in surprise, first at Billy Quirter and the gun in his hand, then at the faces of the others, sitting silently, staring back at him.

Billy Quirter grinned. "Welcome to the party, Doc. It's the left arm— busted. I'm real glad you could make it. Come on over here and start working, huh? Jelly roll there'll get you some breakfast. Hop to it, fatty. How do you like your eggs, Doc? Sunny side up or over one time?"

# Chapter Twelve

The storm was wearing thin with the brightening of morning. Snow had drifted like nicely placed dollops of whipped cream. Traffic had been eased to a thin trickle all around, and would not return to any degree of normalcy until the snow plows had cut through; there was one beginning its slow push from Graintown to Arrow Junction right now.

Still, with a half-ton truck and chains, it was possible to get around fairly easily; and Ted Burley, when he lurched from Greta Blummer's farmhouse did not think about whether or not he could make the drive back to his own farm without trouble. He simply ground the starter until the engine caught and turned over, the muscles of his jaw standing rigid along his cheeks.

Deep in his stomach Ted Burley felt a nauseous distress. For one thing he was suffering a crushing hangover. The night previous he'd drunk three-quarters of a bottle of whisky all by himself, and Ted Burley did not normally drink. For another thing, he had, in his own opinion, just degraded himself to the bottom of the pit by spending the night with Greta Blummer. Anybody in or around Arrow Junction knew well enough what Greta was.

Yet he'd kept up that drinking—taking one final swig from the bottle as he'd driven the pickup into the drive of her farm. Then he'd lurched on to the house and grabbed Greta, while she giggled and kept asking him what in the world he was doing. She'd known exactly what he was doing and was happy as hell over it.

In the cab now, shuddering as he drove away from that house, Ted Burley remembered where he'd put that bottle of whisky; it was just behind him on the ledge behind the seat.

He got it and took another drink, blinking as the whisky seared down to his empty stomach. He'd tripped the emotional lever again, done it by imagining how it was with Ann and Dr. Hugh Stewart, an image that had built up the previous late afternoon and finally suffused him completely, until he'd vented his rage and building desire on the soft flesh of Greta Blummer.

"Damned dirty whore!" Ted Burley repeated of his wife. He hunched behind the wheel, drunkenness resuming instantly with the first drink. He propped the bottle beside him, driving with instinctive accuracy along the snowy road. "I'll show her when I get home," he muttered. "I'll show her!"

But his own farmhouse on the west edge of Arrow Junction was still empty. Ann Burley had remained in the office of Dr. Hugh Stewart. She had finally slept that night. Now, early this morning, she was awake and thinking. "You can't keep on running," Hugh Stewart had told her. "You've got to stop sometime...."

She stood in the silent office and looked out over the snow-covered smallness of Arrow Junction. Two cars had appeared and parked beside her sedan. One of them belonged to Reverend Andrews, she knew; the other was unfamiliar. And now, as she looked, Dr. Hugh Stewart's car also appeared and stopped near Bob Saywell's store.

Her throat tightened a little. She wondered if Hugh Stewart were going to talk to Bob Saywell. How he would, she did not know. A hope fluttered up in her, then died suddenly. She was once again turning to Hugh Stewart when in reality, she knew, the problem was totally hers. "You've got to tell the sheriff," Hugh Stewart had said to her.

Ann Burley pulled the shade down and turned away from the window, the fright returning in full force.

In the sheriff's office of the courthouse in Graintown, Sheriff-elect Jenkins had calmed a little. Fatigue was catching up with him as a result. He sat and looked at his deputy, Wade Miles.

Deputy Miles said, "I can't figure how he busted out!"

Deputy Miles was twenty-one years younger than Sheriff-elect Jenkins. He was the same height, the same weight, in fact—six feet tall and two hundred pounds. But Deputy Miles was lean, muscle making the bulk of poundage which was in Sheriff-elect Jenkins's body pure flab. The contrast in sinewy toughness, however, went deeper than framework; it went deep inside to spirit and courage. Sheriff-elect Jenkins was a bluff. Deputy Miles was not. Deputy Miles had been a paratrooper in World War II. He'd jumped into Holland on D minus one. Deputy Miles was afraid of nothing. He was deadly with either knife or gun, and he was physically quick as a cat.

The prime trouble with Wade Miles was that he did not have the mental ability to match his spirit and able body. His mind simply would not organize properly. He often acted without thinking, because thinking was a terrible chore. Thus he'd been a fine trooper, but never a leader.

He had a leader now, in official terms: Sheriff-elect Harvey Jenkins. But the trouble was that despite the officialdom of the command, Sheriff-elect Jenkins was, at this moment, capable of leading nothing. Due to an inherent lack of sensitivity, Wade Miles did not know this. He did not know, for example, that Sheriff-elect Jenkins was no more capable of figuring out the next move than he was himself—not from lack of intelligence, but rather from a lack of guts.

Sheriff-elect Jenkins shook his head in mock, but convincing, sadness. "He must have, Wade." He hoped, in truth, that Billy Quirter *had* busted out. He had visions of a stolen car, not yet reported, somehow gotten past the roadblocks, souping down a highway at high speed, please God, far away from Graintown.

"Figured the State Police ought to do better on their own than they have," Deputy Miles said sullenly. "They don't do nothing, nothing at all!"

The fact was the State Police were doing as well as they could. The fact was that Sheriff-elect Jenkins, by virtue of county jurisdiction, was in charge of this manhunt. Even with Deputy Miles working hard behind him, Sheriff-elect Jenkins was the weak link in an otherwise strong chain. You couldn't work at peak performance with a drag at the very top of the chain of command.

"Tough cookie," Sheriff-elect Jenkins said. "Slippery as an eel." He was full of triteness this morning, because his mind was dulled by fatigue.

"All roads plugged up," Deputy Miles said, smacking one large fist into one large palm. "How far can he get on foot?"

"Maybe," Jenkins said, suddenly hopeful, "he tried it that way. Got himself caught in the snow somewhere out in the fields. Stuck there right now, frozen—"

"Billy Quirter?" Deputy Miles said, incredulous. Before the previous morning, Deputy Miles had never heard of Billy Quirter. But he'd now heard all he needed to hear to respect him. "No, sir. Not Billy Quirter!" Deputy Miles said, as though he'd known Billy all his life.

"You can't be sure."

"I'm sure enough about that. You don't get Billy Quirter that way. You shoot him down is how you get him. You put so much lead in him he can't stand up for the weight is how you get Billy Quirter!"

"He's not that good."

"You say," Miles said, his enthusiasm created out of his respect for Billy outweighing his politeness to a superior.

"I say we'll get him if he's around," Sheriff-elect Jenkins said brusquely. He'd said that so many times by now that the word-forming was purely mechanical.

"Can't figure out where he got to," Deputy Miles said, pacing. "Covered this town like we was combing out hair. Looked in every niche and cranny. He just ain't turning up!"

"I say he could be gone," Jenkins insisted stubbornly.

"How then? Not in any car! He didn't get out in nobody's car!"

"Well, maybe he got away on that train."

Wade Miles snorted. "How, I wonder? Those boys didn't see a soul at the station. Train didn't stop between here and Arrow Junction. We had the station master in Arrow Junction alerted by the time it did stop. Nobody got off. No trace of anybody on that train. No, sir. He's around here. He'll show his hand one way or another. And we'd better be ready, that's all I got to say. We'd better be good and ready and not miss when we go for him. He'll get some of us if we do, I'll tell you that. You think about that hole in Corly's old head, and then you think what he'll do when we spook him out—"

"Wade," the sheriff-elect cut in, feeling that trembling start inside him once again, "we've got to get some rest. Why don't you just take off home and get some rest?"

Miles looked at him, blinked. "I don't need no rest, Harvey. I'm feeling fine!"

Jenkins rubbed a hand over his mouth. "Well, I'll tell you, Wade, I've got to think a little by myself. All right? I mean, I want to relax just a little in here on that leather couch and get my thoughts straightened out—kind of try to think like this Quirter, so maybe we can outfox him and get him. You get yourself something to eat or something and come back in about an hour, all right?"

Reluctantly Miles nodded. "Okay, Harvey. About an hour. I'll see you then."

When Deputy Wade Miles had gone, Jenkins walked wearily to the leather couch. Folded neatly on the bottom were a pillow and an Army blanket he had used on National Guard camping trips. His wife had brought them the night before.

Harvey Jenkins picked up the pillow and placed it at one end of the couch, then lay down, his stomach knotted so hard it was making him physically ill. He licked his lips. His tongue, his whole mouth, was dry. He reached down and pulled the blanket over him, thinking about what Wade Miles had said: "We'd better be good and ready and not miss when we go for him. He'll get some of us if we do, I'll tell you that...."

A small shudder ran through Sheriff-elect Jenkins, and he pulled the blanket around him a little more. In fact, he pulled it all the way over his head.

# Chapter Thirteen

Dr. Hugh Stewart stared at Billy Quirter. He stared at the quick eyes glinting at him from across the room. He knew instantly who Billy was and why he was here. "Billy Quirter," he said aloud.

He walked across the room and around the counter, approaching Billy. Billy grinned at him, but the eyes were careful, sizing the doctor up. "I'm getting famous, huh?"

Dr. Hugh Stewart said carefully, "Do you want to explain why you're holding a gun on me?"

Billy Quirter kept grinning. "No, Doc."

Hugh Stewart looked around the room. "Anyone else?"

Reverend Andrews stood up. "He is obviously a gangster. Whatever reason he has, it is for some evil reason."

"Sit down, Reverend," Billy said disgustedly.

"I think," Reverend Andrews said stoutly, "it's time for you to explain this thing."

"I think you're going to get in some real trouble, Reverend," Billy said tightly, "if you don't do what I tell you!" He stared at Reverend Andrews until the reverend finally sat down. Then Billy looked straight at Hugh Stewart. "The only thing it's time for is you to start fixing this broken arm. I'd advise that, Doc."

"It's my job to treat you. But not at gunpoint."

"At gunpoint. Or without. Either way. It's still your job. I've just told you it is. Do you want to start?" Billy's voice had softened, but the flash of his eyes indicated a growing anger. Hugh Stewart saw that. He put his bag down, opened it.

"You'll have to get that coat and jacket off."

Billy examined him carefully. He finally nodded. "All right." Billy got off the stool and stepped backward.

Hugh Stewart opened his bag, drew out a syringe. Billy, his suit jacket half shrugged off now, shook his head. "Oh, no, Doc. No, thanks."

"It's going to hurt."

"Let it. See, I just think you might try something if you had half a chance, Doc. Like load up that needle with something that might not really be good for Billy Quirter. It's just a feeling I have."

Hugh Stewart shrugged. "It's up to you, Quirter."

Billy smiled. "That's the whole truth." He had the jacket off now. He stepped forward, looking much skinnier than he had in the coat and jacket. He wore a holster over his white shirt, strapped under his left armpit.

"Okay," Hugh Stewart said, "let's check it."

Billy Quirter, his arm in Hugh Stewart's practiced hands, watched the doctor's eyes with steady, catlike tenacity. Pain flickered through his nervous system; but his eyes showed nothing except a slight tightening of the rims.

"Lucky," Hugh Stewart said. "You could have had it worse than a simple fracture. But I told you. It's going to hurt."

"Fix it. Talk don't get it fixed, does it?"

Hugh Stewart's hands expertly snapped the bone into place. He counted on the shock of pain to take Billy off his guard. He made his try.

He swept his left hand sideways, striking for the gun in Billy's right hand. He brought up his own right hand in a short, but powerful chop at Billy's chin. It was a co-ordinated movement, mind blanking only to the attempt to destroy this man in front of him, the kind of emotion he'd known all his life in times of stress. To those watching, it was a swift, capable movement: left hand sweeping sideways, right hand chopping up....

Half the attempt was successful. The left hand barely missed, because Billy had been waiting for that attempt. Despite the shot of pain as the bone was locked into natural junction, Billy's reflexes reacted. He shifted his right hand out, getting the gun out of line of Hugh Stewart's sweep toward it.

But Billy could not move his head in time to escape the chopping right hand driven up at his chin. The blow grazed along his left cheek, catching his cheekbone hard enough to drive him slightly off balance.

But Billy had already made up his mind about his defense.

He did not attempt to bring the gun back into position to fire at Hugh Stewart. Instead he twisted back and away from the doctor, left arm instinctively loose at his side. He took his eyes completely away from Hugh Stewart, momentarily off balance. He bent over a little toward the counter, swinging the hand with the gun around. He looked straight at Gloria Dickens and brought his gun over the counter and pressed the muzzle against her left breast.

He looked at her with dark glittering eyes. Gloria blinked once, when the barrel touched her, but she didn't move a fraction. Billy remained locked in this position. He didn't look to see if the doctor were moving again. He knew quite certainly he wasn't. Billy was right. In a half crouch, hands preparing for other blows, Hugh Stewart froze, stopped by the lightning action of Billy Quirter.

"Wasn't smart, Doc," Billy breathed. "Wasn't smart at all."

Gloria took a breath, the breath forcing her left breast against the gun barrel more tightly. "It was a nice try anyway, Doctor," she said. "Real beautiful. I thought you'd made it for a second."

Hugh Stewart let his breath out slowly. "Take the gun off her. You have my word. I won't try it again."

"Words," Billy smiled. "I'd never have lived this long on words, Doc." He twisted his head slightly. "Come on, baby—off the stool and start moving around the counter."

Sam Dickens came alive. He straightened and put his palms against the edge of the counter. "Now, see here—"

"Cut it off, Dickens," Billy snapped. "You can't do a thing about it!"

Gloria stood up and came around the counter. Bob Saywell stood staring, transfixed by the action.

Billy stepped back so he could view both Hugh Stewart and the far end of the counter with safety. He said to Bob Saywell, "Okay, Farouk— I told you to get the doc his breakfast!"

Bob Saywell, once again, scurried.

Gloria came down the back side of the counter. Billy allowed her to pass, then said, "Far enough. Now turn and face me."

Billy, lifting his gun, resumed his chair in front of Hugh Stewart. He kept his eyes constantly on Gloria, standing now just beside him.

"Side vision," Billy said. "I've got real good side vision, Doc. Took an eye test once, and they told me that. See, I'm looking at Gloria here, only I can see you too." Then again he put the muzzle of the gun directly against the left breast of Gloria. "See, Doc, you go for me again, I just squeeze the trigger. Bang. End of Gloria. You don't want that to happen. Old Sam over there don't want that to happen. I don't want that to happen." Billy grinned. "You know, baby, you're the prettiest target I ever had in my life?"

Gloria met his look unwaveringly. "Where do you find pretty things in sewers?"

Sam Dickens choked. "Gloria—!"

Billy's grin disappeared, the eyes flashed. Then the grin appeared again. "Gloria, you are the end. You are way out there." He pushed the gun very slightly. "Okay, Doc. Finish the arm, huh? I'm going to sit here and look at Gloria. I'll never feel a thing. Do you know Gloria, Doc?" This, as Hugh Stewart resumed his work on Billy's arm. "You know the reverend and his wife over there, I guess. And fatso back in the kitchen. Do you know Gloria? She's Sam's wife, see? Sam Dickens. He makes movies. How about that? Sam's real smart. He makes movies and he's got Gloria. Sam's the smartest man in the world. Is that why you married Sam, Gloria? Because Sam's so smart?"

"No," Gloria said crisply. "I married him because of his rare courage. I call him Ivanhoe."

"No kidding," Billy said, his eyes barely flickering with the pain as Hugh Stewart worked on his arm. "How come?"

"You'd have to know about Ivanhoe," Gloria said. "Maybe they skipped that where you got your education, Billy-boy."

"Maybe they did, at that," Billy grinned. "You tell me. I'm willing to let you educate me, Gloria."

Gloria's eyes, for the first time, flickered down to the gun pointing at her; but it was only a flashing indication that she realized the proximity of that weapon. "Ivanhoe was a knight. He rode a white horse and carried a spear. He rescued damsels when they got in distress."

"Like how?" Billy asked.

"Like when they were captured by dragons."

"Oh," Billy said, nodding. "I got it now. That's Sam, huh?"

"That's Sam. See, all the girls wait around and hope they can get their own Ivanhoe. It's kind of—symbolic, do you know what I mean?"

"I know what you mean," Billy said. "But I don't grab Sam here for that."

"Maybe you don't. Maybe a lot of girls wouldn't either. But I do. I knew Sam was Ivanhoe the minute I set eyes on him. There's my knight, I said. There's my lover in shining armor. If a dragon ever gets me, I knew Sam would come on his white horse and slay the dragon with his spear and I'd be safe again."

"The minute you laid eyes on him," Billy said. "That was old Sam here."

"Right," Gloria said. "Sam Dickens. Ivanhoe himself."

"Then how come," Billy asked, "he didn't pick up his spear and get on his white horse and come around the counter? I'm like a dragon, huh? Sam's Ivanhoe. What's holding him up?"

"Maybe," Gloria said, switching her eyes coolly to Sam Dickens, "his horse broke a leg."

"Maybe," Billy said, delighted, "it did, at that. Or maybe his spear got bent. Or maybe his armor's wearing out."

"Maybe all three," Gloria said, eyes flashing. "Or maybe—"

"Don't Glory," Sam Dickens said tightly, looking down at his clenched hands. "Don't, or so help me I'll do it. I'll come over this counter and try for him and we'll both wind up dead."

He looked back at Gloria suddenly, with equally flashing eyes. She met his gaze all at once curious. "If you meant that, Sam, maybe I wouldn't mind dying that way. Maybe I'd die happy that way."

Sam raised his brows, as though he were surprised that, in this instance, she cared at all about him anymore. He licked his lips, carefully separated his hands.

Gloria examined him for a moment, then said, "Don't do it, lover. It's like Billy-boy says. Your spear's bent. You don't want to fool around with Billy-boy with a bent spear. The doctor here just tried it with a good horse and fresh armor and a brand new spear. He didn't make it."

Billy laughed good-humoredly. "And the doc's fast. Did you notice?"

"I noticed," Gloria said. "So relax, Mr. Dickens. Maybe I gave up believing in Ivanhoes."

Sam looked at her hopefully to see what, exactly, she meant. Whatever it was, he was certain she did not mean what she said. Gloria, he was positive, had not given up believing in Ivanhoes by a long shot....

"Okay," Hugh Stewart said, "it's fixed."

Billy nodded. "Right. That's fine, Doc." He looked at Hugh Stewart, eyes bright and appraising. Hugh Stewart knew he had been accurately categorized by Billy. The attempt on Billy had been so nearly successful that Billy had made up his mind: of those in this room, Hugh Stewart was the one Billy would watch most carefully. Oddly, in this man's scale of values, Hugh Stewart would also be the one Billy would treat best.

But Hugh Stewart felt a cold clutching within his stomach. The attempt to overpower Billy done, the job of fixing his arm finished, the instinctive flaming within Hugh Stewart settled to a steady glow of coals. Once more he had acted impulsively. And the impulse might have driven this man into wanton killing. There were five other people in this room besides Billy Quirter and himself. He could have gotten them all killed. Mouth dry, he tried to steel himself to absolute control now.

Billy slid off the stool, drawing the gun away from Gloria. "All right, Gloria," he said brightly. "Go back and sit down with old Sam, all right? Doc, you go along with her. That's right. Right around the counter and back up here. Have a seat, Doc. Right there beside Gloria where I can keep my eyes on you. I always respect a man who's fast. Now Sam there, he'd like to be fast, see? But he just ain't got it. Some do, some don't. Sam just ain't got it. Right, Sam?"

Happily, Billy looked beyond Hugh Stewart, Sam and Gloria Dickens. He smiled pleasantly at Reverend Andrews. "How're you doing, Reverend? All right? Saying your prayers and all? I'll bet you're sending up prayers like they shoot up ack-ack, like I seen in news reels. I'll bet that's how heaven looks right now, all black with those prayers exploding up there. I'll bet, if you keep it up, you're going to ack-ack heaven right out of the sky." Billy laughed delightedly.

Reverend Andrews said, "Heaven help you."

"Don't count on it, Reverend," Billy said. Then he called back to the kitchen, "Farouk! The doc's had a tough time setting this arm. He's hungry! How about the breakfast!"

There was almost a magical quality in the way Bob Saywell, normally slow and lumbering, could instantly appear on Billy Quirter's command. He did so, carrying a plate of eggs and bacon, almost running along behind the counter.

"That's right," Billy said. "That's the old stuff, Roly. Now give him some coffee, huh? I need some myself. Give everyone some coffee. Eat, Doc. You ain't going any place. You might as well relax and enjoy yourself. You want something more to eat, Gloria?"

Gloria lit a cigarette, blew the smoke upward, her old self again. She was not looking at Sam Dickens any more. Sam Dickens looked tense, but glum, at the same time. "Thanks a heap, but no," she said.

"You tell me when you need anything, Gloria," Billy said pleasantly. "I'll fix you up."

"Fine," Gloria said. "Don't call me. I'll call you."

Billy laughed. "Sam, you're smart, all right. What a broad!"

Sam Dickens brought his head up. "I think I've had about enough from you."

Billy blinked. "Is that right?"

"That's right. I'll thank you to quit the comics with my wife."

"Quit the comics, huh?"

"That's right," Sam Dickens said, straightening a little more. "That's exactly right."

Billy's eyes narrowed. "Now, Sam, I just told you you were smart. Now you're going dumb again."

"What are you after anyway? Why don't you get it done, whatever it is, and get out of here?"

"Look, Mr. Dickens," Hugh Stewart said quietly, "don't push him. Just don't do that. I don't think he'll hesitate to use that gun."

"See?" Billy said, smiling tightly. "You hear that, Sam? Now Doc don't get confused. He knows what's what. Now you've got brains, Sam. How come you don't use them?"

"I mean it," Sam Dickens said, gripping his hands into fists. "If you've got something to do here, do it! Otherwise, get out!"

Bob Saywell had paused in his pouring of coffee for Reverend Andrews and Lottie. The room was deathly silent. Billy shook his head very slightly, a shiver of a muscle twitching beside his mouth. "You stupid son of a bitch! You're ordering me?"

Billy's lips went thinner, then suddenly his gun swept through the air. Sam Dickens ducked just as the barrel swung by his right cheek. He was not hit. But Sam Dickens's face went white. He froze, half bent, hands clutching the counter, eyes shut, waiting for the next blow.

It didn't come.

Billy Quirter spoke across the counter to Bob Saywell, "Relax, butterball. Sam here is relieving you on the coffee. Sam here's feeling frisky. He wants to pour again. You hear that, Sam? Go get the coffeepot and start pouring. Butterball, you come over here and sit down. Move, Dickens!"

There was only a second's wait before Sam Dickens stood up and walked slowly over and took the coffeepot out of Bob Saywell's quivering hand. Quietly, Sam Dickens filled up Lottie's cup, while Bob Saywell edged to the counter and sat down on a stool, eyes bulging in petrified fear.

Gloria now looked at the lengthening ash of her cigarette, then ground the cigarette out. She said quietly, so that her voice did not reach back to Sam Dickens, "I wonder how you'd look without that gun in your hand, tough boy?"

"Don't bother your brain about it, Gloria," Billy said. "You ain't going to see it that way for a while."

Gloria started to retort, then did not. She sat there, still unnecessarily grinding the cigarette in an ash tray.

"What's the matter?" Billy asked her, his smile finally reappearing. "You surprised to find out old Sam there's weak in the belly? I thought you knew that."

"Shut up," Gloria said.

"Now, Gloria—"

"I said shut up or you'll have to pistol-whip me next!"

"Okay," Billy said quickly and engagingly. "You know I'd hate to do that, Gloria. I honestly would!"

Gloria said nothing more, nobody said anything more. Stiffly, Sam Dickens continued his chore of pouring coffee.

Billy nodded and smiled. "Now then. We're all relaxed."

Still the room was silent. Billy smiled apologetically. "Now I've gone and got everybody upset, haven't I? I didn't hurt old Sam, did I? Did I, Sam?"

Sam was about to pour coffee into the cup in front of Hugh Stewart.

He paused, holding the coffeepot just over the cup. He stood like that for perhaps two seconds. Then he resumed pouring.

"No, now see?" Billy said. "Sam's not hurt. Nobody's hurt. Let's all relax."

Billy looked around, elated over this absolute control of an entire group of people in front of him. Real people. Right here where he could see them, and where they could see him. He was delighted. He felt bigger, taller.

"That's fine," Billy went on. "Now this is all right. Good for everybody to relax. Because I've got a problem and I need a little help." Billy bent over his knees, holding his gun loosely, letting the barrel swing back and forth. The four people in front of him at the counter waited silently. Equally silent and unmoving at their table were Reverend Andrews and Lottie.

"There's this girl I'm looking for. Oh, I guess she's about five-three. Weight? I don't know. But shapely. Like Gloria here. She had dark hair once. Only she's a blonde now. She changed that, and she also changed her name. First it was Rodick, see? Then she went from the Coast to Omaha and changed it to Brown. Then she married some guy and changed it again.

"Now that's what I don't know. She met this guy in Omaha and he took her home. See, he's a farmer—lives right around here, they tell me. Only I don't know his name, and that's exactly why I'm here—to find out. Now this is just a little place, huh? How many good-looking dolls with dyed blond hair come in here married to one of the local plowboys, I wonder? This shouldn't be hard, right? I can even tell you when she came here. About a year ago, see? Just about a year ago—"

Dr. Hugh Stewart said quickly, voice strong and clear, so that nobody in that room would miss what he was saying, "What do you want her for, Quirter?"

"What's the difference, Doc? You know who she is, where to find her? Just tell me. That's all you have to do."

"And then what?"

"Then the party's over. You all go home. Simple, huh?"

Billy Quirter grinned. He was very certain of himself now. His eyes brushed over Gloria; he had the answers now. Someone here was going to tell him where to find the girl. He would then find her. He would do the job. Tony would get the news and release the information of where he'd stacked the dough. Then what?

Simple. Gloria and that Chrysler out there. Take both and he had it made. All he had on his tail were these country hick cops, and they'd already proven how good they were. He could ditch the Chrysler. Switch cars. Keep moving. They'd never get him. He would make the Coast in four days, easy. And then?

Tony's fifty thousand! Tony croaked by that time. But the hell with him. No loss. Because Billy would have those fifty thousand beautiful clams! And Gloria?

He looked at her. She was cool and lovely on the outside, but he had an idea what she was like underneath. Like a wild mink, he would bet. What the hell was she getting out of Dickens anyway? Money. No more, no less. And Billy was going to have some real money himself pretty soon. And what did that mean?

Billy's elation grew. What did she want out of life anyway? A dull tool like old Sam here? Or some excitement? A girl like this? She'd do anything to get some kicks, Billy was certain. So she liked to spit around a little before she made up her mind. But that, Billy was sure, was just a warm-up. And Billy knew just the one who could give her some kicks like she'd never had in her life! You could produce a lot of kicks with fifty Gs!

So it wouldn't last. Who cared? So she'd get tired and go looking somewhere else. Fine. Who wanted to waste his whole life with one broad? But while it was going on...!

Billy had seldom rationalized himself into such a grand escape from reality. But his power had taken away his skepticism. The proximity to the lovely Gloria had finally taken away his reasonableness. Billy was very certain everything would go entirely as he was planning.

Billy licked his lips, warm with pleasure. "See? You see how it is? I just want this one thing, and then it's all over. It's just like none of this ever happened. So how about—?"

The handle of the front door was suddenly rattled. Everyone in the room, including Billy, froze. The rattling was repeated three stubborn times. Then it ceased. Billy took a breath, relaxing again.

"Like I said," he repeated, "how about it?"

"Look," Hugh Stewart said clearly, "you're well known around here already, Quirter. Bob Saywell knows who you are. I do. I don't know about Reverend and Mrs. Andrews. I don't know about Mr. and Mrs. Dickens. I know you're a killer. You killed two people in Graintown yesterday—"

Billy's face had become sharper with the setting of muscles around his mouth. "You're getting pretty talky, aren't you, Doc?"

"I just want the facts clear, that's all." And that was exactly what Hugh Stewart wanted. He wanted to make it clear to everyone in this room exactly what Billy Quirter was—even if it meant inciting him. "And the facts are you're looking for this certain girl—but why? To kill her? Because her testimony put your brother in death row in California?"

Billy's face paled in anger. His mouth was a hard, thin line. Hugh Stewart glanced to his left, saw that Gloria was looking at Billy Quirter with a new evaluation. Sam Dickens also looked at Billy for a moment, then down at his hands, as though he too were adjusting to this new information. Hugh Stewart glanced to his right. Bob Saywell had known all along who Billy Quirter was, and had already reached the peak of his fright.

"Do you want to tell me where she is, Doc?" Billy asked, voice cold.

"Who?" Hugh Stewart said, looking at Billy steadily, meeting the man's eyes.

"The girl, Doc," Billy said softly.

"I don't know who you're talking about."

"You don't? You live in this community, and you never heard of a girl like I just described?"

"Never."

"You're a goddam liar, aren't you, Doc?"

"You call it. You've got the gun."

"So I have. Where's the girl? What's her name now?"

"I told you. I never heard of her."

Mouth whitening at the corners, Billy controlled himself. "All right. Reverend? How about you, Reverend?"

Hugh Stewart turned and looked at Reverend Andrews, sitting slight and insignificant beside large Lottie. The minute Billy Quirter identified Ann, Hugh Stewart reminded himself, she would become a certain target for his gun. She was still in his office, he was sure. But how long would she stay there?

Surprisingly Reverend Andrews seemed to be no more frightened of Billy Quirter now than he had been before he'd learned Billy's true deadliness. He lifted his chin and said, "How about me? How about me what, sir?"

"You didn't hear the question?" Billy snapped. "I'll repeat it. Where's the girl? What's her name now?"

Reverend Andrews shook his head blandly. "I'm afraid I don't know what you're talking about."

Hugh Stewart let out his breath, a very faint smile touching his mouth despite his effort to stop it.

Billy stood up suddenly. He walked down the counter until he was even with Bob Saywell. He stared at Reverend Andrews over the top of Bob

Saywell's head. "Tell me, Reverend. You really believe in that heaven kick?"

"I do."

"You really want to go, in other words?"

"Indeed. When my span is done here."

"Well, maybe you're going to go sooner than you figured, Reverend."

"That's a threat, I presume?"

Billy, anger apparent, lifted his gun a fraction. Then suddenly he smiled. "Okay, Reverend. Have it your way. The truth is I don't need the information from you. I've got it right here."

He continued to smile and lowered the gun again, so that the barrel was pointing straight between the wildly frightened eyes of Bob Saywell.

"How about that, Farouk?" Billy said. "You ain't going to clam up on me, are you?"

Hugh Stewart now stared tensely at the quivering Bob Saywell. "Saywell, listen—" he began.

"Shut up, Doc. Let the human balloon speak for himself. How about it, Farouk? Who's the girl? What's her name? Where is she?"

Bob Saywell swallowed, almost choking. For a moment Hugh Stewart thought that Bob Saywell was going to keep confidence with the rest in that room.

Then Hugh Stewart realized that the only thing that kept Bob Saywell from speaking was the fact that his voice had been momentarily frightened out of him. Finally Bob Saywell said, voice trembling up in pitch, "I'll tell you! Yes, sir! I'll tell you exactly who that girl is!"

## Chapter Fourteen

Ann Burley had finally made up her mind. She was not dedicated to Ted Burley, had, in fact, never been—not honestly. Running? Yes, she'd been running. Running not only from the threat of Tony Fearon, but running from everything else too—even from the fact that she did not love Ted Burley. She did not and had not loved Ted Burley, she told herself now. Not remotely...

She picked up the telephone in Dr. Hugh Stewart's office and rang Marie Pringer at the switchboard. "Miss Pringer, would you please—" She paused. She visualized Marie Pringer, white-haired, prim, capable, the hub of every bit of news or gossip that was ever made by telephone in Arrow Junction. If you said anything at all on the telephone, Marie Pringer was likely to hear it—the switchboard was never so busy that there wasn't time to listen to the parties she had connected. But Marie Pringer, Ann knew, was no gossip. She took her professional responsibility seriously.

"Miss Pringer, this is Mrs. Burley. Mrs. Ted Burley."

"Oh, yes, Mrs. Burley. I just didn't recognize your voice coming from Dr. Stewart's office."

"Yes, I am in Dr. Stewart's office. But I would rather nobody else knew that just now, Miss Pringer. It's very important."

Marie Pringer paused only a moment. "All right, Mrs. Burley. But I certainly wouldn't be telling anyone anyway—"

"I didn't mean that, Miss Pringer. What I mean is that I believe I'm in danger."

"In danger?"

"I want to talk to the sheriff in Graintown just as quickly as you can connect me."

Marie Pringer was quick in emergency. "Is there anyone else I can call for you first? Your husband—"

"Please, no. I—I would rather he didn't know where I am either. If you'll listen to what I have to tell the sheriff, I think you'll understand at least part of it. Hurry, Miss Pringer."

"Yes, ma'am."

Ann Burley waited tensely, listening to the clicking, the humming; then Marie Pringer said, "I'm sorry, Mrs. Burley. I can't get through. The lines must be down between here and Graintown."

Ann Burley bit her lower lip. "Keep trying, Miss Pringer. Please. This is very important. It has to do with the killer who escaped yesterday morning in Graintown. Please, Miss Pringer!"

Miss Pringer hesitated only a moment, assimilating the information. "Stay on the telephone, Mrs. Burley. I'll keep trying."

Ann Burley hung up slowly, just in time to hear the heavy footsteps on the stairway outside the door that led to the office.


In the sheriff's office in Graintown, Sheriff-elect Jenkins sat at his desk, while Deputy Wade Miles paced impatiently. "He's got to be around here somewhere!" Wade Miles said angrily.

Sheriff-elect Jenkins didn't want to hear that. Just before Deputy Miles had returned and awakened him, he'd been dreaming that the day before the last election, he'd withdrawn from the race at the last minute. He'd seen himself making his statement, heard the words: "Due to personal commitments, I now find that I will, if elected, be unable to perform the duties of sheriff of this county. I regret exceedingly..." Then

Deputy Miles had come bursting into the office, so eager it made him sick to his stomach, awakening him from that dream. Now he was sitting by his desk, feeling groggy from finally having slept so deeply those final few moments after almost an hour of restless tossing and turning.

"If he is," Jenkins said, "we'll get him." The words again, this time spoken between dry lips, spoken with a tongue yet thick with sleep. He felt washed out, half numb. His mouth was bitter, a slight ache drummed somewhere back of his forehead.

"Saw another newspaper fellow on the way in here." Harvey Jenkins nodded dully, put a cigarette between his lips, lighting the cigarette.

"Those fellows are piling up in town. You'll have to talk to them again, I guess."

"I guess."

"Told this last fellow you would, in fact. Said you'd probably hold a conference pretty soon, but you didn't want to be disturbed now."

"That's right. I don't want to talk to him now."

"Got Chet Blake down the hall at the stairway there. He's not to let anybody in that ain't got business."

"That's right. That's fine, Wade."

"You heard anything from the State Police since I left?"

"Not since you left, Wade."

"Damn! We got to get that squirrel!"

"We'll get him," Sheriff-elect Jenkins said, inhaling deeply from his cigarette. The cigarette tasted terrible. It made his mouth more dry and bitter. He felt terrible in general.

Then a sharp rap sounded on the door. Jenkins looked up dully, and Deputy Miles strode across the office and opened the door.

A large man in an expensive chocolate-colored topcoat stood there. Beneath the topcoat, he wore a neatly cut suit made of good tan gabardine. He had a broad, good-looking face and quick, alert eyes. His face wore an expression of ultimate confidence and maturity that commanded instant attention—the kind of poised expression achieved very early in life, consciously at first, then unconsciously. He wore on his head a smart Stetson that exactly matched the suit.

"Well!" Sheriff-elect Jenkins said, getting up hastily. "Reverend Styles! Surprised to see you all the way over here."

"Hello, Harvey," Reverend Maynard Styles said. His voice was like a good organ—musical, yet extremely powerful—so that the ringing tones of it seemed to echo in the room. "Bad business here in Graintown!"

Jenkins nodded. "It is, Reverend."

"That's why I'm here, Harvey. Nothing official, you understand. But this is pretty close to my old home! I drove most of the night to get here the minute I heard the news. We just closed out the Babcock Ministers' Conference, and I decided to get over here as rapidly as I could, God willing. God was. I'm here. Terrible tragedy. I don't envy your position, Harvey."

Harvey Jenkins wiped his hands along the sides of his trousers. "Well, these things happen, Reverend."

"They do," Maynard Styles said. "And may God have mercy on the killer and bless those poor souls who have been uprooted from this life ahead of their time by that devil's gun."

"Devil is right," Deputy Miles said. "Shot Corly right through the temple for no good reason. Just mean. Just a killer."

"I heard," Maynard Styles said. "I've already talked to Corly's mother. Talked to Joe Bingham's wife. I gave a prayer for each of them. That's why I've come, Harvey, to do whatever I can. To give a little solace where I can. If I could do more, I'd do it!"

"That's much appreciated, I'm sure, Reverend," Harvey Jenkins said. More talk, more reference to a situation he knew well enough. Why, he wondered, must there be endless talk about it? Stop talking about it, he thought. Maybe it will all be solved of its own accord. Then he felt a vague guilt, thinking that way in the presence of Maynard Styles. Harvey Jenkins straightened his shoulders. "It was good of you to come over, Reverend."

"The least I could do," Maynard Styles said. He paused. "Lots of newspapermen around, I noticed. All the way from Omaha, Kansas City— this is pretty big, Harvey. News dispatches going out on all the wires."

"That's right, Reverend," Harvey Jenkins said. It didn't occur to him that Maynard Styles might be here for any but benevolent reasons. It didn't occur to him even slightly that Maynard Styles had an instinct for searching out publicity outlets for himself that approached the ability of a good hound to search out the tracks of a rabbit. As a matter of fact, this fact did not even occur to Maynard Styles himself. Long ago, he'd cased himself so securely in the belief that he was doing the Lord's work, nothing but the Lord's work, that whatever other convenience he allowed himself was but a manifestation of a far greater motive. Maynard Styles did not really believe himself personally ambitious.

"Gentlemen," Maynard Styles said, sweeping off his broad-brimmed hat, "let us pray."

Harvey Jenkins blinked, somewhat startled by this sudden demonstration. Deputy Wade Miles also looked rather startled; but he came to an instant, if more military than spiritual, attention and put his hands together and bowed his head. Maynard Styles, Harvey Jenkins saw, had closed his eyes and turned his face to the ceiling, arms outstretched in quick abeyance. Harvey Jenkins shook himself into similar attentiveness, bowed his head, and shut his eyes tightly.

The sonorous cannonlike voice of Maynard Styles boomed forth, and Harvey Jenkins prayed silently right along with him. Harvey Jenkins prayed for all he was worth.

Within the locked doors of Bob Saywell's store, Billy Quirter pointed his gun at Bob Saywell and grinned. "I knew you'd co-operate, Farouk. I knew it!" He made a quick thrusting motion with his gun, straight at the paunch of Bob Saywell; Bob Saywell bobbed backward, almost tumbling to the floor. Billy Quirter roared with laughter. "That's the boy, jelly roll! I like to see some eagerness." His laughter died suddenly, his face becoming a fraction more intent. "Okay—spit it out, Farouk."

"Saywell," Hugh Stewart said, "think about what you're doing—"

"Shut up, Doc!" Billy snapped. "Farouk?"

"Her name's Ann Burley," Bob Saywell burst out. "Married a fellow name of Ted Burley. Lives in a farmhouse about one mile west of town. She's the one you're after, all right! I know that. She admitted she was in that trial in San Francisco, admitted it right to my face!"

Dr. Hugh Stewart turned his eyes away from Saywell, looking down at the counter, mouth white at the corners. Billy Quirter smiled at Saywell gently. "Now that's fine, Farouk. You've been a good little soldier. I'm real proud of you."

Reverend John Andrews had gotten up and come to the counter at the elbow of Bob Saywell. He stared down at the flushed pinkness of Bob Saywell's fatty face. "Be careful, Bob," he said. "Be careful of what you're telling this man. I've no doubt that Dr. Stewart is quite right. This man is dangerous. Whoever he's trying to find, he's doing it for no good reason. Be careful, Bob."

Bob Saywell's face jerked up. "It's my duty, Reverend! I've got to tell him! An evil's been brought to this community by that girl—let evil meet evil!"

"Bob," Reverend Andrews said, "I'm the minister here in Arrow Junction. I think my concern is with souls more than yours. Why don't you let me be the judge?"

Bob Saywell shook his head quickly. "No, sir! I know what's what. This fellow wants that evil girl, he can have her! No concern of ours! Let him have her and leave us in peace. This is a God-abiding community, and—"

"It's your own skin, isn't it?" Reverend Andrews said tightly. "That's all you're worried about—your own skin!"

"Now you listen to me, Reverend," Bob Saywell said, his voice trembling shrilly. "You're only as good in the community as this community thinks you are! Now I'm telling you, Reverend, we haven't been altogether impressed with you, did you ever think about that? You don't go telling me who owns the rights on souls. No, sir! We pay you to come in here and repeat the Good Word, Reverend. But that's all! Do you understand? That's all! Now get out of my way!"

Bob Saywell rose, trembling, and pushed past Reverend Andrews, hampered only by his own haste rather than any hindrance from Reverend Andrews, who only stepped aside and looked with disbelieving eyes as Bob Saywell stumbled toward the telephone. "I'll find her for you, sir!" he called back to Billy Quirter. "Yes, sir. I'll find her for you!"

Billy Quirter nodded, smiling, and said, "And tell her to come over here, blubber boy. Get her in here just the way you did the doc." Billy Quirter, eyes gleaming in satisfaction, switched his stare to Reverend Andrews. "You'd better go back and sit down, Reverend. It looks like you don't carry any weight anyway, huh? I'm sorry, Reverend. But this is life. Well, don't worry about it. Pretty soon everything's going to be all right, and you can go back preaching like before—just like nothing happened. You should have seen some back alleys in the cities when you were a kid, Reverend, you know that? Then you'd know something about life. But then you wouldn't be a preacher, would you? You wouldn't have the guts to feed the pigeons all that fancy crap. Sit down, Reverend!"

Slowly, Reverend Andrews moved back to his chair at the table in the center of the room and sat down, staring steadily at Bob Saywell. Bob Saywell cranked the handle to ring Marie Pringer at the telephone office. His jowls were quivering in this eagerness to bring the quarry to the hunter, and so relieve himself of danger.


Marie Pringer, in the time intervening, had again attempted to get through to Graintown. But because she could not get directly through, she decided to try another method.

She rang through to the Bireley farm northeast of Arrow Junction, She asked Mrs. Emma Mae Bireley to make a test call to Graintown via the small town of Linden. Mrs. Emma Mae Bireley, a typical picture of the farm wife, did, and reported back to Marie Pringer. Marie instructed Emma Mae to stay by the telephone with paper and pencil. Then Marie rang Ann Burley.

While Marie Pringer had been doing that, Ann waited trembling as her husband kicked savagely at the office door. He swore. He called her name. Just as the telephone rang, he finally gave up, muttering drunkenly, and stumbled downstairs to the snow-covered street.

Marie Pringer said, "I've got Emma Mae Bireley on her phone. She can get through to Graintown from her place. You can tell Emma Mae what you want to say, and she'll relay it in to the sheriff. How's that, Mrs. Burley?"

Ann knew that the time had come to expose everything publicly. Talking to Emma Mae would be like facing the entire community assembled before her. It was giving in to something she had fought against for all this long time of living with Ted Burley. But there was no other way.

"Yes," she said to Marie Pringer. "Let me talk to Mrs. Bireley."

## Chapter Fifteen

Inside Bob Saywell's store, when the front door had been rattled uselessly for perhaps the tenth time by a discouraged customer ambitious enough to brave the storm that morning, Bob Saywell spoke frantically into the telephone.

"Marie, you mean to say Mrs. Burley don't answer? She don't answer her phone? Nobody does? Not Ted either?"

"I'm sorry, Bob," Marie Pringer said.

"Marie, this is important! This is about the most important thing in the world right now. I've simply got to find Mrs. Burley!"

"Just take it easy, Bob. I'll check around for you."

Bob Saywell replaced the telephone with a shaking hand to look with frightened, imploring eyes at Billy Quirter.

"All right," Billy said softly. "Just keep calling, fatty, until you find her. Then get her over here."

Bob Saywell took a shuddering breath, picked up the telephone again; but his ring didn't get Marie for a few minutes because Marie had cut into the conversation Ann was having with Emma Mae Bireley.

"I'm sorry to interrupt, Mrs. Burley. But Bob Saywell is trying hard to find you. He's at his store. He sounds peculiar. And Hobe Adams was in a few minutes ago. He said Bob's got the store closed up, even though this isn't his closed day. Do you want me to let him know where you are?"

"Thank you, Marie," Ann said, closing her eyes, opening them. "No, don't tell him where I am. Just listen to what I'm telling Mrs. Bireley. Mrs. Bireley, can you hear me all right?"

"Yes," Mrs. Bireley said in her birdlike voice.

"Please tell the sheriff that I'm pretty certain the man who is trying to kill me has contacted Bob Saywell. Tell him that perhaps the man is with Mr. Saywell in Mr. Saywell's store right now...."

As Ann talked, Marie, blinking with attentive purpose, plugged in Bob Saywell's line and began, in response to Bob Saywell's desperate instructions, ringing the numbers he gave her.

It was at the very time, in California, that Tony Fearon looked up from his cell bunk and wondered if he were going to get this last satisfaction in life. It was a single mania with him now, an escape mechanism, in reality, to push all other defeats, miseries and fears aside, to dull the edge of knowing he was going to die very shortly, a total concentration on one thing: to know Billy had done it and the girl was dead, dead, dead.

Sam Dickens sat on the stool in front of the counter in Bob Saywell's store and stared at Billy Quirter. He did so with an odd detachment, finding that he did not hate Billy at that moment so much as he hated himself. Somehow he did not think of Billy Quirter as a single identity, but rather he was a number of people combined: that Carwell punk, Johnny Masters—in fact he had somehow become the symbol for the disease that ate away his first wife. Because, in some fashion, he was a disease himself; and he was slowly but surely eating away this that Sam had with Gloria, a really decent honest-to-God feeling of love that Billy was absolutely ruining. Sam did not want to lose Gloria. But he did not hate Billy. He hated only himself.

Billy turned from watching Bob Saywell's frantic telephoning and looked directly into Sam's eyes. "All right, Dickens. You're staring."

Sam closed his hands into fists on the counter and opened them again with effort. "That's right. I'm staring."

"Well, maybe I don't like it, Dickens."

"That's too bad," Sam Dickens said, his heart going into a crazy banging of fear and self-conviction.

"It will be," Billy said, "if you don't knock it off. You've got something on your mind. I can tell it from your shining eyes. I'd get rid of it. I really mean that."

Gloria, pretty face tired, eyes defeated, looked up. "Why don't you lay off him, Quirter. He isn't going to hurt you, and you know it. What fun do you get out of it?"

Billy smiled meanly. "It comes natural to me. I don't know why. Maybe I should take the problem to a head shrinker."

"Maybe you should," Gloria said.

Sam Dickens, in that moment, saw that Billy was once again diverted by Gloria, saw his eyes switch to her and take in her good looks with a hungry animal look. Sam made up his mind. He didn't hope to succeed. He didn't care if he succeeded or not. But he knew he had to do it.

Quietly, barely audibly, in fact, Sam Dickens said, "Police, Quirter."

Billy, Sam Dickens knew, was open to the simplest ruse, because he thought Sam Dickens would never try anything. Billy's head swung around, eyes going apprehensive.

"The back way," Sam Dickens said.

It was the only chance he would have, Sam Dickens knew; and not much of that. But the chance was not what he was going for. He was going for wiping away the hate for himself in his own mind. He moved. Jamming heels against the rung of the stool, he shoved up and grabbed for Billy over the counter as Billy turned his head toward the kitchen.

In total, it was a clumsy effort, with no chance for success. But it almost worked, because Billy was absolutely unprepared for it. The gun was almost knocked out of Billy's hand, and that would have ended it because Hugh Stewart, with his quick reflexes, would have gotten that gun then.

But Sam Dickens did not quite make it. Instead, Billy was only bumped off balance for a fraction of a second, as Sam Dickens struggled to get the gun from Billy's hand, half draped over the counter, muscles soft from disuse being tried to their utmost.

Then Billy's gun hand came back, and the barrel of the gun whipped down in a swift, snapping motion.

Sam Dickens, lying across the counter, gave a teeth-clenched sound. Gloria muffled a scream with her hand. Blood spurted from Sam Dickens's eyebrow.

He closed his eyes to the whip of the gun, again and again, with Gloria swearing at Quirter, a total sound of gasped shock sounding in the room, Bob Saywell whimpering as though he were being struck instead of Sam Dickens.

And then Billy Quirter stopped. Sam Dickens rolled back, Gloria trying to hold him, but not being able to. Both of them collapsed on the floor across the counter from Billy Quirter. Blood streamed from Sam Dickens's face.

White-faced with rage, Hugh Stewart was up instantly and moving toward Sam Dickens.

"Sit down, Doc!" Billy snapped, almost screaming.

"Go to hell!" Hugh Stewart, with Gloria, moved Sam Dickens away from the counter and placed him carefully just to the side of one of the tables.

Reverend John Andrews, also white-faced, had gotten up.

"Sit down, Reverend," Hugh Stewart said. "He'll kill us all in a minute. I'll take care of it."

Billy, face a savage mask of dangerous fury, sat on the stool behind the counter and watched Hugh Stewart get his bag and start working on the cut face of Sam Dickens. Hugh Stewart worked swiftly, not looking at Quirter once, but thinking that in a moment Quirter might start shooting everyone in the room. You didn't know.

Carefully, Sam Dickens's face was fixed. Gloria, cradling Sam in her arms, moaned softly in her husband's ear. Sam Dickens tried a grin, but his lower lip had been split; the attempt, behind the tape, was grotesque. "Shouldn't have tried it," he said finally.

Hugh Stewart nodded slowly. "That's right. Only I was foolish myself, remember? Took a lot of guts, Mr. Dickens. I had a better chance than you did."

Sam Dickens shook his head faintly, but there was something in his eyes that belied the negative motion. He had the look of a man who had found something in his core that it was not necessary to hate.

"Baby, baby," Gloria said, kissing his forehead tenderly.

Hugh Stewart stared at both for a moment, understanding somehow what had just occurred between them.

Then Billy Quirter snapped, "All right! You've got him patched. Get away from him, Doc. Get back over here. You too, Gloria!"

Slowly Hugh Stewart stood and returned to the counter. But Gloria stared at Quirter with blazing eyes. "You'll have to come and get me, you stinking little monkey. You'll have to—"

Billy, enraged once again, straightened, lifting his gun. Hugh Stewart, seated, said softly to Quirter, "Don't push her, Quirter. You'll have to kill her to make her move right now. Be sensible."

Billy Quirter did not continue his insistence that Gloria leave Sam Dickens and return to the counter, but as Hugh Stewart watched him, he knew that if there was anything in the world at that moment that Billy Quirter was not, it was sensible.

Ted Burley, lumbering drunkenly down the street, ran squarely into Luke Wurton, a shabby, ill-clothed man of indefinable old age. Luke had not been employed for years and lived off the charity of Arrow Junction's church group. He was Arrow Junction's version of a bum. He appeared downtown promptly at six-thirty in the morning and went right around the clock, in and out of the various places of business, standing on the street until late at night, saying a few choice words here and there with those who saw fit to speak to him, watching everything that transpired in a day with faded gray eyes that somehow had never lost their speculative glitter.

Ted Burley ran straight into Luke on the main street, and Luke (who never drank), smelling the whisky on Ted Burley's breath, seeing the drunken look of his eyes, suddenly was aware of more excitement than he'd discovered since the flood in the thirties. All that action in Graintown. Now Ted Burley was drinking!

Ted Burley started on, then turned and grabbed Luke roughly by the shoulder. "You seen my wife, Luke?"

Luke had not seen Ted Burley's wife. But he'd already picked up the news that Bob Saywell, oddly locked up, had been telephoning around for her. He quickly offered that single scrap of knowledge.

"Nope. But it seems like you ain't the only one looking, Ted. Bob Saywell's been telephoning all around for her."

It was all Ted Burley needed. He remembered how Bob Saywell had come out of his house, having been alone with Ann the day before. He'd never liked the fat, quivery-cheeked look of Bob Saywell anyway. Bob Saywell was looking for her. And that meant to Ted Burley that Bob Saywell was somehow mixed up with his wife in a way that he ought not to be.

He staggered down the street to the closed, shade-drawn door of Bob Saywell's store. He put a great hand on the handle and yanked and bellowed, "Open up in there, Saywell! Do you hear? This is Ted Burley! I'm telling you, by God, to open up this door!"

## Chapter Sixteen

Sheriff-elect Jenkins stood up from his desk, feeling his knees begin to tremble the instant he put his full weight on them. The telephone call from Emma Mae Bireley, transferring Ann Burley's message to him, had been completed. Sheriff-elect Jenkins had related the information to Deputy Wade Miles as well as to Reverend Maynard Styles, who had been in the office when the call had come in. The sheriff had told the State Police, who were ready to escort him to Arrow Junction.

Deputy Miles had taken the submachine gun from the closet and stood waiting impatiently at the door beside Reverend Maynard Styles.

"We're going to get that squirrel now," Deputy Miles said, thin-lipped and hard-eyed. He had the look of a man who had tasted blood, a man who was eager. It made Harvey Jenkins sick to his stomach.

"May the Lord have mercy on his soul," Reverend Styles pronounced. He, too, looked a little pale around the jowls. Jenkins had asked the reverend to join them. He'd done so in the personal hope that God would travel nearer that way and so protect him personally. But what he'd said aloud was that perhaps some innocent soul might need the services of Reverend Styles before this was over. Himself, he thought now.

Reverend Maynard Styles really had no choice but to accept, but he already looked badly shaken, less imposing, less the leader, even in his smart clothes and habitually proud bearing.

"Let's go!" Deputy Miles exploded.

"Take it easy!" Jenkins snapped. Then, hating it, he led the way out of the office, hoping desperately that the road to Arrow Junction was still blocked with snow. That last hope fizzled when Paul Jackson, an appointed deputy, called up the stairway, "Road's open, Harvey. There ain't anything to stop us now!"

"There!" Bob Saywell shouted, as Ted Burley pounded on the door of his store. "There's the husband of that woman you're after!"

Billy Quirter, Sam Dickens's try fresh in his mind, looked as though his nerves had been stretched so tightly that each rattle and bang of the door brought him a little closer to maximum tension. He thinned his eyes, glancing from the closed, shade-drawn door to Bob Saywell.

"You see?" Bob Saywell said. "You see?"

"Shut up, fatty. Go over there and let him in. And that's all—just him. If anybody's trying anything funny out there, you'll be the first to go, fats. Hurry up!"

Bob Saywell got up from the counter stool and jounced across the room. Hands shaking, he unlocked the door. That was enough to allow Ted Burley to lurch inside, stumbling as the door gave way in his hand. Billy motioned with his gun, and Bob Saywell shut the door and locked it. He turned to see Ted Burley fall drunkenly to hands and knees a half dozen feet from the door.

Unaware of anyone else in the room but Bob Saywell, Ted Burley, like a large animal viewed in slow motion, rested on his hands and knees for several long seconds. Then, glowering, he slowly pushed himself to his knees, swaying; finally he got to his feet, weaving back and forth. His eyes were murderous, brutelike.

Slowly he turned, believing that only he and Bob Saywell were in the room. He was thinking that he would not ask questions, but simply smash one great paw into Bob Saywell's face. He was not reasoning at that moment, only hungry for a physical release for his resentments. He turned half around, menacingly, slowly. And when he was three-quarters around, as Bob Saywell stood with his trembling back against the closed door, Ted Burley realized that something was very wrong.

"Stop," Billy Quirter said, his whispery voice carrying clearly. "Just like that."

Ted Burley did. He froze, seeing everyone in the room now. The final person he focused on was Billy Quirter—and Billy's gun.

"Back here and sit down, Farouk," Quirter said to Bob Saywell. Then to Ted Burley, "Over here, bumpkin. Behind the counter. What's his name again, fatty?"

Bob Saywell dropped heavily onto a stool, gasping, "Ted Burley."

Quirter nodded. "Over here where we can talk, Burley."

Ted Burley, sobering fast, stood staring, not moving.

"Well, move it!" Quirter said, mouth twisting.

Ted Burley nodded dumbly, all the savage look gone from him. He came around the counter, half tripping, regaining his balance clumsily, then stopping in front of Quirter behind the counter. Hugh Stewart looked at the man carefully and saw that though he had looked drunk when he'd come in, he did not look so drunk now. He was instead the most frightened man in the room, Bob Saywell included. His mouth opened and closed. His eyes bugged.

Quirter faintly grinned, sensing the fear as well as Hugh Stewart. "Where's your wife, Burley?"

Burley shook his head, unable to answer.

"Where is she?" Billy said.

"I don't know!"

"I won't take much time with you, bumpkin. Where is she?"

"Please—"

Billy placed his gun in his lap. His hand flicked out, snapping against Ted Burley's left cheek with the back of the fingers. "Where is she?"

"I swear to God, I—"

"One thing! Where is she?"

"I don't know! I don't know!"

The back of the whipping hand cracked again against Ted Burley's face. Ted Burley seemed ready to give way entirely out of the purest fright.

"Where's your wife, Burley?"

"I don't know!"

The entire action happened with split-second swiftness. Ted Burley did not know why this man wanted his wife, nor, by now, did he care. He knew only that though he was no longer really drunk, his mind was clouded and befuddled. And so it was only by instinct that he realized that this man in front of him was deadly.

Once again Ted Burley reverted to his childhood, a big oxlike figure with great hands, the dark masculine face flushed with fear and the remnants of drinking. He wanted only for Billy Quirter to understand that he would co-operate, that he was friendly and pleasant, that he wanted to be loved the way his mother had once loved him.

So he came toward Billy Quirter, waving his ham-like hands, mouth working in undecipherable sounds, one thing paramount in his wretched heart: to make Billy understand that he was a nice fellow and willing to help, willing—if he had only known why Billy wanted his wife—to throw his wife in a heap in front of Billy's feet, because he was a nice boy grown to manhood.

But Billy Quirter had been accosted twice that morning. This looked like a third attempt to him. He saw only that the great bulk of Ted Burley was coming at him in threatening steadiness, hands clutching, mouth working.

Billy's hand, in lightning motion, picked up his gun. He shot Ted Burley three times in the stomach. When the large figure had stumbled, flailing with arms and legs splayed awkwardly and loosely, the great tree of a body coming down finally and taking with it glasses and plates and cups from the shelves behind the counter, striking the floor with a shaking thump—then Billy fired once again. This time he put a bullet straight through Ted Burley's temple, as accurate and deadly a shot as Billy had put through the head of Corly Adams.

The three shots quickly together were like cannon roars in the room. The last seemed even louder. Then there was a shocked, terrible silence. Outside, where Sheriff-elect Jenkins, Deputy Miles, and members of the State Police stopped their wary approach to Bob Saywell's store, there was a similar silence. All of them stood locked, knowing quite positively that they had indeed discovered Billy Quirter.

# Chapter Seventeen

For a long moment Sheriff-elect Jenkins stood frozen, pressed against the cold brick of the north side of the building. Then, fear sweeping through him, shouting as though to release the awful tension, he yelled, "Give it up, Quirter! We've got you surrounded!"

What he got for that were two bullets smashing through the glass of the front door. The slugs whined across the street.

Harvey Jenkins turned to Wade Miles and the State Police patrolman who stood just behind Miles. His face was deathly white. He didn't know what to say. The cars they had come in were parked well down the street. Ann Burley, whom they had picked up from Hugh Stewart's office, was in one of them. Jenkins ran a nervous tongue over dry lips.

"It's up to you, Sheriff," the patrolman said. "We're leaving this up to you."

"What do you say, Harvey?" Wade Miles asked. Jenkins forcibly swallowed his fear for a moment. "We'll set up a loudspeaker. Tell him he isn't going to get out of there alive if he doesn't walk out, no gun, with nobody hurt in there."

"Let's go," Deputy Miles said. As they hurried back to the cars parked down the street, Deputy Miles added, "Let's just hope he hasn't done some hurting already—four shots he just tripped off when we were coming up. That squirrel don't need more than one."

Wade Miles took it upon himself to speak to Ann in the car. "You just sit tight, ma'am, unless you want to get farther away—"

"No." She sat motionless beside a patrolman. She looked up the block to the opposite side of the street and the front of Bob Saywell's store.

She knew, from the collected information gleaned from residents of Arrow Junction questioned downtown, that Ted was in there. She also knew that Hugh Stewart was in there. And that very probably Reverend Andrews and Lottie along with someone who owned that Chrysler were in there too. Martha Saywell had been informed of possible danger and brought downtown. She now sat in another State Patrol car, sniffling, knowing now that the danger was not only possible, but already very real.

"No," Ann said to Wade Miles, "I'll stay here. This is all my responsibility anyway—"

Her voice broke. Wade Miles looked at her curiously. "Your responsibility, ma'am? That some convict on the West Coast sends his killer brother out hunting for you? It don't figure that way to me."

Ann shook her head slowly, staring at the store front, unable to shake a guilt that she had run out of selfish instinct and, as a result, placed all of the innocent people in that store at the brink of death....

The loudspeaker had been set up in a patrol car. Deputy Miles touched Ann's shoulder in a rough gesture. "Don't worry, ma'am." He motioned with the submachine gun. "We'll get him."

He trotted to the next sedan. Slowly three cars were driven to a point almost directly opposite the closed door of Bob Saywell's store. The drivers hunched low, the men outside walked carefully in the protection of the sides away from the store.

With the automobile barrier formed and the back entrance covered too, Sheriff-elect Jenkins held the microphone in his hand and tried to get control of himself. Finally, he spoke, his electronically magnified words echoing down the snow-covered street.

"This is the sheriff, Quirter. We've got you covered all the way. You can't make it out of there. Do you hear that, Quirter?"

Billy Quirter's mind was whirling with a swiftness it had never achieved before. But it was not a reasonable movement. Billy Quirter, cornered, was not a reasonable man. And the pressure was up to a point higher than Quirter was conditioned to accept.

Thus he thought quickly, but not accurately. And he thought only that he was going to kill the girl, Ann, and make himself and Tony happy. Then he was taking Gloria out with him. He was going to get one hell of a long way from this stinking little dump and pick up Tony's money. How many other people he had to kill in the process made no difference to him. The main thing was to kill the girl, take Gloria, and go. Everything after that would take care of itself.

He looked about the room, totally unemotional about the body of Ted Burley lying at the foot of his stool. He measured eyes. He found fear in every pair of them. Nobody moved.

Sam Dickens rested with his back against chair legs. Gloria held to him tightly. Both of them stared at Billy. Hugh Stewart sat immobile beside the counter. Bob Saywell was shaking on his stool beside Hugh Stewart. Reverend Andrews and Lottie sat very quietly at their table in the center of the room, faces white against the background of red labels of a display stack of large tomato cans.

Nobody said a word. You could not even hear anyone breathing, except for an occasional thin whistling sound from Bob Saywell's nostrils.

Everybody was waiting for death, Billy thought with a fleeting but powerful pleasure. And *he* was death. And so he was God right now. Not what the stinking reverend thought about, something unreal and thought up out of thin air; but a real God! Everybody was waiting for God's decision.

"All right, Farouk," Billy said in his whispering voice. "Turn out the light and raise the shades. It looks like a nice day outside."

Bob Saywell tried to move and could not. He tried to speak and could not.

"I'll tell you, fatty," Billy said. "I'll lay you right out with the Burley guy if you don't move!"

"They'll shoot me! They'll think I'm—"

Billy's voice suddenly went into nearly a scream. *"Move!"*

Bob Saywell shoved his fat bulk from the counter stool and almost fell across the room. He switched out the lights and snapped up a shade on one of the two broad windows, closing his eyes against what would be a certain hail of bullets if he was mistaken for Billy Quirter.

Outside, fingers pressed more tightly on triggers. Deputy Wade Miles's machine gun came up a fraction.

But Bob Saywell's mammoth silhouette could not be confused for the figure of Billy Quirter. There was no shooting.

"Now the other one," Billy Quirter said.

Bob Saywell got the other shade up. Then, stumbling, hands flailing at the air until he'd regained his balance, he returned to his stool.

Billy Quirter grinned faintly, watching his hostages out of the sides of his eyes, but looking through the steamed glass at the daylit street and the three patrol cars lined on the other side. He knew, because of the steaming of the glass and the darkened interior, that no one out there could see clearly into the store. Billy's hand closed around his gun more tightly, then suddenly released it into his lap. He grabbed a cup from the counter and threw it through the large window nearest him. His gun came back into his hand as glass shattered and splattered, leaving a small ragged hole. The cold blew in, and Billy felt better.

He yelled, "Seven people in here with me. Seven live ones! You try to get me, there'll be seven dead ones! And I'll take a half dozen of you with me. Do you hear?"

Sheriff-elect Jenkins, heart hammering, did hear. His men heard. The wind carried Billy's voice down the street, and Ann heard. Martha Saywell heard. A good half of the residents of Arrow Junction, hiding in safety around the edges of the block, also heard. All six with Billy in Bob Saywell's store heard. Hugh Stewart wondered why Billy had chosen to list Ted Burley as one of the living.

Sheriff-elect Jenkins found his voice once more as he stared at the steamed glass, trying unsuccessfully to see clearly into the blurred and distorted interior. "You can't win, Quirter!"

He swallowed, twisting his head to glance down the street where Ann sat in the car. He put the microphone back to his lips.

"We know who you're after, Quirter. You won't get her! We've got the girl, Quirter. Do you understand? Now you'd better come out of there, no gun, your hands up!"

Inside, Billy's mean grin appeared faintly once again. His mind darted with this information just given him by Harvey Jenkins. "All right," he shouted. "I'll make a deal with you. Send the girl in, I'll send everyone else out." Now he was certain he had it—had it absolutely. Make the deal just like he'd now announced—except he wouldn't send Gloria out. He'd keep her and take her with him in the Chrysler just as he'd planned; he would also take the other girl, to kill later...

Harvey Jenkins was miserable, miserable with the realization that he'd just given Quirter an advantage in telling him they had Ann Burley. From behind, a state trooper wriggled up and said, "We brought in a doctor from Graintown. Just in case."

Jenkins nodded dully. "Yeah, that's good." His tone was bitter now, no longer even trying to simulate eagerness. "Maybe we should bring in the undertaker too, huh?"

Billy Quirter shouted, "You hear me, Sheriff?"

"I heard you," Jenkins said through the loudspeaker. "You're crazy, Quirter. We're making no deal like that."

"I'm not crazy, Sheriff. I know what I want. I want the girl! Now I told you—everybody in here is all right now. They won't be if you don't send that girl in here. Seven for one. It's a good deal. Take it. Or you've got seven corpses!"

"Listen, Quirter. Be reasonable. I swear I'll play square with you. You leave those folks in there alone and walk out here with no gun, hands up, there'll be no shooting. I promise. It's the only way you'll come out alive, Quirter!"

"I say you'd better listen to me, Sheriff!" Quirter screamed. "I want that girl! You get her and send her in and everybody stays alive. That's the only way it's going to go, do you hear me? Now I'll give you a deadline to do it. Five minutes. My watch says ten-five. At ten-ten I start shooting in here!"

Harvey Jenkins lowered the microphone and looked wearily at Wade Miles beside him. Miles nodded. "He means it. He'll do it."

Jenkins turned around. Oddly, he was not frightened now. Oddly, he'd come to the end of his fear, and there wasn't any more. He was in a kind of suspension. And he wondered, with the situation in front of his eyes now, how he could have been so frightened. It was really simple, in the end. You had a killer. You had to deal with him. If you won, you won. If you lost, you lost. He did not see how he was going to win, but he kept trying. He said to the state trooper, "Go get Reverend Styles. Maybe he can talk sense to Quirter."

Deputy Miles said, "It's fairly sure he's got Reverend Andrews in there. If he can't do no good—"

"Maybe he isn't good enough. Reverend Styles has got more punch. Maybe he can swing it." Sheriff-elect Jenkins nodded to the trooper. "Be careful. And tell Reverend Styles to watch his step coming back with you."

"Right," the trooper said, and wriggled away.

Inside the store, Billy Quirter listened to the small ticking of his watch. He examined the faces before him. One minute had gone by. Two. No one said anything for another thirty seconds. Then Dr. Hugh Stewart said, "You're crazy to think they'll send her in, Quirter."

"Shut up, Doc."

Three minutes were up. Outside, the trooper wriggled back alone. Jenkins looked at him.

The trooper shook his head. "The reverend said he couldn't make it. Said he wanted to. But he said there was something important he had to get back to at home. Said he was saying a prayer for you."

Jenkins nodded, eyes smoldering. "Yeah." He turned and looked at the store front. Beside him, Deputy Miles said, "Thirty seconds left, Harvey."

Inside, Billy Quirter looked at his watch. Ten seconds left. Eight. The room waited in strained silence. Five.

"Will he do it?" Jenkins whispered to the cold breeze. "Will the bastard really do it?"

The seconds were running out. Three left. Two. One...

Billy Quirter fired a bullet into the supine corpse of Ted Burley.

Bob Saywell came a half a foot off his seat, then collapsed in a dead faint, tumbling to the floor in a soggy heap of perspiration. Hugh Stewart held his breath, swearing inside. And Billy said softly to him, "Let fatty be." Then he raised his voice.

"That's one, Sheriff!"

Sheriff-elect Jenkins did not swear silently, but loudly and steadily.

Billy jerked his head first at Hugh Stewart, then at Reverend Andrews. "Both of you—around here. Drag the plowboy over to the door and heave him out. Make a try for it, you'll wind up just like the country hick here. Now do what I say, and fast!"

Hugh Stewart looked at the man's eyes and knew there was only one thing they could do: what he told them, and quickly.

He stood up, glanced at Reverend Andrews. The reverend, amazingly calm, walked around the counter with him. They dragged the heavy body of Ted Burley toward the door.

"Okay," Billy Quirter said, "heave him out now. Then back to where you were."

They did just that. They got the door open, shoved the body out, then closed the door and returned to their seats.

Outside, Sheriff-elect Jenkins leaned limply and defeatedly against the car and stared at the sprawled figure in front of the store.

"It's like I said," Deputy Miles breathed. "He meant it."

Billy Quirter's voice knifed out again.

"You get the picture, Sheriff? Now send the girl in. Because if you don't, another one gets it. You've got five more minutes!"

## Chapter Eighteen

Inside the store, there was no doubt that Billy Quirter would keep it up. Another of them was going to die in five minutes. Every one of them, including Bob Saywell who had revived in a heap on the floor, knew it.

Bob Saywell tried desperately to faint again, certain he would be the next; but it wouldn't work. Hugh Stewart sat at the counter, stone still, heart beating fast, looking for some slight chance to go for Billy and finding none. Sam Dickens sat unmoving, soothing with words a terrified Gloria, whose bluff exterior had at last crumbled. And Reverend Andrews sat with Lottie, his hand tightly clasped around one of her plump wrists as though to feed her the necessary strength and courage to keep this up.

Two minutes went by.

Outside, Sheriff-elect Jenkins, in hurried conferences with the State Police, realized that there was absolutely nothing they could do. If they tried rushing the store, there was no telling how many would die. Deaths were a certainty that way. And they couldn't, certainly, give the girl to Quirter.

So they had simply to wait for the second five minutes to go by and another body to be thrown out. Jenkins cursed the fear that had initially forced him to make the mistake of revealing the fact that they had the girl. He was wondering, with great guilt and self-accusation, why he had been afraid all of his life of things that could not have been half so bad as he had thought they would be....

Three minutes were gone.

Jenkins was not alone with a feeling of guilt. Ann sat in the car down the street, staring at the store and at the crumpled body of her husband. She felt as though blood were running off her own hands, the blood of Ted Burley, the blood of whomever else Billy Quirter was going to kill in the next two minutes. She sat there silent and still, face beautiful in the cold winter light, certain in the guilt that she had brought this terror to this place.

Four minutes gone. And who would die next? Hugh Stewart...?

She bit her lip until she tasted blood. The trooper beside her said, "Easy, Mrs. Burley. Maybe you'd better not look any more. Maybe—"

Her movement was so fast that he didn't have a chance to stop her. She threw open the door and ran down the snow-covered street. "All right! I'm here! I'm the one you want!" Tears stung her eyes as she shouted, "Get it over! Hurry!"

With Jenkins swearing as he watched her, a half dozen troopers yelling for her to turn back, Ann kept coming. Inside, Billy Quirter finally saw and heard her and knew, at last, that he had his target.

A fixed, deadly smile on his lips, he raised his gun carefully. He watched her run in the peculiar method of a woman, watched her come closer and closer to afford him the better target. Then he saw her exactly through the hole he'd smashed in one window.

Two things happened at almost the same second.

With the diversion, Reverend Andrews, who had been waiting for the right moment, picked up one of the large tomato cans from the stack behind him and sent it flying over Hugh Stewart's head straight at Billy Quirter. It was a good, accurate throw, and the can caught Billy squarely on the left cheekbone just in time to throw off his aim a little.

Billy swore with surprised pain, as his gun exploded. The bullet, instead of catching Ann in the heart, was off to the side. She sprawled on the street. Billy, despite the blood spurting from his cheek, started to fire again, aware of only one thing now: to kill that girl.

But Hugh Stewart, in motion almost at the moment that Reverend Andrews had thrown the can, came over the counter, followed by a swift Reverend Andrews. Hugh Stewart knocked the gun from Billy's hand.

But Billy, back to reality, suddenly squirmed away. Reverend Andrews dived at him. Billy reacted like a crazed jackrabbit. He was not thinking any more, but simply reacting in purely animal terms. He went straight for the front of the store and threw himself through the already punctured window, smashing through it with his broken arm, spinning on the snow outside, then scrambling to his feet and running straight down the street.

"Get him!" Sheriff-elect Jenkins breathed to Deputy Wade Miles.

And Wade Miles, with smooth and professional dexterity, flashed out from behind a car with machine gun in hand.

He danced to the side in beautiful rhythm in order to get Billy Quirter into a range where he would hit nobody else. Then he fired. He moved, fired, moved, fired, the staccato jerk of his gun matching the short crazy chops Billy Quirter, being cut to pieces, made with his legs.

Billy went sprawling as the bullets licked at him. And Deputy Wade Miles kept it up, reinserting one more clip and putting one final burst into the now motionless form of Billy Quirter, as Billy's blood turned the snow red.

Wade Miles finally quit, standing just a few feet from the sprawled body. He wiped a hand across his mouth, eyes colder than the winter wind blowing in from the fields around.

Harvey Jenkins came up and put a hand on his shoulder. "Nice going, Wade."

Wade Miles nodded briefly, then turned and walked evenly with the sheriff back to where Dr. Hugh Stewart knelt beside an unmoving Ann. A few seconds later, the doctor from Graintown, Dr. Edward Orwell, came up and bent beside Hugh Stewart. He examined the wound with Hugh Stewart and finally said, "Bad, I'm afraid."

"That's right," Hugh Stewart said softly.

Dr. Orwell shook his head. "I'm not that good a surgeon."

Hugh Stewart straightened. "I am."

## Chapter Nineteen

When the surgery was over, Dr. Hugh Stewart stood in his office beside the still figure of Ann and smiled at Dr. Orwell. Dr. Orwell put out his hand and shook hands solemnly with Hugh Stewart. "I'm truly amazed. The finest work I've seen. Tremendous nerve and control—after what you've been through, knowing what you told me about how you feel about this girl. Perfect skill. You shouldn't be here, Doctor. You should be somewhere where that kind of talent can be used every day."

Hugh Stewart stood silent for a moment, then turned to look at the beautiful still face of the girl he loved. "I think," he said, "we will be moving on, Doctor."

Below, inside Bob Saywell's store, Bob Saywell lay shaking on one of the tables, while his wife kept sniffling. One by one, the natives of Arrow Junction filed in, looking at the blood on the floor, at the shattered window, then quietly, respectfully, after a curious glance at the quivering Bob Saywell, shook the hand of a calm Reverend John Andrews—the word of his conduct had spread as quickly as any word had ever spread in Arrow Junction.

Reverend Andrews, sitting with Lottie, looked his subjects in the eye, knowing that never again would he feel insufficient in front of them and thanking the Good Lord for that knowledge. At the same time he was praying for the soul of Ted Burley, even for the soul of Billy Quirter, and hoping that some purification might sometime come to Bob Saywell before his time was up.

Sheriff-elect Jenkins drove back to Graintown with Deputy Wade Miles beside him. Just a mile out of town, as they watched the new Chrysler of Sam Dickens pull into a motel on the outskirts of town, Wade Miles said calmly, "I been thinking, what with you taking over now, and me behind you as deputy, this ain't no county to fool with any more. What do you think, Harvey?"

Harvey Jenkins smiled briefly, feeling a tremendous calm. He nodded. "I think you're right, Wade."

And Sam Dickens, as he helped Gloria out of the car in front of the motel unit he'd just rented, looked at her with a tender, happy smile that was obliterated by the tape on his face.

She looked back at him, detecting the smile nevertheless and returning it rather shyly, dropping her lashes just a bit, just as she had when he'd first talked to her.

He felt awfully good, despite the cuts on his face. And he was no more worried about things coming up than Harvey Jenkins was. He was ready. Ready for anything, including Johnny Masters at the studio, or anyone else who came along after Johnny Masters.

They walked slowly up to the door. Then suddenly—just at the precise time Tony Fearon knew finally and totally that Billy hadn't made it, *knew* it somehow, and started screaming his bitterness to the walls and bars—suddenly Gloria stopped Sam Dickens, looked up at him, blinked, and said, "Why don't you carry me in, Sam? You know. Like we did the first time? Like the first time after we were married?"

Sam looked at her and nodded. "That's not a bad idea, Glory. That's not a bad idea at all."

THE END

# THE LONG RIDE

by James McKimmey

# Chapter One

At 7:25 that Friday morning Loma City was already oppressed by a wilting, humid early-August heat. Bright midwest sunlight flashed against the automobiles streaming onto Lodge Boulevard, the city's central six-lane thoroughfare. The boulevard ran from west to east, stopping at the ancient bridge where the downtown area abruptly sheared off at the edge of the broad muddy river that formed Loma City's eastern limits.

At the opposite end of the boulevard, at the western limits of town, rested an aging motel. It was a thousand yards from the entrance of a city recreation area called Elswith Park, no more than fifty yards from a small shingled roadhouse, painted barn-red and known as the Chicken Cottage.

The motel was called Sleepy Lodge. This fact was announced by a large red and black sign mounted on the roof of the motel's office. The sign was new and managed to underscore the tawdry, weary, unhealthy look of the fading green cottages placed in a U behind the office cabin and new sign. A blue 1958 Plymouth sedan was parked in front of one of those fading green cottages. The court, which was in the center of the U, was silent, lonely looking; there were a few pieces of chipped, re-painted lawn furniture resting dolefully on summer-browned grass. There was only one other car on the U-shaped concrete. It was a '54 Dodge with a Kansas license plate. Between the Plymouth and the cabin marked 6C was a short dust-coated walk and a worn rubber mat whose nubbed inscription, WELCOME, had been almost worn out of recognition. The fading brown drapes of Cabin 6C had been pulled.

Inside the cabin, standing with his back to the locked door, was a lean but strongly built man. He wore a freshly pressed tan suit. The suit was a cheap wash-and-wear. But because the man's frame, even after forty-one years of wear, was so well proportioned, the suit hung perfectly. He wore tan oxfords which had been shined to a brilliant luster. His white shirt was carefully pressed; at the collar a plain brown tie was neatly knotted. He owned a flat, cleanly planed face with hard, alert, somewhat stupid-looking blue-gray eyes. His mouth was wide, thin-lipped and gave no expression to the stony look of his face. He had dark brown hair, lightly flecked with gray, clipped short at the temples and combed flat and straight back on top.

He wore soft yellow-tan pigskin gloves. In one hand he held a .30 caliber pistol. He now shifted the pistol so that it was pointing directly at the head of the youth lying on one of the two beds in the room. The youth was dressed in white underwear. His skinny wrists and ankles were bound by new white clothesline. There was a wide strip of flesh-colored adhesive tape across his mouth, a similar strip across his eyes. His long, straight, corn-yellow hair was spread in wild disorder on the pillow under his head. There were a dozen bruises and small cigarette burns scattered over his legs and arms. He lay silent, unmoving.

The man in the tan suit looked down the sights of the pistol at the youth's head. Then he suddenly moved the gun down and strode erectly to the door of the bathroom at the back of the cottage. He opened the door, as a second youth whirled around, a frightened, apprehensive look going into his brown eyes. This youth was also clad only in underwear. There was a thick decoration of fine black hair on his thin legs and arms, but his head carried a thatch of yellow hair very similar to that of the boy lying on the bed in the main room. There was a bottle of peroxide on the shelf above the bathroom sink.

The man in the tan suit motioned his gun angrily. "You'd better get the lead out, boy, or you're going to wind up on a slab this morning."

"Listen, Harry," the youth with the bleached hair said. "I'm trying to hurry."

"It's seven twenty-eight. What are you dreaming about? Get that kid's clothes on. Move it!"

"All right, Harry," the youth said, a faint quivering in his voice. "Sure ..."

The man snapped the door shut and walked back to the front of the cabin. He looked around the room carefully. The iron he'd used to press his suit against the side of the large Samsonite bag resting beside the bureau was still on top of the small glass-topped writing desk. He touched it. It was cool. He opened the large suitcase and put it inside with his other carefully folded possessions. The second suitcase in the room, which belonged to the boy in the bathroom, lay open, its contents stuffed in carelessly. He examined that haphazard packing, an angry look going into his eyes; then he walked back toward the bathroom. He looked at his watch and rapped the gun sharply against the door.

"Okay, Harry," the youth inside whined.

In a moment the youth came out dressed in an inexpensive chocolate-colored gabardine suit. The suit had been tailored with shoulders much wider than the current fashions. There were irregular patterns in the padding where it extended beyond the boy's own shoulders. The boy, in his early twenties, wore a white shirt with a widely spread collar and a large Windsor-knotted red tie. His face was pale. There was a slight tic in his right eyelid. He might have been handsome, but a slight chin and weak eyes and a look of fear had destroyed it. His bleached hair had been oiled and combed into a high pompadour. He looked surprisingly similar to the way the boy on the bed had looked when they'd brought him in the night before, having picked him up going into his rooming house at the north end of town. The boy went straight to his open bag and pulled a half pint of Early Times from under the pile of carelessly thrown clothes.

The older man said, "Put that back."

"Harry, I'm going nuts!"

"Put it back!" A muscle flickered in the man's sturdy neck, the first sign of emotion he'd shown that morning. "Let's go through that first part again. Everything hangs on that, do you understand?"

The boy took a breath. He put the whisky bottle back in his bag, shutting it futilely.

The man in the tan suit walked to the boy on the bed and ripped the adhesive from the boy's mouth. He put the muzzle of the gun on the boy's cheek. "Repeat. And keep your voice down. Good morning, Mike. How do I look? Some stupid woman driver ran into us last night. It's not serious, but my buddy's car is a mess. Listen, Mike, this is a friend of mine Mr. Mason wanted to see about hiring as a new teller."

The boy on the bed did not hesitate. He opened his untaped mouth. In a rather high voice distinguished by a nasal drawl common to the central part of the state he repeated what the man in the tan suit had just said.

The man turned and nodded at the boy in the gabardine suit. In a reasonable facsimile of the voice used by the boy on the bed, he repeated the sentences. The older man said, "All right." Then he retaped the mouth of the boy on the bed and said, "Get, that bandage and the glasses on. And don't forget the handkerchief. We've got to move."

With trembling hands, the boy in the gabardine suit took a handkerchief from his pocket, looped and tied it around his neck, then stuffed it beneath the collar of his shirt. From the top drawer of the bureau he removed a prepared bandage and secured it over his left eye. He took a pair of heavy-rimmed dark glasses from the drawer and put them on.

"Harry, this isn't going to work. I'm telling you—"

The man stared at him. "Get those bags out to that car. Hurry up."

The boy in the gabardine suit started shaking. His whole body trembled visibly. The man stepped over and struck him smartly across the cheek with an open hand. The boy's head snapped back. His glasses fell sideways, slipping down on his nose. He looked frightened and pathetically comic because of it. He pushed the glasses back in front of his eyes. The shaking of his body stopped.

"Get out there and start the car," the older man said.

"All right, Harry," the boy whispered. "How about that kid? What if he gets loose? What if he—"

The older man turned back to the youth lying on the bed. He put the gun against the boy's cheek again. "Now, listen. You're going to lie here just like this until the motel people come in. Do you understand? That'll be about ten o'clock. You try anything before that, I'll come back and hunt you down. I'll find you and really go to work. You'd better be right about everything you told us. That satchel better be filled and ready to go in that bank at eight-five, the way you said, or you'll wish you were in hell sizzling like a piece of bacon. I'm telling you."

He pushed the gun brutally against the boy's cheek. The boy let out a muffled scream.

The older man turned around, looking at his companion levelly. "He won't do anything but just what he's doing—nothing."

The boy in the gabardine suit nodded shortly, very pale. Then he picked up the two suitcases and walked out of the motel, shutting the door behind him.

The older man stood waiting until he heard the sound of the Plymouth's engine turning outside. Then he put his gun inside a shoulder holster under his cheap well-pressed jacket. He walked back to the silent, unmoving, bound-and-taped boy lying on the bed. He put his thumbs down directly under the boy's Adam's apple....

Harry Wells carefully opened the cabin door and looked out. The court was silent. Drapes were drawn on all the cabin windows. He moved out swiftly and got behind the wheel of the Plymouth, as the younger man slid out of his way. He drove out of the court, using the rear exit. He drove around the block and back, stopping at a red light, where he waited to enter Lodge Boulevard, watching the heavy traffic moving downtown.

Willy Tyler sat with his hands doubled in his lap, his eyes staring straight ahead. "Listen, Harry," he whispered, "are you sure that kid ain't going to get free too quick and blow the whistle on us? Are you?"

A flicker of a smile quirked Harry Wells's wide, cruel mouth. "I'm sure," he said. "I'm damn sure."

# Chapter Two

By a quarter to eight that morning the small three-room apartment downtown was sticky hot. Twenty-four-year-old Allan Garwith stood at the second-floor window of the ancient Kennemore Arms Apartment-Hotel and observed the magnificent view that came with the cheap monthly rates, the three badly furnished rooms and bath and the odor of a half century of transients who had left their marks on what had once been considered one of Loma City's smartest abodes. The hot morning breeze rippled the empty folded left sleeve of Allan Garwith's sport shirt as he marveled at the view.

Only their apartment had the privilege, because the building, long nick-named The Flatiron, was but one apartment in width. Below the apartment shared by Allan Garwith and his bride of twenty days was the custodian's equipment room. The third and fourth floor apartments did not begin until twenty feet back of the rear wall, allowing the Garwiths their own gritty, soot-covered tar roof to themselves, with only the apartments of the floors behind and the rest of the tall buildings all around looking down on it.

Allan Garwith's bride had bravely and brightly said, "It'll be like our own penthouse, darling!" And he'd said, "With as much privacy as you'd get if you sat down in the middle of Lodge and Sixteenth."

Nevertheless the view looking back from their apartment was exclusive, because the walls and angles of the alley below cut off the pleasure to anyone else looking from one of the surrounding buildings; Allan Garwith had not ceased to comment on this wonder since the day they had moved in.

"Look at that view!" he said now, while Cicely, dark-haired and pretty-eyed but somewhat large-nosed, slipped a dress over her thin figure, hurrying to make her typing job with a downtown insurance company on time. "That view kills me." Bitterly he stared down, a rangy, well-built young man with loose dark hair that curled damply over his forehead; a dark beard was showing under his temples and around his jaw, and the muscles of his right arm were ridged tautly as he leaned against the sill of the open window.

The view was comprised of a back lot that was walled on either side by a high fence of aged and rotting boards. The lot was as wide as the Kennemore Arms building and was perhaps twenty-five feet long. Beyond that, across the opening, ran the alley that connected 17th and 18th

Streets. There the eye was finally stopped by a high, solid red brick wall, behind a court of the Guffrey Building, once a hotel nearly as rich as the early Kennemore Arms, but now a structure that housed a laundry and cleaning establishment. The lot directly in front of Allan Garwith's angry stare was a museum of rubbish. There were old, rusting pieces of machinery no one could identify, two discarded car fenders of mid-thirties vintage, three stacks of worn tires, a vast collection of bottles, half a dozen thrown-away garbage buckets, the whole array sooty and dusty and rotting from countless seasons of abandon.

Cicely came up behind him, slipping her frail arms around him. "Allan, don't be bitter. We have each other, don't we? And so much more too?"

He turned his head, seeing her reflection in an ancient gilt-edged mirror hung above a worn sofa as she held to him.

He did not know why he had married her. He'd known her for almost all of his life, but he did not know, for the life of him, why he'd married her. She was not pretty. He'd always been attracted by the olive-skinned, full-bodied Italian girls with their warmth and natural gregariousness and white-toothed smiles and husky, sensual laughter. But Cicely, maiden-named Anchovelli, had never owned any of those qualities. Her skin was pale, a white-chalk kind of paleness. And she was skinny with almost boy-hips and hard little breasts. She had the white teeth, but her smile was shy, her laughter tinkling like a lightly struck glass rather than being full and throaty with the hoarse Italian sound. Above all she was not sensual. Beyond the fact that Allan Garwith had known since high school that she'd been desperately in love with him, he could not give himself any solid reason that August Monday morning why he'd committed the ultimate foolishness of actually marrying her.

Of course, he'd been shaken up when he'd come back from New Orleans, an arm gone, a robbery rap missing him by a hair, his mother dead. But he could have had her without marrying her. Now he wondered if he were losing his mind. The cold-water tap in the kitchen was dripping again. He could hear it plainly: a liquid popping sound as it left the lip of the tap, over and over, over and over....

"That damn dripping," he breathed.

"I'll get it, darling," Cicely said swiftly.

She hurried to the kitchen and tightened the faucet. The dripping stopped.

"There," she said, coming back.

He did not thank her. He went over to the sofa and sprawled on it, picking up last evening's newspaper with his one hand.

"Listen, darling," Cicely said, recombing her hair in front of the gilt-edged mirror. "We can leave. I wouldn't mind."

"Your family would blow two dozen corks."

"I wouldn't care if they did. I'm married to you, darling. I'd go anywhere with you. Why couldn't we go? California—they say it's very cool and lovely right now. They say San Francisco's the most beautiful city in the world. Wouldn't that be nice? It would be like starting out completely fresh!"

"How do we get there—flap our arms and fly?"

She sat down beside him, looking at him with her pretty eyes. "Just listen. When we got married Daddy gave us something. I know you don't get along with him very well. And that's why I didn't tell you right away. But he gave us some money and I put it in the bank."

He blinked. "How much?"

"You won't be mad because I took it? He wanted us to have it, Allan."

"How much?"

Her eyes sparkled. "A hundred dollars."

He looked at her for a long moment. His profit for that job in Mexico that he'd never gotten to would have been eight thousand dollars, and it would have taken only a few days. Now she was telling him her old man had opened his great big Italian heart and laid a hundred on them. He couldn't answer her.

"Isn't that wonderful, darling? You're not mad about my taking the money, are you?"

He laughed bitterly and reached for her, pulling her over on him roughly, squeezing her left breast tightly.

"I can't now, darling," she whispered, her breath coming very quickly. "I'll be all mussed up. When I get home—just as soon as I get home."

He let go of her suddenly.

She stood up and had to recomb her hair. "Beast," she smiled. "But I love it." She finished combing her hair again and smoothed her dress. "Anyway—remember we've got a hundred dollars in the bank."

"Let's fly to Paris," he said thinly.

"Allan, don't be discouraged. You'll find something you like one of these days. But you don't have to worry about it. I like to work. And, if I do say so myself, I'm a very good typist. Aren't we getting along all right? Now look in the want-ad section of the paper. I've got another surprise for you."

"I don't think I can stand it."

"Go on. Page sixty-two in the want-ad section."

Carelessly he placed the newspaper on the sofa and flipped the pages.

"First column, third item down."

"'Wanted,'" he read, "'to share ride to San Francisco with widowed lady. Call Mrs. Landry. Walnut seven five nine one.'"

"Now. You see? I'll bet it wouldn't cost very much that way. The things we couldn't carry with us, we could ship—there isn't much, only the wedding gifts. And I'll bet I could get a good job the day we got there. They pay more there too, I've heard. So you think about it, dear husband of mine. All right?"

He shoved the paper aside.

She bent down and kissed his cheek. "Don't be depressed, darling, because I love you." Then she was gone.

He sat silently for a moment, drumming his fingers on the newspaper. Then he gathered the paper into his one hand, crumpled it and threw it viciously across the room. Finally he got up and walked to the window, staring down at the litter of the back lot. Two people appeared walking quickly along the alley crossing in front of the lot, east to west.

One was a rather solidly built man in a tan tropical suit whose shoes glistened in the sun as he walked. The other was a younger man in badly fitted gabardine who wore dark glasses and a bandage over one eye. Allan Garwith looked at them disinterestedly.

He turned his eyes back to the lot beneath his window. A large yellow and tan Tom had suddenly appeared on the edge of one of the side fences. It came down into the lot with a smooth, off-handed grace and prowled toward one of the discarded garbage buckets.

"Christ," Allan Garwith said aloud, the increasing heat of the city beginning to burn his face, "What a view!"

# Chapter Three

The Midwest Federal Trust Bank, at the end of the alley that bordered the lot below Allan Garwith's apartment, was a modern building. A vintage business building had been condemned and knocked down five years ago. Now the Midwest Federal Trust had taken its place and rested in imposing contrast to the otherwise old and fading buildings of that downtown block. Heroic Grecian figures were frozen in sandstone bas relief on its exposed sides. Its front entrance, just around the corner from the alley, was a pair of very thick glass doors, attended by a white-haired guard named Mike.

Before turning the corner, Willy Tyler and Harry Wells stopped near the 17th Street mouth of the alley. Their car was a block behind them through the alley, on 18th. Willy Tyler's nerves were going crazy. And he was thinking how pleasant it would be in his own bed at home right now, right here in Loma City, if so many things hadn't happened.

If he hadn't been drafted, he'd never have been sent to that California camp where Harry Wells was stationed. If he had never drawn Harry Wells for a sergeant, Harry wouldn't have known him. If Harry hadn't been transferred to Fort Allison outside Loma City to finish up the last year of his twenty-year hitch, Harry would have never gotten interested in that fort payroll money, waiting inside this bank right now to be delivered to the fort later in the morning. If Willy hadn't come back to Loma City to live at home after his discharge, Harry couldn't have looked him up. And if that kid lying on the bed in that crummy motel hadn't gotten a job as a junior teller at the Midwest Federal Trust three weeks ago, if he'd been short and fat instead of Willy's build, then Harry might have let it go and not got Willy into it and instead re-enlisted to finish out ten more.

But all the ifs had dropped into a neat pile, one upon the other, and they had added up to what was going on right now. It was all Willy could do to stop himself from turning and running back down that alley to jump in the car and get away before they'd gone any further with this. But the hard, frightening look in Harry Wells's eyes held him.

"Harry, this isn't going to work!"

"Shut up," Wells said thinly.

Willy was having trouble talking through his dry mouth. He tried to dredge up a little courage thinking about what he could do when this was over and he had his share of the money. He thought about girls. He thought very hard about girls. He could have models and dancers, maybe even a movie starlet or two. He would find them in Vegas and Hollywood and New York, you name it. Because you could do anything with enough money.

But his courage failed again. You couldn't think right about girls when you were so frightened your mouth felt like it had been packed with cotton. He opened his mouth and nothing came out. Finally he managed, "That kid we left in the motel, Harry. They might find him any minute and he'll blow the whistle on us—right in the middle of it. He knows everything we've got planned!"

"That kid won't blow the whistle on us," Wells said softly.

Willy looked at his eyes, and something snapped inside of him. All at once he was no longer trembling. It was though somebody had pumped cold water into his veins. He shuddered once, then stood very motionless, staring at that look in Harry Wells's eyes. He breathed, "You killed him, didn't you?"

"Now," Wells said, "you're growing up."

"How?"

Wells lifted his hands, smiling coldly.

Willy shook his head once. He wanted to scream and pound on the man, condemning him for ruining everything—Harry had promised nobody would get hurt....

But Willy said nothing.

"You're into it now," Wells said, looking at him with hard eyes. "Let's do it and do it right. Move."

Willy nodded woodenly and moved ahead of Wells to the door. It was exactly one minute after eight. Behind the thick glass doors, the guard, large and white-haired in a blue uniform, peered out. Willy felt his breath speeding until he thought he might choke, then he was suddenly almost lifeless again. He didn't give a damn now. He just didn't give a damn at all.

The door was unlocked from the inside. Willy waited for the guard to draw his gun and point it at them; instead he said, "Morning, Norman. What happened to the eye?"

Willy stepped inside. Harry Wells waited behind him. Willy had a peculiar feeling that if he did anything wrong now it would not be the guard who would gun him down, but Harry Wells. "Good morning, Mike. How do I look? Some stupid woman driver ran into us last night. It's not serious, but my buddy's car is a mess. Listen, Mike, this is a friend of mine Mr. Mason wanted to see about hiring as a new teller." He said it all almost mechanically, just as he'd practiced, in the twangy drawl of Norman Austin, who now lay dead on a bed in the motel. He thought for a moment the guard might start laughing, then Harry Wells would gun him from behind and run off, leaving him in a pool of blood on the marble floor at the doorway.

"Women drivers," the guard said in disgust. "Sure—bring your friend in. He can wait here. Mr. Mason won't be in until eight-thirty. Better hurry, Austin—you're four minutes late right now."

Willy walked through the entrance alcove which was bordered on both sides by low leather-cushioned benches. Willy looked at the interior of the bank as though he were dreaming. He and Harry had been in here separately three times in the last two weeks; it should have been familiar. But it was as though he'd never seen it before.

The loan department was forward on the right side behind a railing. Back of that were the deposit boxes and vault. The vault, Norman Austin had told them, was electronically opened at 8:05, just forty-five seconds from now. On the left were the rows of teller cages.

Head down a little, wondering who was going to be the first to recognize that he was not Norman Austin, he moved slowly past the central desks with their ballpoint pens and fresh stacks of white forms ready for the public that would come in at ten o'clock.

He looked up briefly at the clock built into the stone of the rear wall. Thirty seconds left. He stopped and got out a handkerchief, suddenly aware of the weight of the gun strapped inside his overly large suit jacket. He blew his nose, then returned his handkerchief to a hip pocket. He looked at the clock again. It was exactly 8:05. A slim man in a gray suit walked to the vault. Willy moved again. He reached the back right corner of the room, just as the man in the gray suit swung open the vault door and turned around. Willy stopped again. It was thirty seconds past 8:05. He put his right hand inside his jacket and around the gun. At the same instant he heard the hard, penetrating voice of Harry Wells echoing through the large room:

"Everybody stand right where you are. This is a holdup. It'll take only a few seconds. Don't touch an alarm. If it sounds we'll start shooting. We'll kill as many as we can. All of you at the teller cages step back two steps. Now!"

The alarms were at the teller cages, Norman Austin had told them. They were also at some other points Norman Austin didn't know about. But that was a chance they had to take. The people at the cages moved back as instructed. Willy stood with his gun in hand now, looking at them with a peculiar detachment. Faces had gone white. Some looked angry. Some looked frightened. Some looked bewildered. Nobody moved.

Willy yanked the handkerchief inside his shirt up around his face and looked back down the distance of the room, feeling alone and vulnerable and self-conscious, as though he'd suddenly found himself in the center of a stage watched by an awed audience. Shades had been pulled over the front glass doors. The guard was backed against a wall, hands above his head and away from the holster at his hip. Harry Wells stood with his feet spread apart, his gun held close to his side, face now masked like Willy's. He nodded to Willy. Willy walked through a swinging gate built into the low railing in front of the vault.

He moved quickly, but he did not run. He saw a half dozen employees staring at him as he passed. Then he was moving into the vault. He looked to his right, and there, on a wooden chair, rested the black satchel, just as Norman Austin had told them.

Willy picked it up and walked out of the vault, into the main room.

He was certain nobody had moved. He went straight down the center of the marble-floored rotunda, his footsteps echoing in the silence. Ahead of him Harry Wells, eyes dark and mean, motioned his gun impatiently for him to hurry. Willy continued to pace evenly, halfway to the door now.

"Come on, come on!" Harry Wells called angrily.

Then the guard moved. He dropped his hand to the gun in his holster, closing his big hand around the handle. Harry Wells turned and pulled the trigger on his pistol three exploding times. The guard pitched forward, tumbling to the floor heavily.

"Run!" Harry Wells shouted, and slammed open a glass door.

Willy ran, hearing the sudden and jarring sound of the alarm going off. He had a mental picture of himself running through that large interior, knowing he looked foolishly out of place, clumsy and awkward like a child who has got caught stealing cookies.

As he neared the door he looked at the fallen guard and realized that the old man was still alive, dragging the gun from his holster. It did not occur to Willy that he should fire at that old man.

A dozen people were yelling as Willy passed the guard and reached the sunshine. The alarm rang with ear-piercing, nerve-shattering steadiness. Harry Wells had reached the mouth of the alley. He turned to yell hoarsely, "Move, move!"

"Sure," Willy breathed foolishly, knowing that this surely was a dream. "Sure ..."

A slug caught him in the shoulder. He whirled, dropping the satchel, and stumbled to a stop. He looked back, surprised to see the guard lying in the doorway on his stomach, holding his gun with a badly shaking hand. Another bullet whined in Willy's direction. But the guard's aim was off now. Having fired the second time, the guard let go of his gun. His head fell against the cement of the sidewalk. Willy blinked, realizing that a uniformed policeman was running toward him from the end of the block, tugging his gun out.

Willy shoved his gun in its holster and picked up the satchel. His left shoulder was beginning to burn. He tore off the fake bandage and colored glasses and ran again, heading down the alley, wondering when the nightmare was going to end and he would wake up safely in his own bed.

Harry Wells was far ahead of him now, almost to the other end of the alley. Willy followed, feeling his breath come shorter for the effort. Now Harry disappeared. "God ..." Willy Tyler gasped.

Suddenly the sedan appeared at the far end of the alley. Harry Wells waited behind the wheel, gunning the engine. Willy could hear the hard voice, "Faster, faster!"

"Yeah ..." Then something bit him in the left leg. He stumbled awkwardly and realized the cop behind had shot him. He tried to keep his footing. He whirled again, looking back along the alley. The cop ducked into a doorway, firing again. This time Willy felt the bite at his forehead. He fell to his knees as blood poured into one eye. "Oh, my God ..." he said, thinking of how much he'd loved his poor parents when he'd been a very little boy.

Almost blinded, feeling the world tip upside down, he fell sickeningly sideways until his head slammed into the pavement. He knew it was all just a bad dream, just a terrible and frightening nightmare.

"This way!" Harry Wells was screaming in fury from the car waiting at the mouth of the alley. Then Harry Wells was firing at the cop behind Willy.

Willy lifted his head and shook it, trying to get the blood out of his eyes. He was thinking: I've got to get out of here, that's what I've got to do.

Another bullet licked his right shoulder. He began to crawl. He crawled blindly, knowing that this was the way it always was in dreams. You tried to move fast and you couldn't—all you could do was crawl, crawl....

The shooting was behind him now. No more bullets were trying to find him. He kept crawling until he bumped into something hard. It was not just the blood blinding him now but a blackness that kept washing in front of his eyes.

He shook his head and saw with one eye that he still had the satchel in his hand. Well, he thought, and rolled over, throwing it from him. It was that which had brought this rotten dream around. If he got rid of it the bad dream would end.

He lay on his back, dark waves hitting him, as though he were lying on a beach and the ocean was slowly folding over him. Okay, dream, he thought, end.

It did. He lay there very silently in the early morning sun, while the shooting went on in the alley, unheard by Willy, who had absolutely dreamed his last dream.


Allan Garwith was at the window of his apartment when the sound of the bank alarm, then the shooting, began. He saw first the man in the tan suit running by, shoes flashing, face now masked by a handkerchief. Bullets whined and ricocheted and whined again. Allan Garwith stood frozen, ready to duck, a furious pumping of fright going through him. He suddenly remembered how he'd felt when he'd tried to hold up that service station just outside New Orleans.

Then the youth with the yellow hair appeared in the alley, running, spinning, as a bullet struck him in the leg. He too was wearing a handkerchief. It came undone as the boy was hit again. Blood spurted over his face from a head wound. Allan Garwith sucked in his breath, crouching now, looking over the window sill. He saw the boy start crawling, coming right into the lot below, dragging a black satchel.

Then everything cleared in Allan Garwith's brain. He knew positively what had just happened. The bank was at the end of the alley. The men wore masks. There was shooting. A satchel was clutched in the hand of the boy now crawling through the litter of machinery below.

Allan Garwith ran out of the apartment with swift, athletic grace. He hit the back stairway fast, thinking that Brogan, the custodian, would be up the street eating breakfast, that nobody else would or could see that kid crawling through the back lot.

He reached the door, as bullets continued to whine back and forth through the alley. Teeth beginning to chatter, he saw the kid, not twelve yards from him, roll over and throw the satchel weakly from him. The satchel lay directly in front of Allan Garwith.

In spite of a wild fright clutching at him, he dived forward, grabbed the satchel and ducked back into the doorway.

The boy lying in the lot was silent and unmoving. Allan Garwith pressed himself against a wall of the back stair well. The man in the tan suit suddenly appeared, throwing himself behind a fence inside the lot. The man searched desperately with his eyes over the entire lot, but he did not see Allan Garwith. Fast hands inserted a new clip in his gun, then the man leaned around the fence, firing up the alley again. Finally he broke into a run back down the alley and disappeared. In a moment Allan Garwith heard the loud roar of a car, the wild shrieking of tires.

Allan Garwith, trembling all over, took a breath. He spun and ran up the stairs to his own apartment, shoved the satchel beneath the bed, then ran out of the apartment and down the front stairway to the street. Outside, people were hurrying along the street, totally concentrating on the sounds of the bank alarm still ringing and the echoes of the shooting.

Allan Garwith trotted across the street, away from the apartment. He cut through the next block, went down an alley and continued two more blocks until he came to a cafeteria. He went inside, still trembling, aware that the people here had been out of earshot of the firing and alarm.

He picked up a cup of coffee and two doughnuts, then sat down at a table, still shaking. It was a number of minutes before he could calm down enough to pick up his coffee cup; but his mind kept whirling, fitting one piece of judgment to another. Slowly he finished the coffee and ate the doughnuts, as his hand finally stopped shaking. Then he got up and walked to the cashier with his check.

While the cashier waited for the money, he went through one pocket, then another, beginning to look rattled. The cashier, a girl with dyed blond hair, looked at his armless sleeve and waited patiently. "I think I forgot my money," he said.

The girl paused. "Well, you can pay me the next time."

"I'm awfully sorry. I—" He suddenly brought out a dollar bill and put it on the counter. "There it is. Just missed it, I guess."

The girl smiled and thanked him, handing him his change. He walked outside and down the street, away from his apartment. He walked on to the public library and held a book in front of his eyes for a half hour, seeing nothing. Then he walked again aimlessly for another half hour. Finally he started back toward the apartment. Two uniformed policemen were standing in front when he came up.

He looked surprised.

"You live here?" one of them asked.

"Sure."

Brogan, the custodian, fat and disheveled, his reddish face even more flushed than usual, came out. "Allan, all hell's been breaking loose around here. Midwest Federal was robbed!"

"You're kidding!" Allan Garwith said.

"Hell, no. I miss everything!" He turned to the police officers. "This is the guy who's got the back apartment."

"You didn't see any of it?" one of the officers asked. Allan Garwith shook his head. "Me? No. When did it happen?"

"About eight-five. Two guys. They both ran down the alley back there, away from the bank. Got one of them. He ran out of gas in that lot back there. We thought maybe you saw some of it."

"Not me. You mean he died right back there?"

"The other one got away."

"Hell," Allan Garwith said. "I was over at Brock's Cafeteria on Farley Street, when it happened. Did the guy get away with anything?"

"A hundred thousand. That's all. Well, thanks. I guess you can't help us."

In another minute Allan Garwith had escaped from the excited Brogan and returned to his apartment. He went in and locked the door and sat down on the sofa. He was shaking again, breathing quickly.

He sat there for perhaps two minutes, then he got up and went into the bedroom and pulled the blind. He slid the satchel out from under the bed and opened it. It was stuffed with currency. He closed it suddenly, shoved it back under the bed and went into the bathroom and was sick. Finally he came out and lay down on the bed right over where the satchel lay hidden. He was still shaking, but presently he was under control again. He rubbed his hand over his mouth, staring at the ceiling. "My God," he whispered. "My God almighty!"

# Chapter Four

Willy Tyler died in that vacant lot among the rusting machinery on Friday. Sunday afternoon John Benson stepped off a Loma City bus at 34th and Cherry. The neighborhood was clean, old and substantial-looking. The houses were two-storied, with deep front terraces and generous back yards. It was mid-afternoon, and the sun's angle was beginning to lengthen the shadows of poplars, oaks and elms lining Cherry Street. John Benson crossed 34th and walked west on Cherry, a tall man of thirty-six wearing a neat light-weight brown suit and straw hat. His face was lean and reasonably handsome, if not memorable.

In front of the third house from the corner, he stopped, checking the shiny metal numbers fixed on the front siding. The house was white with an old-fashioned swing hung from chains on the front porch in front of a bay window. There was a scraggly hedge bordering the walk, carelessly trimmed; a huge growth of red roses spread along the railing of the porch. A large oak rose from the center of the lawn and put the front of the house in shade.

John Benson moved up the walk toward the porch. He pressed the button beside the door and listened to the sound of chimes inside.

In a moment the door opened. A rather heavy-set, scrubbed-looking woman with gray hair and sparkling blue eyes appeared behind the screen. She wore a brilliantly flowered, blue house dress. "Yes?" she said, smiling.

"Mrs. Landry?"

"Yes—I'm Mrs. Landry."

"I'm John Benson. I called earlier."

"Of course! Come in, Mr. Benson—please come in!" Mrs. Landry led John Benson through a hall into a cheerful living room. Overstuffed furniture had been covered with brightly flowered slip-covers. Fresh flowers were displayed in vases in half a dozen places. There was an upright piano in one corner with stacks of sheet music on its rack. John Benson immediately noticed the woman sitting in a chair opposite the sofa.

She was of rather indeterminable age, even to John Benson's eyes—

somewhere in her thirties, he judged. Her figure was full, but extremely well proportioned in an inexpensive but neat-looking blue suit. Her hair was ash-blond, shaped in an off-hand style that was so effectively simple that it dramatized the good looks of her face. Her eyebrows were dark, and she had brown eyes that examined John Benson with a straightforward, somewhat lazy curiosity. The planes of her face were bold and well-defined. There was a relaxed air of confidence and maturity that made John Benson feel immediately attracted to her.

"Mr. Benson," Mrs. Landry said. "I want you to meet Mrs. Moore. Margaret Moore."

"How do you do, Mrs. Moore?" John Benson smiled, noticing that she wore no wedding ring.

"Mr. Benson," she said in a quiet, husky voice, staring at him with a soft smile. A cigarette was in her left hand, held limply against the arm of the chair; a tall glass rested on the end table beside her.

"Now then," Mrs. Landry said, "you sit right down there on the sofa, Mr. Benson. You and Mrs. Moore can get acquainted while I get you a glass of lemonade."

"Well, you don't have to bother, Mrs. Landry."

"Of course, I do. Unless you don't like lemonade. I think it's good, isn't it, Mrs. Moore?"

Mrs. Moore motioned a hand toward her glass, smiling. "Delicious, Mrs. Landry."

"Well, all right," John Benson said. "I would like some, if you don't mind."

"Of course, I don't mind. Now you two sit there and get acquainted." She bustled out of the room. John Benson smiled at the woman seated across the room from him. "Very nice, isn't she?"

"Very," Margaret Moore nodded.

"An old friend, or—"

"No. I met her ten minutes ago. I feel like I've known her for twenty years."

John Benson nodded. "You're riding with her to San Francisco then?"

"Yes. I've just been accepted. And you, Mr. Benson?"

"I don't know. That's what I'm here about."

"She'll take you. She likes you; so she'll take you."

"Well, I hope so." He paused. "If she does, do you think we'll be the only ones?"

"Well, no," Mrs. Moore said, smiling faintly. "Not quite, Mr. Benson. With you, I think that makes a total of seven."

"Seven?"

"So far." Mrs. Moore laughed softly, and John Benson found himself delighted by her laugh. It seemed to slip past the guard he'd built around himself over the last year, and it bothered him that it did. But he was nevertheless delighted. He suddenly relaxed a little.

Mrs. Landry came back with his lemonade, saying, "Now, you just go ahead and smoke if you want to, Mr. Benson. Mr. Landry, God rest him, smoked in this house and I never minded. If a man or a woman wants to smoke, it's their privilege. Women who waste their time forbidding people to smoke in their homes ought to be investigated mentally. Now then." Mrs. Landry sat down, clasping her hands together, looking at John Benson with bright, merry eyes. "You want to go to San Francisco with me?"

John Benson nodded. "Yes, I do, Mrs. Landry."

"All right then. You tell me a little about yourself. I've already made up my mind. But I promised my daughter, Ella June—she's in California, you know, and that's why I'm driving out, to visit her and her family—I promised that I'd have everybody tell me about themselves. She was worried to death when I wrote her I was driving out there and was going to advertise for someone to ride with me. She called right up, long-distance, and told me I was taking an awful chance." Mrs. Landry laughed. "Well, imagine—such nice people have wanted to ride with me. But I promised her I'd find out about everybody. So you tell me something about yourself, Mr. Benson."

"All right. I'm a widower, Mrs. Landry."

"Oh, my goodness. You poor boy. How long, child?"

"A little over a year." John Benson looked at his hands. "My wife was killed in an automobile accident. One of those things that should never have happened. But it did. We lived in Lafayette, Indiana. It was icy—" He shrugged. "She was alone. The driver in the other car was killed too."

"Poor fellow. I shouldn't have asked."

"It's all right," he said. He shrugged again. "I have two boys—seven and eight. They're with my wife's parents right now. My own family is dead."

"And where are your wife's parents?"

"Chicago. I had a small advertising business in Lafayette. I was doing pretty well as a matter of fact. But when my wife—well, everything went flat. I decided to go west. I left the boys with their grandparents in Chicago. I stopped here in Loma City to see an old friend of mine I went to college with at Indiana. When I was ready to go on, I decided I'd had my fill of being alone. I saw your ad in the paper. I decided I'd much rather travel with someone in a car than as a stranger on a train. I don't like to fly, so—"

"Wonderful, Mr. Benson," Mrs. Landry said, nodding positively. "That shows very good sense. When Mr. Landry died in nineteen forty-nine I felt the same way. I felt all lost and so depressed, and I sat around in this house and didn't even want to see my friends and neighbors. Then pretty soon I realized that you just can't do that. It isn't healthy. You've got to go right on and be with people. And I'm just so glad you're riding along with us, Mr. Benson. Aren't you, Mrs. Moore?"

Mrs. Moore nodded, an amused smile on her wide, handsome mouth. "Of course."

"Well, then. It's all settled. Now, let's see. That'll be you two. And Miss Kennicot. And—"

The door chimes sounded.

"Just a moment," Mrs. Landry said, and hurried off to the front door. In a moment John could hear the high, rather loud voice of a woman alternately laughing and talking.

Mrs. Landry returned with a very tall woman who had large legs and wide hips and a thin, long torso. She wore a pink suit that somehow did not seem to fit well, although John could not immediately tell what was wrong or where. She wore a small black hat above a flushed, rather long-nosed face. She looked around, then laughed loudly. Mrs. Landry began to search the room and came up with a slender book. "Here it is, Miss Kennicot."

"Oh, my, thank you!" Miss Kennicot's voice boomed around the room. "Oh, dear, oh, dear!" She clutched the book tightly. "My Shelley, you know. I don't know how I could have forgotten it. I missed it when I got on my bus, and I had to get off and come clear back."

"That's a shame, Miss Kennicot," Mrs. Landry said.

"Well—'Memory is the diary that we all carry about with us,'" Miss Kennicot said, laughing. "That's Wilde, of course. But I must have even forgotten my diary!" Miss Kennicot laughed so hard that tears formed in her eyes. John Benson suddenly realized she was looking straight at him, speaking as though for his benefit alone.

"Miss Kennicot," Mrs. Landry said, "these are two more of my guests on our drive to California. Mrs. Moore. Mr. Benson. This is Miss Kennicot. She's a librarian for the Loma City Memorial, and she's riding along too."

Miss Kennicot flashed a dangerous glance at Mrs. Moore, then fastened her stare on John Benson again, laughing violently. "The great adventure, isn't it! Well, it's just a lark for me. To California and back! 'Round the world and home again. That's the sailor's way.' W. Allingham. I've just decided to go ahead and do it! I haven't done anything so headstrong since four summers ago when I decided to lead our Robins—that's our teen-age girls' group—on a hike clear across the state and back!" Miss Kennicot tipped her head back and roared. "Well, I'm just girlishly foolish, I guess." Miss Kennicot lowered her head, grinning with large teeth, and gazed straight at John Benson until he felt vaguely nervous. "Well, my goodness!" she said finally. "I've got to run. 'A sorry breaking-up!' T. Moore. Tuesday morning then? I know it'll be simply loads!" Roaring, she allowed Mrs. Landry to escort her to the door.

John Benson looked across the room at Margaret Moore. They met each other's eyes for a moment, then both of them laughed softly. Mrs. Landry reappeared.

"Miss Kennicot," she said. "She's so smart and so healthy-looking. Don't you agree?"

Mrs. Moore nodded and John Benson said. "Indeed."

"Well, then," Mrs. Landry said. "Where was I? Oh, yes. I was saying it's all settled now. You two. Miss Kennicot. And then I have the sweetest young couple—just married!" Mrs. Landry laughed gaily. "Makes us all feel a little younger. That's the Garwiths. The girl is so sweet and shy, just the way a bride ought to be. The boy—Allan, that's his name—lost an arm somehow, poor boy, but he seems to do awfully well anyway."

John Benson nodded, glancing at Mrs. Moore, who was studying him casually with a faint smile.

"Well, then. And that's all, I think. Oh, no. Mr. Wells! He's the retired Army man. Very soft-spoken and dignified and not very old. And he's so very neat! Yes, with Mr. Wells, that'll be all. And I'll have my station wagon looked over so they can do whatever they're supposed to do when you leave for a long trip. My goodness, isn't this going to be fun? Friday morning, eight o'clock, and away we go! How could I be so lucky as to have such a wonderful group of people with me! And my daughter was so worried! Imagine!"

John Benson and Margaret Moore left together. A bus was just approaching the corner down the block, where Miss Kennicot was still waiting.

"Shall we run and catch it?" Mrs. Moore said. "They're about ten minutes apart out here."

"Well," John Benson said, "I don't know. What do you think?"

They both strolled very slowly, as the bus hissed to a stop. Miss Kennicot, her back to them, snapped shut her book of Shelley poems.

"I don't know," Mrs. Moore said, smiling. "We could make it if we run."

The bus door opened. Miss Kennicot stepped in, reminding John Benson of a large colt boarding.

"I just can't make up my mind," he said.

"Too late," Mrs. Moore said. The bus roared off. She laughed her husky, full laugh. It made John Benson feel more alive than he'd felt in many long months.

As they waited on the corner, he said, "Well, now I've explained why I'm going west. How about you? Tired of Loma City?"

"I don't think I thought very much about it," she said. "I haven't been here long. I've moved around quite a bit. One job, then another. I'm a natural wanderer, I guess. Compulsive. Never satisfied. Not for long anyway."

"You mean you just arbitrarily came to Loma City? Why?"

"Well, I'd been living in New York, working in a rather good clothing shop, as a saleswoman. It started out being enjoyable. A small, pleasant group of friends. The city to prowl and enjoy. Then one day everything seemed shallow, brittle, so I left. I'd lived for a time in the midwest before. From New York, this part of the country seemed more solid, closer to the earth, so to speak. So I picked out Loma City. It was fine, for a while. Then—" She motioned a hand. "I don't know. Restless again. I had a job in a real estate office here. I just told them I was leaving. I read Mrs. Landry's ad in the paper. San Francisco sounded fine. So that's it."

"Well," he, said, smiling, "I admire your independence. And I'm glad you decided to go west on this ride. The trip is going to be that much more pleasant."

"Thank you, John Benson."

The bus was approaching, and in a moment they had boarded. Seated, he said, "You live downtown?"

"On the edge of downtown. A small apartment. And you?"

"I'm staying at the Walton Hotel."

She nodded, looking at him. "Very nice, very respectable. That's a very nice suit you're wearing, Mr. Benson."

He looked at her carefully. She met his gaze straight-on. "Well, thank you."

"It just seems to me," she said, "that you're the type to use taxis, Mr. Benson."

He smiled. "John, all right? And yes. We could have taken a taxi, but a bus ride takes longer. I enjoy talking to you, Mrs. Moore."

There was a flicker of sensuality in her eyes that John Benson could feel deep inside, and there was at the same time a remote kind of mystery about her. She was saying, in effect, that she did not understand his being in a situation like this, regardless of his explanation. But he could not really figure her position in it either. She was puzzling.

"Margaret," she said. "Even my friends, when I have them, don't call me Marge, thank God. And if you're wondering about the Mrs., which I rather hope you are, I'm divorced, John. I'm a free agent. But if I told you everything you might not be interested any more. I hope you're interested, John."

He nodded, enjoying her directness. "I'm interested."

She smiled softly. "This is my stop coming up. It's been very pleasant."

He watched her walk down the block toward an apartment house. There was a fine poise and confidence about the way she moved, as though the world could tumble down around her and she would take it as it came. He leaned back as the bus moved forward, rubbing his chin with the back of a hand. He was still aware of her presence, and he had not felt that way about a woman since the first day he'd met Maggie. He'd been certain he would never feel that way again....

Five blocks farther into the downtown section, he got off and strode briskly to the Walton Hotel. He went directly up to his room. Ray Hannah was inside, waiting for him.

"You make it, John?"

"I made it. The last one. Seven of us altogether."

"Wells?"

"He'll be there."

"Good. I just talked to the mother of that kid who was killed in the motel. We want to get that son of a bitch and get him all the way. Sit down. I'll mix you a drink from your own booze."

# Chapter Five

Ray Hannah was blond, square-shouldered, with the full, healthy-looking face of the born athlete. At 32 he was the head of the Loma City FBI office, and carried out his responsibility with animal energy.

When John Benson had been called into the office of his chief, Frank Terrill, in Washington, Frank had explained the situation briefly and quietly. "They want someone from out of town, John. Hannah's a good man and I trust his judgment. I think he's right. We've had you locked up in this office for four years—how about going into the field again?" John Benson knew that he might be right for this job, but he also knew that Frank was worrying about him, purposely urging him into something that might break him out of the shell. Frank Terrill was a wise man.

Ray Hannah mixed two drinks hastily, then began pacing. John took off his jacket and sat down on a straight chair, propping his feet on the bed. "How about going over it again?" He'd come in last night. Ray Hannah had given him the facts briefly. But he wanted to get everything securely in mind. He would be all the way into it in two days. He couldn't afford any mistakes after that.

"From where?" Hannah asked.

"From the beginning."

Hannah nodded. "All we've got since it happened. The kid who was choked to death, Norman Austin, didn't know how much that satchel had in it—nor where it was going. We're sure of that, because the bank was definite about who knew about it. I don't know whether I explained or not. But when that money was put together for the Fort Allison payroll, it was moved from the big Federal on 13th to the Midwest Federal, in the satchel, to hold until the armored car picked it up and carried it out to the fort. They figured it was a simple enough dodge to keep things safe—especially since only three people at the Midwest Federal knew how big it was."

"And you've checked them out?"

"Positively. Norman Austin sure as hell wasn't one of them. He could have known about the satchel itself, that it contained some money. But he wouldn't have known it was a hundred thousand."

"So you started figuring it from the fort side?"

Hannah nodded. "Somewhere in the finance section. Harry Wells, as a top sergeant out there, knew what was going on in the finance section. He could have known about the satchel. He could also have found out what bank it came from."

"But nobody else?"

"No. But we've checked out everybody else who could have known about it. We, at least, got a general description about Wells's build, the sound of his voice. Only the guard saw his face directly. But the guard's dead. The cop he shot it out with in the alley didn't get a clear picture in that kind of action. But we got his build, and Wells's build fits. We got his voice, and his voice fits. Nobody else who could have known about that payroll at the fort fits the description as closely. All of those that are hairline were accounted for during the time of the holdup."

John Benson sipped his drink thoughtfully. "But no record on Harry

Wells?"

"Not a thing. He was clean before he went into the service. He was clean for twenty years in the Army."

"Not even an AWOL?"

"No."

"Then he does this."

Hannah shrugged. "He's tough. Leans to the sadistic side. But nothing you'll get in a record. No emotion. No compassion. Everything all down the line."

"Good combat record?"

"Hell of a combat record."

John Benson shook his head. "What triggers a thing like this?"

"Maybe it isn't just triggered. Maybe this is where he was heading all the time. Man like that can stand at attention for twenty-four hours and never twitch a muscle. Then tear things up. I figure he went by the numbers all his life, then, when he was ready, went for it all the way. A hundred grand, tax free. To a guy like that, it wouldn't matter if he had his whole life invested in it, this would be worth it."

"How smart?"

"Not too smart. Medium IQ. That probably accounts for the mistakes he made."

"Like the kid he brought in—Willy Tyler?"

"That's the big mistake. It's the positive tie that hooks him. We checked back. Wells had Tyler under him in California. When he started figuring on going for the payroll, he just naturally thought of Tyler. Tyler doesn't have a record either, but he must have been ripe for a deal like this—the report on him indicates he was hungry to make it big but hadn't done much about it, kept looking for something for nothing. Wells could have leaned him into the deal, all right. We figure it that way."

"But no evidence they were together anywhere, anytime, since Wells came out here and was discharged?"

"No. But remember this was the big one for Wells. He would have been careful from the beginning."

John Benson nodded. "So when this kid, Norman Austin, got a job in the bank, Wells realized he was pretty close to Tyler's build and looks, and figured it out that way."

"Yeah. Kidnaped Austin, tortured as much information out of him as they could get—I think Wells did that—and then you know how they pulled it at the bank. It was Tyler who screwed it up."

"He didn't fire his gun at all?"

"Not once. It must have been Wells, all the way. He got the money, all right. But we know who he is. And that's going to nail him."

"And you think this is the right way, Ray? Let him run? Let him trip himself?"

"How else? If we pick him up now, how much can we get him for? He's no doubt got an alibi figured for his time. He's got no record. We could pull him in, hope to crack his alibi. But if we don't have enough, we lose not only the money but Wells too. Identification by the people at the bank just isn't enough. He was masked, and it won't hold up. What we've got to do is get him with the money. We've got the serial numbers, all right. But we can't wait until it starts showing up spread all over the country, maybe. We've got to get him with the package. Then we can really slam him.

"Hell, he killed that Austin kid in the purest cold blood. I'm certain of that. He also killed the guard. He's responsible for heisting one hundred G's of Uncle's sugar. We're going to get him, John. It's going to be a sweet, dangerous job for you. But it's the only way. This bastard may not be an old pro, but he's damn cagey. He left no fingerprints anywhere. We couldn't get a particle of anything out of the car he ditched. It's going to be a real job."

"The money—the Tyler kid was the one who took it out of the vault?"

"Had it going out of the bank. Still had it when the patrolman knocked him down in the alley. The kid crawled into a lot off the alley. Then Wells came back and got it."

"Did the patrolman see him get it?"

"No. Wells was splattering so much lead he couldn't get a good look. He was flat up against a wall, backed up in a little recess, just firing in Wells's direction. But Wells didn't run back through that fire for his health. There's one apartment that looks over that lot—a young couple live in it. But the wife was at work. And the husband was eating break-fast at a cafeteria a couple of blocks away. We checked the company where the girl works, and they verified her. The cashier at the cafeteria remembered the husband being in there about the time the robbery came off.

"We're sure Wells got the satchel, high-tailed it up the alley, took off in that stolen sedan, then ditched the car. That's where we stand with it right now. We've had a tail on Wells, ever since we got it down to him. He hasn't done one solitary thing out of line—only put in for a ride to California with your new friend, Mrs. Landry. And that is going to sink him. He's going to make a move for that money, and you're going to be there when he does."

John Benson sat silently, studying his glass. It had been four years since he'd done any field work. He felt rusty for it. But there was a small flicker of excitement deep in his middle. It was a welcome feeling—he'd been too long absolutely dead-numb inside.

"You're playing it pretty close," Ray Hannah said. "Using your own name and some of the other things. Your wife's parents living in Chicago, your kids staying with them."

"I know," John Benson nodded. "But I've been out of this end of it too long. I've got to have an advantage, to give me less room for a slip. If somebody called me by a phony name, I'd forget to turn around. This is better."

"Did you really go to Indiana University or live in Lafayette at any time?"

"I didn't graduate from Indiana—I graduated from California. But I was at Indiana for a while during the war. I remember Bloomington. I was in Lafayette a couple of times. I had some dates with a girl whose home was there. I've got some folders on the town. I've memorized the map. I'll be all right."

"How about the advertising? Know anything about it?"

"I had a part-time job with a small ad agency while I was in college. I don't think I'll run into trouble, unless—"

"Unless what?"

"Well, I haven't met everybody that's going on that ride. If—"

"I wanted to get into that. We don't want to spook Wells any way at all. So we've allowed nothing to leak. As far as the news outlets are concerned, the city cops and the FBI are purely stupid and don't have a lead to their names. The tail on Wells has been a careful thing, buddy. When Wells went into the Landry lady's house, we walked very softly. Had a guy show up in the neighborhood as a telephone repairman until he found out she was advertising for riders to go to the Coast. Then we checked Mrs. Landry, very roundabout, then we laid off. You're all of it now. We'll check the people riding for you as well as we can. Seven? What the hell is she going to drive? A bus?"

John Benson smiled faintly. "Station wagon."

Hannah shook his head. "Well. Mrs. Landry. If there's any connection between her and Wells, we don't see it."

"If my instinct's any good, there isn't."

"Do you know the rest of them now?"

"There's a Miss Kennicot. A librarian at the Loma City Memorial. I met her. She looks genuine."

Hannah got out a pencil and a small pad of paper. "Okay."

"Then Wells."

"Amen."

"And a woman named Mrs. Margaret Moore. She lives in an apartment on Twenty-first Street, just off Lodge. I've talked to her. Says she's divorced. Hell of an attractive woman, but she doesn't seem to fit in with this group. She doesn't think I do either, by the way." He paused, then: "I'd check her heavily, Ray."

"We'll try. But we've only got two nights and one day. Who else?"

"A young couple. I didn't see them. Newly married. Mrs. Landry said the boy had one arm."

"Which?" Ray Hannah said quickly, staring at John Benson. "One arm."

"Name?"

"Allan Garwith."

Ray Hannah put a hand to his forehead, closing his eyes. "That's the kid who's been renting that apartment that overlooks the lot where Willy Tyler died!"

John Benson blinked once, staring back at Ray Hannah. He whistled softly. "Wow."

"Yeah," Hannah said, starting to pace again excitedly. "Wow, indeed, brother ..."

## Chapter Six

Late Monday afternoon wind and rain swept down on Loma City with such intensity that windshield wipers were pressed motionless for seconds at a time and drivers were forced to stop their cars in mid-street blinded by the wash of water over their windshields. Lightning flashed and thunder rumbled like large beaten drums in the dark sky, an aged elm on Carter Street at the north edge of the city was split down the center and dead limbs were torn from other tree trunks and strewn over the city's residential avenues. The storm lasted for twenty minutes and was followed by a gray, airless lull of intense humidity. By Tuesday morning the air was cooler, less humid, and the early sun had evaporated the last silver rain puddles on sidewalks and streets. Birds were calling. The sky was blue-white and clear except for a scattering of fragile floating clouds to the west.

When John Benson got out of his cab and stepped onto the broad front porch of Mrs. Landry's house with his suitcase, the door was open. There was an odor of freshly made coffee coming from the interior, mixed with the smell of baking. The station wagon was parked in the driveway, and several bags were resting on the grass beside it. Inside there was the sound of laughing female voices.

"There you are!" Mrs. Landry called, coming through the house. "Here's Mr. Benson, everybody! We're all set now!" She was wearing a brilliantly patterned blue and orange dress. Her gray hair was neat and shining.

"I hope I'm not late," he said.

"Of course not, Mr. Benson. Come in and have some coffee."

He followed her through the living room. Dust covers had been thrown carelessly over the furniture. Numerous vases had been emptied and the lack of flowers gave the room an entirely different look. Drapes had been pulled together, and the interior was lighted only by shafts of bright morning sunlight that escaped through the few spaces where the drapes had not come entirely shut.

The kitchen was flooded with light, however, and everyone was standing around a yellow-painted kitchen table loaded with freshly filled thermoses of coffee, a large sandwich basket and an equally large box of fresh-baked cookies.

"Here he is, everyone," Mrs. Landry said gaily. "The last one."

Miss Kennicot, a cup of coffee in her hand, was wearing a black skirt and an extremely lacy white blouse that was transparent and showed, quite primly, a similarly lacy white slip. She tipped her head back and laughed loudly, eyes on John. "As dear William said, 'All's well that ends well!'" She laughed again, looking at him in a way that made him feel faintly nervous. He then noticed her eyes flicker to Margaret Moore with an unmistakable look of distaste.

Mrs. Moore, in a simple white dress that emphasized the handsome mold of her body, looked at John with a lazy smile. "Welcome, John. Can I pour you coffee?"

"I'll do it!" Miss Kennicot said shrilly.

"Let's see now," Mrs. Landry said. "You've met everyone, I think, Mr. Benson, but the Garwiths and Mr. Wells here. Mr. Wells, I want you to meet Mr. Benson. Mr. Benson's in the advertising business. And Mr. Wells is the retired Army sergeant I was telling you about."

Harry Wells, dressed in his well-pressed washable suit, looked at John with cold, expressionless eyes. He shook hands briefly. "Benson."

John smiled at him, thinking: alert, in tremendous shape, and with, I'm damn sure, blood that runs as cold as a mountain stream. Don't make any mistakes with him. It won't be good if you do. "Glad to meet you, Sergeant."

"And here are the Garwiths. Allan and Cicely Garwith, I want you to meet Mr. John Benson."

John looked at Allan Garwith carefully. He was dressed in dark gray slacks and a blue and white short-sleeved sport shirt. He had the look of an athlete, John thought: neck straight and muscular, body held with an unconscious grace, his one arm smoothly muscled. He put down a coffee cup to shake hands with John.

John noticed that when he placed it on a saucer on the table it rattled. His handshake was firm, but he would not look at John straight-on.

Cicely smiled at John. She was not pretty, but her smile was. She had a look of freshness, of untroubled innocence, standing beside her husband in a new, inexpensive yellow dress. Garwith said nothing, but Cicely said, "I'm so delighted, Mr. Benson, to make your acquaintance."

"Thank you, Mrs. Garwith," he said, thinking that Garwith looked nervous, certainly. And so did he have the money? Or did Wells have it? Or were they working together? Was that the reason they were traveling this way? Maybe Garwith did pick up the money and Wells knew he got it—figured it out by going back to that lot and rechecking who could have seen that satchel dragged in there. He could even have done that the same day of the robbery, before Ray Hannah got the tail on him. But who knew? Garwith looked like he had it—frightened-looking, as though he were ready to bolt any minute. They knew from the state registration that he bought a pistol. But that didn't really prove anything. One thing was certain. If he spooked one, then he spooked the other. He had to wait until he was sure. Then he would, he knew, have to move very fast or it would be too late. "It's my pleasure, I'm certain."

Miss Kennicot handed him a cup of coffee, giggling coyly, so loudly that it made John's ear hum. He thanked her and looked again at Margaret Moore. The main thing, he thought, was to look calm, wait and be ready. And while he was doing that, concentrate on something to help keep the pressure off. Margaret Moore?

Yes, he thought, she's easy enough to concentrate on so that he didn't give anything away. But how would Maggie look at that? Is that how Maggie would like him to learn to live again?

But Maggie was gone, and there was no use trying to figure any more what she would or wouldn't want him to do. He had to face it alone. It was hard to do, after all the years. To give up on Maggie, even if she was dead. To try to stop worrying about how the boys were doing without her, in Chicago. Very hard. But there was no other way.

So go ahead, he thought. Enjoy that look Margaret Moore was giving you, the fine warmth of it. Who was she, really? Ray Hannah hadn't been able to get much on her, and he would still, he knew, have to worry about where she fitted into this picture. But he was still going to enjoy the pleasure of her presence, as he stood beside Harry Wells, the murdering butcher, smiling with polite respect at everyone as this group prepared to board the waiting station wagon and move on its cross-country way….

The sandwich basket and cookie box were packed, the coffee percolator and the cups that had been used washed, dried and put away. The group moved out to the front lawn. There Harry Wells volunteered to load the bags. John Benson helped him. Allan Garwith, nerves jumping, volunteered to do nothing, but instead stood off to the side, wishing Cicely would stop hanging on to his hand, looking up at him every five seconds like a sick dog. Think of the money, he told himself, and how it'll be pretty soon. He was going to ditch, he knew, and that would be the end of Cicely. Could she tell anything? He'd bought that pistol, packed it in the bag. But she'd taken his word for it when he'd explained that they ought to have it on a trip like this. No. He was certain she didn't suspect anything. She was just being herself, and that was enough against her. Ditch her, he thought, just as soon as he could. So long, Cicely. And good-by.

He turned his head and looked at Margaret Moore standing beside Mrs. Landry as Benson and Wells loaded the baggage. Concentrate on that, he thought, and the nerves'll stop singing. She looks so soft, so capable, so easy—she could stop your nerves from singing, all right.

But the money—he knew he should have mailed it to Cheyenne right away. Friday, not yesterday. But he'd had trouble thinking clearly. His brain kept spinning. How long, he wondered, did it take first-class mail to get to Cheyenne? And why, he thought, hadn't he sent it airmail? He couldn't afford to make any more mistakes like that.

What if the package broke? What if the stupid post office people stuffed the package into the parcel mail by mistake? No, he thought. Don't think about that. It'll be there today. It's got to be. Tomorrow walk up to the general delivery window and it's mine. That's when I ditch. They'll never get me after that.

What was it about that Wells guy loading the bags into the wagon? Something familiar. But, no. Imagination. Caused by the way his brain kept spinning. He had to think clearly, he knew, every minute, every second.

Harry Wells loaded the suitcases into the station wagon carefully. He placed one bag in the rear and then decided it should go in later. He handed it back to John Benson and took another. Benson, he thought, looked out of place somehow. But that wasn't the thing to worry about. The only thing to worry about was that kid. And there it was, the kid's bag. Heavy, he thought, fitting it behind the rear seat. Was that where he'd put it? In that bag? One hundred thousand dollars....

Wells's face became a fraction more grim. Did Garwith think he could get away with it? Picking up Harry Wells's money, the money he'd worked and planned so hard and so carefully to get? Didn't he think he could go back? Figure out that only one place looked out on where that foul-up Tyler crawled to and died? That Garwith had to pick up that bag? That he could trail him out here and watch him go into Grandmother's house? That he could buzz Grandmother on the telephone and ask to talk to her under a phony name and have her ask right away if it was about the ride to San Francisco and then know, all of a sudden, what Garwith was trying to do? That he could come up later, in his own name, and jump on too? Was he as stupid as Tyler? The cops didn't know Harry Wells had failed to get that money. But Garwith knew it, because Garwith had it.

All right, Harry Wells thought. It was better if he was stupid. It was going to make it easier to follow him around, wait for him to make one small mistake, his last.

Oh, he was going to have had it then, Harry Wells thought. Just like that punk kid in that motel. Three dead, and he didn't feel a thing. It was no different than the rotten Heinies dead by his gun, the rotten Gooks dead by his gun. What was the difference? It was the way the world turned around. Some lived, some died.

He was going to get that money, all right. Because he was going to do it right and very damn carefully. And that kid would never know what hit him, once he made his mistake. But where, he asked himself, had the kid put it? In that bag? Right there, at the end of the wagon? He was going to sit on the back seat, he told himself, and lean against that bag and watch that kid. And all he had to do was breathe wrong. Then it was over for him, absolutely over....

When the baggage was loaded, the riders selected their seats. Mrs. Landry got behind the steering wheel and started the engine. Beside her, in the front seat, Miss Kennicot plumped down, clutching her collection of poems, the cover blotched from her perspiring palms, giggling loudly. Behind them, in the next seat, Allan and Cicely Garwith sat on the left side, Margaret Moore on the right.

Cicely took hold of her husband's hand, failing to notice the slight rhythmic tensing of muscles that had begun on the right side of his mouth. Mrs. Moore waited for the station wagon to move, holding her hands loosely in her lap, a calm but alert look of awareness on her face.

Behind them, on the last seat, John Benson sat on the right, Harry Wells on the left. John leaned back, watching that flickering muscle at the side of Allan Garwith's mouth. Directly behind Garwith Harry Wells rested one arm on top of a bag which contained a leather-framed tag strapped to the handle, announcing: *This belongs to Allan Garwith.*

Carefully Mrs. Landry put the car in gear, drove out of the drive and rolled the station wagon very slowly down the quiet residential avenue. Mrs. Moore lit a cigarette, then John Benson also lit one. Miss Kennicot suddenly laughed for no apparent reason. Mrs. Landry said, "Oh, I just wonder if I turned off the stove after we made the coffee?"

Cicely Garwith leaned forward and said in her clear, youthful voice, "I checked as we were going out, Mrs. Landry. The right front burner was on a little, but I turned it off."

"Oh, that was so sweet of you, dear. I always seem to forget something."

"I think everything's all right now," Cicely said positively.

Allan Garwith detached his hand from his wife's and turned to John Benson, saying in a harsh whisper, "Does she figure on getting to Cheyenne tonight? Isn't that what she said?"

John Benson nodded. "That was the plan."

The station wagon moved very slowly onto Lodge Boulevard and started west, toward the outskirts of town. Allan Garwith turned his head impatiently forward. Cicely smiled at him worshipfully and reached for his hand again. He moved it out of her reach.

Miss Kennicot switched around in her seat, suddenly laughing again. "Isn't this fun, everyone?"

Allan Garwith looked at her with thin eyes and then stared disgustedly out of the window to his left, that muscle moving steadily beside his mouth.

At the city limits the flat brown prairie fields stretched ahead. The land was almost treeless, and the highway, narrowing to two lanes, moved in a straight line ahead, the flatness creating the perspective of a painting. Faint mirages glimmered ahead on the blacktop. The telephone poles and wires running down on either side of the highway added to the sharp look of perspective.

"Our ship of adventure!" Miss Kennicot shouted. "'She starts—she moves—she seems to feel the thrill of life along her keel.' Longfellow!"

"I'll Longfellow her right in her mouth," Allan Garwith whispered to

Cicely. Cicely caught his hand and pressed it tightly, smiling brightly at Miss Kennicot.

As Mrs. Landry drove past the white sign marking the outer edge of Loma City she said, "All right! Here we go now!"

"Away and away!" Miss Kennicot yelled.

"Let's," said Mrs. Landry joyfully, "everybody sing: Altogether now. California, here we come…!" Her voice lifted in lusty off-key exuberance. She suddenly floored the gas pedal.

The station wagon lifted its nose and leaped down the highway. Mrs. Landry removed one hand from the steering wheel and waved it in time to her singing, now joined by Miss Kennicot. The speedometer needle moved to seventy. Mrs. Landry did not remove her foot. Allan Garwith paled, staring straight ahead at an old truck lumbering ahead of them. In the distance there was the dark form of a car approaching.

"Everybody now!" Mrs. Landry shouted, waving her free hand, as Miss Kennicot, singing lustily, turned toward the front again. Miss Kennicot finally realized the mounting speed. Her voice cracked. She laughed more loudly than before, then started singing again, grabbing the front edge of her seat tightly.

Harry Wells blinked once, then sat motionless, observing the truck ahead and the car they were about to meet. An eyebrow arched faintly above Margaret Moore's eye, as she watched the speedometer move up to eighty. John Benson rubbed his chin, staring down the highway.

Mrs. Landry suddenly one-handed a slight turn on the steering wheel, singing joyfully with the nowyelling Miss Kennicot. "California, here we come …" Miss Kennicot emphasized the word as though hit in the back with ice water, just as Mrs. Landry shot around the ancient truck and snapped back in her own lane inches ahead of smashing head-on into the approaching car, whose angry horn could be heard only for a brief moment. Then they were sailing down the highway, the truck far behind them, the speedometer needle quivering just under ninety.

"Now don't be bashful!" Mrs. Landry shouted, while Miss Kennicot went into a steady giggling, trying to unloosen her fingers from the seat. "California, here we come …!"

# Chapter Seven

The Wyoming state line behind them, John Benson checked his watch as they whipped over the last miles approaching Cheyenne. It was 4:20. They would be in Cheyenne by 4:30, and Mrs. Landry, who had gaily waved away offers to relieve her at the wheel, had managed to average an even seventy miles an hour the entire distance.

John shifted in his seat, looking out at the changing countryside. They had swept swiftly over the flat plains, slowing only to observe the speed limits of the small prairie towns spread far apart through the corn and wheat country. Yellow goldenrod and sunflowers had livened the otherwise dry-looking brown fields. They had moved through innumerable weary-faced small agricultural towns with their invariable water towers and grain elevators; the clusters of white frame houses looking lonely to the stranger's eye as they lay another season beneath the hot, blinding sun; the service stations cluttered and uninviting on the edges of the highway; the ever-present café signs looming large and unmistakable and which, without fail, would advertise a building long closed, its windows boarded with gray lumber, a screen door hanging awry on rusty hinges, as a dog or cat ambled in front of it, semi-numbed from the beating of the white-hot sun.

Now the rolling grazing hills had begun, clear of everything but the brown pasture grass, supporting only the lean western cattle and the Black Hills coyote and rattlesnake. Traversing the Bad Lands, they had risen from the low elevation of Loma City to an altitude of 6,000 feet, as they now moved onto the eastern slope of the Rockies. The air was cooler. The sun seemed less glaring as the bluish dark shadows lengthened along the weathered faces of the yellow buttes.

During the past seven hours Mrs. Landry and Miss Kennicot had led a series of endeavors intended to entertain the occupants of the hurtling station wagon. Mostly the endeavors had been songs, sung primarily by the women. When he could hear over Miss Kennicot's blasting contralto, John Benson had discovered that Margaret Moore owned a low, husky singing voice that might have, professionally trained, served well in a small supper club. The selection of songs, however (they had sung "Friends" seventeen times), was not a good one for Mrs. Moore. Rather it was Cicely Garwith who had, even beneath the competition of Miss Kennicot's volume, demonstrated a high, beautiful singing voice notable for its absolute pitch. John had joined with a baritone on a few selections.

Neither Harry Wells nor Allan Garwith had made the attempt.

Between songs Miss Kennicot had led in games. They had played Twenty Questions from the edge of the Loess Plains through the Sand Hills to the Bad Land buttes. In this Allan Garwith had participated but once. After two hundred miles, he'd seemed to be able to remove his eyes from the road, finally immune, John thought, to Mrs. Landry's rampaging speed. He had admitted to the others that he was thinking of a subject. When the twenty questions had been exhausted, failing to reveal the answer, he had announced in a tight, bitter voice that he was thinking of an arthritic bang-tailed Mexican monkey vaccinated against yellow jaundice.

There had been a pause. Then everyone but Harry Wells had laughed. After that Allan Garwith had fallen into an oblique silence, staring grimly out of his window.

They had also played games which involved seeing how many words could be constructed out of the letters in Constantinople (won by Miss Kennicot); who could name all the capitals of the United States (again won by Miss Kennicot), and a version of charades that had been limited by the cramped positions of everyone in the car.

This last had been dominated by Mrs. Landry's performance. At a speed of seventy-nine miles an hour, she had lifted her hands from the steering wheel and pressed her elbows against it to maintain control. She had put a finger outside either eye, stretching the skin outward and upward, speaking in high Oriental-sounding gibberish. John Benson had instantly guessed that she was a World War II Jap pilot committing harakiri in a dive bomber. The guess was absolutely correct, and it fortunately got Mrs. Landry's hands back on the wheel. Everyone, including Harry Wells, agreed that it was a dramatic performance.

Now they were approaching the outskirts of Cheyenne, the breadth of Wyoming ahead of them with its two ranges of the Rocky Mountains lifting on either side of the blue-purple sagebrush flat of the Great Divide Basin.

Mrs. Landry seemed not even faintly weary from the long drive. But Miss Kennicot had, at the ceasing of the games and songs, instantly dropped her head back and fallen soundly asleep, her mouth dropping open, issuing slight snoring sounds. During this period John Benson had talked to Margaret Moore of the countryside. Cicely Garwith had nestled her head against the side of her silent, withdrawn husband. Harry Wells had remained equally silent, sitting very straight on his portion of the rear seat.

But now, as they approached Cheyenne, there was a faint stirring. Miss

Kennicot had awakened, startled that she had fallen asleep; she began rearranging her hair, laughing. John Benson carefully noted that Allan Garwith seemed to tense again, straightening in his seat, forcing his wife's head away from him by shifting his wife's shoulder almost rudely. He's nervous, all right, John Benson thought—really nervous.

And as Allan Garwith straightened, Harry Wells, John noted, also stiffened, sitting at even more rigid attention, his eyes staring steadily at the back of Allan Garwith's head. John had talked to him only sparingly during the trip, because of the economy of Wells's responses; but he decided to try again:

"You say you're going to look around the San Francisco area for a job, Sergeant?" He noted Wells's quick swing of head, the wary look going into his eyes. "It's all right if I call you Sergeant, isn't it? Even if you've retired?"

"Yeah, that's all right, Benson." He nodded faintly. "Look around for something to do. They don't retire sergeants on generals' pay, you know."

"I guess not," John said. "You like it out there?"

"I like it out there."

"Were you stationed around San Francisco?"

"Close as I got was Camp Roberts, down the coast. But I was through San Francisco when I went out, then came back from Japan."

The facts were right, according to Ray Hannah's report. And that was what was going to be tough about this, John thought. Harry Wells was simply playing himself. He had to hide only one deviation from the norm—killing one kid with his hands, getting another killed by talking him into that robbery, gunning down a guard, and trying to get away with a hundred thousand dollars.

That was one hell of a deviation, John thought, but that still was all Wells had to cover—one day of wanton destruction. If he were a con with a history, it would be far more simple. His habits would be formed, and they would know them. You could trip him somewhere along the way. But Harry Wells was a one-shot artist. It was going to be very tough to find a weakness.

"Ever been in Cheyenne?" he asked.

"Through it on a train, but that's all."

They were inside the city limits. The town was small, old and undistinguished looking, despite the grandeur of the surrounding countryside.

"It doesn't look like I've missed anything," Wells said and turned his head away. John gave up the conversation.

In a moment Mrs. Landry was driving the station wagon down the center of the business section. John watched Allan Garwith remain very alertly straight. That muscle beside the corner of his mouth was working again.

Mrs. Landry said, "Well, I'm just so surprised! I thought Cheyenne was a much bigger city. I don't even see any cowboys, does anybody else?"

Miss Kennicot, fully awake now, said, "'Appearances are very deceitful.' Le Sage, of course. I looked up Cheyenne in our historical section at the museum just two days ago. At the last printed census it had a population of thirty-one thousand, nine hundred and thirty-five. It is, of course, the capital of Wyoming. It was selected as the Union Pacific Railroad division point in eighteen sixty-seven. Cattle ranching and gold started its growth in the eighteen seventies. And it's a center for sheep and cattle. So there ought to be some cowboys around somewhere. Isn't that terribly interesting?"

"Listen," Allan Garwith said, speaking for the first time since he'd revealed his monkey subject during the Twenty-Questions game, "where are we going to stay in this town?"

"Well," Miss Kennicot said, digging into her very large white purse, "now just a minute. I took the trouble of asking the three A's to give me their catalogue on hotels and motels before we left. The three A's are very good to get recommendations from, doesn't everybody think? I can read you the whole list."

Allan Garwith, John saw, looked annoyed, almost desperate. Mrs. Landry had stopped the car now, near the center of the downtown section. There was a billiard parlor ahead. A trio of young men in wash-bleached Levis and faded cotton plaid shirts strolled by, their eyes stopping on Margaret Moore. One of them paused to put a brown cigarette between his lips, his eyes never leaving her.

"Any place is all right with me," Allan Garwith said. The man with the brown cigarette moved on. "How about that hotel over there?"

The hotel he indicated was visible over the tops of the low business buildings. There was a sign across its top that read, *Hotel Plateau.*

"Let's see," Miss Kennicot said, running her finger down the list of hotels. "Now a friend of mine, Alice Gregson—she runs a little book store out on the west edge of Loma City—told me about a darling motel in Laramie, simply darling, where the rates are just unbelievably low for how nice it is. But of course Laramie is around another sixty miles, I think, and here we are in Cheyenne." She frowned studiedly, as she searched for the listing of the Hotel Plateau. Then she said, "Oh, here it is! Isn't that nice? It's approved by the three A's. Of course it is. Oh, but heavens! Look at those rates! Oh, I just don't know about that!"

John Benson studied Allan Garwith's reaction. Garwith twisted in his seat angrily. "It doesn't make any difference to me. I'm just getting tired of riding."

"Well, but those rates are *very* strong," Miss Kennicot said. "Why, I believe that place in Laramie Alice mentioned—the Sleep Tight Motel—is down at least three or four dollars over this one. Of course, that looks like a very nice and new hotel over there. But—"

"Well, now," Mrs. Landry said brightly, "I'm just feeling fit as could be. If Laramie's only another sixty miles or so, maybe we could just shoot on and stay in that nice motel there. What does everybody think about that? Mrs. Moore?"

Mrs. Moore shrugged pleasantly. "Whatever you like, Mrs. Landry. It's quite all right with me."

John Benson was certain Allan Garwith's face had paled. Harry Wells, he noticed, continued to watch Garwith carefully.

"Whatever everybody else wants to do," Cicely Garwith said politely, "that's what Allan and I want to do."

Garwith turned his head, looking at her with angry eyes, that muscle shivering beside his mouth.

"Mr. Benson?" Mrs. Landry said.

John Benson spread his hands. "Anything's all right with me. If we go on to Laramie, though, we've cut that much more off the journey. I wouldn't mind going on." He watched Allan Garwith intently.

Allan Garwith suddenly bent forward, hugging his one arm to his middle. He made a short gasping sound, then started moaning. Cicely at once put her arms around him, fright going into her eyes.

"Oh, goodness!" Mrs. Landry said. "What's the matter?"

Garwith shook his head back and forth. "Pain—just a sudden pain ..."

Mrs. Moore moved out of her seat swiftly, saying to Cicely, "Let him stretch out, Mrs. Garwith."

In a moment Allan Garwith was lying along the second seat, Cicely hovering worriedly above him. Mrs. Moore put her hand on his forehead, looking at him carefully.

"I'll just bet it's appendicitis!" Miss Kennicot yelled.

"Is the pain severe?" Mrs. Moore asked.

"Yeah," Garwith managed.

"Where you've got your hand?"

"Where I've got my hand." He gasped again.

"We'd better get him to a doctor," Mrs. Moore said.

"I'll ask somebody where the closest hospital is," John Benson said, and started to open a back door.

"Just a minute," Allan Garwith said. "It's easing up."

John Benson paused, looking at him. Then he looked at Harry Wells, whose eyes had narrowed faintly as he studied Garwith.

"It's going away," Allan Garwith managed. "I don't know—just tired, I guess. I'll be all right."

"Are you sure?" Mrs. Moore asked.

"Yeah. But I'm still kind of weak."

"I'd better find out about a doctor anyway," John Benson said.

"No, it's all right now," Garwith insisted. "Just a little weak, that's all. I'll be all right."

"Well," Mrs. Landry said, "I guess we surely shouldn't drive any more today. We'd just better stay right here in Cheyenne. Maybe we can find something besides that hotel over there. But I think that poor boy ought to get into bed and rest."

"Maybe," Cicely Garwith said worriedly, "we should just go to the nearest place." She blinked. "Quickly."

"Of course," Mrs. Landry said definitely, and drove directly to the large, new Hotel Plateau, while Miss Kennicot looked at the rates again. Miss Kennicot looked back at Allan Garwith, worriedly, then stuffed the AAA listing into her purse in a pronounced motion, obviously forcing away thoughts of what the Plateau was going to do to her budget.

The lobby of the Hotel Plateau was light, cheerful and air-conditioned. Checking in was far smoother than John Benson had expected. Miss Kennicot's worries about higher rates seemed to dissolve when she and Mrs. Landry decided to take a room together. Mrs. Moore preferred a room of her own, as did Harry Wells. Mrs. Landry explained to the desk clerk in her familiar chatting fashion that Allan Garwith had suffered an attack of something or other, and the clerk had instantly suggested that it had been the altitude. Allan Garwith had quickly nodded, as though relieved to find the source of his trouble. Cicely had also looked relieved. Mrs. Landry, apparently overjoyed with the simplicity of the explanation, had gone on to explain to the room clerk that the Garwiths were newly married. The clerk registered the Garwiths first, so that they could retire quickly to their room, while Cicely blushed and Miss Kennicot went into a peal of laughter, looking at John Benson coyly.

They were all assigned to the fourth floor. John followed the bellboy into his room, noting that the Garwiths were two doors down, Harry Wells four. Mrs. Landry, Miss Kennicot and Mrs. Moore were on the opposite side of the hall. John tipped the bellboy, examining the room quickly. It was small but carefully arranged and newly furnished.

When the bellboy had gone, John waited beside the door. After a few minutes he heard a door down the hall opening and closing. He walked to the telephone and got the desk. "Manager, please."

In a moment a nasal-sounding voice said, "Yes? Mr. Brander speaking."

"This is John Benson. Room four-oh-eight. I just checked in."

"Yes, Mr. Benson. Is anything wrong?"

"The plumbing seems to be in trouble up here."

"The plumbing?"

"That's right, Mr. Brander. I'd like you to come up and look at it."

"What is it? A worn washer? I can send our maintenance man up immediately—"

"It's more serious than that, Mr. Brander. I don't want your maintenance man. I want you to come up personally, at once."

"Well, but I—"

"Now," John said, and hung up. He walked to the window. His room faced the street bordering the front of the hotel. He saw Harry Wells step to the curb and stand there, unmoving. He picked up the telephone again, opening his wallet with his free hand and looking at one of the numbers written in pencil on a business card announcing his own name and his advertising agency in Lafayette, Indiana. He gave the number to the PBX operator and in a moment heard a woman's voice saying, "Hello?" A baby was crying behind her.

"Is Mr. Harnet there, please?"

"Yes, I'll call him."

The baby stopped crying. A man's voice sounded: "Yes?"

"Mr. Harnet, this is John Benson. I stopped in Loma City for a few days on my way west to see a friend, and I met Don Harkert. He said he was an old friend of yours. When I told him I'd be going through Cheyenne, he asked me to give you a ring, to send on his regards."

"Well, that's very nice. Yes, Don and I are old friends. How is he?"

"Very good. He says he hopes to get over here this fall and do some hunting. Jackson Hole was all he could talk about."

"Well, we'll be glad to see him. How are you traveling, Mr. Benson?"

"Car. I'm riding with several others."

"I see. Where are you staying?"

"The Plateau."

"Well, listen. Couldn't you drop over this evening, Mr. Benson? How about dinner? We could—"

"Thanks very much, Mr. Harnet. I'm afraid not."

"Well, anyway, I'm glad to hear Don's fine and that he's coming along this fall. Going to Los Angeles, Mr. Benson?"

"San Francisco. Don tells me you're in the florist business. How's business?"

"Excellent, Mr. Benson."

"I'm glad to hear it. Some day I'd like to try my luck at Jackson Hole myself."

"I hope you will, Mr. Benson."

"Good-by, Mr. Harnet."

"Thanks for calling, Mr. Benson."

He hung up and looked out the window, noting that Harry Wells was still standing at the curb, motionless, watching the occasional cars passing. The neighborhood was quiet. A small park was across the street, with a fountain in the center and green benches along the diagonal walks. Beyond that were old but neat frame houses.

What, John thought, am I doing here? And why isn't Maggie here with me?

He shook his head, forcing himself back to reality. Maggie's dead, he thought; whip yourself with that fact until you bleed enough to know it, once and for all. Strange city, strange people all around, everything you've gotten used to, grown to love, either smashed or somewhere else. You've got to start over. There's no other way.

He thought of telephoning the boys in Chicago. But he gave the thought up quickly. One thing he was sure of: Garwith had faked his attack. And that meant that he'd wanted to stop in Cheyenne for a definite reason. Whether or not this hotel, the Plateau, had anything to do with it was the problem. If it did, then he could not allow himself to telephone his sons in Chicago, because they might just very well innocently give something away, something that could be picked up on the switchboard. And for the same reason he had not done so with the call to Harnet a few moments ago, he did not want to go to a public booth—with a telephone in his room, it might look suspicious. And he could not afford to alert either Garwith or Harry Wells. Or, in fact, Margaret Moore, if she were possibly mixed up in this some way.

There was a tap at his door. He opened it. Margaret Moore stood smiling at him.

"Well," he said. "Hello."

She nodded. "Nice room, John?"

"Very nice, Margaret. Come in?" He looked down the hall and saw the elevator doors open. A small man in a white linen suit and brilliant blue tie stepped out, and moved with a quick, nervous stride down the hall.

Margaret Moore followed the direction of his eyes. "I didn't stop to invite myself in, John. I simply wanted to induce you to invite me downstairs for a cup of coffee. That could lead to dinner. I'm not particularly backward, if you haven't guessed."

He smiled. "I've always hated backward people. Sure. I'd like to."

The man in the white suit and brilliant blue tie arrived. He had wispy gray hair and a look of disbelieving hurt in his eyes. "Mr. Benson," he announced, "I'm Mr. Brander, the manager of the Plateau, and I find this very distressing."

John looked at Mrs. Moore. "I'm having a little trouble with the plumbing."

"Really," Mrs. Moore said.

"What," Mr. Brander said, "could possibly be wrong with the plumbing? We simply don't hire out our rooms in a state of disrepair. We—"

"I'll show you in a moment," John said to him. Then to Mrs. Moore: "Could you wait a moment in your room for me, Margaret? I'll pick you up just as soon as we get this straightened out."

"This truly dismays me," Mr. Brander said. "I don't know when one of our customers has insisted that I, as manager of this hotel, come up to check faulty plumbing. We've just never had any plumbing problems at the Plateau."

"All right," Mrs. Moore said, nodding, looking at Mr. Brander curiously. "Fine, John." She crossed the hall. John shut the door gently as Mr. Brander strode into the bathroom.

"Now," Mr. Brander called in his hurt voice, "what is it here that's gone wrong?"

"Mr. Brander," John said, "come back, will you?"

Mr. Brander came back into the room, staring at John haughtily. "This is *most* peculiar, Mr. Benson. I—"

"Just a moment, Mr. Brander." John stepped to the suitcase rack and opened one of his bags. Carefully he pulled the lining open at one side. He removed a card and handed it to Mr. Brander. Mr. Brander examined it, then looked up blinking. "FBI."

"That's right," John said, and replaced the card, shutting the bag.

"Well," Mr. Brander said nervously. "We wouldn't want the plumbing defective for anyone, Mr. Benson. Especially for the FBI. If you'll just tell me—"

"The plumbing's fine, Mr. Brander."

"It is?" Mr. Brander said, blinking. "Well, but—"

"I wanted to talk to you, Mr. Brander. Sit down, won't you?"

"Oh," Mr. Brander said. He stood there for a moment, nodding, then suddenly sat down. "Oh, I see." He nodded again. "I see it all now! My goodness! What's gone wrong, Mr. Benson?"

"How long have you been managing this hotel, Mr. Brander?"

"Twenty-two years, Mr. Benson. That is an absolute accurate statement. It was twenty-two years day before yesterday."

"This looks like quite a new hotel."

"We moved in here five years ago. Before that we were two blocks down. But it was always the Hotel Plateau. And I've managed it without serious trouble for twenty-two years. I just hope nothing's gone wrong now to destroy the reputation I've worked so hard to build up. This hotel is owned by Mr. Emil Crabbe, one of Wyoming's principal cattle men. I've always been able to look Mr. Crabbe straight in the eye because I've run the hotel as conscientiously as I know how. I'm married, Mr. Benson, to a wonderful girl I met in nineteen thirty-five right here in Cheyenne, and she's given me two fine boys, one of whom is now a doctor in Phoenix, Arizona, the other of whom is a lawyer in Pasadena, California. I am the grandfather of seven boys and girls. I take pride in my life, Mr. Benson. I just hope nothing has gone seriously wrong."

John examined him closely, then smiled. "I'm sure it hasn't as far as you're concerned, Mr. Brander. All I want is your co-operation."

"By golly, you'll get that, Mr. Benson."

"Good. Now, who runs your PBX board?"

"Alice Begley. Same fine woman who's run it for the past fifteen years."

"You recommend her character, Mr. Brander?"

"I'd put my life on it."

"And your desk clerks?"

"Joe Curry, Albert Thompson. I've known them both as long as I've lived in Cheyenne, which is all of my life."

"The rest of your employees?"

"There isn't anyone in this hotel who has less than ten years of service, Mr. Benson. Except Albert Thompson's son. He's sixteen and only works for us summers."

"All right. Fine."

"What is it, Mr. Benson? What is it all about?"

"Just a routine check, Mr. Brander. That's all I can tell you. This is, of course, a private conversation."

"Yes, sir. I understand that. How about my wife? Can I tell my wife?"

"It you make sure it's just going that far."

"I promise."

"All right. Now all I'd like, Mr. Brander, is that you tell me anything that goes on that might seem unusual concerning any of the people I'm riding with. Again—this has got to be kept just between you and me. You came up here to check the plumbing, nothing more. If you discover anything—and you are positive you can trust your PBX operator or whoever's on the switchboard—then call me when I'm in my room. Your Miss Begley doesn't work around the clock, does she?"

"No, sir. Daytimes is all. Albert takes over both the desk and the board after eight o'clock. But you can trust everybody in this hotel, including Albert—I guarantee it. Just anything unusual at all?"

"That's right, Mr. Brander. Anything at all unusual between now and the time we leave, which will be tomorrow morning."

Mr. Brander stood up, looking determined. "You can count on me, sir."

"I'm sure I can, and I thank you very much. You've been very kind and co-operative."

"Yes, sir," Mr. Brander said, moving to the door. He stopped, looking quite serious. "I, of course, don't know what you're going after, Mr. Benson. I suppose it's murdering, thieving, dope, something like that. But I'll tell you I'm relieved to find out there isn't anything wrong with the Hotel Plateau's plumbing."

"I'm sure," John said, "that the Plateau's plumbing is undoubtedly in superb condition, Mr. Brander."

"I feel I can breathe again," Mr. Brander said, and disappeared.

John stepped to the window and looked out as the last light of the day escaped a dimming Cheyenne. Harry Wells was still standing below, unmoving, a cigarette between his lips, the faint breeze picking up the smoke and curling it away from him. John looked across the street at the park. A blue Chevrolet came to a stop on the opposite side of the block. A man in a light gray suit and matching straw hat got out, a newspaper under his arm, and strolled into the park. He stopped and sat down on a bench and opened the newspaper.

All right, John thought. That's taken care of.

He washed his hands, brushed his hair, then stepped out into the hall and walked to Margaret Moore's door. He'd done all he could do for the moment. Until tomorrow morning it would be up to either Allan Garwith or Harry Wells, or both, to do something. Until then all he had to do was wait, keep calm, and be ready to act if he had to. Right now he could afford to concentrate on Margaret Moore. And that, he thought, knocking lightly on the door of her room, remembering the look in her eyes when she'd come straightforwardly to his room, was not going to be difficult.

# Chapter Eight

Harry Wells finished his cigarette, standing beside the street running in front of the hotel. The breeze was definitely cooling now. Wells was grateful for that. When he was tense, he sweated. And that took the creases out of things, clammed up his clothing. He liked things crisp and fresh and well-pressed. Well, he thought, when he got his hands on that money, he was going to pick some place in this world where it was cool all of the time.

He turned, looking up at the fourth floor. He would like to kick Garwith's door down and walk in and throttle him just like he had that kid in the motel back in Loma City. But he couldn't do it. He had to wait until Garwith made a slip. He lifted a hand and rubbed a cheek angrily. He was getting tired. He hadn't really slept since this thing started. And now he certainly couldn't relax. What was he going to do next?

There was a small dull ache in the back of his head. That always happened when he was perplexed and couldn't immediately figure out what to do. He had to keep track of that guy, every minute. He was certain Garwith didn't slightly suspect who he was. But Garwith just might pick up and leave, any time. He couldn't afford to lose him.

But what to do? The small ache in his head was annoying, as he tried to sort out the possibilities. He couldn't stand here all night.

He turned around, looking up the broad steps at the hotel. He frowned a little, then got his wallet from his hip pocket and removed a ten-dollar bill.

He walked into the lobby, the bill folded in his left hand. He stopped at the desk, trying to make his brain work, so that he could do this right.

The man behind the desk was a different clerk than the one who had registered them. He was tall, massive-shouldered, with a weak, stolid face. He stood in stoop-shouldered dignity, looking as though he had handled this job long enough that he no longer had to apologize for anything in this world.

"You the clerk for the night shift?" Wells asked.

"Yes, sir."

"Listen, how would you like to make yourself ten bucks?" He looked around. The lobby was empty.

"You're with the large party that just checked in?"

"I'm riding with them. How about it?"

The clerk's eyes had narrowed slightly. There was a very faint twitching of his nose. "I think you misunderstand this hotel, sir. We have been in business, honorably, for a good number of years now."

"Listen," Wells said. "I don't care how long you've been in business."

"I'm afraid I can't help you. This is definitely not that kind of hotel. I wouldn't consider involving myself."

Wells blinked, finally understanding. "I'm not talking about that." He shook his head angrily. "This is something personal between me and one of the people I'm riding with." He nodded, growing more positive with each second that he had figured this out right. "Did you see that guy who's got one arm?"

"I'm afraid not, sir," the clerk said, still suspicious and haughty.

"Well, that's all you have to know. He's got one arm. You can't miss him, even if you're half asleep."

"I guarantee you, sir," the clerk said, eyes flashing, "that I'm never half asleep on this job."

"All right. Only it's the guy with one arm. Now. He borrowed some money from me." His nerves jumped a little, when he said that. Then he felt calm again. This was the way to handle it, he was sure of it. "He borrowed five hundred bucks. I somehow got the feeling I might have made a mistake. Do you follow me?"

The clerk shook his head, frowning. "I'm afraid not, sir."

"I don't want him running out on me with that five hundred. It's worth ten bucks to me to see he doesn't. Now I'm tired. I'd like to get some sleep. So—I give you ten bucks. Put it on the counter for you just like this. And I go up and go to bed and get myself some sleep. You call me if the guy with one arm comes down. You see what I mean?"

The clerk was nodding, at last. "Well, now that's quite another matter. I thought at first—"

"I know what you thought. How about it?"

"Of course," the clerk said, putting his hand on the ten-dollar bill. "We're always happy, at the Plateau, to be of any reasonable and honest service that we can."

"All right," Wells said. "One thing more. Don't tell anybody about this. The guy's got a decent wife. I don't trust him, but his wife's okay, see? So I got to ride with these people to the Coast. So I don't want to get people upset thinking I'm afraid maybe that one-armed guy would run off with that money he owes me. Follow?"

"Now," the clerk nodded, "I follow you perfectly." He tucked the bill carefully into the breast pocket of his suit.

"This is just between you and me," Wells said. "If it gets any other way, I'm not going to like it."

"Of course not, sir. You may rest assured."

"I hope so," Wells said. "Otherwise I'll come down here and break your neck with my bare hands."

The clerk blinked, realizing the intensity with which Wells had spoken his last words to him. Then Wells made a brisk about-face and walked to the elevator. In a few moments he was in his room.

There, he considered it and was positive he'd handled this right. Relaxing a little, finally, he was more weary than ever. He looked at his watch and realized he hadn't eaten. But he was tired, tired....

There was a knock on his door. He opened it carefully. Mrs. Landry stood in the hall.

"Hello, Mr. Wells!" she said brightly. "How is your room? All right?"

"What?" Wells said. "Oh, yeah. It's all right."

"That's wonderful! I'm so glad to hear it. What do you plan for dinner, Mr. Wells? I'm just out gathering up those who want to go to dinner together. Miss Kennicot's freshening up, and I thought I'd go around and ask everyone. I haven't asked the Garwiths, you understand. I felt so sorry for that poor boy. But I'll just have to leave it up to them if they want to have dinner with any of the rest of us. How about you, Mr. Wells? Would you like to join us somewhere?"

"I'm a little tired. I'm just going to bed." And how was he going to explain that, he thought, if the clerk downstairs told him Garwith and his wife had gone out, say for dinner, and he'd have to follow them? Why didn't the old lady mind her own business? They ought to throw a net over both her and that Kennicot woman. "I think I'll just skip dinner. I'm just not hungry right now."

"Oh, you do look tired, Mr. Wells. But it isn't good to skip your dinner. An Army man like you? I've heard how Army people eat lots and lots of good food." She snapped plump fingers. "Of course—I just thought of it. We didn't eat all of those sandwiches I had packed. They won't last for tomorrow. Now you just wait a minute. I'll get those sandwiches for you."

"Mrs. Landry—" Wells began.

"No argument, Mr. Wells. I'll just be a minute."

She hurried down the hall and disappeared into the room she shared with Miss Kennicot. As the door opened and shut, he could hear Miss Kennicot singing lustily. He closed his eyes and swore silently. Then Mrs. Landry reappeared, carrying a basket. She handed it to him, patting his hand. "Now, you just take that, Mr. Wells. You just go into your room and eat those sandwiches and then get yourself a nice long rest. We won't be leaving until eight o'clock tomorrow morning, remember, and I'll bet that's late in the day for a good Army man. Sleep tight, Mr. Wells. Pleasant dreams."

Wells stepped back into his room. He put the basket on the bed angrily. Christ, he thought. The damn stupid woman.

His single suitcase was resting on the rack at the foot of the bed. He opened it and looked at it carefully. Socks had been rolled into pairs, the top of one fitted around the whole to make a neat bundle. The bundles were carefully lined in a tight row. White shorts and T-shirts had been similarly rolled and fitted in absolute rows. Everything in that bag was precisely placed, including his gun, and Harry Wells was ready for a complete showdown inspection any second. The iron, the item that severely weighted the bag, was at the back end of the bag. He removed it and placed it on the top of a bureau. Then he took out a thick, browned length of heavy cloth that he used to place over whatever surface he used for his pressing.

He removed his billfold, Zippo lighter, keys and change from his pockets, then took off his suit and shirt and underwear, standing in lean, bare hardness. He hung the suit in the closet. He wouldn't, he thought, do any pressing until tomorrow, so he would be leaving here with everything in its best shape.

He carried his shirt and underwear into the bath and filled the washbasin with lukewarm water, to let the clothing soak. Then he returned to his suitcase and removed a large bar of Ivory soap; you couldn't beat Ivory, he'd decided a long time ago, for the suds. Finally he took out a clean T-shirt and a pair of shorts and placed them carefully on the bag. Before he snapped the bag shut, he looked at the gold-framed picture he'd placed on the bottom of the bag. He took it out, careful to rearrange the socks he'd disturbed.

It was a picture of himself in khakis faded almost white from the sun and constant washing; there was a short strip of neatly laced leggings beneath the bloused trousers, and his hair was clipped neatly at the temples. He'd looked very lanky, brown and bone-young. He'd been a staff sergeant then, and you could see the stripes on the sleeve the girl was holding with one possessive hand. The girl was small, dark, with high cheekbones and large, animal-bright eyes; she had long black hair and wore a thin dress that showed the good lift of her breasts, the thick, ripe set of her hips. The picture had been taken in Panama in 1943.

He placed the picture on the bureau and returned to the bath, to hand-scrub the clothing in the sink. A long time ago, Panama and Pooli. Pooli—what a name. But she'd been fine. Part French, part Chinese, part Spanish, part Indian—the best of all of those bloods. Panama had been no good otherwise. Stinking hot, and he'd been nervous down there in an RA garrison, drinking PX beer and local rum, while the war got into a full-scale operation.

But there'd been Pooli, eager, soft, lazy, spitting, seductive, abandoned, loving, all wrapped up into one little French-Chinese-Spanish-Indian girl.

How long had it been? Too long. She'd written him some pathetic letters in horrible grammar that had made even him wince. He'd never answered them. All he had to do was think of that stinking heat down there, and he didn't even want to write to her. But she'd been the best woman he'd ever had, worth that fight he'd had in the beginning to get her.

He paused, soapy white shirt in hand, and remembered that Panamanian bar, dancing with Pooli, and that sergeant from another battalion who'd come up and announced Pooli was his and had been for six months. His eyes narrowed a little, as he remembered how they'd gone at it, all over that bar. How the sergeant, a tall, blond, blue-eyed, mean son of a bitch from New Jersey, had finally pulled a knife.

He'd really had to go for him then, smashing the bastard's head with a bottle, finally slamming him against the railing of the bar. They carried him out of there. Dead. And he'd been ultimately glad for that knife, because the knife made it self-defense on his part. The Army hadn't wanted trouble down there, and the bastard from New Jersey had a reputation for trouble. They hadn't even put it on his record, let alone shaved his stripes.

He shrugged, dipping his shirt. Long time ago. But when he got this done, got the money from Garwith, he might go down and see how fat Pooli had gotten, how many illegitimate kids she had running around after her.

But, he thought, probably not. Too hot down there, even for a short visit. No, he was going where it was cool, where you could put on clean clothes and have them stay neat and fresh and well-pressed for hours. Alaska maybe. That sounded all right. Iceland, Norway, Sweden. Anywhere where you didn't sweat all of the time.

When he'd washed his clothes, he showered for twenty minutes, scrubbing and rinsing himself steadily. He stretched a cord from his bag between two chairs near a window and hung the clothes to dry. They would be just right for pressing in the morning, he thought.

Then he sat down on the bed in fresh shorts and T-shirt and put a cigarette between his lips, looking disdainfully at the basket containing the sandwiches. He snapped the Zippo lighter. It failed to light. He looked at it carefully.

He tried again, frowning. It failed again. Slowly he took it apart. The flint was all right. But he could see that the fluid was running out. He got the fluid can from his bag and soaked the cotton. He could see, because the fluid had run low, that the wick had burned down. But he didn't have another wick.

He reassembled the lighter, attempting to lift the wick slightly, and tried once again. It sparked, but it wouldn't light. He tried it over and over, a look of stubborn concentration in his eyes, a faint ache starting at the back of his head once more.

He took the lighter apart again, absently taking a sandwich from the basket beside him. He ate the sandwich. Then assembled the lighter and tried again. It wouldn't work. He took it apart again, oblivious of time. He worked for forty minutes, consuming the sandwiches, all of them, without realizing he had. Still the lighter wouldn't work.

That impassive look of stubborn concentration never left his eyes. He assembled and reassembled the lighter, never working faster or slower than he had the first time. Finally he realized an hour had gone by. He placed the lighter on the night stand and turned out the lights and lay back in bed. He would have to get a wick somewhere tomorrow.

He closed his eyes; then, after a few minutes, he sat up and switched on the lights again. He picked up the lighter and took it apart again.

He looked very much as he had when he'd been sitting on his bunk one summer evening at Fort Dix in 1944, just before his division shipped overseas into combat. Then he'd been perplexed with a faulty ejector spring on his carbine. The rifle needed a new spring. He could have walked over to the supply room and gotten a new one. But instead he attempted to make the old one work. He'd repeatedly taken apart and reassembled the rifle's mechanism, the same look in his eyes as he had now.

A twenty-year-old PFC named Brown, whose mother was dying in Biloxi, had sat and watched him. He watched him take apart and put together that mechanism fifty times. Brown, who had been refused an emergency furlough to watch his mother die because he'd already had one a month before when they thought she was going to die and hadn't, kept opening and closing his hands as though wanting to help. He counted the process up to sixty, then got up and tore the rifle out of Wells's hands and threw it against the barracks wall, screaming. They discharged the boy on a Section 8 that week, but his mother had died by the time he got back to Biloxi.

At eleven-thirty, Harry Wells studied his lighter once again, then tried it again. He watched the spark fail to catch in the too-short wick. Carefully he took the lighter apart again.

# Chapter Nine

In the Garwiths' room, Cicely said, "I'd just better have them send something up, Allan. I mean, do you feel like eating? Your tummy isn't bothering you any more?"

"No, it's not bothering me any more." He lay flat on his back on the bed, staring up, his one arm lying limp in a diagonal line on the bed. He was wearing shorts, and his bare chest, arm, stomach, legs were smoothly muscled. He was thinking about Margaret Moore. He didn't know why. Maybe, he thought, because when he'd faked the attack in the station wagon she'd got up and bent down close to him and put her hand on his forehead. He'd been nervous, intent on making his performance convincing and stopping them from running on to Laramie. But he'd still been aware of Margaret Moore's face close to his own, the cool feeling of her hand on his forehead, those good breasts of hers just inches from his face....

"What shall I order?"

"How about a New York, about six inches thick, baked potato and sour cream, French-fried onions and a Roquefort salad?"

He turned his head and watched her carefully. She had showered and spent an unholy time in the bath afterward. Now she was wearing her best nightgown under a flowery housecoat. She had put her hair up in tight curlers and removed her make-up. Her face glistened with cream and seemed especially thin, as though the removal of make-up had allowed the bones to stretch the skin further. Her nose seemed especially large. Marilyn Monroe, he thought.

"Well—" she said, frowning a little. She got her purse from the writing table and took out the small pink wallet where she carried their money. She took the money out and counted it.

"Why," he asked, "do you go through all that? You know right down to the stinking dime how much money you've got. I say I want a New York, baked potato, French-fried onions and salad with a Roquefort dressing, and you've got to get out that damn wallet and count the money."

She looked at him, eyes misting, and put the money back into the wallet blindly. Her mouth trembled. A tear rolled down a cheek. "Allan, I just—" She shook her head, her voice quivering.

"Oh, God," he said. He put his arm over his eyes and lay there, wholly disgusted. "Order me a hamburger." He thought of the money, packed in that box, sitting now either in a train boxcar or in the Cheyenne post office. His nerves jumped, and he knew he would have to keep his mind off that.

He heard her pick up the telephone. In a moment she was saying, "Yes, please. A very thick steak, medium-rare—a New York cut, please. French-fried onions. A large baked potato with sour cream. A tossed salad with Roquefort. And coffee. Yes, please. To be delivered to the room. And one tuna sandwich."

He took his arm from his eyes and looked at her as she put the telephone down. "One tuna sandwich?"

"Allan, I'm just not hungry," she said, wiping her tears away, holding her chin up.

"Oh, God," he said. "You get a kick out of that, don't you?"

"Allan, sometimes I just don't understand. I ordered just what you wanted, and that's what I want you to have. I love you, don't you understand?"

"Yeah," he said. "And you get your giant-sized jolts out of sitting over in the corner nibbling on a tuna sandwich while I gorge myself on steak. What's the fun in it?"

She shook her head, holding her tears back. "Sometimes I just don't understand anything. I want you to enjoy dinner. And a tuna sandwich is all I want, truly."

"All right," he said, covering his eyes with his arm again.

He lay silently. When he got that money, he was going to ditch this one but fast. Oh, but you were going to see some fast ditching when he got that money!

He listened to her moving around the room. In a moment he could hear voices in the hall. Mrs. Landry, he realized. Then that laughing one. Miss Kennicot. God, he thought. Loose from an asylum. The doctor that delivered that one should have put it back where he got it. He shut his eyes beneath his forearm, waiting for the steak he really wanted. After this it was going to be steak every day, and no Cicely to sit watching him eat it while she nibbled like a cow-eyed martyr on her greasy tuna sandwich. And he was thinking of Margaret Moore again. Right across the hall. Just that far away from him.

What, he wondered, was she all about anyway? Where did she come from? Where was she going? Free and easy, that one. Would she take a proposition? A good one, with some money back of it? Yeah, he thought; she would.

He could feel a pulsation of excitement. He suddenly got up and strode to the bath. Cicely said, "Do you feel all right, dear?" He didn't answer.

He shut the door behind him and locked it. He looked at himself carefully in the mirror, thoughts of Margaret Moore putting a little knot in his middle.

He examined himself carefully in the mirror. Good face. Good physique, all except the missing arm. For a moment he kept his eyes off where the arm had been amputated. He didn't mind exposing that to Cicely, but not to himself. When he lay around with it exposed to Cicely, he kept watching her eyes going to it. It still unnerved her, he knew, and he found a pleasure in that. But right now he did not want to look at it himself.

Instead he looked at the rest of his good, well-formed athlete's body. He'd been a good athlete. Nobody could say he hadn't. If he'd decided to pick up one of the three college scholarships he'd been offered, the whole country would know how good an athlete he was. In football ...

His face became grim. Who said he hadn't been one of the best high-school backs in the state? Fast? Skilled? What did you want? So why hadn't he been the best? He closed his eyes, remembering those words of Nick Pomasetto, the beefy fullback who'd played with him in high school and gone on to play varsity at Michigan State. They had been alone in the locker room after a hard scrimmage just before their last game. He'd never got along with Nick. They hadn't spoken much, just played together in the backfield.

That afternoon Nick had said, "You're good, buddy-boy. But you're faking half the time. If you weren't so damn good everybody would know it. You're scared, buddy-boy. You're scared one day you're going to get your face kicked in, your groin punctured, your leg twisted off, just some small accident that's going to ruin it for you. So you're faking. What makes you so scared, buddy-boy?"

He'd threatened to take Nick Pomasetto's head off with one swing. But Nick had only laughed softly and walked off to his shower. He'd never spoken again to Nick. Nick had never again spoken to him. Not after that last game they'd been forced to play together. But he could still hear that soft Italian voice accusing him....

He shook his head angrily. Stupid bastard. So Nick went on to college and worked off his scholarship like any other lump of beef for hire. Now he'd graduated, what would he have? A few years of pro ball? Getting himself smashed up week after week at what kind of money? Peanuts, for a work-horse like Pomasetto—they were a dime a dozen in pro clubs. Then when his brains were shaken loose enough, what then? Coaching some high-school team or some two-bit college team somewhere in the sticks? And the money reduced to a third, maybe less, of the peanuts he'd gotten for the pro ball.

Allan Garwith's mouth curled bitterly. He turned on a faucet, looking at himself in the mirror, rinsing his hand absently. What would Nick Pomasetto think if he knew Allan had a hundred thousand on the hook? One hundred thousand, no tax, free and clear—if nothing went wrong. And nothing was going to go wrong. Somehow, fate had dealt him this chance, and he was not going to lose it.

His eyes drifted to the stump of his arm. He closed his eyes and turned off the faucet and dried his hand. He started out of the bathroom, then stopped to tighten the handle of the faucet. He was nervous again, his nerves singing. He walked back to the bed without a glance at Cicely, dropped on his back and covered his eyes once again with his one arm.

Again he heard movement in the hall. Margaret Moore this time? There was a knock on their door. No, not Margaret Moore moving in the hall; the dinner coming in instead. When the dishes had been arranged, he sat on the edge of the bed. Cicely carefully cut his steak into small portions, and he started eating without a word. Cicely sat in one of the chairs, carefully nibbling on her tuna sandwich as though it were one of the world's rarest delicacies.

"What," he said finally, "did you tip the joke of a waiter who brought this in?"

She blinked. "Ten cents. I had a dime all ready for him."

He stared at her for a moment, then shook his head once and resumed eating. The steak, he had to admit, was delicious. Everything was delicious.

When he was half finished Cicely asked anxiously, "Is it all right, Allan?"

"Remind me," he said, "never to order a steak in this crummy hotel again."

"Oh, Allan. I was hoping—"

"Don't hope. They must have cut this piece of so-called meat off an eighty-year-old buffalo." He glanced at her. Tears were in her eyes again. He felt better. He finished the dinner, then pushed the tray away and lay back on the bed. The food felt good inside of him. It had relaxed him. When he relaxed again, he felt the knot of want once more. The image of Margaret Moore was going through his mind.

Suddenly he knew. There had been something about her, some vague familiarity, as though he'd known someone like her some time, somewhere. Now he knew what it was. New Orleans. New Orleans, with the fear shaking his teeth loose, blood flowing out of him, and Charissa....

He was suddenly there again, in the bar smelling of shrimp and oysters, drinking beer to fortify himself against the pressing heat of the tired, gray city. The sweat had streamed down his face and ribs, soaking his flowered sport shirt. He'd lost count of the number of beers he'd drunk. He only knew that he was running out of money saved from the packing-house job in Loma City. And Charissa, plump, smiling, a mysterious look of pleasure in her dark eyes, had walked by his table. He'd said, more to himself than with an intention to stop her, "That is a beautiful behind—truly beautiful."

He'd been surprised the words had come out so clearly, so loud. He'd known the beer, with the heat, had gotten to him, because he always spoke more carefully, more loudly, when he was getting drunk. Later his words would mush, like anyone else's. But there was that high-glow stage when he spoke very distinctly, very loudly. And he knew he'd just done so.

She'd stopped, broad and full-breasted, the thin dress displaying her ripe body well. She'd be fat, really fat, in a few more years, he'd thought at that moment. But he'd felt a sudden jab of desire that surprised him. She had a broad, copper-tinted face and quick, appraising eyes that looked you over and took you apart and yet never lost their look of pleasant invitation. He'd thought she was going to spit at him. But instead she smiled, showing perfectly even, perfectly white teeth—a beautiful smile—and said, "You are a naughty little boy, do you know that?"

She'd accepted his offer of a drink. Three hours later he'd stumbled into the small, untidy house outside of the city where she'd driven him in a rattling 1949 Ford sedan. He was not sober for five days. In that time he was virtually consumed by Charissa's heavy, vociferous, unholy physical appetite. He'd come back to reality the sixth day. She'd told him, "Now, little boy, you have been fed well, no?" Laughter, low and full, like the sound of a quick stream. "You are all, how you say, pushed out of shape. So?" She nodded. "All right. Now is the time for you to do something else."

It had taken him a while to sober up completely. He remembered only vaguely what the two men who'd come to the shack looked like. But they had talked, and he remembered that talk very clearly. They were planning to run a cache of dope into the country. It had to be smuggled up from Mexico. It now waited for them in a small Gulf-Coast town down there. All they had to do was sail across the Gulf in a boat owned by one of the men and pick it up. He'd never been involved in anything criminal other than stealing junk from dime stores, hubcaps, nothing serious. But the plan had seemed so simple, and his cut would be eight thousand dollars. He'd agreed. They would go in two weeks.

When the men had gone he'd asked Charissa, "Why me? I don't know a boat from a streetcar."

She'd smiled and started his excitement all over again. She unbuttoned his shirt and pulled it from his shoulders, a soft, knowing smile on her lips. "You are young and strong. They know what is what, but you have the muscle, see?" Later she'd said, "But, little boy, we have nothing until you earn your eight thousand dollars. Nothing on the shelves. No food. No whisky. Not even beer. You must do something now, something—ah—little. You know?"

Something little turned out to be a little gas station on the edge of New Orleans. Charissa had had her eye on it for some time. Softly, carefully, she'd explained how simple it was, then brought out a pistol he'd had no idea she owned. It was clean, oiled and loaded.

That night, very late, he'd gotten out of the car Charissa parked beside the pumps of that station. He'd asked for a map of the city and followed the attendant inside. The attendant was a young man with a pimpled chin and hair the color of corn husks. Inside, Allan Garwith had removed the gun from inside his jacket and pointed it at the youth, demanding all the money in the register.

He'd never forgotten how the youth had stared at him blankly, then shaken his head. He'd been amazed and yelled for the boy to give him the money. But the boy simply stood there with a stupid, stubborn look on his face, shaking his head.

"Shoot him then!" Charissa had called, a wild edge in her voice, "and take it!"

But he'd suddenly come apart, staring at that stupid, resolute look on that kid's face. He'd turned and run to the car. He'd screamed at Charissa to drive off. She had, with an angry screech of tires.

She drove across town, into the country, her otherwise soft and full mouth a white, tight line. When she stopped, she looked at him, at the way the gun in his hand was shaking uncontrollably. Her dark eyes glinted. "Ah, little boy—I didn't think you would do that. What you are, that didn't really show before, did it?"

He'd tumbled out of the car and staggered to the edge of the road and been sick. He'd been blind with sickness, shaking so badly he could hardly hold on to the gun in his hand. Then he stumbled back toward the car, and that was when he'd accidentally shot himself in the left arm.

Charissa, swearing bitterly, had pulled him into the car and yanked the gun out of his hand. He'd bled badly on the way back to the shack. The next thing he'd realized was that the sun was up again, hot, smoldering through the dirty windows as he lay in bed. Charissa was quietly and coldly explaining to him that he had not really done very well. They had no money, no food, no liquor.

"This arm," he'd gritted, "is killing me."

"I will do something," she'd said.

She disappeared for twenty hours. He'd lain in pain and utter fright. Finally she'd come back with a tall, raw-boned Negro woman, saying, "You know what one must do, little boy, when one has no money— someone like me, little baby? I do not like to earn money that way."

"What the hell is she doing?" he said, seeing the flash of the knife in the hand of the large, funereal-looking Negro woman.

A glass was pushed close to his chattering teeth. "Drink, little boy. Keep drinking." He had. But it hadn't stopped realization of the nightmare that followed. When it was over, when both the tall Negro woman and his arm were gone, he knew he'd lost more than an arm. He'd lost something inside himself that he was never going to get back.

The days following were painful, dreary, nerve-racking. Charissa had been cool toward him, yet careful to take care of him properly. He was certain he was going to die, but he did not. Finally, when she had bathed him and stood looking at his bare body with a flashing look in her dark eyes, she'd said, "You are getting stronger, little boy. We have held up the trip to Mexico for you to get stronger. But my friends are getting impatient." She'd smiled brightly, then disappeared into the bath. He'd listened to the shower running. Pretty soon she'd come out, her good, full body gleaming in the hot shafts of sunlight flowing into the small room. "Now," she'd said, "let's see just how strong you've gotten again."

He'd finally said desperately, "No use." He could not even keep his mind on it, because he kept hearing drops splattering on the galvanized metal that formed the shower's floor. They hit and splattered in an infuriating regularity, and that was all he could keep his mind on.

She'd smiled sadly and got a bottle of whisky from the cupboard.

"It'll come back," he said, a pleading note in his voice. "Everything'll come back, all of a sudden."

"Sure, little baby," she'd said softly. "Have some of this to help it along."

He'd tasted the whisky. "Can't you stop that shower from dripping?"

"I'll see," she'd said. "Have some more whisky while I do. There is nothing else to do anyway, is there?"

He'd gotten drunk lying in bed. He'd finally gone to sleep, listening to that dripping in the shower that Charissa had been unable to stop. He woke up realizing he was being moved from the bed, through the house, to a car. He was certain that he was being moved by the two men he was supposed to accompany to Mexico. But it was vague; he'd drunk too much. The last he'd remembered was Charissa's face close to his, those bright, white teeth gleaming. He'd heard her voice, soft, polite, "You are good for nothing, eh, little baby?" Then felt her long, sharp fingernails gouging down the side of his face.

He'd awakened on the edge of a swamp, muddy, face bloody and sore, arm-stump hurting because he'd been rolled down to the edge of that swamp; there was a fever in his head.

He'd stumbled, staggered, crept into town, to the Salvation Army and claimed he had been the victim of a hit-run accident. He'd refused a doctor's examination and been able to hide the fact that the arm was newly gone. They gave him food, a bed. Slowly he'd got control of himself and got some decent strength back. They had loaned him a ticket for a bus back to Loma City. He went back to discover that his mother had died while he was gone. He'd lived on the money from a small insurance policy she'd had, in Loma City. When that ran out he'd married Cicely, who'd idolized him when he was a football hero in high school.

Now they were together in a room in Cheyenne. And he was thinking that one of the things he was going to do with that $100,000 was return to New Orleans. He was going to find Charissa. She was going to know what kind of money he had. She was going to get down on her knees and plead for his favor. And then he was going to enjoy her again, because he'd never forgotten what she was like. Then she was going to pay for the way she'd left him by that swamp. The fingernail scratches had healed, but not the wounds inside. And she was going to pay for them....

But New Orleans was a long way off. He could not keep his mind on Charissa right now. He was thinking of that money, how it had better be there when he went to get it in the morning. Then ditch, only maybe not before he'd made a try with Margaret Moore, just because she reminded him of Charissa....

He suddenly thought of Mrs. Landry, how she'd stood down there in front of the desk when they'd checked in, running on about when they were leaving in the morning. His entire body tensed.

"When," he said to Cicely, "did they say we're leaving in the morning?"

"Eight o'clock," Cicely said, looking at him hopefully, as though wishing desperately for his mood to shift and place her in greater favor.

He swore softly.

"What's the matter, dear?" she asked, the hope going from her voice.

"Why is that damn faucet dripping in the bathroom?" he asked angrily, thinking: eight o'clock. Why didn't I pay attention to that before? The post office won't even open before nine o'clock.

"I don't hear any dripping, dear."

"Well, check it!" He would, he thought, have to stall some way.

Cicely hurried to the bathroom. He watched her peering at the sink, trying to tighten the faucet. She came back. "It wasn't dripping, dear, really."

"You say," he snapped bitterly, his mind spinning back to that moment when Charissa had come out of the shower in that shanty house outside of New Orleans, her body gleaming. He said to Cicely harshly, "Aren't you ever coming to bed?"

She blinked at him, wholly confused.

"Why," he said, "don't you turn the lights out?" When she had gotten into bed, in the darkened room, he put his hand on her savagely.

Later, perspiration on her upper lip, her teeth tight together, she lay with her eyes closed, the fury of it over. She was content. So long as it was this way, then nothing else at all mattered. She turned to him again, kissing his cheek lightly, tenderly. But he was already asleep.


# Chapter Ten

When the elevator had brought up the boy with dinner for the Garwiths, John Benson and Margaret Moore rode down to the lobby, just in time to miss the invitation by Miss Kennicot and Mrs. Landry to join them for dinner. There, Mr. Brander, standing beside his desk clerk, had motioned to John.

"Will you wait for me at the door?" John asked Margaret Moore, and crossed the lobby to the desk.

Mr. Brander bent forward, his excitement showing through his effort to look nonchalant. He spoke in a hoarse whisper, "Mr. Benson, you asked me to report to you anything unusual and telephone you. Now I just did telephone you. But you didn't answer, you see, and so—"

"What is it, Mr. Brander?"

"Well," Mr. Brander said, voice quivering a little, "Albert here just told me that one of your party, Mr. Wells, stopped at the desk earlier and gave him, Albert here, ten dollars to report if and when that young fellow with one arm in your party left his room and came down here. Now what do you think of that? Wouldn't you put that down in your book as unusual,

Mr. Benson?"

John nodded slowly. "Yes. It might be. That's very good to know, Mr. Brander." He smiled at the desk clerk. "I think you've both done a fine job."

"What are we going to do now?" Mr. Brander asked.

"Just," John said, "keep ourselves calm. Act quite naturally. If the boy with one arm goes out of his room, why, you, ah—" He looked at the desk clerk.

"Albert Thompson," the desk clerk said positively.

"Mr. Thompson, you inform Mr. Brander here and then telephone Mr. Wells, just as he asked." He looked at Mr. Brander. "Then, when I come back, if that's happened, why, you let me know, Mr. Brander."

"That's all?" Mr. Brander asked.

"That's all."

"Well, but are you leaving the hotel now? I mean, if you're gone—"

"Let me know when I get back," John said. "If there's anything to let me know. And one thing more. The boy who delivered the food to the Garwiths' room—he was coming up just as we were going down. Who is that?"

"That's Albert's boy. Albert, right here. That's his boy."

John nodded. "Fine." There was one thing he was certain of—Mr. Brander and all of his employees including Albert and Albert's son were trustworthy. And it would be quite a trick to smuggle a hundred thousand in small currency underneath a few silver warming covers on a food tray even if you had an accomplice in this hotel, which John was certain Allan Garwith did not have. He knew a good deal more about Allan Garwith now, but he looked at both of the men behind the registration desk calmly. "Thank you both very much. You've been very cooperative. But remember, we have to be careful. No unnecessary contacts."

Mr. Brander nodded excitedly. "I understand, Mr. Benson. I absolutely understand!"

John smiled at them and returned to Margaret Moore, who was waiting at the door. They walked outside, into the cooling twilight. She looked at him curiously.

"I guess I overdid my complaint. I've got the manager, Mr. Brander, worried."

"Somehow," she said, "that doesn't fit into my impression of you. Your calling a manager of a hotel to complain about something."

He looked at her quickly, then grinned. "No? Well, everyone has his peculiarities. I have a temper, you know."

"No," she said, "I wouldn't have known."

They crossed the street and started through the park. "Still hungry?" he asked.

"Famished."

The man in the light gray suit and straw hat who had driven up in the blue Chevrolet was sitting on a bench, newspaper folded now on his lap. He looked at them idly, as they passed.

"Well," John said, "I am likewise. I wonder if we should have eaten at the hotel?"

"It could be crowded," Margaret Moore said, smiling.

"Yes," he said, nodding. "I've got that feeling. Did you hear Miss Kennicot singing when we passed her door?"

"I still hear her," Margaret Moore laughed.

"Well, all we need is a good restaurant. Maybe—" He stopped. "If you want a good restaurant, ask a native. Excuse me a moment, Margaret."

He turned and walked back to the man sitting on the bench. Out of earshot of Margaret Moore he said to the man, "Harnet called you?"

The man looked up, a friendly, polite look on his face. "That's right. Benson?"

"Yes."

"Good. I'm Dornig."

"I saw you get here from the hotel. It was fast. Harnet's really a florist?"

"That's right. We use him for things like that now and then. Nobody'll trace it."

"Well, I don't think they'll try. I don't think any body's suspicious of me yet. But I just found out something. It's important. Wells bribed the desk clerk to tell him if Garwith left his room. We know now that either Garwith's got the money and Wells is waiting for a chance to get it back or they're in this together but Wells doesn't trust him. I swing to the first. I don't think they're in this together."

The man nodded casually. "I'll relay it back to Loma City."

"Have you got the back of the hotel covered?"

"Yes. But all we can do is watch and let you know what happens. We don't want to make too much noise and screw it up for you. When do you leave tomorrow?"

"Eight o'clock."

"Where do you stop then?"

"Mrs. Landry drives like she's on fire. We'll make Salt Lake, at least. I'm not sure we won't go beyond it. They're set up in Salt Lake?"

"Yes. But maybe it'll take all the way to the Coast before anything breaks."

"Could be. But I think Garwith faked a stomach attack to stop us in this town. Keep a close watch. Where's a good restaurant, by the way? That's what I'm supposed to be talking to you about."

"There's a good place straight ahead two blocks and a half block to your left. Best we've got. Good steaks. Good-looking woman. Which one is she?"

"Margaret Moore."

"The one we don't have much background on. You're not worried about her? I mean, as far as—"

"I don't know. We'll see. Thanks, Dornig."

"All in the job."

John turned and walked back to Margaret Moore. He smiled at her. "They're talky in Cheyenne. He said there's a good place a couple of blocks away."

"Well, let's merely run then, before I faint from undernourishment."

The restaurant was small, cool, dim, with round, leather-covered booths. John asked, "Drink?"

"Beer. I thought about a beer all the way across Nebraska in that desperate heat."

"I know what you mean. How about a steak?"

"Please, God. The thickest. We split this, by the way, since I trapped you into it."

"I'm willing to be trapped like this any day, any time. Don't forget that."

"I won't."

She leaned her head back against the leather of the booth, closing her eyes. He studied her face when he'd ordered for them, noting the clear, smooth complexion, the fine lines of time at the corners of her eyes and mouth that did nothing to destroy her beauty, only gave it a durability, a depth that he had seldom seen in a woman. Not even in Maggie, he thought guiltily.

She turned her head, opening her eyes, meeting his stare directly. "Now tell me about yourself, John Benson."

"I was going to ask you to do the same."

"You told Mrs. Landry you were from Lafayette?"

"That's right."

"Well, I've been through Indiana. Very lovely in the fall. In the south part especially. All those rolling hills, yellow with flowers, the trees with their leaves golden and red. I was there with my husband."

He nodded. Then waited.

An eyebrow flickered. "We had a very pleasant and agreeable parting."

She smiled faintly. "I was very fond of him. I still am."

"Maybe it's none of my business, but you said you divorced him? Why?"

"We separated by mutual consent. We got a divorce to make it legal." The beers had been brought and poured. She lifted her glass and tasted. She shuddered happily. "Delicious, no?"

"Yes. Do you want to tell me about him? Maybe I'll understand you better if you tell me about a man you were fond enough of to marry, then divorce amiably, and still feel fond of. What kind of man is this?"

"Or," she said, "what kind of woman is this? That might make more sense." He gave her a cigarette and lit it for her. "He was sixty-four when I met him, a nice gentleman's gentleman, with a white mustache and impeccable manners and soft, far-away eyes—like a child dreaming on a summer day." She looked at him. "Make sense?"

"No," John said. "I mean, I hadn't figured it that way."

"Neither had I," she said. "I'd gone along all my life, skidding off from the marriage entanglement at the last minute perhaps a dozen times, and always glad, later, that I had. Not that I didn't love each one of them in a certain way. I think I did, a little bit anyway. But never enough to settle down and say this will be it with this particular prince charming. But Edwin was different. You don't call a man sixty-four years old with a beautiful white mustache and child's eyes a prince charming. He was a good deal more. I married him."

"Just like that."

"Just like that."

"Where did you meet him? And how? And what did he do?"

"He was an English professor. I met him at a party in Chicago. He was teaching at Iowa State. I was a buyer for a large department store in Chicago, and he'd come into the big city to relax before the next term started. He had great dignity and a fine, razor-sharp mind, yet an ability to reflect on things. I was tired of the job. He was tired of living alone. He'd lost his wife a few years before. They hadn't had children. So—it just happened. We got married and I went back to live in an old, very wonderful white house with him. It was very nice."

John shook his head. "It doesn't sound right, somehow. I don't mean that critically. I just don't see it."

"I think it was very good while it lasted. I liked the books, the contentment, the hard winters around us, snug in that old house, with the fire in the fireplace, a little wine, talking about literature. I hadn't got to college. I was born in England, brought here when I was two, orphaned in Arizona when I was fifteen. I got jobs and moved around. There wasn't a chance for college. But I read a great deal and thought about things, and Edwin believed I thought sensibly."

"I'm sure of that."

"But," she said, "the intellectualism wore thin. At least for me. After the newness wore off, Edwin retreated to what he'd known before I came along. Evenings, he'd go to his desk, wearing the elbows out of that invariable tweed jacket, reading and studying and working over his students' papers. Finally, after two years, I said, 'You don't need me.' And he said, 'I love to have you here. It's very comfortable when you are. But not if it's not enough for you.' It was agreeable. That's when I went to New York. He insists on sending me a check every month, though I didn't ask for it. He does quite well with royalties from the texts he's written and edited and his income from the college. I think it was a fair bargain, both ways. I hope so."

He nodded, looking at her. He saw her in better perspective now. But he still did not know if she might be involved with Wells, or with Garwith, or both. Perhaps in the same unreasonable fashion she'd been involved with the man she'd married, she might be involved in this. She intimated she didn't need money. Maybe she simply needed excitement. He did believe that, above and beyond her fine sensual attraction, Edwin, the aging English professor, had found a strong attraction in her mind too. Put this with the good face, the rich body, and you had a good deal of woman, a very good deal.

"All right," she said, "now you. You lived in a university town too. Edwin and I were in Lafayette twice—he had a friend on the Purdue faculty. Does it hurt to talk of that? Your home, life? I mean, because of your wife? I won't press if it does."

"No," he said. "It's all right." And he realized that now, with Margaret Moore, it was all right to talk about it for the first time since Maggie had been killed in that accident in Washington. Whatever Margaret Moore was, whether or not she was involved with this, she had a strong way of relaxing a man, because she was, unconsciously, so complete a woman. "Well, I'd still be in Lafayette if—" He shrugged. "It was a good life."

"You hadn't grown tired of it at all, in other words?"

"Not at all," he said softly. "Nice town, nice family, nice business." It was easy, he found, to mix the lie with the truth. It hadn't been Lafayette, and he hadn't been in business—but it had been a good life...

"You loved your wife very deeply, didn't you, John?"

"Yes," he said.

"Do you still?" she asked directly.

He looked at her, flushing a little, as her eyes examined him carefully. "In memory, yes."

She suddenly smiled. "Did you have a nice house in Lafayette?"

"Yes," he said. "We did." And they had owned a nice house, he thought. The quiet Anacostia neighborhood, far out from downtown Washington. Washington had been too hot in the summer, often too cold in the winter. But he'd been glad to give up the field work and settle into the routine of the Washington office. The quiet of the home, evenings. Now and then a sitter for the boys and dinner at the Wharf; perhaps a drink at the old-fashioned, ornate bar in the Willard; Sundays, often, driving down through Alexandria, enjoying the golden Virginia countryside, stopping wherever suited them. Maggie had owned a child's eagerness to enjoy every minute. He remembered how they'd stopped one Sunday in a little town called Blackstone and bought the boys ice cream sodas in a corner drugstore and watched the citizens amble lazily down the main street. He lit a cigarette and tasted his beer. "Lafayette," he said, "is a very pretty town."

"Where did you live? Near the campus?"

He was back with the present quickly. He looked at her eyes and said, "We lived in the Hills and Dales District in West Lafayette. Do you remember that?"

"Yes," she said. "Beautiful homes there."

He nodded. "We were able to get an older home on Forest Hill Drive. I had my business on the east side, on Kosuth."

He thought her eyes flickered faintly, but it was only, he thought, imagination because he was now trying very hard to be careful.

"Advertising," she said. "Did you like that?"

"That's what I trained for at I.U. after the war. I started out thinking that I was going to be an engineer. I grew up in a little town near Lafayette, and I was around Purdue some—an engineering college primarily—you know that. So I just naturally thought I'd be an engineer. I started in it, and then I enlisted in the Army. After basic they sent me back to Indiana, at Bloomington, to study engineering for a while. I was really no good at it. After the war, I switched to advertising. I liked it, yes. I still like it."

"What did you do in the war?" she asked.

"What an awful lot of other men did." He smiled, and now he was telling the entire truth. "Enlisted private, knocked around camps for a while, along with that short-lived AST Program, then went overseas with the infantry as a rifleman. I worked up to squad leader, mostly because I stayed alive. Came home after the war ended, put my uniform in a trunk and haven't seen it since."

"Not like our friend, Mr. Wells?"

"I'm afraid not."

She nodded, smiling a little, studying her glass. Then the steaks arrived. "My God," Margaret Moore breathed, "they look beautiful!"

"Indeed," he said, relaxing again, not knowing how much he had to worry about her, but simply glad to be with her, the two of them in that small leather booth, cutting into the best-looking steak he'd seen in years.

Suddenly he heard a familiar, but startling, sound. He looked up and saw, coming in, Miss Kennicot followed by a beaming Mrs. Landry. The sound was Miss Kennicot laughing. She was roaring, red-faced with exertion, coming down on them with flashing eyes and large display of white teeth.

"There you are!" she shouted, as the other diners looked up. "Now wasn't that naughty of you to run off and not even tell us where you were going! My goodness, steaks! Well, they told us at the hotel this was the best restaurant in town. And I just knew we'd find you two naughty children when we couldn't find you at the hotel. Didn't I say that to you, Mrs. Landry?"

"Yes, dear," Mrs. Landry said happily, "you did."

"My goodness," Miss Kennicot said, laughing, "aren't you two ashamed of yourselves running off from us like this!" She looked at John with gleaming eyes. Then she looked at Margaret Moore. In that second, her laughing stopped, and a vicious cloud of anger flashed visibly across her face as she stared accusingly at Margaret Moore. But then she laughed again, and in a moment she and Mrs. Landry pressed themselves into the booth.

After checking the menu carefully, Miss Kennicot noted that she rarely ate steaks. ("Now the price of these here—now that's what I'd call quite firm!") She really preferred soups, she said, and small sandwiches and things made out of eggs. But since steak was the specialty, and since John and Margaret Moore had ordered them, she was just going to go ahead. Mrs. Landry also ordered a steak and attacked it with relish. Miss Kennicot, seeing the beer glasses before John and Margaret Moore, ordered a beer too.

And long after everyone else had finished his steak, she was letting hers get cold, finishing the last drops of one bottle of beer with ceremonious tippings of the bottle and tastings. John was startled to realize that she actually seemed to be getting tipsy. She ate only a little of her steak then. And when they returned to the hotel, she laughed all the way back, weaving a little, finally grabbing John's arm and hanging on to him across the lobby, up in the elevator, right down the hall to the door of the room she shared with Mrs. Landry.

John, when everyone had gotten into his respective room, returned to the lobby. He spoke briefly with the desk clerk, who had nothing new to report, then reported to Ray Hannah in Loma City from a public booth in the lobby.

Ray Hannah said, "Okay, John. And I've got a little more on Margaret Moore now. She was married to an English professor at Iowa State. Lasted a couple of years and dissolved about eleven months ago. Before that she was buyer for a store in Chicago. That's all I've got yet."

"All right, Ray," John said, relieved to find that much was working out, as he had thought it would. "And I don't think I'll be in touch with you from here on. I've got the hotel staff alerted, the local men covering the hotel, now I'm talking to you. It's getting too much like a circus. We can't afford it. I'm going to play it closer from now on."

"Okay, pal. And good luck."

When he'd returned to his room and lay in bed, looking at the flat bars of light on the ceiling coming from the street lights through the tilted Venetian blinds, he thought of Margaret Moore, just across the hall, also alone, perhaps looking at a similar pattern across her ceiling. A driving pain of loneliness went through him. He wished he could get up and cross that hall.

Then he thought of Miss Kennicot, also across the hall. He remembered how she'd clung to him on the way back, so hard he could still feel her fingernails pressing into his forearm.

"Lord," he whispered, and got up suddenly, making certain his door was locked. Then he returned to bed, laughing softly, feeling the tensions ease a little because of the laughter. Down the hall was Harry Wells, a known murderer. Also Allan Garwith, possibly just as potentially dangerous. Yet he'd gotten up to check the door to make sure it was locked against Miss Kennicot! "Lord, Lord," he whispered again, laughing long and hard, trying to keep the sound muffled, grateful for that ability to laugh. Then he fell into a sudden and deep sleep.

# Chapter Eleven

At eight o'clock the following morning, the sky was clear, the sun was shining and there was a faintly cool breeze. Mrs. Landry, Miss Kennicot, Margaret Moore, Harry Wells and John Benson had assembled at the station wagon in front of the hotel with their baggage. Harry Wells again volunteered to load the bags. John Benson helped him. The job was finished by eight-ten. The Garwiths had not yet appeared. Harry Wells, though he packed the baggage carefully, was visibly nervous.

At eight-twenty, Mrs. Landry said, "Well, I'm just worried that they haven't come down. I just hope that poor boy isn't feeling badly again."

Casually John said, "Want me to check?"

"Yeah," Harry Wells said, voice cold and rasping, "check." He leaned against the station wagon, looking up toward the fourth floor. He lit a cigarette. He'd bought a new wick for his lighter at the cigar counter early this morning.

"Mr. Benson—I mean, John," Miss Kennicot said quite loudly, "I'll go along. I mean, I'm concerned too." Nervous laughter, and then: "Anyway, 'A merry companion is as good as a wagon.' Lyly, of course. And I shall try to be merry!" Solid booming laughter now, while Harry Wells looked at her angrily, then stood staring upward again.

"Fine, Miss Kennicot," John said smoothly. "We'll go up together."

Miss Kennicot strode with him up the front steps of the hotel, saying, "And just no more of that Miss Kennicot business, John. Vera. I insist. After all, we are boon companions now, on this adventure of ours. 'Distinct as the billows, yet one as the sea.' J. Montgomery. And perhaps there's more truth in that than meets the eye."

"I wouldn't wonder, Vera," John said, as they boarded the elevator. "I'll have to say you show a wonderful ability to find a quotation for every occasion. I think that's making our trip very pleasant, Vera."

"Oh, John!" Miss Kennicot breathed. She reached out and squeezed his left bicep tightly. He tried not to wince. Her face was blushing, he saw, and she was suddenly quite nervous. The hand that had pinched his arm flew back to her purse and started twisting the catch open and shut rapidly, making loud clicking sounds. Her eyes were frozen on him. "John, John," she said. He was relieved when they got to the fourth floor.

They walked down the hallway. He knocked on the Garwiths' door, and Cicely opened it. Her eyes were red.

"We were a little worried, Mrs. Garwith," John said.

"Yes, I know we're late," Cicely said. "But Allan—" She motioned a hand at Allan Garwith lying on the bed, dressed, but quite motionless, his eyes closed.

"He isn't feeling well again?" John asked.

"Yes, and I'm so worried. Allan," she said, moving to him. "Won't you let me call a doctor, please?"

"I don't want a doctor," he said, keeping his eyes closed. "I just need a little time to lie here. I'm all right. It's the damn altitude."

"Allan, if you'd just let me—"

"No. Just let me lie here a little while. I'll be all right."

"That might be the best idea, after all," John said finally. "We're not trying to break a speed record on this trip, I'm sure."

"Why, of course not!" Miss Kennicot said. "You know how Shake-speare, that dear Bard, said it. 'He tires betimes that spurs too fast be-times.' Now doesn't that make you feel better?"

"Yeah," Allan Garwith said, putting his forearm over his closed eyes.

"You relax too, Mrs. Garwith," John said to Cicely. "I'm sure he'll be all right."

They returned to the elevator. On the way down, John realized that Miss Kennicot was staring at him again, a smile trembling nervously on her mouth. "John—" she began, then bit her lip, flushing deeply.

"Yes?" he said, puzzled.

"John, I—" She started snapping the clasp on her purse again. "I just—" Then she suddenly laughed and her hand shot out, whacking him in the arm. "Isn't this fun though?"

As they crossed the lobby below, he gave up trying to figure out Miss Kennicot and thought: Garwith's going to try something, and very shortly. I had better be ready.

Outside, when they had reached the station wagon and explained the Garwiths' delay, he carefully moved away from Miss Kennicot, to stand a good dozen yards away. He had a feeling that if she were too close to him in an emergency, she would, somehow, manage to trip him, foul him, prevent him from action at the proper moment, just out of her inherent nature.


At five minutes before nine, Allan Garwith stood up in his room.

"Allan," Cicely said, "do you feel better now?"

"Allan, do you feel better now?" he mimicked. "You talk and talk, don't you?"

"Allan, please don't be mean to me. I know it's because you aren't feel-ing well. But I'm only trying to do things right."

He lifted the telephone and said to the operator, "Let's have somebody come up and get the bags." He dropped the telephone. He could feel that muscle twitching at the side of his mouth. That money, he thought, had better be there; it had absolutely better be there.

"Are we leaving now?" Cicely asked, blinking.

"I'm leaving," he said. "You wait for the bellboy. I've got to have some air."

"Allan, I just hope—"

"Don't hope," he said.

He strode swiftly down the hall. When he came out of the lobby downstairs, he looked at the group standing, around the station wagon. They were all looking at him. It only made his nerves jump again, until he picked out Margaret Moore. She was wearing a fresh white dress that showed her body perfectly. If it weren't for her, he thought, he would walk off now. The hell with the ride. But no, he thought, that wasn't entirely true. If the money wasn't there, if it had gotten fouled up some way so he couldn't get it, then he had to have this ride—they couldn't afford anything else. But if he got to the post office and did get the money, which he had damned well better do, then there was still Margaret Moore. For her, he was going to hang on a little while longer. One try for her. He had to have that....

"Are you feeling all right now, Mr. Garwith?" Mrs. Landry was calling.

"I've got to have a little air," he said. He realized then that the Army guy, Wells, was looking at him with hard, mean eyes. He met Wells's eyes for a moment, defiantly. He was thinking: Well, spit out an order, soldier boy. You don't like my holding things up? Then put out an order on it. He motioned with his arm. "I've got to take a little walk. I'll be all right then. I don't want to hold you up. If you want to go on without us, I guess we can manage." Now he was looking at Mrs. Landry.

Quickly Mrs. Landry shook her head and said, "Why, that's ridiculous. Now don't you worry about a thing! You just go have your little walk and get yourself some of this nice Wyoming air. There isn't a thing to worry about. When we get out on that Great Divide, why, I can just make up all kinds of time!"

"All right," Allan Garwith said. "If you don't mind, that's what I'm going to do."

He crossed the street and walked through the park. He glanced idly at a man sitting on one of the benches, then turned left on the far side of the park, walking toward downtown. He had to restrain himself now from breaking into a run.

Downtown he stopped an elderly woman and asked for directions to the post office. While she gave them to him, he looked back and saw Harry Wells moving swiftly up behind him. Harry Wells then stopped and turned and looked into a shop window. Allan Garwith frowned. Again he sensed that same familiarity about Wells that he'd noticed just before they'd left Loma City. There was something about him. But what? And why was he following him?

Once again his nerves jumped wildly. He shook his head and moved on in the direction of the post office. He was imagining things now, and he couldn't afford to do that. Wells wasn't following him, he was simply killing time wandering around downtown until the station wagon started rolling again. That was all it was.

Inside the post office, he paused to look out a window, back in the direction from which he'd come.

His heart seemed to stop for a long moment, then started pumping wildly. Harry Wells was moving swiftly toward the building. His tropical suit pressed perfectly, his freshly shined shoes glistening in the sun, he moved with quick determination.

Allan Garwith blinked, his mind spinning back to that moment when he'd watched those two men stride down the alley toward the bank. One of them had worn a well-pressed tropical suit, his highly polished shoes had flashed brilliantly in the sunlight....

"My God," Allan Garwith whispered.

John Benson, after Allan Garwith had crossed the street toward the park, had stepped over to Mrs. Landry and said, "If it's all right with you, Mrs. Landry, I think I'll look around a little bit too. Maybe we can just move up our leaving time, say, an hour. Is that agreeable?"

"Why, of course, Mr. Benson," Mrs. Landry had said cheerfully. "You just go right ahead."

"Good. I'll get some cigarettes first and then get some exercise."

He'd been able to note Allan Garwith's general direction. Then he'd gone swiftly into the hotel. Margaret Moore had looked at him expectantly. He'd merely smiled at her. Miss Kennicot was turned away, talking vacuously to Harry Wells, who obviously did not hear a word she said. John saw Cicely stepping out of the elevator as he came into the hotel. Then he went swiftly out the rear exit. A dark blue Chevrolet was parked on the opposite side of the back street, a tree-lined boulevard that was very quiet. John glanced at the man sitting in it; he was certain that it was the local office's man, but there wasn't time to check.

He circled the block and walked swiftly back in the same direction Allan Garwith had taken, a block up from where the station wagon was parked. Then he saw Garwith cross the street a half block beyond, moving in the direction of downtown. John paused. In a few minutes, looking straight ahead, Harry Wells strode across the same intersection, behind Garwith. John moved forward, following both.

He was a half block behind Harry Wells when he saw Allan Garwith go into the post office. Wells seemed to speed up. John was perhaps a hundred yards behind him when he heard the loud cry behind.

He turned and looked, anger pulsing in his temples, as Miss Kennicot, laughing and gasping, bore down on him once again.


Inside the post office, Allan Garwith did not see either John Benson or Miss Kennicot. He was only aware of Harry Wells.

Throat dry, hands trembling, he swung around and went directly to the general delivery window. He asked for a package bearing his name. He'd made up his mind how he would get it back into the station wagon. He would stop somewhere and have it wrapped as though it were a gift purchased in a department store. He would tell everyone it was a present for Cicely, which he was going to give her in San Francisco. But he'd figured that out before he'd realized what was familiar about Harry Wells. Now he didn't know what he was going to do. Now he didn't know anything.

The clerk came back to the window. "How do you spell that name?"

"G-a-r-w-i-t-h! It's a package!"

He turned nervously, looking at the doorway. He could not see Harry Wells.

"No," the clerk said, returning. "No package material for any Garwith."

"It's got to be there! It's a package this big." He motioned his hand, shutting his eyes against the awful fear drumming through him, remembering how he'd thrown the satchel into the river and then carefully packed the currency into a stiff pasteboard box. "It's a box, wrapped in heavy brown paper, first-class mail stamped all over it. I'm telling you—"

"Oh," the clerk said. "I assumed you meant fourth-class surface mail when you said it was a package. First class. I'll check again."

Sweat was now gleaming on Garwith's face. He could feel himself trembling all over. The clerk came back with the package.

"Here we are. I'm sorry. I thought you meant—"

Garwith grabbed the package and turned swiftly. Harry Wells now was standing at the doorway, looking at him with icy blue-gray eyes. Garwith's eyelids flickered spasmodically. He suddenly moved to a mailing window. He looked back at Wells. Wells had not moved, only stood there, blocking the doorway.

Garwith shoved the package into the window and said, "Give me that heavy pencil!"

The clerk blinked, looking at him.

"The pencil!"

The clerk handed him a thick pencil. Garwith crossed out the stamps and address, turned the package over and started to write his name. He paused, his mind spinning into blankness because of his wild fear. He forcibly got control of himself. He finally wrote, *Raymond Jones.*

He stopped again. Next stop would be in Utah probably. Probably Salt Lake. But he couldn't be sure, not the way that grandmother, Mrs. Landry, drove. He'd have to send it beyond that. He wrote, *c/o General Delivery. Reno, Nevada.*

"Okay," he said, shoving the package at the clerk.

The clerk examined the address, then turned the package over where Garwith had lined out the previous address and cancelled stamps. He shook his head. "It won't go like this, of course. It should be rewrapped, by all means, and—"

"Send it! Airmail!"

"Well—" The clerk finally pulled several wide strips of brown paper tape from a roller and carefully pasted them over the old stamps and address. "There. That ought to take care of it." He looked at Garwith, smiling in satisfaction. "Airmail?"

Garwith had gotten out his wallet and now opened it. There were no bills in it. My God, he thought, and remembered how, before they'd left Loma City, Cicely had asked for all the currency he had, so that she could count the money and make sure they spent it correctly. That stupid bitch, he thought. He reached into a pocket and drew out his change. He'd accumulated some silver that Cicely hadn't gotten. "How much?" He turned and looked at Harry Wells, who now was moving from the doorway toward him.

The clerk quoted the cost of airmail stamps. Garwith shook his head weakly. "Make it regular."

He shoved the silver at the clerk. It took all but three pennies to buy the postage. Swiftly the clerk stamped the package and snapped it into a large canvas bag, smiling. "Thank you, sir."

Allan Garwith turned from the window just as Harry Wells reached him.

Garwith finally found his voice. "What do you say, Wells?"

Harry Wells stood looking at him, eyes hard and hating.

Miss Kennicot fitted her hands around John Benson's arm like a wrestler about to try for the first fall. She grinned wickedly and said, "Why, imagine, John! I guess we both had the same idea, didn't we! Coming down here? I felt so sorry for that poor boy, of course, but I said to myself, 'Vera, you just haven't even seen very much of Cheyenne.' And so I just tripped right downtown. And here we are, both of us! Two minds with but a single thought. I'd call that a mental marriage, wouldn't you, John? And marriages, as Tennyson says, are made in heaven!" There was a full, long gale of laughter, as Miss Kennicot's fingers tightened on John's arm to the point of pain. "John," she said, looking at him. "John, John."

He forced himself to smile at her, eyes flickering to look toward the post office. He could break her hold on him, forcibly, trip her, slam her to her back. He would have liked that. But he could not do it. And he did not know what he was going to do about her. Because he was certain that anything less than physical violence was not going to get rid of her.

Harry Wells, he saw, had disappeared into the post office.

Miss Kennicot loosened her fingers for a fraction of a moment, then dug in even harder, laughing loudly again.

Allan Garwith knew he was visibly shaking, but he stood his ground as Harry Wells stared at him. A smile flickered off and on, then Harry Wells said to him, "Needed a couple of stamps. I thought you were pretty sick, Garwith." He looked inside the postal window, but the bag which contained the package was now being carried toward a rear loading dock.

"That's right," Allan Garwith managed. "Had a package to mail—something Cicely's mother sent on here to Cheyenne. I just remembered it this morning. I decided to mail it on to San Francisco and save packing it in the station wagon. You pack pretty good, Wells, but it's still crowded."

"Yeah," Wells said, staring at Garwith. "You feeling better?"

Garwith shrugged. He was not. He truly was not now. He'd been faking before. But he was not now. He was trembling so hard he was certain that he was going to be ill. "I don't know," he said. "This altitude must really be getting me."

"Yeah?" Wells said. Then, after a moment, "Well, how about it?"

Garwith felt his heart jump again. "How about it?"

"How about letting me by so I can buy those stamps?"

His head suddenly bobbed. "Yeah. Sure."

When he got outside and felt the sun on his face, the breeze drying the sweat on his face, he felt a moment of relief. Then he went weak. His knees almost buckled, and he had to stop walking, to get back enough strength to continue.

He couldn't be certain that Wells was the one who'd robbed that bank. But it was a possibility, and that possibility had thrown everything awry. He may have been in trouble before. But it was nothing, he thought as he forced himself to move weakly down the street in the direction of the hotel, to what he was into if Harry Wells really were the man he'd seen racing down that alley in Loma City....

# Chapter Twelve

It was four that afternoon before the station wagon rolled out of Cheyenne.

When Allan Garwith returned to the hotel, Cicely had insisted once again that he see a doctor. This time he didn't argue. The desk clerk recommended a clinic. Then Harry Wells and John Benson, accompanied by a fawning Miss Kennicot, returned to the station wagon. All the riders climbed into the car. Mrs. Landry drove to the clinic.

While the others remained outside, Cicely and Allan Garwith went in. They waited an hour, during which time Garwith sat silently opening and closing his hands. At last he went into the doctor's office, alone.

The doctor, a brisk, capable-looking young man, checked Garwith's blood pressure and pulse. He looked into Garwith's eyes carefully, with a light. He questioned him at length and finally said, "I think you've just got a bad case of nerves. Any particular reason for it?"

Garwith shook his head. "Maybe just making this trip. I got to worry about getting a job when I get to California. I guess I've been worrying about that." He was careful, despite the raw feeling of extreme nervousness, to look the doctor in the eyes when he spoke, careful to make his voice sound extremely sincere.

"Well," the doctor said, "perhaps you're just worrying too much. Things always work out, don't they?"

Garwith nodded. "Yeah. I guess so."

"I'll give you a couple of things to take. Some tranquilizers, a few sleeping pills." The prescription was written. Garwith returned to the waiting room.

"What did he say?" Cicely asked anxiously.

"The altitude," Garwith said shortly. "Pay these people and let's get out of here. And give me some money, will you? You stripped me back in Loma City, do you know that? What do you think I'm going to do with it? Spend it on wild women?"

"I'm sorry," Cicely said.

"Don't be sorry. Don't be anything. Just pay the broad at the desk over there and let's get these goddam pills."

Meekly Cicely paid at the desk. Mrs. Landry drove them to a drugstore. There was a forty-five minute wait for the drugs. When the prescription was finally filled, Cicely and Allan Garwith returned to the car. "Are you feeling better now?" Mrs. Landry asked. "I certainly hope so, poor boy."

"How about swinging around by that park across from the hotel again?" Garwith said. "I've got to take some pills—there's a fountain in there."

"We've got some water in the car—" Mrs. Landry began.

"I don't want to hold you up," Garwith said. "But I need a little air before we start again. I mean, I'm sorry about it, but I've got to have some air first. It's okay if you go without us. We'll manage somehow."

"Now don't be ridiculous!" Mrs. Landry said, and drove to the park. "Now you just relax. We've got plenty of time, haven't we, everyone?"

Garwith walked into the park with Cicely. He took one of the tranquilizers with water from the drinking fountain. He closed his eyes and thought of Harry Wells sitting directly behind him every time he was in that car. He looked across the park and saw Wells now leaning against the side of the station wagon, staring at him. Christ, he thought, and took another tranquilizer.

"Did the instructions say two, Allan?" Cicely asked, blinking with worry.

"Go over and tell them I've got to rest before we take off." He turned abruptly and walked across the grass to a point behind one of the green benches. He lay down on the grass, on his back, and covered his eyes with his arm.

He waited for the pills to go to work. Mentally he damned the fact that he'd had only enough money to send that package on by regular mail. That Landry woman really might beat the postal service this time. But that wouldn't happen if he stalled long enough.

He would like, he thought, simply to junk the station wagon altogether. Buy Cicely a one-way ticket back to Loma City on the bus. Tell her to stay with her parents until he got located. Take all the money they had and use a train for himself to Reno. There was just about enough to do that, he figured.

But if he did that, and Wells really was the one who'd lifted the money from the bank, then he would be putting the finger on himself. So far

Wells, if he were the one, didn't have any more on him than he had on Wells. But busting out that way would be like a red light blinking in front of Wells's eyes. And the thought of the man on his back from that point on, searching for him, coming out of nowhere some day, some minute, was too much. Wells had seen him pick up and mail a package, but that was all, so far. Thus, if he stayed on with the ride, then got the money, he would be able to ...

But what, he thought, was he going to do when he got to Reno? How would he handle it then, even if he slowed this up enough so that the money would absolutely be there by the time they arrived?

I don't know, he thought, realizing that the pills were going to work finally. I don't know anything. And he felt, for the first time, a relaxation. It got into his system and spread and left him with a pleasant, detached feeling. In a moment, his nerves finally calming, he dozed. He awakened when Cicely came over and sat down beside him. She put her hand comfortingly on his forehead. He didn't protest. He lay there until three-forty-five, really not caring at all. Then finally he stood up and looked at the station wagon.

Some of the others were out of sight. But Harry Wells was still standing beside that wagon, just as though he hadn't moved, staring straight at him. The hell with you, Garwith thought. He walked back to the fountain and took two of the sleeping pills. What do I care about anything? He said to Cicely, "Let's roll it, what do you say? I'm sick of this town."

After John Benson had followed Allan Garwith back to the station wagon that morning, Miss Kennicot clinging to his arm like an eager oversized bear cub, he'd known that he should have counted on Miss Kennicot even more accurately than he had. But there was, he knew, nothing he could do about that now.

When they'd driven to the clinic, he was able to walk down the street, into a store and telephone Dornig. He instructed Dornig to check the post office for anything bearing Garwith's name. When Allan Garwith had stretched out on the grass in the park, he'd made a second call to Dornig from the public booth in the lobby of the hotel,

Dornig reported, "It was a package. Garwith picked it up at the general delivery window, then remailed it. But the clerk on the mailing window doesn't remember where it was going. The package was gone by the time we got on it. But it had to be shipped out on a westbound train. Nothing has gone east in that time. And it was first class, the clerk remembers that much. He said Garwith readdressed it. Crossed out the old address and stamps and turned it over and put on the new name and address. The clerk said he couldn't accept it that way, so he put some paper tape over the old stamps and address. But he doesn't remember the name it was mailed to or where."

"But its sure going west?"

"Yeah. The package was the right size for the dough. But there're a lot of packages the right size, even with brown paper tape on them. We'll start the check. I'll alert all the points on your route. If he figures to pick it up while he's on this ride of yours, and he's sent it to his own name again, maybe we can nail that money. But they'll have to contact you before they fool with it. *If* they find it."

"If," John said. "Wells was right behind him. Maybe they're in it together. But maybe Garwith's trying to keep it out of Wells's hands. Maybe that's why he mailed it again." He paused. "If the package is located, maybe we can put a dummy in its place and save the money no matter what happens. But I don't know. I don't want just that kid and the money—I want Wells too."

"Well," Dornig said, "remember the kid could have sent the package anywhere. It's a large postal service. But it ought to be on one of two trains going west. We'll alert both of them. If we get the package, you'll know it when you check in, wherever that is. Good hunting, Benson."

Allan Garwith, with Cicely, returned to the station wagon at three-fifty, when the sun had burned away all of the mountain coolness of the night before. A short conference was held by the riders before Mrs. Landry started the engine.

"It's late," Mrs. Landry said. "But remember it's summer and we've got a lot of good light left. I can make ever such good time once I get out on that Great Divide."

"I just think we ought to go on!" Miss Kennicot said, laughing heartily. To John Benson's dismay, she had climbed into the seat previously used by Margaret Moore, just in front of him. Margaret Moore now sat up front with Mrs. Landry. Harry Wells was still at John's left. The Garwiths were sitting in the same place. Allan Garwith had stretched out, leaning his head back against his seat. He looked calm, even sleepy, John saw. He's either certain he is going to get away with this, he thought, or those pills have gotten to him.

"What do you think?" Mrs. Landry said to Cicely. "Will the poor dear ride all right now?"

Allan Garwith had closed his eyes and seemed to have fallen asleep. "Well," Cicely said, "I think we've caused an awful lot of trouble. But I think everything will be all right now. Whatever everyone else wants to do is fine with us, I'm sure."

"Mrs. Moore?" Mrs. Landry asked.

"Somehow," Margaret Moore said, "I'm getting weary of Cheyenne."

"Of course," Mrs. Landry said. "Mr. Benson?"

"I'm ready," John said.

"Mr. Wells?"

"Let's move it," Harry Wells said.

Seven minutes later, Mrs. Landry rolled past the western city limits. Once again she floored the gas pedal. The station wagon's nose lifted. Everyone was pushed back into their seats. Then Mrs. Landry was whipping the car down the highway at a little less than eighty-five miles an hour.

"Would it bother your husband if we all sang again, dear?" Mrs. Landry called to Cicely.

"I'm sure it wouldn't," Cicely said. "I think he's sleeping very soundly."

"All right," Mrs. Landry said happily. "What'll we sing this time?"

"Why don't we just warm up with 'Friends' again?" Miss Kennicot shouted. She had paled a little, John noticed, and was gripping her seat with white-knuckled tension. She laughed uproariously, then pealed into the song at the top of her lungs.

Allan Garwith, John Benson saw, had begun to snore softly. When Mrs. Landry reached the Great Divide, she really opened the station wagon up.

# Chapter Thirteen

The singing had gradually died as Mrs. Landry took Granite Canyon, Laramie, Medicine Bow and Rawlins like a skier running down a hard-packed snow slope. The riders simply settled into silence as she sent the car winging swiftly over the purple sage-clustered land, as the sun yellowed and dipped closer to the horizon ahead.

Everyone but the Garwiths had eaten lunch in Cheyenne while Allan Garwith had been stretched out on the grass in the small park. Cicely had bought sandwiches during that time, and now had them ready in the event her husband awoke and was hungry, though she had not eaten herself. This fact obviously bothered Mrs. Landry. After covering the basin in what was undoubtedly one of the fastest crossings in Wyoming history, she began talking of dinner. "You can't go without fuel, you know!"

"This friend of mine I mentioned," Miss Kennicot said, "Alice Gregson? You remember? Well, she said there's a perfectly wonderful little roadhouse to eat in in Green River, just as cheap as anything, and awfully good food. Let me look it up in the Three A's. Here it us. It's right in Green River. That isn't far ahead is it, Mrs. Landry?"

They arrived in a half hour. It was dark when the station wagon stopped outside the roadhouse. Everyone climbed out except Allan Garwith.

"My goodness," Mrs. Landry said, peering at him stretched back on the seat, "he certainly sleeps, doesn't he?" She looked at Cicely. "Do you want to wake him up, dear?"

"Well," Cicely said nervously, "maybe, since he's sleeping so hard, I shouldn't. I mean, the doctor gave him some pills and maybe it wouldn't be good to wake him."

"All right, dear. You just come in with the rest of us, and let him sleep."

"Maybe I should stay out here and be with him, in case he does wake up."

John Benson watched Cicely Garwith carefully. He had felt certain from the beginning that however Allan Garwith was mixed up in this, Cicely was innocent. She had to be a superb actress to be anything else. And the background Ray Hannah had given him on her did not indicate that she was anything but what she seemed to be. He was even more certain now that whatever Allan Garwith was doing, she had no part of it.

"Now, dear," Mrs. Landry said in her best mother's tone, "I know you haven't eaten lunch. I don't know if you've even eaten breakfast."

"We had it in our room. I really haven't been hungry since."

"Well, it isn't good for you not to eat all day. Now that young man's going to be all right. If he wakes up and gets hungry, he can eat those sandwiches you have. Now you come inside with us."

Still Cicely looked hesitant, and John Benson thought: It's a matter of money, as much as her concern for him. Garwith hasn't spent any of that bank money, or he would have known it by now. She just can't afford very much.

He said, smiling at the girl, "Would you have dinner with me, Mrs. Garwith? Let's make your husband jealous, shall we? I think grooms take too much for granted. Do I have a date?" Cicely looked at him for a moment in surprise, then a smile broke forth, bright, appealing, so honestly direct that it was irresistible. She laughed. "I think you're quite right, Mr. Benson. I think I should keep him a little jealous." There was a glow in her eyes, he saw, as though what he'd just said to her was the most pleasant thing she'd heard in a good while.

He gave her his arm. They all moved into the roadhouse, leaving Allan Garwith sleeping deeply, snoring softly.

He awoke a few minutes after they had gone inside. He looked around the interior of the otherwise empty station wagon, light from the neon of the roadhouse illuminating it. He then looked out at the roadhouse and saw the others at a booth by a window. He realized that the station wagon was clearly visible from that window. He shrugged and shifted his position into one more comfortable. He closed his eyes and in a few moments was snoring softly again.

When they returned to the car, Miss Kennicot again plunged into the seat originally occupied by Mrs. Moore. She waited expectantly for John Benson to get into the one just behind her. She had, during the last leg of travel in the dark, taken to swinging her hand down and cracking it against John's knee whenever she quoted something. His knee had become quite sore.

Thus he was relieved when Mrs. Landry finally admitted a vulnerability. She did not like to drive at night. She couldn't see well enough, she explained, to get the kind of speed she liked. When John volunteered to take the wheel, she agreed.

Driving out of Green River into the mountains that preceded Salt Lake, Miss Kennicot kept up an endless flow of quotations, songs, and anecdotes about her Robin experiences. In time, John realized that she increased the volume of her voice whenever he and Margaret Moore, who now sat beside him in front, started to exchange a few words.

But finally Miss Kennicot's head fell back. Her mouth fell open. And she began snoring softly, in harmony with Allan Garwith.

As he ran the curves looping into the mountains, John said to Margaret Moore, "Do you think you'll like San Francisco?"

"I'm sure of it," she said. "I have a feeling about it. I've read about it, seen pictures. I love the ocean. Fog. Hills. The water all around. It's my kind of place, I think."

"Well," he said, "I think any place you liked would become your kind of place, Margaret. You have an awareness, a control. I think you're above places, really. I admire you."

"Do you?" she asked very quietly.

He glanced at her in the glow of the dash lights. "Yes," he said very seriously, knowing he meant that regardless of whatever she was, "I do."

He felt her hand placed gently on his knee, left there, as he drove on, the car silent now, as the miles dropped away. They were in Utah now, curving through the night along the mountain highway. He enjoyed the closeness of her, the feeling of her hand. He held off thoughts about what might happen in Salt Lake City if Garwith, with Wells behind him, went for that money. He forced himself to think only about the pleasure of Margaret Moore sitting beside him this way, silently. It was, he thought, a tremendous improvement over the pounding of Miss Kennicot's fist against that same knee....

Lights of Salt Lake were first visible by the white glow in the night sky; then, before the sharp descent from the high mountain road to the low flat of the land beside the lake, they looked down on the lights themselves, spread in a large silver-dotted cluster.

The others began to stir as John drove down the grade toward the city. In a moment he heard Miss Kennicot laughing again.

As they came into the city limits, Miss Kennicot got out her Three A's book. She was given a flashlight from the car's glove compartment. She began searching for the proper place to stay and said, "What about a motel this time, everybody? I do think they're generally a bit down on rates. Wouldn't a motel be nice?"

But after covering a long number of blocks it was obvious there were no vacancies at that hour.

"Oh, dear," Mrs. Landry said from the back of the station wagon. "I just feel this is all my fault somehow. Maybe I should have sent ahead for reservations before we even left Loma City. My goodness, I did want this to be such a pleasant trip."

"We'll take another run through the city," John said. "We still might find something."

"The thing is," Miss Kennicot said worriedly, "when everyone's filled up this way, and you're desperate, why, then they can just charge anything they want to. Highway robbery, in other words."

Now Allan Garwith finally awakened and said, sitting upright, "Where are we?"

Cicely said, "Salt Lake, Allan."

"Already?"

"You've been sound asleep, dear," Mrs. Landry said.

"Well, where are we staying?"

"Maybe no place," Harry Wells said in his flat voice. "The motels are filled. Maybe we ought to keep on going."

Garwith switched around, looking at him. Then he turned to the front again. "If we're in Salt Lake it's time to take a break, isn't it?" His voice was fuzzed with sleep, but mean-sounding.

"We can do just what anybody wants to do," Mrs. Landry said. "I just want everybody to be happy."

"I could use a break," Garwith said sullenly.

"Well, Allan, maybe—" Cicely began.

"I mean, two days. We're in Salt Lake? That's not dragging our feet, is it?"

"It isn't," John said. "But I still don't see any vacancies."

"Maybe," Cicely said, "we can just go on and then—"

"What are you talking about?" Garwith said. "You always said you wanted to see Salt Lake, didn't you?"

"Well—" Cicely said. "It sounds interesting. I guess if—"

"There *is* so much to see!" Miss Kennicot said. "I, of course, read a good deal on it before we left Loma City. It's the home of the Mormons, you know, right here at the foot of the Wasatch Range. It was founded in eighteen forty-seven by Brigham Young. The Temple and Tabernacle are right in the heart of the city. And it's called the City of the Saints. Isn't that poetic?"

"Well, I just don't know what we should do," Mrs. Landry said.

"But," Miss Kennicot said, "I wouldn't want to find some awful motel that was the last thing anybody wanted to rent, not even clean, I mean, and find out they've skyrocketed their rates just because they know they can take advantage of you at this time of morning. People can be so awful about that. Just take terrible advantage, because they know you're stuck with it."

"I have an idea," Margaret Moore said. "It's going to be daylight in a little while. When we leave Salt Lake we'll cross the desert, and that's going to be very hot when the sun comes up. If we want some rest before we go on, why don't we wait until people start checking out of the motels—that ought to start in a couple of hours. Then we can check in, rest until this evening, and start driving when it's cool again. If we left, say, at midnight, it's going to be a lot more comfortable driving between here and Reno."

There was a moment's pause, then Allan Garwith said, "That's the most intelligent thing I've heard all year."

"Yeah," Harry Wells said quickly. "Let's stop and get some coffee and wait it out."

They had coffee and waited in an all-night restaurant, then returned to the car. Sunlight had finally begun washing over the city, revealing its broad, clean streets, the old but neat buildings; the sun crept over the mountains they'd left behind, clearing the last webs of darkness and soon the city was splashed in a bright, shimmering morning light.

John Benson started the search along the highway running through the city. At last they found a motel with neat stucco cabins. Three had just been vacated. These were taken by the Garwiths, Margaret Moore, and Miss Kennicot and Mrs. Landry together. The motel's manager assured John that two more cabins would open up shortly, and he waited in the station wagon with Harry Wells.

Wells, John noticed, kept checking his watch, then staring at the door of the cabin taken by Allan and Cicely Garwith. He kept thinking: I would like to slam you right into death row, Wells, and watch you squirm while you wait for the same thing you gave that kid in that Loma City motel and that guard, but ...

He said conversationally, "I hope they don't take too long checking out. I can use some rest."

"What?"

He met Wells's eyes and tried to decide whether or not Wells had suspected him when Miss Kennicot had revealed his position near that post office in Cheyenne. Wells stared at him coldly, unemotionally, with no clue whatever. He didn't know. But he was fairly certain that Wells was not suspicious about him. He was only concerned, John was certain, with that money.

"I said," John repeated, "I hope we get into a cabin pretty quickly. I can use some sleep."

"Yeah," Wells nodded and resumed his silence, checking his watch, then staring at the Garwiths' cabin.

At seven thirty-five two more cabins were vacated. Fifteen minutes later, when they had been cleaned, John and Harry Wells each stepped into a cabin.

Inside, John pulled the drapes of his front window almost shut, leaving a slight opening. Through this he looked at the other units. Margaret Moore's was beside his own. The one shared by Mrs. Landry and Miss Kennicot was next to it. Across the small green-grassed court was Harry Wells's and the one used by the Garwiths. He waited, watching.

A half hour later two people owning a car with Maine license plates checked out. He watched the manager roll a cart up to the door of the vacated cabin and disappear inside with fresh towels and sheets. Five minutes later he reappeared and rolled the cart into his own unit and disappeared again.

John lit a cigarette. His mouth was dry. He was beginning to feel a dull ache at the base of his skull. Finally, at ten minutes to nine, Harry Wells stepped out of his cabin.

He did so carefully, looking at the other cabins, staring at the Garwiths' for several seconds. Then he moved away swiftly. He went around the corner of his cabin, away from the one used by the Garwiths. In a moment he was striding down the sidewalk, heading downtown.

Seconds later the Garwiths' door opened. Allan Garwith came out quickly. He ran in a trot to the corner of Wells's cabin, then stopped and looked after the retreating Wells. When Wells was far down the block, he moved off in the same direction, hurrying with brisk, nervous strides.

John opened the door of his own cabin and walked across the court to the public telephone booth beside the manager's unit. He checked the number of the local FBI office in the telephone book and dialed it. A man named Sands came on: "Benson—yes. Glad to hear from you."

"Wells and Garwith both just left on foot from where we're staying, the Restwell Motel, and they're going west on Norfolk Avenue. Have somebody pick them up and watch, only don't, for God's sake, let them know it."

"Hold on." There was a pause, then, "Okay. It's done. We'll have a man on them in seconds."

"Good. Did that package show up here?"

"No. But we've got someone on both trains right now, checking. We may pick it up by Reno."

"How about the post office here? Have you got it covered right now?"

"Can do, very quickly."

"I would. And at least one man on this motel, all the time we're here. I think Wells and Garwith will be back. I've got a hunch about what's going on. I'll check with you again in a few minutes."

He returned to his cabin and waited. In ten minutes, neither Wells nor Garwith had returned. He walked back to the telephone booth and called Sands.

Sands said, "They showed up at the post office, just now."

"That's where I thought they were heading."

"Wells walked up to the general delivery window at nine o'clock. He asked for a package addressed to Allan Garwith. When they told him there wasn't one, Wells left. Three minutes later Garwith came in and asked if anyone had checked for a package in his name. They told him yes and described Wells. Then he took off."

John nodded, brain turning. "I think that gives us the picture all right."

"Garwith's got the money. But he sent it somewhere else. Wells isn't hooked up with him. He just wants to get the money. Now Garwith knows who Wells is and what he wants."

"That ought to be about it." John looked out of the booth and saw Wells coming down the street swiftly. "Thanks, Sands. Wells is coming back."

He hung up and moved quickly back toward his cabin. As he did he thought he saw one of the drapes move behind the front window of Margaret Moore's cabin. He went into his own unit, then looked out between the drapes. He wasn't certain. But unless his senses had played tricks on him, that drape at Margaret Moore's window most certainly had moved.

Wells then appeared and moved into his cabin. Minutes later, sneaking in from the back, Allan Garwith turned the corner of his cabin and hurried inside.

Then it was very silent.

# Chapter Fourteen

Allan Garwith sat in his cabin, smoking, staring with hard eyes at the gently sleeping Cicely. It was early evening. The air-conditioner, though it hummed steadily, seemed to do little good. The sweat kept streaming down Garwith's forehead. He could see the beading on Cicely's face. She was covered with a single white sheet to a point just above her breasts, nothing else. That morning he had tried to go back to sleep, after he'd returned from the post office when he'd absolutely proven who Harry Wells really was. That, of course, hadn't worked. But Cicely had awakened neither when he'd left nor when he'd returned. He'd begun tossing in the bed angrily at noon and finally awakened her. She'd gotten up, put out the sandwiches for him, showered, and then asked, clad in her housecoat, if there was anything she could do for him.

"Yeah," he'd said. "Take off the housecoat."

When she got into bed again, he'd started thinking of Wells once more. He'd finally said, "To hell with it." He hadn't really started anything. She didn't seem to mind very much. She'd said, "I'm just so tired, Allan. Maybe we're just both tired."

"Well, sleep," he'd said bitterly.

Since then he'd stalked back and forth in the cabin, eaten a sandwich, and periodically gotten out the pills and looked at them. They had taken on an extreme significance since they'd come into this motel. He kept remembering the pleasant way he'd stopped caring when he'd taken them in Cheyenne, the beautiful way he'd slept all the way to Salt Lake. But now, having verified who Wells was, he knew that he could not afford going out on that stuff again. Yet, the temptation to return to that pleasant state of dreams, not caring about a damn thing, was heavy.

Now, as darkness began to settle over the city, he got out the two bottles and looked at them. His hand began to tremble as he did, and he suddenly got up, walked to the bathroom and flushed all the pills away. He stopped on the way out and yanked viciously at the handle of the hot-water tap of the sink. There was a faint drip there. He looked at the yellowish stain on the white porcelain where the drops had been striking. He wrenched the handle again. He waited. Another drop fell with a soft, barely detectable sound.

He went out of the bathroom, shut the door and sat down. He listened very intently. He could hear nothing for long moments. Then he was certain he could hear the faintest plop of water striking the porcelain. He sucked in his breath, trying to shut it out of his ears. He remembered how that dripping had gone on and on in that small dirty house outside New Orleans, after Charissa had attempted to see how much strength he'd gotten back. He turned that out of his mind and leaned his head back, closing his eyes.

But he still remembered the same sound, years ago....

He'd been twelve and they'd lived in that crummy Italian neighborhood, on Third Street, just off the river. Allan Garwith had been one of only a half dozen non-Italians in his grade school four blocks away. He'd tried to please, and worked hard to compete at the games. And he'd been accepted. Italians, he'd learned early, took their time accepting you; but when they had it was a lifelong acceptance. Still he had not liked that neighborhood. It was tough, dirty, and you never knew when something was going to go wrong.

But it was not really the neighborhood that was always going wrong. It was, he would later admit in moments of clear reasoning, his father, who had been a large blond man, half-Swede, half-English, with huge shoulders and large, muscular arms. The best thing he remembered about his father was a crooked front tooth that protruded slightly from an otherwise even line of large white teeth. Somehow, his father, with his short-clipped hair and athletic frame, had always seemed very handsomely young—except when he smiled. Then that crooked tooth gave him a mean look that had always frightened him, as though his father had lived an eternity and could even see right into his young-boy mind and discover any disloyalty and punish him for it.

His father was always punishing him for something. He drove a gravel truck for a city quarry. And when he came home, always with beer on his breath, he would, within an hour, find something for which to punish Allan. Allan could not even remember all the things that he'd found, but he did remember that one thing, that one particular evening when his father had come in, eyes glazed, wide mouth slack and mean-looking, that smile flickering on and off.

He'd come into the small, cramped apartment, knocking a chair over. And Allan Garwith's mother, a large, dark, handsome Irishwoman, with a placid face and a plumply spacious figure, had appeared from the small kitchen, looking and saying nothing. Allan had been sitting on the maroon mohair sofa, playing with a gyroscope he'd gotten the day before. His father had said, "What do you think you're doing?" Just that, and that was all, but it had been the way he'd said it.

His mother said, "Roy, don't start on him. Now please don't start on him."

"I want to know," his father said, teeth gleaming, "what he's doing sitting there playing with toys like some damn infant when he ought to be learning how to fight."

"What are you talking about, Roy?" his mother had said. "It's good for him to play with that—it teaches him science. They told me that at the dime store when I bought it."

Allan Garwith had looked at his father apprehensively, waiting for his mother to make it all right.

When his father started this sort of thing, she had always made it right for him.

His father laughed nastily. "I talked to Frank Panzarri down at the Eagle Club about thirty minutes ago. Do you know what Frank Panzarri told me?"

"Why would it make any difference what Frank Panzarri told you at the Eagle Club? I've got dinner ready."

"I'll tell you what Frank Panzarri told me. He said they were teaching the kids boxing lessons down at the school today. And this little mother's boy wouldn't fight."

Very quickly Allan Garwith again concentrated on his gyroscope. He looped a heavy string between his thumb and little finger, got the gyroscope spinning and then put it on the string. He had never concentrated on anything more carefully in his life.

"Why should they be teaching little boys to fight at school?" his mother asked. "Don't they do enough of that in the streets anyway?"

"Not this mother's boy," his father said. His father smiled and stepped to him and knocked the gyroscope across the room. "Boy, you're going to learn something now. Stand up."

"Roy, you leave him alone, do you hear?"

"Get up, boy. Get up on your feet. You're going to get your first real lesson. Right now."

He stared at his father, blinking slowly. It was true that he'd refused to put on those oversized boxing gloves at gym class that afternoon, re-fused to box with Nick Panzarri. He'd been afraid to. But this was even worse. He could feel himself trembling very badly inside.

"Get up," his father said.

"Roy, no!" his mother said.

His father reached out, grabbed his shirt and snapped him to his feet.

"Put up your hands, boy," his father whispered. Allan Garwith watched the way that crooked tooth made his father's smile look pecu-liar, so that he was even more frightened. "All right," his father said, and slapped him hard across the cheek.

"Roy—!" his mother had called.

After that he remembered the slaps coming harder and harder, until, though he wasn't seriously hurt, he'd fallen down. But he still had refused to bring his hands up. Then, because he knew his mother was struggling with his father, he ran. He ran like a mouse searching for an opening in a cat-prowled house. He finally found himself in the bathroom, listen-ing to the struggling of his mother and father. He was shaking very badly. He squatted down, underneath the sink, trying to make himself very small.

He could hear the thump in the other room as his mother and father bumped into a wall. He heard the grunting, the sharp intake of breath, a crack of a hand against skin, a table tumbling over. He heard the foot-steps, heavy and menacing, coming toward the bathroom. He squeezed himself even tighter beneath the sink. He saw his father's work shoes ap-pear, the heavy white socks, the khaki trousers. He was afraid to look any farther up, to see that look on his father's face. Then he heard his mother coming, grabbing his father again. He held his breath and closed his eyes, listening to the struggling again as his mother pulled his father out of the bathroom.

Finally he heard a rapid swearing from his father, the slam of a door. For a few minutes it was absolutely silent. In those minutes he realized that a tap above him was leaking. Right above his head he could hear the faint plops of water striking the sink rhythmically, as he huddled there shaking, waiting for his father to reappear.

At last his mother came in and pulled him to his feet. He put his arms tightly around her generous body. She had been forced to push him away, in order to examine him.

"You're not hurt," she said, her voice a flat, weary sound. She turned and left him. She went into the kitchen and sat down wearily at the small table. He followed her and looked at her for a while. Then he went back to the living room and picked up his gyroscope.

It wouldn't work any more. He went back and looked at his mother.

At last he opened the front door and peered out cautiously. He could not see his father on the two flights of steps that ran to the lower level of the ancient apartment house. He ran down them swiftly. Outside he jumped to the sidewalk and ducked into a doorway and waited. He could not see his father anywhere.

He finally returned to the sidewalk, moving cautiously. Then he shoved his hands in his pockets and swaggered a little, whistling, ready to run any second, He went down the street and around the block.

And that was when he found his father. He was down the alley, struggling with someone again. Allan Garwith was prepared to run again, but he was compelled to watch. When he realized that his father had not discovered him, he pressed himself close to the corner of an old building and stared down the alley in the yellow light of a street lamp.

His father, this time, was struggling with one of the women Allan Garwith had often seen around the neighborhood, a woman who wore a lot of powder and lipstick, someone the older fellows always snickered about and said things about that Allan Garwith didn't understand. The woman laughed, he was surprised to hear, as she struggled against his father. Suddenly Allan Garwith turned and ran. He ran all the way back to his apartment.

He came into the kitchen, puffing, sweat streaming down his cheeks. When he'd caught his breath, he told his mother, who was sitting exactly as he'd left her, precisely what he'd seen downstairs in that alley.

She didn't say a word.

He'd thought she didn't hear him properly, so he started repeating the description. She suddenly brought a hand hard across his mouth.

He'd been too stunned to move for several seconds. During his description he'd felt a fine feeling of discovery, of having come on to something that would make his mother love him more than ever. Now this had happened. He was barely able to turn, blindly, and stumble to bed. He lay there, eyes smarting, hating everything in the world.

He hadn't stopped hating the next day, nor the next, nor all of them after that. His father had been killed in a truck accident a week later. He had gone to the funeral and hated him lying dead in the casket. His mother had grieved for his father a long time, which he'd also hated. And he hated her personally for being able to grieve that way. When he got back from New Orleans and found that she was dead, all those years later, he felt no specific hate; he simply didn't care….

Now, in the motel cabin in Salt Lake City, as darkness came down from the mountains and blanketed the city, Allan Garwith stood up suddenly, slamming his chair back against the wall. He strode into the bathroom and shoved at that faucet. He could not stop the dripping. He walked angrily back into the room. Cicely was sitting up in bed, holding the sheet close to her chin.

"What's the matter, Allan?"

He paced, silent, mouth and eyes grim. He kept thinking of Harry Wells. Harry Wells, on their first stop out of Cheyenne, had gone directly to the post office and tried to collect that package in his name. Harry Wells knew what was in that package, and Harry Wells was a cold-blooded killer. Oh, God, he thought, trying to hang onto his nerves.

He tried to get his mind off that. He thought of Margaret Moore. He thought of how he'd watched her walk to her cabin early this morning; it was the way her body moved, the flex of her good legs, the whole of her just plump enough to start a pounding excitement deep in his middle. He stopped pacing and looked at Cicely.

He stepped over to her and pulled the sheet from her with one snap of his hand. He looked at her, while she looked back at him, blinking a little. Then he bent down and put his mouth on hers, hard and brutally....

Minutes later he said angrily, "The hell with it, the hell with it...!"

He got out of bed, face flushed, and listened to her saying, "Allan, it's just my fault. I'm sure of it. If you can't—"

"Shut up!" he said, whirling.

He stood there, trembling with fury. He could hear that steady dripping, the sound that had come through to him minutes ago, when he'd thought he'd be above any kind of sound. It had gotten into his ears, his brain, and there wasn't anything else. He'd finally given up. Now she was trying to feel sorry for him.

"Allan—" she began again.

"Stop," he said, his voice rising. "Just stop!"

Dressed, he walked out of the cabin, shutting the door. He stood in the warm air, leaning back against the door, away from that damning sound of the dripping, tipping his head up to look at the stars sweeping across the black sky. He saw the lights in Harry Wells's cabin go out. He knew Wells was checking him. Well, check! he thought. Check!

He shook his head, blinking, trying to shake his mind into calm. He felt stripped of all courage, trapped.

He suddenly looked in the direction of Margaret Moore's cabin and saw the glow of a cigarette. It came up in an arc, glowed more brightly, then went down. She was standing, he realized, in the shadows, alone....

His throat tightened. He pushed himself from the door and began walking slowly across the court in her direction. What he'd lost with Cicely a few minutes ago was back with him, full force. He could not hear the dripping sound now. Nothing was bothering him, except that she was standing there, alone, in the night, and he was walking toward her....

She saw his door open, saw him silhouetted against the light from inside the cabin. Then the door was shut and he was only a dim outline in front of it. She had tired of the inside of her cabin and had come out, to the fresh air, to look at the stars, at a moon just showing along the tops of the mountains. She was calm. She felt no anxiety when she realized he was walking toward her.

When he was in front of her, she looked curiously at his face, hazy in the dim light.

"Nice night," he said softly.

"Yes," she said. "It is."

He said nothing more for a few moments. Then she felt a faint apprehension, only instinctively. Somehow she did not like his silence, his immobility. She dropped her cigarette. He said, "I'll get it." When he'd ground the cigarette out with his shoe, he'd come another foot closer to her. He was directly in front of her. She suddenly moved sideways a step, toward her door. He shifted so that he was between her and that door.

"Are you feeling better?" she asked, keeping her voice very polite, knowing now that something was very wrong.

"Yeah," he said. "I'm feeling great."

"Well, that's very nice. I'm glad to hear that."

She started to move again. His hand dropped on her shoulder.

She looked at him. "I think—" she began.

Then he was shoving her backward, along the wall, forcing her to the back of the cabin. She didn't call for help because she was too surprised. She only struggled silently against the savage strength he was displaying, using his one arm.

"Don't be foolish," she gasped finally, as he pressed her against the back wall of the cabin. "I can call for help. I can—"

His hand went over her mouth. His body pinned her to the wall. She struggled harder this time. But he held her locked.

He breathed, close to her ear, "Don't fight it. Do you hear? Relax! I'll make it right for you. Don't you understand?"

She kept fighting him, determinedly, pulling on all of her strength now.

"Listen," he gasped, "I can give you anything—anything you want! I've got the money. You name it—"

She suddenly got his hand from her mouth, then twisted so that he'd lost his command over her against the wall. She ran back toward the front of the cabin, listening to his footsteps behind her. She did not go to her own door, but instead to John Benson's. She rapped on his door and turned, as Garwith came toward her. He stopped as the door opened, and ducked back out of sight. Margaret Moore moved inside swiftly, looking at the surprised eyes of John Benson.

# Chapter Fifteen

He looked at her standing there, looked at the tear at the neck of her yellow dress. Her hair had been disarranged. There was an alive, tense, frightened look in her eyes. She was breathing fast. She was, he decided, one of the most beautiful women he'd ever seen. He also knew that she had come to his cabin in extreme fear. He closed the door and said, "Are you all right?"

She nodded. "Yes." She walked across the room, arranging her hair with one impulsive motion. She turned around, beside a chair near the bed. A smile flickered. She was, he knew, getting control of herself rapidly.

"What happened?"

She shook her head faintly, her smile flickering again. "May I sit down?"

"Of course." He came over to her. "Cigarette?"

"Please."

He gave it to her. He held a match for her. She put her hand against his while he did. He could feel the trembling in her hand. He wanted suddenly to put his arms around her. But he did not. She inhaled the cigarette deeply.

"That's better," she said.

He sat down on the edge of the bed, looking at her eyes. "What happened?"

She took a deep breath, let it out, smiled at him. "Our young groom, Allan Garwith, just tried to rape me."

His eyes, he knew, were steady. He was silent for a moment. He lit a cigarette for himself and finally the anger came. His professional calm shattered for a moment as he realized completely what she had just said. "How did it happen?"

"I went outside for a cigarette. He came out of his cabin and crossed the court. He said it was a nice night. Then he dragged me back of my cabin—" She shrugged. "I didn't call for help because I couldn't realize it was really happening. Then he got his hand over my mouth. I got away from him. I came here. He ducked into the shadows when your door opened."

"I see," he said flatly, thinking of what Garwith had attempted, feeling the anger once more. "I can call the police. I'll—"

"No. I'd like to think maybe he just got an idea and got carried away with it. I'm sorry he did, but it didn't work out. I like his wife. I wouldn't want her to be hurt. I'm afraid she will be anyway, one of these days. But I don't want to do it."

He stood up. "I haven't got a drink to offer. The best I can do is coffee. Instant, with hot tap water. Will that do?"

"Yes," she said. "That'll do fine."

He fixed two coffees, using the cabin's glasses. He sat down again with her. "You didn't see this coming? I mean—" He paused. "Maggie used to know certain things. The way a man would look at her, certain things another man would never see or detect that a woman does."

"I guess so," she said. "Not rape. I didn't see that coming. But the little things, yes. It's puzzled me. The boy was just married, after all." She looked at him directly. "There've been a lot of things that have puzzled me about this trip, John."

He put his coffee glass down. "Yes?" Now he was being careful again.

"You, for instance. Something. I don't know. Except you seem two different people to me."

He shook his head, looking puzzled, knowing that he'd lost some of the ability he used to have for this kind of thing, knowing that he'd shown too much of himself to Margaret Moore. But he'd been unable to help that. "I don't think I follow you."

"Just a feeling. I'm sensitive to certain people, especially those I like. For instance, that complaint of yours in Cheyenne, bringing the manager into it. That didn't fit. Then the way you've been watching people—Allan Garwith, Harry Wells, especially."

He spread his hands. "I didn't realize that." And he was thinking, if she had detected it, had Garwith? Had Wells?

"Maybe," she said, "it's my imagination. But there's something. I don't know what. In Cheyenne, when Allan Garwith went for that walk after he came out of his room, Harry Wells disappeared. So did you."

"So did Miss Kennicot," he said, finally smiling.

"After you did, yes. After she'd inquired of everyone if they knew where you'd gone."

"She seemed to know. She found me."

"Yes," Margaret Moore said. "She's a pretty good bloodhound, I think.

Anyway, Allan Garwith's been acting peculiar all through this trip. Now this tonight. Maybe he's simply a psycho, but I think he's into something. When we checked in here, this morning, I couldn't sleep. I was awake when he left his cabin. Did you know he left this morning?"

"No," he lied. "I didn't."

"He did—after Harry Wells left. Same thing as in Cheyenne, only in reverse. Both of them off. And then what?"

"I don't know."

"You left your cabin and made a telephone call. Two of them, in fact, in fifteen minutes. I watched you. It isn't because I'm so very damn snoopy in general. It's just that I sensed something going on. I think Allan Garwith has been deliberately stalling on this trip. He said his wife had always wanted to see this city to get us to stop here. She hasn't left her cabin. I think something's going on that's tense and serious."

"Well," he said. "What Garwith tried was tense and serious, I admit that. But the rest of it—" He shrugged. "I have an old Army buddy who lives in this town. I called him up. He wasn't in the first time. He was the second."

"I'm sure it's none of my business," she said. "But things still seem peculiar to me. I don't, for example, really see you on this kind of ride. I know what you told Mrs. Landry. That you simply decided not to travel alone. But I rather think you're not the type to do that—unless you had a more important reason."

"Like?" he said.

"I don't know. But there're things that just don't seem to add up to me about you."

"Be specific," he said. "Please."

"All right," she said. "You say you had your advertising agency on Kosuth in Lafayette?" She shook her head, looking at him directly. "You pronounced it Kosuth with the hard o. The natives pronounce it Kahsuth, and with the accent on the last syllable."

He smiled at her again, hating himself for the blunder. But he motioned a hand and said, "Not really good evidence, Margaret. That's an old habit. A switch on the usual way of saying it. We used to do it. We called Lafayette Laughayette. Maggie and I had a few things like that—a kind of rustic humor. But I'm glad to hear you have a good imagination. It makes you more complete in my mind."

"What Allan Garwith did a little while ago wasn't imagination," she said. "Nor what he told me."

"What did he tell you?"

"That he could give me anything I wanted. That he had the money."

Very carefully he lit another cigarette. That, he thought, absolutely sealed it as far as Garwith was concerned. But he frowned, puzzledly. "He said he had the money to buy you anything?"

"That's what he said. I got the impression the Garwiths were making this trip on the proverbial shoestring."

"Yes," he said. He shook his head. "I don't know. If he tried what he did with you, I imagine he'd say almost anything, wouldn't he?"

"I guess he would," she said slowly.

"I wouldn't try to read things into this that aren't there, Margaret. One thing's certain. Garwith did attack you. What do you want to do about it? We've still got the rest of the trip ahead of us. You can't just ignore it."

"Yes," she said, "I can. Because maybe there's something wrong between him and the girl, something that might have made him try what he did. I don't know. But I'll respect the possibility. He may regret it very deeply right now. And, as I said, I don't want to hurt his wife. As long as I'm safe, I won't reveal it."

"All right," he said softly. He looked at her carefully, feeling the strong pump of his own blood, a building want in himself. If he could risk telling her who he really was, then it would be so much simpler. But he couldn't. He was almost certain that she was all right. But if she were somehow connected with this, then this might be a last-ditch effort to find out who he was. If she were connected with Wells, for example, this would have been a good attempt to do that. The story she'd told about Garwith might or might not be true. He thought it was. But he couldn't be sure, and so he had to keep on playing the game. "I want you to be safe too. How can we make sure of it?"

"Right now," she said, looking at him in a way that he could not fail to understand, "I feel very safe with you."

"Right here," he said softly, "in this cabin."

"Yes," she said.

He bent forward and kissed her. Her response was sudden, almost explosive. She put her arms around him, digging her fingers into his neck, her breath coming short all at once. He felt her lips on his ear, cheek, as he held her tightly. Then his mouth was on hers again, feeling it open....

The hands on his traveling clock announced that it was eleven o'clock that evening. She stood in front of a mirror, buttoning the yellow dress, a soft smile on her good mouth. Then she combed her hair. She is radiant, he thought, lying in the bed, watching her, taking these last few minutes with care, to enjoy them fully.

"You look truly beautiful," he said.

She turned to him. "I feel truly beautiful." She came over to him and he kissed her again. Her lips were warm, soft, the fury of passion replaced by a quiet contentment, the result of what they had had together during the past dark hours. "I'd better hurry," she whispered. "I can't leave here just as the caravan is gathering outside."

"Will you be all right?"

"If there's any more trouble, I'll call this time. You could hear that, couldn't you?"

"Yes," he said and kissed her carefully again. She moved away from him then, applied new lipstick, touched her hair once more and finally came over and took his hand. "The best thing about this," she said softly, "is that I'll see you again in an hour. But don't feel obligated, John. Anytime. Anywhere. But no strings. Remember that."

She left swiftly.

Miss Kennicot had been awake for three hours, puttering about the cabin, while Mrs. Landry slept contentedly. Packed, ready to go, with a little over an hour to kill, Miss Kennicot got out the poem she'd written after she'd returned from her tour of downtown Salt Lake City. It was written on a sheet of purple stationery, in a fine, swirling script. It read:

TO A SUMMER PHEASANT ON THE WING

*(For one loved and dear)**

Oh, hail to thee, blithe fleeting pheasant
In the sky. So full of all colors in your
Coat so gay. Dost thou know the burning
In my heart, whilst thou flees through the
Scudding clouds up in the sky of blue? Oh,
Pheasant, do you carry the secret of this
Tortured love so bright and flaming, going
Through the scudding clouds in that sky of
Blue?

*Written summer of 1961 to John Benson, unknown to him.

Tears formed in Miss Kennicot's eyes when she had finished reading. A smile trembled on her lips. She folded the paper carefully, then thrust it lovingly down the front of her dress. She turned out the lights and stood breathing hard for a moment, then opened the door, ready to sniff in the deep nectar of nature's summer night.

As she did, she saw the door of John Benson's cabin open. She saw Margaret Moore step out and close the door carefully behind her. Miss Kennicot watched from the shadow of the door, while Margaret Moore, in the moonlight, returned to her own cabin. Then she stepped back, doubling as though punched in the stomach. She shut the door and spun, clutching herself in the middle, making a low strangling sound. Finally she pulled the poem from her dress and ripped it viciously into small bits.

Mrs. Landry, awakening, stumbled out of bed and snapped on the light switch. "My dear, what's the matter?" She blinked, trying to come awake completely. "My goodness, I heard the most peculiar noise—like somebody had got stabbed or something...."

Allan Garwith had not stopped shaking since Margaret Moore had got away from him and knocked on John Benson's door. After she had gone inside, after he'd ducked back into the shadows, Harry Wells had come outside.

Garwith had pressed back against the side of Margaret Moore's cabin. But Wells had walked straight toward him. He thought he would faint when Wells stopped in front of him, looking at him in the moonlight.

Wells said, "Thought I saw you out here. How're you fixed for cigarettes?"

There had been seconds before Garwith was able to reach inside his shirt pocket and draw out his pack.

Wells took the pack and shook several cigarettes out. "Thanks. I ran out. Mind if I take a few?"

Garwith shook his head silently, swallowing over and over. Wells returned the pack to him. With a shaking hand, Garwith put it back in his pocket. Wells turned and walked slowly back toward his cabin. He stopped in front of his door, lit the cigarette and continued to stand there, looking in Garwith's direction. Slowly Garwith returned to his own cabin.

Inside, Cicely said, "Did the air make you feel better, Allan?"

"Oh, shut up," he whispered.

She began to cry, hunched in the bed. She cried softly and steadily. He didn't care. As long as she was doing that, she couldn't talk to him. He couldn't stand any more talk from her. He paced for a while, the sound of Cicely's sobbing a vague echo in his ears.

What had come over him anyway, he thought, trying that with the Moore woman? He must have been out of his mind. The only thing good about it was that she hadn't started screaming. That would have really fixed everything.

But why, he asked himself, hadn't she started screaming? Hadn't she told Benson what happened? He'd expected to see Benson come charging out of there. Well, maybe she hadn't told him, he thought. Maybe she hadn't because she hadn't minded it so much, after all. Maybe he'd just pushed it too fast. She didn't mind, but she'd gotten stubborn, that was all. Maybe she'd really gone for it, including that promise he'd made that he could get her anything she wanted. Yeah, he thought, maybe that was it.

He felt a little better then, more certain, stronger; and the shaking began to disappear. Okay, he thought, thinking of Harry Wells. I can handle you, friend. Reno—that's where it's going to count. Only that package has got to be there by the time I get there. And I've got to shake you, buddy.

He was thoughtful for a moment, then he walked into the bathroom and took a new razor blade from its holder. Cicely was still crying when he came back through the room and stepped outside. Once again, the lights in Wells's cabin went out. The stupid bastard, Garwith thought. He's too damn obvious. It's no wonder he screwed up that bank job. He's stupid. Well, all right.

He stood in front of the cabin for a moment, then suddenly broke to the left, away from Wells's cabin, dodging around the corner. He moved swiftly, hearing Wells's door flying open. Blade in hand, he went over a short fence, into an alley, then ran with a swift athletic speed half the distance down the block. There was a closed appliance shop at that point. He cut back along its wall and stopped. He could hear running behind him.

He stood very motionless and silent against that wall, out of sight in the shadows, and watched Harry Wells moving down the alley. You are really stupid, he thought.

When Wells had gone out of sight, he returned to the motel, to the front of the court, where Mrs. Landry's car was parked.

He got the hood up quickly, then ran his hands along the engine until he found the fuel line. Carefully he sliced it thinly with the razor blade, then closed the hood.

He hurried back to his cabin and shut the door behind him. Cicely looked at him with tear-filled eyes. "Allan, I—"

He smiled at her, feeling better now, much better. "So I've been in a lousy mood," he said. "So it'll all be all right pretty soon." He grinned widely, knowing that was an absolute fact. "What's to cry about?"

"Oh, Allan," Cicely said. She got out of bed and ran to him. She put her arms around him tightly.

In a few moments, there was a knock at their door. Garwith opened it, to face a hard-eyed Harry Wells. Wells's forehead was wet with perspiration. He extended a fresh pack of cigarettes. "Thought maybe I was using up your last cigarettes. Went out and bought some."

Garwith looked at him and smiled tightly and thought: The hell you say—you just about busted something until you made sure I was back in here, and you go right on being so stupid it's astounding. "Thanks, but I've got plenty."

"Sure," Wells said. "I didn't disturb you, did I?"

"No," Garwith said. "You didn't."

Wells walked back toward his cabin. Garwith shut the door and turned around. He took Cicely in his arms once more, still smiling. Reno, he thought. Then I start again, fresh and new, without this broad to make me sick every time I look at her.

"Allan," Cicely said, holding to him like a child, "all I want is to know you love me. You do love me, don't you, Allan?"

"Cicely," he said, "you know it. But listen. How about letting me carry the money, all of it, from here on? Just so I don't forget what it feels like."

Before they vacated the cabin at midnight, while Cicely was turned the other way, he was able to take the gun from the bag and fit it under his belt beneath his jacket.

## Chapter Sixteen

The station wagon rolled away from the motel a few minutes after midnight. After the usual shock of Mrs. Landry's flooring the gas pedal as they left the city limits of Salt Lake City, the inside of the car became silent. John Benson sat again in his usual place in the back. Miss Kennicot, who had returned to her place up front beside Mrs. Landry, was strangely silent. She sat woodenly, John noticed, chin tilted up as though she had sniffed something foul in the air. Everyone else sat in their original places.

As they raced past the Great Salt Lake, the water reflecting the moon as a train lumbered slowly across the lake over dark pilings, Mrs. Landry started humming her favorite song, "Everyone Is Beautiful in Someone's Eyes," a song which Miss Kennicot had particularly liked and learned from Mrs. Landry. Tonight, however, Miss Kennicot did not join in. Instead she turned her head, gazing out at the night, and Mrs.

Landry's cheerful voice gradually died away.

They left the lake and moved onto the desert. Traffic was extremely thin. Cool air had relieved the blinding heat of the day. The station wagon sailed smoothly over the salt-flats highway.

The car began to lose power when they were nearing the far, western edge of the desert.

In sudden frustration over the loss of speed, Mrs. Landry tromped on the accelerator. The car jumped ahead, faltered, jumped ahead, then finally rolled to a stop at the edge of the highway.

"The darn thing," Mrs. Landry said.

"Well, what's the matter with it?" Miss Kennicot said, speaking for the first time. "Aren't we ever going to get this trip over with?" Her voice had a note of anger, sharpness and whining distress in it.

Mrs. Landry looked at her in surprise. John Benson said quickly, "Why don't you try it again, Mrs. Landry?"

Mrs. Landry did and shook her head. "Darn thing."

"Well," Allan Garwith said in a full, clear voice, "it isn't the gas. You got a full tank in Salt Lake."

"I'll take a look under the hood," Harry Wells said. "How about that flash in the compartment?" Miss Kennicot gave him the flashlight with one angry movement. Harry Wells climbed out and opened the hood. Allan Garwith followed, then John Benson also got out.

The beam of the flashlight went over the engine slowly, while the howling of coyotes echoed over the desert. John Benson saw Allan Garwith start when that howling reached their ears; he turned quickly, looking out over the moonlit flatland, his eyes flickering apprehensively. Wells shook his head. "I don't know. I never ran a motor pool. I wouldn't know what it is. How about you, Benson?"

"I'm afraid I don't know much about cars, Sergeant."

"Garwith?" Wells said.

"Let me take a look," Allan Garwith said, taking the flashlight. He moved the beam around, poking and shoving at wires gingerly. "Hell, I don't know."

"Maybe a vapor lock," Wells said doubtfully. He walked back to the window beside Mrs. Landry and asked, "How's the temperature gauge?"

Mrs. Landry checked. "Normal. Right on the little line."

Wells walked back to the opened hood. No car had passed or met them. "The car's not overheated so it isn't a lock in the fuel pump. Somebody'll have to get help."

John Benson stepped to Miss Kennicot's window and said, "How far is the next town, Miss Kennicot?" He smiled at her, certain, somehow, that someone—probably Garwith—had tampered with the car. He hadn't wanted to risk another telephone call in Salt Lake, or he might have found out through the report of the man the office there had placed on the motel. But it made sense that Garwith was stalling—perhaps to make certain his package arrived before the station wagon. That would mean that Garwith had sent it somewhere along the line of travel, perhaps Reno. And that, John told himself, was good news. He was, he was certain, going to get his chance to get both of them, and very shortly. But it was not, he knew, going to be easy.

Miss Kennicot flashed him a withering look. She snapped, "Ten miles. Ten miles straight down the road. What's the matter? Can't you fix the car? I thought men were supposed to be able to do anything. That's a laugh, isn't it?"

"Thank you, Miss Kennicot," he said politely, surprised by her reaction. He returned to the front of the car. "There's a town ten miles ahead."

"Well," Allan Garwith said quickly, "you fellows relax. I'll hitch a ride and send somebody back." He smiled engagingly and walked back along the car. "Cicely, I'm going to get help."

"I'll do it, Garwith," Wells said, stopping him. "You better stay with your wife. If I had a wife, I wouldn't want to leave her out here in the middle of nowhere."

Garwith turned around. "I don't think there's anything to worry about. I mean, I trust you fellows to take care of things. A good Army man like you? Why would I worry? I'll be glad to go."

"Why," John said, "don't I do it? The sergeant's right. You'd better stay with your wife. And I think you're right—a good Army man like the sergeant here ought to be around too, just in case."

"All right," Wells said swiftly. "You go on, Benson. We'll stay here, both of us."

Allan Garwith opened his mouth, as though preparing to protest, then closed it and climbed into the station wagon, slamming the door behind him.

"Here comes a car, Benson," Wells said thinly.

The car bore down on them, slowed slightly, then whipped on. The howling of animals across the desert continued. The fifth car going in their direction stopped. Mrs. Landry called after John, "I'm a member of the Three A's too, Mr. Benson, just like Vera here. If there's a Three A's place, that'll be the best thing."

John got into a new Ford driven by a white-haired man with a good tan who explained, as he drove on, that he was a soup salesman.

"They've got a tow-in service up ahead," he said. "Both auto clubs."

Fifteen minutes later John was let out at an all-night service station and garage on the edge of a small town. A lank youth in white coveralls explained that the tow truck was on another call, that it should be back in twenty minutes. John stepped into the public telephone booth and called Reno. A man named Ryan came on with a rasping voice, after the call had been switched to his home.

"Benson? Good. Where are you?"

"West of Salt Lake on the edge of the desert. Little town ahead of Toand Range. The station wagon fluked out about ten miles back. I hitched a ride in here to get a tow truck. I think Garwith's stalling for time. I think he jimmied the car one way or another."

"I got the report from Salt Lake. The man on the motel there said he had the hood on the car up before you left."

"Well, you'd better have the police alerted in both directions, just in case that station wagon can be fixed while I'm gone and Garwith or Wells tries something."

"All right. But I think Garwith just wants to get to Reno. We located the package—it's in the Reno post office right now. He sent it to a phony name, Raymond Jones. Either that or he's got an accomplice by that name. I doubt that, because he hasn't had enough time to set a partner up."

John blinked once. "How about the money? Did you open the package?"

"We didn't want to touch it until you checked in with us."

"Have it opened, very carefully. I'll check back with you in ten minutes."

"Right."

He hung up and stepped out. The tow truck had not arrived. The youth in the white coveralls was relining the brakes on a white 1958 Thunderbird.

In ten minutes John called Reno again. Ryan said, "Money's there—all of it. The boys were careful opening it. We've got Garwith now, the minute he asks for it."

"But not Wells."

"We can wrap up the package again, with phony money inside."

"Yes, and maybe tip off either Garwith or Wells. We can't afford that." He was silent for a moment. "There's only one way to do it. Let Garwith get the package with the real money in it. Let Wells make his move. Once Wells gets his hands on that money, we've got him. There's supposed to be identification on general delivery material, isn't there?"

"Supposed to be. They don't always do it. Depends on the clerk or whether they think they know the customer. Did they check him in Cheyenne?"

"Maybe I should have asked, but I didn't. I don't think they did, so I think he doesn't know what the rule is supposed to be, hasn't even thought about it. If he has, then maybe he's got some false identification ready. Or maybe he's got a friend involved in this. I don't think so. But no matter what it is, I want him to get that package. If someone else asks for it, let them have it and tail them. But I don't figure that any more than you do. I think Garwith will ask for it. When he does, have them give it to him. Make sure they rewrap it carefully."

"You're giving away good odds."

"I have to."

He closed his eyes, visualizing the post office in Reno. It was on Virginia Street, the main downtown street, on the Truckee River. The Riverside Hotel was directly across the street. He'd been there several times during his college days, a few times on the job before he went into the Washington office.

"All right," he said. "Cover the post office. Put a man in the lobby of the Riverside. Have him ready with a gun for me. I'm going unarmed right now. I'll be wearing the blue suit I've got on, a striped yellow and blue tie. If I need help, I'll wave. Otherwise leave it alone. If Garwith picks up the package and goes out, I'm going to wait until Wells goes for it. Have a man behind me. I figure if Garwith takes the money out, Wells'll make his move pretty fast. But maybe Garwith will mail it again. If he doesn't, and Wells hasn't made his try by the time we leave Reno, better put a car behind us. But nobody moves in until I signal. All right?"

"All right, Benson. Good luck."

The tow truck had returned when John stepped outside. Minutes later he was riding in the cab with a short, swarthy man, who said nothing all the way back to the station wagon. There the mechanic lifted the hood and silently examined the engine. "Fuel line," he said. "Shot. Have to put in a new one. Better tow you in."

The station wagon was hitched to the truck. Thirty minutes later, after a creeping journey, the wagon and passengers arrived at the all-night station. The fuel line was replaced. The short, swarthy man held the old one in his hand. "Looks like it was cut." Within range of his voice were John, Allan Garwith, Harry Wells, Cicely and Mrs. Landry.

John said, "I don't know how that could have happened." He looked at Wells's eyes, saw them switch to look at Garwith.

"Who knows?" the mechanic said. "Maybe it just looks that way. Anyway, it's ready to go."

When they were once more whipping down the highway, west, toward Reno, Mrs. Landry said gaily, "Now that wasn't so bad, was it, everybody?"

There was a murmur of agreement by everyone but Miss Kennicot, who remained stonily silent, as she had been during the entire process of towing in the car and repairing it.

Miss Kennicot, in fact, did not speak until they rolled into Sparks, Nevada, just ahead of Reno. Then she said, "I don't see why we don't just keep going, right on through Reno. What's so much about a dirty little town just full of gambling and heaven knows what other kind of filth! It's a disgrace, and it ought to be outlawed!"

There was a moment of surprised silence in the car. Then Mrs. Landry said, "Are you feeling all right, Vera? I mean—"

"I'm feeling perfectly fine," Miss Kennicot said. "I'm simply offering my opinion on this absolutely sinful state we're traveling through. Six more hours and we could be in San Francisco. I'm just very awfully tired of this trip, if anybody cares to know. I don't see why we can't just keep on going."

Allan Garwith spoke next. "Maybe we're just going to stop in that sinful town, regardless."

"Allan—" Cicely began.

"I mean," Garwith said, his face flushed with anger, "since when is one person running this show, I wonder? When did that start anyway?"

"Now you just listen to me for a moment, young man!" Miss Kennicot said, switching around to glare at Allan Garwith. "I have every right to—"

"Vera," Mrs. Landry said quickly, "maybe a good, hot cup of coffee would make you feel ever so much better. Mrs. Moore, isn't there some coffee left in one of the Thermoses?"

"I think so," Margaret Moore said. "Would you like me to pour you a cup of coffee, Miss Kennicot?"

Miss Kennicot's face twitched visibly. "No, I would not like you to pour me a cup of coffee!" She twisted around, facing the front again, her face a deep pink. "I wouldn't care, this minute, just what we ever did, whether or not we stopped in that miserable town, or whatever we did or didn't do. I really wouldn't care! I hope I make that completely clear. It just absolutely doesn't make a particle of difference to me one way or another. And I've made my last statement on that!" Having finished, she clamped her mouth shut and sat rigidly, staring straight ahead, as Mrs. Landry, completely befuddled, drove into Reno.

Downtown, the sign stretching above Virginia Street announced, "The Biggest Little City In The World." In the bright, warm sunlight, the casinos lining both sides of the street looked lifeless without the contrast of darkness to intensify the flash and glitter of their signs. But the sidewalks were busy with people hurrying from one casino to another.

"Well," Mrs. Landry said worriedly, "I'm just willing to do what everybody else wants to do. If you want to stop, or just go right on, why—"

"We're going to stop," Allan Garwith announced decisively.

"Well, but Allan," Cicely said. "If nobody else wants to stop, we—"

"Why," John said carefully, "don't we stop for a little while? We can look around—say, for an hour or so—and then we could keep on going and get to San Francisco this evening."

"Well, that sounds just right!" Mrs. Landry said, relieved to hear a positive suggestion. "Is that all right with you folks?" she asked the Garwiths.

"Yeah," Garwith said.

"Mrs. Moore?"

"I think an hour is all I'll need here, Mrs. Landry. I've never had any luck gambling."

Miss Kennicot whirled around again, glaring at Margaret Moore. "Do you mean to tell me that you'd shamelessly go in and support one of those havens of sin by actually gambling?"

"Well," Mrs. Moore said. "Yes."

"I don't know what I could possibly say about that!" Miss Kennicot shouted, and turned to the front again. Margaret Moore turned and looked at John curiously. He shook his head, spreading his hands. Harry Wells, he noticed, was silent, tense, simply watching Allan Garwith.

"Well, we'll just stop then, for an hour," Mrs. Landry said. "Only first I'll have to find some place to park—it's so crowded on this street."

"I think I saw a sign pointing to a parking lot back a couple of blocks, Mrs. Landry," Margaret Moore said. "On the other side of the tracks."

"All righty," Mrs. Landry said. A few minutes later, two blocks off the main section of downtown Reno, she rolled the station wagon into a self-park lot. John Benson, as they came in, offered to pay for an hour at the small entrance booth manned by a disinterested attendant. When the car stopped, Allan Garwith was the first one out. He waited impatiently while Cicely climbed out, then took her arm and hurried off, toward Virginia Street.

Harry Wells remained in the car for a few moments, opening and closing his suitcase swiftly. Then he got out and strode off in the same direction the Garwiths had gone. Margaret Moore came up to John, smiling. "Any particular plans, sir?"

"I'm afraid so, Margaret. I'd like to take you downtown, but I've got a small errand first. I'm sorry."

She looked at him, eyes flickering. "All right. And no need to be sorry, John."

He moved off quickly, listening to Mrs. Landry trying to urge Miss Kennicot from the car. "No, I will not!" Miss Kennicot was saying loudly. "I will simply not set foot in this dirty town!"

Allan Garwith moved quickly ahead with Cicely. Wells was pacing rapidly behind them. John felt his stomach tighten. He knew what Wells had taken from his suitcase—a gun. And he was very certain when they had the car repaired that he'd detected the shape of a small gun beneath Allan Garwith's jacket. It was all going to explode, and very quickly....

## Chapter Seventeen

A short distance from Virginia Street, Allan Garwith saw a small sports shop. He stopped and dug a dollar bill from his pocket. He said to Cicely, "Go try your luck somewhere. Here's a buck. All right?"

She looked at him in surprise. "By myself, Allan? I mean, aren't you—"

"How about not arguing with me today? How would that be? Would that be too much to ask? I've got something to do. I'll see you back at the car."

"But, Allan. I—"

"Listen," he said. "I want an hour, all by myself. Is that too much? What is the matter with that anyway?" His mouth was a tight, white line. The muscle beside it was shivering.

"Are you all right, Allan? You look so pale, and I—"

"Take the buck, right? Right in the little hand. Then go. Trippy, trippy, down the street! Move!"

She took the dollar, her eyes misting once again. She walked on quickly, stumbling once because she was obviously unable to see past the tears. She righted herself, while he stood looking after her with angry eyes. She turned the corner.

He'd known Wells was behind him when they'd left the parking lot. He could not see Wells now. Stupid bastard, he thought. Right to the post office. Only he won't get it. But he'll show again when he doesn't. So all right. I'll be ready for him.

All right, he thought, and stopped the first person he met. "Which way to the post office?"

"Straight down the street."

He moved down Virginia Street, his pulse beating at an even one hundred and twenty-five pulsations per minute.

Harry Wells walked away from the general delivery window in the post office and stepped outside, the sunlight making the planes of his face harsh and masklike. He put his hand against the jacket of his suit, feeling the pistol strapped against his chest in its holster. He would like to use it. He would truly like to use it, just take it out and start pulling the trigger on everybody in sight....

He moved down the steps and walked around the building. He stopped and looked back. Garwith was not in sight. He stepped hack, putting a tree between himself and where he expected Garwith to appear, if he were coming. Maybe, he thought, the bastard had sent the money to San Francisco. Maybe Los Angeles. Maybe anywhere in the world. My money! But he was not going to shake Harry Wells until he led Harry Wells to that dough. Then he was going to get a present for his trouble. A nice, fat, deadly present, to be enjoyed once, that's all.

Harry Wells waited motionless, silent, habitually patient even against his frustration and anger.

Across the street, unseen by Harry Wells because he had used the entrance on the Truckee River side, John Benson walked into the lobby of the Riverside Hotel. He strode past the slot machines, a crap table, a roulette wheel, into the section that contained the registration desk and a small alcove that housed a magazine counter and a set of telephone booths. Glass doors looked out on the street, allowing a view of the post office across the street.

John walked to the doors, not looking at the chunky man in the light gray suit who stood to his left. A bellboy in a cowboy costume removed two bags from a white Jaguar and accompanied a small chic brunette to the desk. Behind, there was the faint sound of the croupier's chant from the casino.

The man in the gray suit edged closer to John and said in a rasping voice as he looked across the street, "Benson?"

"That's right."

"Ryan."

"In person?"

"I wouldn't sit in the office at a time like this. Here."

The gun was slipped to John swiftly. He tucked it under his belt, buttoning his jacket again. He felt two extra clips sliding into his left jacket pocket.

"Wells went into the post office about two minutes ago," Ryan said. "He came out and walked around the building. He's standing behind a tree down the block. I've got a man in the telephone booth to your left. We're hooked to the post office. Wells asked for the package. He was told it wasn't there. If Garwith asks, he'll get it and we'll know it."

John looked past Ryan. A man in a blue suit and matching hat sat in one of the telephone booths. John looked back across the street at the post office. "No sign of Garwith yet?"

"No. You decided not to cover him over here?"

"I don't want to take a chance on spooking him now. The money's where he's going. If he gets cold feet now and tries to disappear without picking up the money, that'll surprise the hell out of me. He'll—" He stopped, looking to the left, as a figure appeared on the bridge running over the Truckee River. "Here he comes now."

Garwith walked slowly, his one arm straight at his side, as he crossed the bridge. His eyes looked straight ahead, almost as though he were in a daze. A large woman in a wide-brimmed straw hat came toward him from the opposite direction, a small child tugging against her hand. She held on to the child stubbornly. But the child got away at the bridge and headed off in a zigzagging run, bumping squarely into Allan Garwith.

Allan Garwith crouched, his hand flying to his middle. His eyes opened widely, as the child ran on ahead, his mother calling after him loudly. Quickly Garwith straightened and dropped his hand away from his middle.

Ryan let out a soft whistle. "Something goes wrong, he'll blow sky high."

"And he's armed," John said flatly. "Carrying a gun just about where I'm carrying this one. That's too bad."

"You're sure this is the way you want to do it? We can grab Garwith the instant he puts his hands on that package. No sweat."

"Then we lose Harry Wells. No thanks."

They watched silently as Garwith walked up to the doors of the post office. He disappeared inside. A minute went by. Two. They were both looking at the man in the booth to their left. The man pressed the receiver of the telephone closer to his ear. Then he looked at them and nodded.

"Okay," Ryan said. "He's got the package."

Swiftly John moved outside into the bright sunshine, followed by Ryan. He stepped close to a cab parked at the curb and said to the cabbie, handing him a bill. "Just stay parked here." The cab was a cover between himself and Garwith as well as Wells. Ryan flashed his identification at the cabbie, then stood beside John and said, "What do you figure he'll try to do?"

"Try to shake Wells. That's all right now."

Allan Garwith walked out of the post office. He walked in that same dazed manner, and now he was carrying the package.

John felt a flicker of nervous tension running through his entire body. There was a wild, peculiar look on Garwith's face.

He reached the sidewalk and walked back in the direction from which he'd come. He moved at a careful, even pace, toward the bridge that led to the main part of the casino-clustered street.

"Here comes Wells," Ryan said.

Harry Wells appeared from behind the tree down the block and walked in their direction with a brisk, military stride. Garwith had crossed the bridge and was even with the lobby entrance of the Mapes Hotel.

"All right," John said to Ryan. "Stay behind me."

He rounded the cab, following Wells toward the bridge. At that moment Garwith suddenly spun, looking back at Harry Wells, then ducked into the Mapes lobby....

Allan Garwith had been certain that Harry Wells, though he hadn't yet seen him, would be behind him when he came out of the post office with that package in his hand. He had felt it, as he'd walked over the bridge that crossed the Truckee River. Then he had made up his mind. In crowds he would be safe. In crowds he could lose Harry Wells. And then, he thought, his brain turning better than it had ever turned because he was pitched to a point of near-explosion, he would do the last thing Harry Wells would expect him to do—return to that station wagon in the parking lot on the other side of the business district. He would simply tell them that he had run into Wells downtown and Wells had sent the message he was staying in Reno. He even thought that he could tell them Wells had instructed him to check his bag into the bus station in San Francisco to be picked up later. It was clear, fast thinking, better, Allan Garwith thought, than any he'd done in his life.

Then he turned around swiftly, and actually saw what he knew would be the fact: Harry Wells behind him. That was when his thinking collapsed and he'd turned and darted into the Mapes lobby, not thinking at all suddenly, simply going on instinct, because the panic had risen up in him and was nearly choking him. He had seen that look in Wells's eyes, as Wells came after him across that bridge. That had turned him to jelly.

And he was simply moving now, like a hunted animal.

The casino of the Mapes was directly off the lobby to his left. He had two choices. Either go through the casino. Or try for an elevator straight ahead. But he was certain the elevator would not be fast enough.

He moved into the casino at almost a trot. The casino was in use, as always, but not crowded. He passed the slot machines, the gaming tables. A roulette dealer looked at him, eyes cool and impersonal, and said, "Black eight, a winner." At the glass doors at the far end of the room, Garwith looked back. Wells was coming into the casino, bumping into a couple just leaving for the lobby.

Garwith slammed through the doors into the sunshine again. He set off at a swift athletic run, to his right, past the coffee shop entrance of the hotel. He ran with the same speed he'd demonstrated on the football field in Loma City.

Midway down the block, he crossed the street, dodging between cars. He turned to his left at the corner at the end of the block. When he'd reached the end of that block, he looked back again. Wells was coming down the street from the opposite corner. The street, one block off the main street where the casinos were grouped, was almost deserted. Garwith moved past the entrance of the Cal-Neva Club and cut across the street diagonally, heading back toward the crowds.

At mid-block, across the street, he moved into a short T-shaped pedestrian avenue, converted from an alley, paved with multicolored stones, with silver dollars imbedded in the surface. The back entrance to the Golden Hotel was to his right, the rear entrances to Harrah's Club, the Nevada Club and Harold's Club were all lined along his left. He hesitated, turned, saw Wells entering the short avenue. He plunged into the rear of the Nevada Club.

The club was packed with people, lined elbow to elbow at hundreds of gleaming slot machines. He shoved his way through, holding the package with his one arm, using it as a wedge. There was angry muttering. But nobody stopped gambling. He pushed his way clear through the casino and looked back. Harry Wells was halfway through the crowd.

Garwith stumbled out to the sun-splashed Virginia Street, moved down the block, and swung into Harold's Club through its front entrance. A narrow escalator was running upward. Garwith stepped onto it and ran up the steps. In a moment he was on the second floor. Wells was just coming in, at the street-level entrance, as Garwith stepped out on the second floor.

He looked around wildly. More slot machines spread away from him. A girl in a cowboy hat and a fringed black vest looked up from her wheel.

The eyes were bored, disinterested. A male croupier to her right chanted, "Hard-way four." Garwith looked down the escalator—Wells stood below, looking hesitant and furious, then he stepped toward the escalator. Garwith moved swiftly to the one moving down, at the opposite side of the room.

He went down the steps quickly, almost tumbling a very old woman, who was just reaching the lower floor. She called after him sharply. Then he saw Wells, halfway up on the up-going escalator. Wells wrenched around, having seen him, and came down the steps against the upward motion. Garwith ran for the back entrance, a wild, unreasonable, insane fright almost blinding him....

John Benson, sweat streaming down his face, came out of the Nevada Club just as first Allan Garwith, then Harry Wells, moved into Harold's Club. He was followed by Ryan. He stopped outside the entrance and saw Harry Wells pause at the foot of the escalator. He backed a step and said to Ryan quickly, "Better stay out here. Both of us inside, we could lose them altogether in these mobs."

"Right," Ryan said.

John looked inside Harold's Club again, just as Harry Wells was going up the escalator. He started to go in. Then Wells looked down, as Garwith came down the other escalator.

John stepped back, out of sight again, until Wells had turned and come back down the escalator. Wells started after Garwith, who was running toward the back exit. John went in.

Garwith, followed by Wells, reached the T-shaped pedestrian avenue again. They were heading out along the upper leg of the T, when John pushed his way outside. They disappeared around the corner to the left, on the back street that ran parallel to Virginia Street. John ran swiftly after them.

When he'd reached the corner, he saw Garwith, with Wells fast behind him, sprinting toward the railroad tracks. In the distance a train whistle sounded. John realized that Garwith, for some reason, was heading back in the direction of the lot where the station wagon was parked.

Breath burning his chest, he followed. Garwith was now crossing the tracks, running swiftly, with his inherent athlete's ability. Behind him, Wells stumbled once, then regained his footing. But he was also fast.

John was in the open now, exposed to both of them, he knew. But Wells had never looked behind once. If he'd suspected John, or anyone else on his trail, he'd forgotten it in this dogged chase, John was certain of that.

They were moving back toward Virginia Street, along the tracks. In a moment, John thought, he would be crossing the street, where he could signal Ryan.

But as he reached the street, a train came rolling toward the station, slowing, moving directly between John and where Ryan waited on Virginia in front of Harold's Club. John hesitated, then ran on as the train stopped, blocking him from Ryan's view. He would have to go on by himself, he knew. Then he realized, as he ran, that he had failed to take time to tell Ryan where the station wagon was parked. If Garwith were leading them there, there was not going to be any help; not now, he knew, snapping the sweat from his eyes with one angry motion of his hand. He was in it all alone.

# Chapter Eighteen

John Benson saw, as he ran, that Allan Garwith had reached the edge of the parking lot, that Harry Wells was coming up fast behind him.

Garwith suddenly disappeared among the cars. The lot was silent. The attendant was now reading a paperback mystery. Mrs. Landry's station wagon was parked at the end of the row where Garwith had disappeared. An hour had passed since they left the lot, John knew, and waiting quietly around the car were Mrs. Landry, Margaret Moore, Cicely; and inside was Miss Kennicot, her mouth a firm, haughty line.

John Benson pulled the gun from his belt, slowing, as Harry Wells's hand came out of his jacket with his gun. Wells paused briefly at the edge of the cars, head swinging from left to right. Then he plunged ahead.

John saw Garwith leap out between cars halfway down the row. The package was out of Garwith's hand now, replaced by a gun. But Garwith did not fire. He came in sideways on Wells, whose reflex was too slow for the catlike speed of Garwith. The gun in Garwith's hand slammed into the side of Wells's head. Wells sprawled to the ground, his head spurting blood.

John lifted his gun and swung it down to firing position. "Hold it, Garwith!"

Garwith spun, seeing John for the first time. Behind him came Cicely, running from the station wagon. "Drop the gun, Garwith," John snapped.

Garwith did not. John would have fired instantly, but Cicely was just behind Garwith now. Behind her came Margaret Moore and Mrs. Landry. They were all in the line of fire. Then Cicely had reached Garwith. "Allan—"

Garwith moved with unbelievable speed. He stepped back and grabbed Cicely around her waist with his one arm, holding the gun in front of her stomach, pointing at John. She froze. Garwith, behind her, nodded, eyes blazing. "Cop, Benson? It figures. Bastard! Well, drop the gun yourself!"

"I mean it, Garwith—I'll start shooting."

"You'll start shooting her then," Garwith said, his voice a trembling sound of nerves, fright and desperation. "Get rid of that gun and quick!"

John stared at the look in the youth's eyes. He would murder, he knew, anybody and everybody, including his own bride. There was nothing else to do. He dropped his gun.

"Kick it this way," Garwith snapped.

John did. The gun skittered over the concrete and stopped just in front of the sprawled Wells. Slowly one of Wells's hands moved toward it. Garwith stepped around Cicely and kicked him at the base of the skull. Wells gave a short, pained gasp.

"Pick up those guns, Cicely," Garwith said, releasing her. "Quick."

Looking bewildered, frightened, Cicely picked up both Wells's and John's guns.

"Put them in my jacket pocket," Garwith said. "Then pick up that package between the cars. Hurry up!"

"But, Allan, I don't understand! What's happening? What's—"

"Move!"

Cicely put the guns in her husband's pocket, then picked up the package.

Margaret Moore and Mrs. Landry had come up now. Allan Garwith said to them, "Back to the car. Don't make any noise. Just do what I tell you! Benson—walk around me, back toward the wagon!"

Margaret Moore looked at the crumpled Wells, then at Garwith's eyes. She turned and started back. Mrs. Landry, however, stood and stared at Garwith. "My goodness, whatever is wrong, Mr. Garwith? Why, you look—" Then, for the first time, she saw Wells lying on the concrete. "Oh, my goodness sake!"

"I told you what I want you to do!" Garwith said. "Now do it!"

"Hurry up, Mrs. Landry," John said, moving past Garwith and taking her arm. "Do what he says."

"But I just don't—" Mrs. Landry began.

"Quickly, Mrs. Landry," John insisted.

They moved back toward the station wagon. John paused to look back. Allan Garwith had turned the pistol in his hand down and was pointing it at Harry Wells. Cicely suddenly clutched his arm. He shook her hand free. "Allan, you can't—I mean, whatever this is about, you can't—"

"I won't," he breathed. "But only because I don't want to wake up everybody around here." His mouth whitened, then he kicked Wells's head again. A gasp rose up in Cicely. There were tears in her eyes. Blood poured out on the concrete around Wells's head. "All right," Alan Garwith said, shoving Cicely with the barrel of his gun. "Let's go."

He herded them back to the station wagon swiftly. Then he said, "Inside. Hurry up. Cicely, get behind the wheel."

Miss Kennicot, who had been looking straight ahead in the same stiff mood she'd demonstrated since they'd left Salt Lake City finally turned around, frowning. She had obviously, John realized, missed everything that had just gone on. "What is going on here anyway?" she demanded.

"Get out of that seat and move back," Garwith said harshly.

"What in the world are you doing with that gun in your hand?" she said archly.

"Miss Kennicot," John said. "Please do what he says and very quickly."

"What is going *on*?" Miss Kennicot said, her voice rising.

"I'm telling you, you stupid loud-mouthed excuse of a damn woman!" Allan Garwith said. "You get the hell out of that seat and move back and now!"

Miss Kennicot's mouth fell open. She stared at him in disbelief.

"Move!"

She suddenly fell out of the open door and plunged back into the car, into a back seat. She started a low continuous moaning, as though she had just been branded.

John Benson got into the seat where Garwith and Cicely had ridden during the trip. Margaret Moore resumed her old seat. Mrs. Landry sat in back with Miss Kennicot. Garwith got in front beside Cicely.

"All right," he said to her. "Let's get out of here."

"Allan, if you'd only tell me what—"

"Don't talk. Drive!" There was a thread of pure insanity in his voice now, that raked against John's nerves. He glanced back to where Wells had been left, as Cicely drove the car toward the exit. He thought he saw Wells move, but he wasn't sure. He brought his attention back to Garwith. He tried to think of some way he could jump him. But Garwith was leaning back against the door, looking at them, saying, "This gun's right in my lap. I'll use it on the first one who winks at me wrong. Do you hear that?" There was nothing, John Benson realized, that he could do....

As the station wagon rolled out the exit, the attendant barely looked up from his book. Harry Wells pushed himself up against his hands. Then he fell forward. The world spun around him. The pain seared through his head. He tried again. This time he got to his haunches, just in time to see the station wagon turn left, rolling down the street out of sight.

He shook his head desperately. He could not think well. He could not do much of anything but try to keep going. After several long and painful moments, he pushed himself to his feet. The lot remained silent. The attendant was deeply immersed in his book.

Harry Wells staggered from car to car, falling to his knees, pushing himself up again. Ten cars down the row he saw a key in an ignition. The car was a 1957 Pontiac. He got the door open and fell inside. He sat there for a moment, getting over his dizziness, then looked at himself in the mirror. His face was a mass of blood.

He snapped the glove compartment open. There was a box of Kleenex there. He pulled out tissue after tissue, wiping the blood from his face. Finally he pressed together a collection of them in a makeshift pad and fitted them against the wound Garwith had created with his swinging gun. Behind him, on the back shelf, was a man's straw hat. He reached back, teeth gritting, got the hat and put it on his injured head. The hat was too large, but it covered the wound.

Then he started the car, backed, swung forward, and drove toward the exit. He checked the gasoline gauge. There was three-quarters of a tank of gas. As he rolled through the exit, the attendant did not even look up.

Forcing himself above the returning dizziness, Wells turned left, taking the same street he'd seen the station wagon turn on. He pressed the accelerator down. In minutes he was on the motel-lined street that led out of town, west. Must have gone this way, he thought, a dark anger pulsing deep inside him. West, in the direction of San Francisco. The anger gave him strength. Traffic was light. When he reached the last scattering of motels on the outskirts of town, he looked at the flat highway ahead. To the left were purple plateaus. Straight ahead the Sierra Nevada Mountains loomed darkly, a bluish black silhouette. He speeded up. He passed a log truck with an empty flatbed. He passed a white pickup. The car had power, he realized, plenty of it. The needle of the speedometer quivered at ninety. There was one more car ahead, a dark object in the distance, just at the point where the road started up the steep grade.

He came up hard on the car, just as it started up the narrow road that would climb around the edge of the sheer rock, to the top of the mountain and Donner Pass.

Then he was on the tail of the car. It was the station wagon.

He saw the riders turn around and look at him. Mrs. Landry. That damn Kennicot woman. Margaret Moore. John Benson—a cop that one, and I should have figured that out, he told himself, at Cheyenne. But no matter now. Garwith in front, holding the gun. And his wife driving. Look at them, he thought. Scared out of their skins.

All right, he told himself, as the two cars moved up the winding grade, tires shrieking, hang on, suckers. He swore savagely and floored the accelerator. The Pontiac rammed the left edge of the station wagon's rear pumper. The station wagon bounced, skidded, then continued up the grade.

There were no other cars in sight on the drive. And Harry Wells's brain was finally working well for him. One thing to do, he thought. Bump that station wagon over. It'll roll to hell and gone, lost down there in that rattlesnake brush, and that's that. Only I'll know where they are, where that money is. I can come back, pick up the money, take off again, and not one of them will be alive to worry about it.

He swore again, then picked up speed, slamming his front bumper into the wagon again. The wagon careened wildly, back and forth. Hang on, suckers, Harry Wells thought, it's just about over.

# Chapter Nineteen

John Benson turned from looking at Harry Wells. He felt the station wagon swerve sickeningly, saw that they had skidded too close to the edge of the steep, narrow grade, knew that they were high enough now that if they went over, none of them was going to live.

Miss Kennicot was now virtually howling, a steady, nerve-shattering moan with her mouth wide open, eyes closed, face pale to the color of white paper. He looked at Allan Garwith sitting tensely against the door, gun in hand, visibly shaking. He looked at Cicely, obviously so frightened, she could not even think, but pressing up that mountainside on her husband's command like a colt being whipped ahead by a savage, panicked master. John's mouth had gone dry. He felt helpless and sick because of it. He looked at Margaret Moore. Her mouth was set in a tense line, but she was under control, he knew. Mrs. Landry was merely hanging on, blinking, obviously trying to get it straight about what was happening.

Suddenly the station wagon was jarred again. John whirled around, seeing a flash of Harry Wells's wild-looking face. Miss Kennicot picked up the volume of her howling, as the station wagon swerved from the inner rock side to the edge.

"Faster!" Allan Garwith yelled at his wife. "Faster!"

"Garwith, listen—" John began.

"Shut up! Do you hear me? Just shut up!"

John licked his lips. Cicely had increased her speed and lost some of her driving control because of it. She took a tight turn, barely skimming along the edge of the road. The drop was long now. And John visualized the rest of it ahead. He'd taken this road, many times before. It went up sharply, then curved in a hook at the top, at the snow line, above the timber. Donner Pass was a narrow bridge between two mountain peaks. The drop-away on either side of its low concrete sides was immense.

Cicely was running along the edge of the road again. He could see her blinking, confused, frightened tears blurring her vision. My God, John thought, his own nerves singing—she won't be able to see at all in a moment.

Then, as Cicely ran the wagon along the outer edge, Wells brought the Pontiac up again, getting his bumper between the wagon and the inside of the road. He turned out slightly. There was a grinding of metal. The rear bumper of the station wagon tore loose at one side and the car jumped back toward the edge.

"He's trying to get inside!" John shouted. Cicely added speed and Wells was forced to drop back.

Allan Garwith waved his gun wildly. He yelled at his wife, "Hurry up, do you hear me?" He suddenly aimed his gun to the rear. John reached around and slammed Miss Kennicot sideways into Mrs. Landry, ducking. Garwith fired two shots. The bullets whined through the space where Miss Kennicot had been sitting, through the rear window, flying harmlessly into space.

Shrieking like a drunk Indian, Miss Kennicot tried to untangle herself from Mrs. Landry. John Benson shouted, "Garwith, listen to me. You'll get us all killed, including yourself. Give me that gun! I can—"

"Oh, you bastard!" Garwith shouted back. "I'll—" He lifted his gun again as Cicely bore down on the gas pedal in a wild surge of speed that sent them ahead of the trailing Pontiac.

Instantly Margaret Moore reached out and put her hand on Garwith's wrist, shoving his hand down. Swearing, he shook her hand free. But she said, "Allan, listen to me—"

"Touch me again, and I'll—"

"Allan, listen. We've got too much together to throw it away, don't you see that?"

John Benson stared at her, wondering if she had been involved with

Garwith all along.

Garwith was shaking his head, eyes wild-looking.

"Allan, please," Margaret Moore pleaded. "Remember when we were together in Salt Lake? Outside in the dark? When you told me how you felt about me? Don't you remember, Allan?"

John suddenly understood. He looked at Allan Garwith, as the station wagon whipped wildly up the grade, gradually increasing the space between it and the Pontiac. He saw in Garwith's expression the look of a frightened child, desperately waiting for someone to tell him it was going to be all right. He looked at the wild-driving Cicely. Tears were streaming down her cheeks.

Margaret Moore's voice was warm, urging, "Allan, we can have everything together. I want that, don't you see?"

From the back of the car came Miss Kennicot's howling voice, "You dirty thing! You'd do anything, wouldn't you? You—" Then the words melted back into a continuous howl.

"Allan," Margaret Moore begged as they neared the top, "please listen to me. Together, just you and I. Just like you wanted in Salt Lake. That's the way it's going to be."

As they came around the last curve at the summit, the station wagon rocking right on the edge, Cicely took her foot from the accelerator, a weary, defeated look crossing her tear-stained face.

"Cicely," John said, leaning forward, "that bank robbery in Loma City just before we left—your husband got the money when it was left in the lot behind your apartment. Harry Wells was the one who held up the bank, and he knows your husband got that money. I'm an FBI agent, and—"

"Shut up!" Garwith screamed and swung the pistol at John. The barrel grazed a fraction of an inch away from his head, as he threw himself back, out of the way.

They were losing speed. Wells, behind, was closing the distance between them again. Garwith yelled insanely at Cicely, "What are you doing? Move it, move it—!"

"You never," Cicely said in a dead-flat voice, "loved me."

The station wagon rolled onto the bridge that spanned the peaks and came to a stop. Wells's car swept around the curve behind them, approaching fast. Garwith stared at his wife, mouth working, fury darkening his face, aware of nothing else for that moment. "You miserable little—"

John dived forward and hit Garwith's wrist with the back of his hand, sending the gun flying to the floor. He hooked a left fist hard into Garwith's middle. Then, as the youth doubled with an anguished gasp, he chopped the side of his hand against his neck.

He grabbed Garwith's gun from the floor and turned, slamming himself back through the station wagon. Wells's car approached the short, narrow bridge. John fired six times. The front right tire of the Pontiac exploded. Wells's eyes opened widely. Then the Pontiac whipped sideways, smashing over the concrete wall, end over end, sailing into the clear, sun-warmed air. It struck the rocks far below with an explosive, shattering impact.

Slowly Cicely snapped off the ignition of the station wagon and sat there, dull-eyed. Miss Kennicot continued howling loudly. Allan Garwith moaned and shoved himself up, shaking his head. He looked at John Benson, saw the gun in John's hand. He sat there for a moment, then suddenly knocked open the door and leaped out of the car. His feet started chopping in a wild, panicked run.

"Garwith!" John called.

He pushed out of the wagon after him. Garwith was running back across the bridge. John fired over his head. Garwith spun, throwing his arm out wildly. He turned, mouth working, then threw himself sideways, in absolute fright.

He stumbled into the bridge's railing, and because it was in his way, he instinctively started to scramble over it.

"Garwith!" John shouted.

Allan Garwith seemed suddenly to realize, as he poised at the edge of the railing, where he was. He clawed wildly at the air with his one hand. He screamed. Then he went over.

He hit the rocks approximately a dozen feet from where the Pontiac containing Harry Wells had disintegrated.

# Chapter Twenty

Rear bumper rattling, Mrs. Landry drove up the ramp to the entrance of the terminal building of San Francisco International Airport. She and Miss Kennicot were the only occupants of the car. When she stopped, Miss Kennicot fairly tumbled out of the car. She reached in the back and grabbed her bag and the thin sweat-stained volume of Shelley.

"Well, it just seems awful, dear," Mrs. Landry said. "Why, you've really only got out here. Now you're flying right back home to Loma City."

"I've got to hurry," Miss Kennicot said acidly.

"But, dear, you'll just lock yourself up in that library again and—"

"Good-by!" Miss Kennicot snapped, looking at Mrs. Landry darkly. Then she ran toward the terminal, clutching her bag and book of poems.

"My goodness!" Mrs. Landry said, when she had disappeared. "The poor thing!"

She wheeled the car off the ramp and drove back to San Francisco. She came off the Skyway and drove to the Greyhound Station. She parked and hurried inside. Standing in the lobby were John Benson, Margaret Moore and Cicely Garwith. Cicely turned, seeing her coming, and smiled wanly. She looked drawn, dark smudges running under her eyes, but she also looked bravely determined. Two bags were at her feet. There was a bus ticket for Loma City in her hand.

"I'm so glad you could make it, Mrs. Landry," she said. "My bus is just ready to leave."

"I'll carry your bags out," John Benson said.

"We'll all go out and see you off!" Mrs. Landry said to Cicely positively. "Only I just feel so sorry about everything, child. But that's all over now, isn't it? Will you be all right?"

"Yes," Cicely said. "I'll be all right. Did Miss Kennicot get off?" They walked out to the loading platform.

"She's in the air right now," Mrs. Landry said. "The poor thing—all she wants to do is get back to her library. I don't believe she saw one single thing in San Francisco!"

Cicely nodded politely, then shook hands with everyone. "Good-by."

Mrs. Landry kissed her on the cheek. Margaret Moore smiled at her, then bent forward and kissed her too, saying, "You find something good for yourself, won't you?"

Cicely nodded. "I will, thank you."

"Promise?"

"I promise."

She boarded the bus. Minutes later, it pulled out and disappeared into the traffic.

"The poor child," Mrs. Landry said. "She deserves better than she's gotten so far. I just hope she finds somebody real nice now."

"I think," Margaret Moore said, "she will."

They returned to the lobby. Mrs. Landry shook hands with both John Benson and Margaret Moore and said, "Now you two—you're going to stay out here awhile, aren't you? And remember, if you want a ride back to Loma City, why, just call me at my daughter's. I'll be ready and willing in two weeks! You remember where Ella June lives, don't you? Only, of course! I keep forgetting. You're really a G-man, aren't you, Mr. Benson. You'll be going clear back to Washington, won't you?"

"Well, I think," John Benson smiled, "they're going to give me a short vacation out here anyway, Mrs. Landry. You say hello to your daughter for us, won't you?"

"Of course, I will! And to my grandchildren too. They're so excited! And I'll always think of what an exciting time we all had together! Wasn't that something? Well, my daughter's been so upset, and I just keep telling her—Ella June, you're going to get old before your time, worrying that way. My goodness! A little excitement is what somebody needs to stay young, that's what I say! Good-by, you two. I've got to run. And don't forget—keep in touch!"

Mrs. Landry hurried out of the lobby. They watched her cross the sidewalk, get into the station wagon and drive off. Margaret Moore turned to John Benson. She extended her hand. "Good luck, John. It was nice."

He took her hand, looking at her eyes. He could feel the past slipping away. It was a new day now, he thought. Time to start over. He said, "Just like that? Good luck, it was nice?"

She shrugged, an eyebrow flickering. "I told you. No strings."

"Well, maybe," he said, "I wouldn't mind a few strings."

She blinked once, then her smile warmed, her eyes turned radiant.

"How about dinner somewhere?" he said. "A thick steak? Maybe this time we won't be interrupted. Or maybe you'd just like to wander around the city first?"

"A steak sounds beautiful," she said, eyes bright. "And I think, John Benson, that I'm suddenly tired of wandering."

THE END

## Crime classics from the master of hard-boiled fiction...

# Peter Rabe

**The Box / Journey Into Terror $19.95**
978-0-9667848-8-6
"Few writers are Rabe's equal in the field of the hardboiled gangster story." –Bill Crider, *Twentieth Century Crime & Mystery Writers*

**Murder Me for Nickels /**
**Benny Muscles In $19.95**
978-0-9749438-4-8
"When he was rolling, crime fiction just didn't get any better." –Ed Gorman, *Mystery Scene*

**Blood on the Desert /**
**A House in Naples $19.95**
978-1-933586-00-7
"He had few peers among noir writers of the 50s and 60s; he has few peers today." –Bill Pronzini

**My Lovely Executioner /**
**Agreement to Kill $19.95**
978-1-933586-11-3
"Rabe can pack more into 10 words than most writers can do with a page."—Keir Graff, *Booklist*

**Anatomy of a Killer /**
**A Shroud for Jesso $14.95**
978-1-933586-22-9

"*Anatomy of a Killer*...as cold and clean as a knife...a terrific book." –Donald E. Westlake

**The Silent Wall /**
**The Return of Marvin Palaver $19.95**
978-1-933586-32-8
"A very worthy addition to Rabe's diverse and fascinating corpus."—*Booklist*

**Kill the Boss Good-by /**
**Mission for Vengeance $19.95**
978-1-933586-42-7
"*Kill the Boss Goodbye* is certainly one of my favorites."— Peter Rabe in an interview with George Tuttle

**Dig My Grave Deep / The Out is Death**
**/ It's My Funeral $21.95**
978-1-933586-65-6
"It's Rabe's feel for the characters, even the minor ones, that lifts this out of the ordinary." –Dan Stumpf, *Mystery*File*

**The Cut of the Whip / Bring Me Another**
**Corpse / Time Enough to Die $23.95**
978-1-933586-66-3
"These books offer realistic psychology, sharp turns of phrase, and delightfully deadpan humor that make them cry out for rediscovery."—Keir Graff, *Booklist*

In trade paperback from:

**Stark House Press**
**1315 H Street, Eureka, CA 95501**
griffinskye3@sbcglobal.net
**www.StarkHousePress.com**

Available from your local bookstore, or order direct with a check or via our website.